George Andropolous looked around his ice cream and scowled. It was too damn early and he still had to purchase supplies today. But he had to be here to keep people from robbing him blind.

Cherries, chocolate sauce and now the nuts were starting to go too.

At this rate he was going to have to raise his prices again and that was bad for business.

"How we fixed?" he demanded of Lance.

"Okay. We're a little low on vanilla and I had to open a new can of cherries last night, but . . ."

"A new can? Jesus, that's three this week."

Lance shrugged.

"How in the hell . . . ?" Andropolous stopped. There was a distinct rattle, like metal on metal.

"What was that?"

Lance opened his mouth to reply, but Andropolous motioned him to be quiet. Again the rattle.

There it was again. This time he could pinpoint it. The rattling was coming from the hot-fudge pot.

Slowly, carefully, Andropolous edged up to the pot and eased the lid back. He lifted it perhaps an inch when something small, manlike and liberally smeared with chocolate sauce popped the lid back and went running across the counter, leaving tiny chocolate footprints in its wake.

"WHAT THE HELL WAS THAT?" Andropolous screamed as the tiny creature scuttled out of sight, leaving a brown trail behind.

"I'm not real sure," Lance said slowly, "but I *think* it was a chocolate-covered brownie."

MALL PURCHASE NIGHT

Baen Books By Rick Cook

The Wizardry Cursed
The Wizardry Compiled
Wizard's Bane
Limbo System

Mall PURCHASE NIGHT

RICK COOK

BAEN

MALL PURCHASE NIGHT

Copyright © 1993 by Rick Cook

All rights reserved, including the right to reproduce this book or portions thereof in any form.

A Baen Books Original

Baen Publishing Enterprises
P.O. Box 1403
Riverdale, NY 10471

ISBN: 0-671-72198-4

Cover art by Gary Ruddell

First Printing, December 1993

Distributed by Simon & Schuster
1230 Avenue of the Americas
New York, NY 10020

Printed in the United States of America

DEDICATION

Besides the usual list of helpers (Jaison, Cynthia, the mall rats at Metro Center, the Circle Of The Desert Willow and the folks at Jan Ross Books) there's someone who deserves special mention. Over the years I've "borrowed" his life story, ripped off a character name and picked his brains on various arcane matters.

Since he and I were security guards together a long time ago, it's particularly appropriate to dedicate this one to Cary.

Chapter 1

His leg hurt.

It wasn't two A.M. and already Fogerty's leg was giving him hell.

It's all these goddamn stairs, he told himself as the golf cart whined through the night. Never mind that he usually took the elevators, it was the principle of the thing. A man his age shouldn't have to be climbing all over something this big.

At least tonight he had outside duty. He could spend most of the shift riding the cart to check the lots and the mall's exterior. Except he still had to get out every so often to look over the dumpsters and planters.

Black Oak Mall was built on and into a ridge and the parking lots were laid out stair-step fashion up the sides. Each level had to be checked separately.

He tried to rest the leg on the cart's dash, but it was too high. He couldn't drive with his leg on the seat and some sonofabitch had taken his box out of the cart. It had taken him two days to find a box just the right height to support that leg.

He breathed deeply and then coughed. *Christ, even the air stinks*. Even after six years in California the damn air still smelled wrong. He should have stayed in Pennsylvania, lousy economy, snow and all.

He reached the turnoff for the highest lot and stopped for a minute. The full moon was riding high in the sky, only slightly blurred by the thin haze. Below, the lights of the valley spread out in all directions, the streetlights running off into the smog like a net of

jewels. The sight just reminded him that he was on a hill
and made him even more sour.

Fogerty still weighed 250 pounds, same as when he
was the pride of the Altoona, PA, police force. Of course
that had been thirty years ago and a continent away.
Now he carried more of it around his waist and less in
his chest and legs. But he still thought of himself as Big
John Fogerty.

He looked at the empty lot and hesitated. There was
a bottle in his car in the employees' lot. Fogerty swallowed hard at the thought. But no, he'd already been
warned twice about drinking on duty, and that prick
Morales would turn him in if he smelled liquor on him
when he checked in at the security center. *Besides,* he
thought, looking up at the security camera mounted on
one of the light standards, *that sonofabitch could be
spying on me right now.* He jammed the cart in gear
and lurched off into the lot.

It was all the goddamn high-tech. These assholes
thought you could substitute a bunch of cameras and
radios and stuff for patrol officers. Well it didn't work
that way, and he had twenty-two years of experience
that said so. All that shit was good for was spying on employees. Suppose there was some junkie or crazy hiding
in one of these fancy planters? Suppose he got jumped?
What the hell good would those fancy security cameras
do? There were only three guards in the whole damn
mall after midnight. He could be dead before help got
to him.

He noticed once again how quiet it was. Not even
traffic noises this far up the hill. Just the whine of the
cart's electric motor and the occasional buzzing of a
lamp. The lot was brightly lit by the even pinkish radiance of the high-pressure sodium lights, but there were
dark contorted shadows around the dumpsters and in
the planters.

He reached down and patted the butt of his .38. A
man's best friend if you knew how to use it and Big John

Fogerty had two medals in his dresser drawer that said he knew how to use it. Just stay alert and don't spook yourself and you'll be fine.

He pulled up next to one of the chest-high planters that separated areas in the lot. A quick sweep of his flashlight convinced him there was nothing in the planter. He climbed back into the cart and jammed the pedal down.

Fucking pissant Morales. Fogerty hawked and spat. The golf cart whined in protest as it climbed to the next level. *I'm a better man drunk than he is sober.*

A rattle pierced the warm night air, as if something metallic was being dragged over pavement, or wheels on asphalt.

He stopped instantly. *What the hell . . . ?* Must be those damn kids again. Skateboarders, trying to avoid Fogerty and the security cameras so they could break their goddamn necks on the sloping access roads. It was fine with Fogerty if they scraped their whole hide away, too good for them. But his job was to run them off.

As quietly as he could, Fogerty reached for the radio on his left hip. "Base, I've got something on Level Four-H." Only the hiss of static in reply. "Base. Base?" Still only static. Fogerty snorted in disgust and jammed the radio back in its holster. Just like that asshole to be off taking a leak when he needed him.

He left the cart and eased forward on foot, keeping three steps from the retaining wall on the downhill side of the lot — close enough to dive behind it if he needed to but not so close that someone behind it could reach up and grab him.

There was another rattle. Fogerty froze, hand on his gun. It was definitely coming from the dumpster alcove up ahead. He felt naked out under the pink glow of the parking lot lights. He eased diagonally across the lot and toward the dumpster bay.

He drew his six-cell flashlight from its belt ring and grasped it tightly next to the head. With that grip he could flash the light in someone's eyes or reverse with a twist of the wrist and use the heavy aluminum case as a night stick.

He got his back to the inside retaining wall and moved toward the alcove crabwise, making as small a target as possible.

Something moved in the darkness next to the dumpster. Fogerty swept his light into the alcove. He saw nothing, but something moved in the narrow space between the dumpster and the alcove wall. He unsnapped his holster strap with his thumb.

"All right, you little bastards," Fogerty called. "I see you in there. Come on out with your hands up."

Then the intruder moved and stepped into the light.

Fogerty's eyes widened and he screamed.

He was still screaming his throat raw when Morales found him ten minutes later.

Chapter 2

Andy Westlin fidgeted as the man across the desk scanned the application. His shirt was scratchy with newness, and the tie he had bought for the occasion was too tight. The tiny office seemed too hot. He wondered if the shock of red-brown hair at the back of his head was sticking up again. He almost reached up to plaster it back down, but he decided that would be too obvious.

Christ, he thought, *I wasn't this nervous going after speed freaks in abandoned buildings.*

The nameplate on the desk read "J.D. Dunlap, Chief of Security." Behind it sat a blocky man with a hard face and thinning gray hair. An ex-cop, Andy thought, one of the ones who was tough rather than efficient. But he was losing the tough look as the layers of flesh accumulated. Now he just looked mean. Andy wondered what he would be like as a boss.

Dunlap finished the first page and looked up.

"You still have a permit to carry a gun on duty?"

Westlin nodded.

Dunlap turned the page and went back to reading.

"Two years on the force, I see."

Andy nodded. *Here it comes.*

"What precinct?"

"Southeast," Westlin said woodenly.

Dunlap looked at him sharply. "You involved in that?"

"I was a goddamn rookie. I didn't even know what was going on." The lie didn't come easily and Westlin was sure he'd said it so clumsily he had given himself away. But Dunlap only grunted and nodded.

"Why'd you leave the force?"

"Like it says there. I decided I didn't like it."

The security chief smiled for the first time in the interview. Andy didn't find it particularly reassuring.

"Long hours, low pay and spending your time dealing with scum, huh? Well the hours aren't much better here and the pay's less. But most of the people don't hate your guts and not many of them will try to kill you." He glanced through the rest of the application.

"Westlin, I think you'll do nicely." Dunlap gave him another unsettling smile. "You'll have to submit to a polygraph and urinalysis, and go through a background check, but those are pretty much formalities. When can you start?"

"Any time."

"Fine. Be here at 9 A.M. tomorrow to draw your uniform and we'll get you squared away." He looked over at a clipboard hanging on the wall. "You'll be on days for a couple of weeks until they get the reports back on you. Then you'll be floating. Probably mostly nights cause you're the new guy."

When Andy pulled his old Toyota into the employees' parking lot at 8:45 the next morning, there was already a sprinkling of vehicles in the regular lots. That struck him as strange since the stores didn't open until 10.

From the employees' lot at the edge of the property Black Oak Mall looked like something out of a science fiction movie. The structure rose like some futuristic city out of the flat terrain of the valley. The planters that rimmed the parking lots on each level drooped greenery like a hanging garden and the heat-reflecting glass roof seemed to glow golden in the morning light. The roof's aluminum framework was anodized gold as well, making even brighter golden highlights in the gleaming mass. Even the white concrete walls were tinged gold by the morning sun. The parking lot was freshly swept and the vegetation was carefully trimmed to look natural without being untidy. It was all clean and bright and wonderfully new, without a trace of graffiti or a broken wine bottle to be seen.

It was a long way from the streets he had patrolled, and the distance wasn't just measured miles. Andy wondered if he'd fit in better here than he had on the force.

Well, the way to find out wasn't to sit here and moon. He reached over onto the passenger's seat and picked up his Sesame Street lunchbox containing a couple of sandwiches and his Taurus .357 revolver with a regulation 6" barrel. Then he started across the parking lot toward the glistening edifice before him.

The main entrance was at ground level. The roof swooped out from the portal and the patterns in the terrazzo pavement converged on the doors as if sweeping the whole world inside. Not just welcoming, sucking you in.

There was a carefully arranged rack of newspaper machines to one side of the mall entrance. *Wall Street Journal, New York Times, USA Today* and the local papers. "Police Scandal Grows," announced the headline on the LA *Times*. "Eight More Indicted in Police Corruption Probe," blared another. Andy tried hard to ignore them and stepped through the glass doors.

Inside, even the air was different. The temperature was about the same as the morning air outdoors, but it seemed cleaner and clearer. Andy walked past the shops flanking the entrance and out into the open space of the main mall. He stopped dead as the full effect hit him.

The open court reached up four levels with planters and cascading greenery to break up the white concrete of the railings. The effect was like a gigantic atrium with ivy and ferns cascading over the waist-high walls every level. There were benches and planters with more greenery scattered about the court before him, including a stand of bamboo that must have been fifty feet high. Around the perimeter, the names of the stores glowed brightly but not garishly above the still-closed entrances. High above, sunlight filtered down softly, the beams catching a plant here and an architectural detail there. In the background, soft music played over concealed speakers.

Andy had been in malls before, but never one like this. When he applied yesterday he had come through a side entrance near the mall offices. He realized he didn't have the faintest idea where those offices were.

"Excuse me."

An old man in T-shirt and shorts pounded by him, breathing heavily, eyes fixed on something infinitely far ahead. Not far behind him came an elderly couple in matching blue warmup suits, striding along in lockstep. A middle-aged man in shorts, running shoes and a Walkman passed them, driving past like a freight locomotive, torso shining with sweat.

Andy stepped out of the runner's way and up to an information kiosk to try to find where he was supposed to report and to meet his new supervisor.

Eduardo Morales was a chunky, swarthy ex-cop with a big nose and tight little eyes that never seemed to stop moving. He greeted Andy amiably enough, shoved a pile of clothing and equipment at him and nodded him toward the locker room.

The uniform was a little loose on Andy's lanky frame, and the combination of dark blue and sky blue with yellow piping made him feel like a movie usher. Still, he was careful to wear it in the style he had learned at the police academy. The patch on the shoulder read "Black Oak Security" over a stylized picture of an oak tree.

When he came out of the dressing room, Morales looked him over and nodded approvingly. Then he handed him a plastic card with a clip on one end and a bar code on the other.

"This is temporary, but don't lose it. It's your real badge. It opens doors and clocks you in when you make your rounds." Andy fumbled a bit as he clipped it to his other breast pocket, across from his shield.

"Come on," Morales said. "I'll show you around in here for a little bit. Then I'll take you topside and LaVonne will show you the ropes on day duty."

He led Andy back into a big gray room behind the main office. In the center was a large U-shaped desk with about fifteen monitors. Another guard in the blue-on-blue uniform sat at the console sipping a cup of coffee and watching the monitors.

"This is the security center. The whole place is watched from here."

"How many guards are on?"

"In the daytime, anywhere from eight to a dozen, depending on the day of the week and the season. At night, just three. One guy here, one patrolling inside and one patrolling outside."

"That's not much for a place this big."

Morales smiled. "Technology, man. They really don't need nobody except the guy in the security center. Those cameras show everything that happens in the whole mall."

The stubby man with jug ears and thinning hair watching the monitors glanced up and then went back to the screens.

Andy did a quick count of the screens. "Just fifteen?"

"Nah, there must be a couple of hundred cameras. You can switch back and forth, see?" He leaned over the console to demonstrate. "But you don't need to worry about that. Senior man takes the security center and the other two guys do the patrolling. One inside, one outside. Be a while before you'll be sitting at that desk."

He turned to the man at the console. "Anything good, Henderson?"

The guard grunted. "Nah, too early. Maybe something later."

"People don't realize the whole mall is covered by those cameras," Morales said as they left the security office. "Sometimes they'll do the damnedest things in the corners and hidey-holes around here. Hell, we've seen people screwing, men going down on men, women on women." He smiled and shook his head. "We made a videotape of some of the best stuff. You ought to see it some time."

Instead of turning left to go back out into the mall they turned right. There were no more offices along the corridor, just metal double doors with store names stenciled on them. The corridor was wide but deserted. The walls of the corridor were unfinished concrete and the baseboards and corners were black with tire marks and chipped from the passage of hand trucks and forklifts. The floor was spotless and buffed to a matte finish. The air was warmer and still, Andy noticed. Apparently it wasn't air-conditioned directly.

"This is the fast way to get to the central elevators," Morales explained. "It runs behind the smaller stores.

"We'll keep you on day duty for a few days until we get your test results back," Andy's new supervisor told him. "Then you'll float wherever we need you. Probably mostly graveyard, but some days too."

"Much happen here at night?"

Morales snorted. "You know why we're here at all at night? It's the goddamn insurance. It's so much cheaper if they have people on around the clock that they can pay a guard force and still save on the fuckin' premiums.

"Night shift's a piece of cake. You make a round every hour, that takes you about forty-five minutes. The rest of the time you sit at the desk in the information center down on the first level.

"Days are tougher cause the mall's full of people. There's lost kids and drunks and shit. LaVonne will tell you about it and it's all covered in the regs book in the security center. Get here a little early for the next couple of days and go over the book. It's pretty straightforward."

"What kinds of crimes should I watch out for?"

Morales looked at him oddly. "Crime? You mean like felonies? Hell, we don't even have much car theft. Not with all those cameras. When the place first opened they had a couple of gangs lifting cars from the lot. But that stopped when they found out we had everything on tape. Not only made it easy to ID the perps, it was real convincing when they played it for the juries." Morales gestured expansively, palms up. "So, no more auto theft."

"And inside?"

"Just about zip. Maybe someone's purse gets lifted. Once in a while we'll get a rape or something, but the cops investigate that. Mostly it's a matter of kids acting up, vandalism, that sort of thing. We keep everyone in line and keep 'em happy. That's our real job."

Morales tapped his head. "It's common sense, man. Use common sense and remember which side your bread is buttered and you won't have any trouble."

"What about shoplifting?"

"Not our problem. The store detectives handle it in the big stores, the clerks take care of it in the small ones and we stay out of it unless they ask. Usually they call the police themselves.

"Most of this business is public relations. You keep your eyes open and show the flag. You won't have any trouble."

They stopped before the door and Morales unclipped his ID card and put it in the slot.

"Easy way is to take the elevator to the top and work down. We'll meet LaVonne up on Level Four."

When they stepped out of the elevator, Andy was stunned at the change. In the time he had been with Morales the stores had opened. The sprinkling of joggers was replaced by streaming crowds of people. Andy looked at his watch and saw it wasn't even eleven yet.

"This is the South Court," Morales said. "LaVonne will be here in a minute." Andy nodded and looked over the railing.

It was like standing on the edge of a canyon. Waist-high planters served as railings at each level. Down at the bottom, water sprayed and tinkled over an elaborate waterfall of artificial rocks and splashed down a tall metal sculpture in the center of the pond. While Andy admired the view, the supervisor spoke briefly into a walkie-talkie and listened intently to the static-filled response.

"That's a real spring," Morales told him. "When they were building this place they hit water. So they put a fountain there and use the extra water for irrigation and the other fountains in the mall. Even when we had the drought that fountain kept going."

"A spring? In a ridge?"

Morales shrugged. "Hey, all I know is, the water's there. Never shuts off. Even at night when the mall's empty. Anyway, like I was saying, the best way to handle trouble is to head it off before it starts. Don't strong-arm anybody but don't take a lot of shit either. If someone causes trouble, your job is to throw him off the property. There's a list of people down in the day book who aren't allowed in the mall. Study it, and if one of them shows up, toss him out."

"Isn't that harassment?" Andy asked, remembering his training at the academy.

Morales grinned mirthlessly. "You don't get it. This isn't a public place. The whole mall is private property and we don't have to put up with nothing. If someone starts causing trouble, tell 'em to leave. If they don't leave, we escort them off the property. And if that don't work, we call the cops and have them arrested for trespassing."

Morales looked at the crowd streaming around them. "When you get right down to it, none of these people have any rights in this mall. Makes keeping the peace a whole lot easier."

"What about nights?"

"On midnight to eight there's mostly no one here. All the regular store employees are supposed to be gone by ten p.m. From ten to midnight no one's allowed in the mall without a special ID. From midnight to six a.m. the guards are the only ones authorized to be in the mall. Cleanup crews finish at midnight or come in before the stores open."

"Why?"

Morales shrugged. "Security, man. There's a lot of valuable stuff in here." He smiled like he had just made a joke.

Chapter 3

Andy started to ask another question, but Morales' eyes shifted over his shoulder to something behind him. Andy turned and saw another guard easing her way through the shoppers to them.

"Lost kid down on One South," she said to Morales and then without preamble to Andy: "So you're the new guy."

Andy extended his hand. "Andy Westlin."

His new mentor took it and pumped it firmly. "LaVonne Sanders."

There was a pause while each of them sized the other up. LaVonne was a stocky black woman who just about came up to Westlin's chin. Her hair was cropped in a tight natural Afro and her shoulders were almost as wide as Andy's. Not young, not old, but she had that look he recognized from associating with street cops, the tough, competent ones.

"Pleased to meet you."

"Well, I'll leave him to you," Morales told LaVonne. He was turning toward the elevators when a shout brought him up short.

"Hey you! Guards." The three of them turned and saw an overdressed but well-groomed man bearing down on them. Six foot, 150 or so. Black hair, blue eyes. Light gray suit, patterned silk handkerchief in the breast pocket. Patterned tie to match against an olive-green shirt. Overdressed to be a businessman. If he'd been flashier, Andy would have pegged him as a pimp. As it was, Andy wasn't sure what the guy was, except upset.

"There you all are," he said as if it was an accusation. "Someone's been messing with my car again."

"How do you know, Mr. Crampton?" LaVonne said in that tone cops reserve for crazies and children.

"Here's how!" He held up his key chain, and the tiny box on one end was flashing an orange light. "That's the intruder alarm. I tell you someone has been fooling with my car and we've barely opened. How the hell am I supposed to keep my mind on business when I've got to worry about my car all the time?"

Morales sighed. "I guess we'd better go have a look."

Without a word, Crampton turned on his heel and led the three into the elevator. LaVonne followed Morales and motioned Andy to join them.

"And someone parked in my space again today," he continued as soon as they were packed into the elevator.

"Mr. Crampton," Morales said, "we've told you there are no reserved spaces in the employee lots."

He brushed that aside. "And I've told you I've got to have a space under a security camera. Instead there's some damn *van* parked there so the camera can't even see my car!" He looked like he'd bitten into something rotten. "A ratty old Volkswagen van covered with flowers!"

The doors opened and Crampton headed for the main entrance at a brisk pace.

"Look," Morales said as he fell in beside the store owner, "you could always leave your Porsche at home."

Crampton looked at him as if he were stupid. "What the hell's the good of having a Porsche if you don't drive it? It's bad enough that you don't have *convenient* parking for the merchants, but then you don't even provide decent security, well . . ."

Crampton had parked in the front row in the employees' parking lot, where anyone driving by would be sure to see his Porsche.

It was quite a sight. The car didn't merely sparkle, it

gleamed. The chrome gleamed. The glass gleamed. Even the body gleamed. The paint job shaded from brownish-maroon above to jet black below.

"That's fifteen coats of hand-rubbed enamel," Crampton said proudly. "You get a scratch in that and it costs more than all of you make in a week to get it refinished."

Andy, Morales and LaVonne took one more step toward it, but Crampton motioned them to stop.

"Stay back," he told them. "Let me disarm it."

He did something with the controller on his key ring. Then he selected a key, unlocked the door, selected another key, turned off something under the dashboard and then punched several numbers on a keypad on the console to the right of the driver's seat.

"You can approach now."

While Morales and LaVonne made a show of going over the car, Andy just admired it.

"I paid eight thousand dollars for that security system," Crampton told them. "It was done by one of the best people in the state. He does Paul Newman's cars and Jay Leno's Cobra. Proximity sensors, motion sensors, voice synthesized alarm, remote alarm and an automatic tracking unit that will report the car's position to the alarm company. It's got some special tricks too. But you don't need to worry about that," he added quickly. "All you've got to do is keep people the hell away from it."

"Well, it doesn't look like anyone has touched it," Morales said finally.

"If no one touched it then why did the alarm go off?" Crampton demanded. "Someone's been tampering with it."

LaVonne ostentatiously knelt and shined her flashlight under the Porsche. "If they did, they didn't leave any signs." She stood up, brushing off her pants.

"Look, Mr. Crampton," Morales began in that ultra-reasonable tone. "We can't do anything if there's no sign of tampering." Crampton bristled but the guard supervisor held up his hand. "Now, if you do find evidence that someone has messed with your car, stop by the security office and let us know, okay?"

Crampton sighed loudly. "No, it is not okay, but I can see that's all I'm going to get from you people. Mall management is going to hear about this. I'll bring it up at the next meeting of the Merchants' Association too."

"That's certainly your privilege, Mr. Crampton," Morales said neutrally.

"Who is that, anyway?" Andy asked as the three of them walked back into the mall leaving the man fussing about the car.

"Name's Crampton," LaVonne said. "He owns Smilin' Jack's, one of the men's stores."

"Pain in the ass," Morales added. "He's nuts about that damn car."

LaVonne nodded. "It used to be anyone parked next to him and the damn siren would go off. Finally we made him turn the sensitivity down, and you should have heard him bitch about that. Then he wanted to bring one of those one-car fiberglass garages down here and set it up in the parking lot." She snorted. "Complete with a goddamn built-in fire extinguisher!"

"From the looks of it, it'd be worth doing just to shut him up," Andy said.

Morales shook his head. "Against the mall rules. Anyway, that stupid silent alarm keeps going off, and every time it does he comes running to us."

"If you ask me," LaVonne put in, "that car's paranoid. Just like the owner."

"I think he's got it confused with his cock," Morales said.

LaVonne struck a hip-shot pose. "Honey," she said in a fruity ghetto accent, "I guaran*tee* he ain't got no cock what needs no eight thousand dollar security system."

❖   ❖   ❖

The guards weren't the only ones who were thinking about Jack Crampton. Just then he was very much on Dawn Albright's mind as well.

Dawn was model-tall and still model-slender although it had been years since she had set foot on a runway. As befitted the supervisor of the Business Boutique at Sudstrom's department store, her white linen suit was as elegant as the wearer. But the suit was cool and unwrinkled and right now Dawn Albright was neither.

Ostensibly she was trying to work out the merchandise floor plan for next week. That meant deciding what items to display most prominently, what to feature in the in-store displays and how to keep up flagging sales of women's business apparel as Sudstrom's at Black Oak moved into the summer doldrums.

What she was really doing was reviewing her date last weekend with Jack Crampton and trying to figure out what was bugging her about it.

Jack was amusing, attentive, well-off and good in bed. He always knew the best places to eat and the latest places to go. Thinking back on it, Dawn couldn't remember ever having a bad meal or a bad time on a date with Jack.

Every girl's dream in a Porsche. So why wasn't she satisfied? She sighed and tried to focus her attention on the layout sheets — and away from irritating questions.

She slapped the pencil down on the diagram and looked up in time to see her assistant approaching with her arms full of clothing.

"Don't tell me we're out of hangers again!"

Pat Loney, almost as tall and almost as slender, younger and brunette, shrugged apologetically and held up the skirt and three blouses she had just taken from the fitting rooms.

"Would you please tell me," Dawn asked, "how we can leave the store at ten-thirty with every garment in the department on hangers and come back in at eight the next morning and four or five of them are on the floor and the hangers are nowhere to be seen?"

Pat only shrugged again. The hanger shortage was an old story in fashion retailing. Merchandise arrived in the departments on hangers, and when the clothing left the store the hangers often stayed behind. Yet everyone always seemed to have more clothes than hangers.

"You haven't got any more stashed, have you?" Pat asked hopefully.

"I ran out yesterday. Have you looked down in Alterations?"

"Casual Shoppe cleaned them out this morning." She hesitated. "What shall we do?"

Dawn considered her options. She could send down to the stockroom for more hangers, but extras were charged against the department's budget. The alternative was to beg some off one of the other departments. Every savvy department manager tried to keep a private stash of hangers, and sometimes they were willing to barter for favors.

"This is getting ridiculous. We've gone through three extra bundles this month. No one's taking them home, are they?"

It was a rhetorical question. At Sudstrom's, hangers were guarded only slightly less closely than the cash drawer.

"No one's shoplifting them either," her assistant said. "I checked that after we had to get that last bundle."

"Well, *something* is happening to them."

"Maybe something's eating them," Pat suggested, then wilted under her boss's glare.

Dawn reached behind the counter for the phone. "We'll get another bundle. And this time ask people to at least try to keep track of them."

"That's one of the problems with this job," LaVonne told Andy after Morales left them. "Merchants like Crampton are a pain in the ass, but they pay our salaries, in a manner of speaking."

"That's why we all went out to look? I've seen fewer officers at a homicide."

The black woman nodded. "That's it. You sure as hell don't have to do everything the tenants want, but you don't give them the idea you're taking them lightly. They'll be all over mall management, and Dunlap will be all over your ass."

"I'll remember," Andy said glumly. Politics and kissing up to important people had never been his favorite part of being a cop.

"It's not that bad," Sanders assured him. "Most of the people are pretty nice. Come on, I'll introduce you to some of them. The employees, mall rats." She turned and strode off toward the escalators.

"Mall rats?"

"You know," she said over her shoulder, "kids who hang out at the mall.

"Are there very many of them?" Andy asked as he caught up and matched LaVonne's easy stride.

"Hundreds. But only two or three dozen you'll see almost every day."

Just like the street, Andy thought. Except most of these regulars probably weren't carrying guns.

"Now we don't have a regular training program," LaVonne told him. "We don't hire that many new people. Mostly it's just common sense, and the rest is in the regs in the security center. Just go by the regulations and you won't have any trouble."

"With as little crime as there is here I don't see why they need us to go armed."

"Who told you we don't have crime?"

"Morales. He said there aren't even any car thefts."

The woman considered. "Car thefts, no. No strong-arm stuff either, what with all the cameras. But let me tell you, when things go wrong around here they can go real wrong. Back when the place first opened they had the guards in blazers and slacks. The nonthreatening look, you know? Turned out that wasn't such a good idea. The badge and gun give you psychological size, and sometimes that's all you've got to keep the place peaceful — and you healthy."

"Have you ever had a problem?"

LaVonne shrugged. "Once or twice. I had some crazy pull a knife on me and a couple of kids tried to give me trouble one time." She made a dismissive motion, like brushing off flies. "The thing is, you're mostly out there alone. Especially at night. You've got to look out for yourself, and the best way to do that is to make damn sure trouble doesn't start in the first place." She shrugged. "It's mostly attitude. When I was an MP I used to break up fights between paratroopers. You just look tough and act like you mean it and you'll be all right."

Looking at her, Andy could believe it. LaVonne wasn't that big but she was stocky, she wasn't carrying any excess weight and she moved like someone who could handle herself.

"Besides," she went on, "there's plenty of crime, don't let Morales kid you. The store dicks say this place has a terrible record for shrinkage."

"Shrinkage?"

"Merchandise that walks off. Shoplifting and employee theft, mostly. Some of it's accounting and inventory mistakes."

"Is that a problem for us?"

"Nah, that kind of stuff comes and goes. It doesn't look good right now, but it will probably even out over the next six or seven months. It's not our problem, anyway."

They turned a corner, threaded their way between two planters, and then they were in front of a set of escalators.

"The escalators are the easiest way to get from one level to another, even when they're not running," LaVonne explained. "During the day they let you watch the whole level as you ride up."

Andy looked out over the level falling away below

them. The open center of the mall let him see over the planters and down the entire leg of the mall. He looked up two more levels to the translucent white ceiling. The sun must be high by now, but the light streaming down was still soft and even. In the background he could hear something he vaguely recognized as Bach played by an orchestra with way too many strings. Then he turned to face the next level and stiffened.

The man was leaning on the rail and looking down over the court. He was surfer tanned and surfer blonde, with a shock of bleached hair that hung down over his forehead. He was wearing a surfing T-shirt, a pair of baggy pants and tennis shoes with no socks. Wraparound sunglasses hid his eyes. From a distance he looked maybe 18 or 19.

It wasn't until you got close enough to see the wrinkles around the eyes and the leathery texture of the skin, the way the hair was coarsened and beginning to thin, that you realized he wasn't nearly that young. And if he took off the sunglasses what you'd see in the eyes would tell you he was older yet.

Andy gave him a professional once-over as he and LaVonne came up the escalator. The surfer gave both of them a single disinterested glance.

"I think I know that guy," Andy said as soon as he and LaVonne were away from the escalators. "I used to see him around sometimes."

"So?"

"So he's bad news."

"As long as he keeps his nose clean in here he's no kind of news at all," LaVonne told him. "He's just a shopper so don't go hassling him."

"Doesn't look like he's buying anything to me."

"Doesn't look like he's doing anything either," she retorted. "Look, Westlin, around here the rule is live and let live. He don't cause problems, we don't give him grief, no matter what he does anyplace else." She snorted. "Hell, there's a bunch of bikers that come in here all the time. As long as they don't cause trouble that's fine."

"Bikers shop here? That sure doesn't square with the mall's image."

"Not so much to shop. They like the video games in the arcade. We've had to warn one or two of them about their language when they start shouting or screaming at the machines, but they're not much trouble."

Andy thought about admonishing a biker to watch his mouth and shook his head. "And they do it? That doesn't square with the image either."

The woman shrugged. "Like I said, you gotta know how to deal with people. Just speak softly and be polite. Do that, don't let them get behind you, keep one hand on your gun, and they don't give you trouble."

Andy grinned. "I'd hate to see what you consider a serious problem."

"There's an example right there," LaVonne said with a jerk of her head.

The only thing to their right was a kitchen gadget store. Andy stared for a moment but he couldn't see anything out of the ordinary. "Where?"

"That." LaVonne pointed at a rack in the store entrance.

Andy bent over to peer at the display of combination corkscrew-nutmeg-grater-garlic presses.

"I admit it's a silly idea, but . . ."

"No." LaVonne pointed again. "That."

Andy looked down at the floor. The rack was at an angle so one corner extended beyond the metal track where the store's sliding door ran.

"That's encroaching," LaVonne explained. "It's against the mall rules."

"What do we do?"

"Unless it's a safety hazard, nothing. That kind of thing's mall management's problem, not ours."

"It doesn't look like much," Andy said. "He's what? Six inches over the line?"

"Around here that six inches is like six feet."

Andy just shook his head.

"There are all kinds of rules like that," the woman went on. "The stores can't use certain colors, their signs have got to be just so, they've got to be open certain hours, they've got to get their sales and promotions approved beforehand. All kinds of stuff."

"And the stores just put up with it?"

"Sure. All the malls have rules like that and they can make a hell of a lot more money in a mall than they could anywhere else.

"It's kind of a deal with the devil. The merchants give up a lot of control and a potload of money, and they get the opportunity to make even more money. Oh, they bitch about it all the time, but they keep signing those leases — if mall management lets them."

Andy jerked his head back at the offending display. "What will they do about that?"

"What they *could* do is throw him out of the mall. The leases let them if the stores don't follow the rules exactly. What they *will* do, most likely, is make him move it back." She shrugged. "Anyway, it's not our thing. If anyone tries to suck you in on something like that, just send them to mall management. Oh, wait a minute, here's someone you should meet."

She led him over to one of the planters and the man working at it. He wore the light blue shirt and dark blue pants of a maintenance worker. He was lean, balding and his silver hair was pulled back in a ponytail that reached down to his shoulders. He was using a pair of hedge shears to trim the bushes in the planter.

"Hi, Billy, how's it going?"

Billy Sunshine turned his head slowly and blinked at the two as if trying to bring them into focus. "Groovy, man," he said at last. "It's like, really cool, you know."

"That's great, Billy," LaVonne said heartily. "You keep it up, you hear? Andy, this is Billy Sunshine. He keeps our plants looking pretty. Now, Billy, this is Andy

Westlin. He's a new guard here so you'll be seeing him around."

Andy offered his hand. "Pleased to meet you, Billy."

Billy blinked at him and then shook hands. He had a surprisingly firm grip. "Peace, man."

"We gotta be going, Billy," LaVonne said. "We'll see you around, okay?"

Billy nodded amiably. "Later." Then he turned back to the hedge.

"He checked most of his brain in Haight-Ashbury in 1967 and lost the claim stub," LaVonne said as soon as they were out of earshot.

"He's not a problem, is he?"

"Ol' Billy? Not if you don't get too close to his van when he's toking up on his lunch break. You know, if anyone was to *find* him smoking dope in the parking lot they might have to *do* something about it, and Billy's too good to lose." She made a face. "He's the only person in the whole damn place who's really happy all the time."

Andy started to move off, but LaVonne laid a hand on his arm and gently steered him in the opposite direction. After a second's disorientation, he realized he'd been headed back the way he had come.

"Easy to get lost in this place," LaVonne told him. "That's deliberate. It encourages people to wander and spend money."

"The crowds don't help. I don't believe this place is so busy this early on a weekday."

"Busy? Hell, this is slow."

Andy looked around. "But the place looks full."

The woman smiled. "It's supposed to look that way. You get even a few people in here and it looks like a crowd. Saturday afternoon we'll have two or three times as many people in here and it will look just as busy, no more.

"A while back Cogswell had one of the architects come out and talk to the mall employees about the way this place was designed. Turns out it's just full of tricks."

She pointed on ahead. "See the way the mall zigzags? Just far enough so no one gets claustrophobic and close enough so it breaks up the sight lines. Personally I think it's just another gimmick to get people lost and wandering."

Andy shook his head. "I'm going to need a map and compass to get around in this place."

"Compass won't do you any good. You know the South Court? It's at the east end of the mall."

"Then why call it the South Court?"

LaVonne shrugged. "Maybe they thought it sounded better. Now, notice something else?"

"What?"

"No windows. Just the skylights and the smoked glass doors at the entrances. They could be having a goddamn blizzard outside and there's no way you'd know it. It's deliberate. The way you'll never find a clock in a Las Vegas casino. It's a gimmick to isolate people from the outside."

"I hadn't noticed it, but yeah." Andy looked around slowly. "Air conditioning, artificial lighting or diffused sun. In here you're completely cut off from the rest of the world."

LaVonne laughed. "That's because this ain't the real world. This is Oz, man."

Andy thought about that for a job description. "Security guard in Oz." He decided it wouldn't add significantly to his resume. He looked around again in wonder. "It's all pretty overwhelming."

"You get used to it." She smiled. "Pretty soon it seems almost normal."

They turned a corner again, and they were in a wide space with white wrought iron tables and chairs on a Tuscan tile floor. There were twenty or thirty food booths along the walls, and the smell of fried food and spices filled the air.

"The Food Court," LaVonne explained unnecessarily. "This is one of the hot spots. People who are just hanging out tend to congregate here, especially the mall rats. And folks will do dumb-ass things like leave their purses on the table when they go back for a refill on soft drinks."

It was barely mid-morning, so there was only a sprinkling of people at the tables, some solitary, some mothers and kids and a few groups of teenagers and preteens.

"You want to keep a close check on the bathrooms back here," LaVonne said as she led him through the maze of tables and chairs. "If something's gonna go down, that's a favorite place for it."

An old man sat at one of the tables. He was hunched over a cup of coffee like a vulture, pale wattled neck stretched out of his dark suit. He glared at them as they walked by. LaVonne ignored him.

"That's one kind of trouble right there," she said quietly once they were past.

"Doodle dasher?"

LaVonne chuckled. "Looks the type, don't he? No, he doesn't expose himself. We call him the Preacher. He thinks he's commanded to witness for God Almighty everywhere he goes."

"What does he do?"

"We've caught him preaching in the mall, putting fliers on cars, even slipping stuff in folks' shopping bags. He's been thrown out of every mall in the valley three or four times, but Black Oak's his favorite. We must have thrown him out eight or ten times."

"Can't you just bar him permanently?"

She looked at him. "Morales give you his little spiel about this being private property? Well, it's not that simple. We can ban a lot of things you can't restrict in public places, but we're not exactly private either. On free-speech stuff we usually have to wait until they do something before we can throw them out."

"Now the Preacher, he's under a court order. He doesn't harass nobody and we let him alone. If he starts preaching or handing out his little pamphlets, then he's violating the order and out he goes." She shrugged. "Anyway, it's all spelled out in the regs down in the office." She looked off past Andy. "Oh, here's someone else you should meet. Hey, Slick."

The kid was skinny, maybe sixteen. He was wearing a pair of baggy blue shorts that nearly reached his knees, a black T-shirt advertising a rock band in indecipherable Day-Glo lettering, and a baseball cap turned backwards. His hair was shaved close to his temples on the side and down over his collar in back, and he wore a pair of funny looking tennis shoes.

"Whoa, like greetings, dudes."

"Slick, this is Andy. He's a new guard here. Andy, this is Slick."

Andy nodded.

"Wow! Like *excellent*, Your Secureness!"

"Anyway, don't be giving him no lip, you hear?"

Slick looked pained. "Ooh, bogus. To think that I would cause problems. That is, like, most bogus indeed."

Andy put on that cop smile which is friendly and intimidating at once. "Oh, I'm sure Slick and I won't have any problems."

"Outasight," Slick agreed. "Well, like later, dudes." He swung off down the mall.

"Skateboarders," LaVonne explained as they moved on. "They're not supposed to bring their boards onto the property, but as long as they leave them outside and don't ride them in the lots, we pretty much leave them alone."

Andy looked after the boy. "I didn't know anyone really talked like that."

"They didn't until the movie came out."

Andy shook his head. "Amazing."

LaVonne looked at him narrowly. "Where you from, Westlin?"

"I grew up around here. Well, in Huntington Beach,

actually. We moved there when I was twelve and I've lived in Southern California ever since."

"You act like you've never been in a mall before."

"Only to shop. And not very often."

"You mean you didn't hang out at the mall with the other kids?"

Andy's lips set in a thin, hard line. "Not all us white boys had time to hang out at malls."

LaVonne led him along the second level past three or four zigzags, then down another set of escalators and along the first level almost to the far end of the mall. Finally they stopped in front of a short arm of the mall.

"Now this is the other hot spot," LaVonne said. "The real name is the Amusement Court but everyone calls it The Pit."

The stub was a neon-lit cave. Glaring red, blue and orange tubes outlined the dozen or so tiny shops along the sides and spelled out "Arcade" over the gaping dark entrance at the far end. The place looked like the anteroom of Hell to Andy, but it was thronged with teenagers.

As soon as they turned the corner they began to hear rock music. It got louder as they walked toward the back, and by the time they reached the arcade entrance it was well mixed with electronic bleeps, squawks and computer music from the games. The din was deafening and the place smelled of cigarette smoke overlaying old grease and cheap food.

The combination of violently clashing neon, noise and blindingly bright lights in the small stores made Andy's head hurt. The kids and the workers seemed oblivious to the racket and the glare. Andy wondered if it was familiarity, nerve deafness or ear plugs and sunglasses.

Without comment, LaVonne led him back to the arcade entrance. There didn't seem to be anyone in the place over 25, Andy noted, and a number of the kids were pointedly ignoring the guards.

At the very entrance to the arcade two kids were not just ignoring Andy and LaVonne, they seemed to be ignoring the whole universe. Each was skinny to the point of emaciation and had hair down past his shoulders, one bleached blonde and one dark. They were dressed in old rock T-shirts and faded, artfully tattered jeans. In the dim light Andy couldn't be sure if they had their eyes closed or not, but they were both playing air guitar to the music.

The blonde one did a knee slide on a particularly heavy riff. The other one duck-walked backwards, holding his imaginary instrument straight out before him. A couple of girls came out of the arcade and stepped past, seemingly as oblivious to him as he was to them.

"What's their thing?" he shouted, gesturing at the pair.

LaVonne leaned up and put her lips close to his ear. "As near as I can figure out, playing air guitar and faking brain damage."

"Druggies?" Andy asked just as the music ended with a drum flourish that sounded like a combination car crash and artillery barrage.

"Huh?"

Andy raised his voice. "I said, are they on drugs?"

LaVonne shrugged. "Not around here."

"Why do they allow this?"

"Huh?"

"I SAID, WHY," but they turned the corner and the sound died away as if by magic, leaving Andy shouting in the quiet mall. ". . . do they allow that?" he finished more softly, reddening. "I mean it looks like trouble to me."

LaVonne shrugged again. "Those kids are going to come here anyway. The Pit gives them a place to hang, keeps them out of everyone's hair and lets us watch them. Did you notice all the cameras in there? Eight of them, just for that little space. You can't make a move in The Pit without being seen in the security center."

Which probably explains why the Surfer is at the escalators instead of down here, Andy thought.

"Besides," she continued as they dodged around a group of middle-aged women wearing identical "Born to Shop" T-shirts, "it makes money. The Pit is one of the highest grossing areas of the mall on a square-foot basis."

"And I'll bet they spend half the money they make on handling trouble in there," Andy said sourly.

"You'd be surprised," LaVonne told him as they maneuvered around two mothers with strollers. "First off, the kids here, they're good kids, most of them. Just ride 'em a little and don't let 'em think they can get away with too much and they stay in line.

"Second thing," she said, stepping expertly between a couple of running kids and a woman with her arms full of shopping bags, "is that if they don't behave we run their asses right out of here. Hey, you kids slow down," she called after the running children. She smiled. "The threat of getting thrown out of here scares most of them worse than jail."

"What about the gang members?"

"We don't allow obvious gang stuff in the mall. Raiders stuff and things like that. There's a list in the duty office. Check it on the way out." She made a face. "Not that there's a real Crip or Blood within five miles, unless he's driving by on the freeway. Out here they're just wannabes. But we don't want them getting any ideas."

By the time they broke for lunch they had made two quick tours of the mall and Andy was thoroughly disoriented. All the stores looked the same, and every direction looked alike.

LaVonne timed it so they finished up back at the Food Court.

"Most of the food stands give discounts to mall employees," she told him. "There's also a mall employees' lunch room down behind the mall offices if you

want to bring your lunch. I'll meet you back here in half
an hour or so and we can go on."

There was an orientation packet in his box when he
got back to the security office. On top was a pamphlet
welcoming him to "the Black Oak family" with a cover
picture of Kemper Cogswell, the mall's developer, and
several hundred words inside that added up to nothing
much. Looking at Cogswell's picture, Andy thought he
looked like he played too much tennis.

Most of the rest were clippings about Black Oak
Mall. How Cogswell had the vision and foresight to take
a piece of land with a prime location but "undevelopable" topography and through daring and genius blah
blah blah.

There was also a booklet of rules for mall employees.
Andy set that aside to read later. The most useful things
in the packet were some maps and diagrams and as he
finished his sandwich Andy went over them.

The mall was built on, or rather into, a ridge that jutted up sharply from the surrounding valley. The site was
too steep to build on by conventional means so the
architects had terraced the whole ridge to make the
parking lots run up the sides of the mall and had built
the stores partially on and partly into the hill.

Looking at the cross sections, Andy saw that there
were between three and five shopping levels in the mall.
According to the material there were over 300 stores in
the complex, which made it one of the biggest malls in
the United States.

The mall ran zigzag along the ridge. At each point
where it changed direction it opened out into a "court."
In addition there were smaller courts along the runs on
the upper levels. The arrangement wasn't complicated,
Andy saw. The thing that made it confusing was that the
same basic plan was repeated over and over. He put a
couple of minutes into memorizing the names and relationships of the courts. That would give him a rough
guide to where he was.

❖   ❖   ❖

Slowly and deliberately Billy Sunshine worked his way down the planter. His shears moved at perhaps three clips a minute, but he left the hedge behind him almost mathematically straight.

The people swirled about him. Shoppers striding by, intent on getting from Store A to Store B. Teenagers in groups of three or five, giggling among themselves and intent on seeing and being seen. Parents trying to herd their children past the carnival of distractions. And over all the concealed speakers poured out sweet, syrupy music.

Since Billy was neither for sale, socially interesting or something to sit on, the people ignored him. Billy's attention was totally focused on the slow, steady movement of his hedge shears.

There was a sound like a tiny giggle.

Billy stopped and looked around slowly. None of the people passing by looked like the giggling kind, and the elevator music certainly didn't include a part for gigglers. He blinked twice and then went back to trimming.

He took two more clips when he heard it again. It was definitely a giggle, like someone was tickling a mouse.

He paused in mid-clip, shears open and poised over a scraggly bunch foliage.

A head about the size of his fist poked out of the greenery almost nose to nose with him. Billy drew back so his eyes could focus.

Whatever it was had big bat ears, a long crooked nose and mouth so wide it covered half its face. Its skin was grayish green and it was parting the branches with tiny hands with long, long fingers. The eyes were enormous, dark and lit by a combination of merriment and madness.

Another head poked out of the leaves next to the first one, and then a third. All three of them looked at each other and then looked back at Billy. Then they giggled in chorus.

Billy did what he always did when he was nonplussed by strangers. He held up his right hand with the first two fingers extended in a V.

"Peace," he said.

All three of the little creatures giggled again and vanished into the bushes, leaving Billy making a peace sign at a half-trimmed boxwood.

He stood frozen for a long minute, right hand in a peace sign and his left grasping his hedge clippers. Then he blinked again as he absorbed what had just happened to him.

"Oh, Wow!" Billy said at last. He reached down to the Bull Durham bag in his shirt pocket, pulled it out and looked at it reverently.

"Outasight shit!" he breathed.

Then he shook his head and went back to trimming.

LaVonne was finishing a slice of pizza when Andy joined her back at the Food Court.

"Think of any more questions?" she asked as she dumped the contents of her tray in the garbage can.

"A few. You said there wasn't much violent crime. What about drugs and prostitution?"

LaVonne shrugged. "Probably some dealing going on, but it's real discreet. As for the working girls, take a look around. Notice anything about the crowd?"

Andy glanced over the now-crowded Food Court. "Mostly women and kids."

LaVonne nodded. "Women, kids and families. That's about eighty percent of it, even weekends and evenings." She chuckled. "Only exception is Christmas Eve and the day before. Then this place is packed to the rafters with men and all of them with this haunted expression in their eyes. Anyway, this just isn't prime hunting ground for hookers."

They turned the corner from the Food Court into the main mall again.

"Now if you do see something suspicious you can use

those extra-legal powers Morales is so fond of. Get an ID and order them off the property. Then post the information in the day book for the rest of us. If you do have trouble, your radio's your best weapon. Or get to one of the information kiosks, punch nine-one-one and your badge number. That'll get you a direct line to the security center."

"They're tied in?"

"They're run off the same computer. Just like the lights, air conditioner and nearly everything else in this place."

Andy laughed and shook his head.

"What's so funny?"

"Just thinking. A few weeks ago I was worrying about drug dealers and armed robbers. Now my biggest problems are likely to be a street corner preacher and a paranoid Porsche."

LaVonne grinned. "Beats working for a living, don't it?"

They walked on a ways in silence.

"Westlin, mind if I ask you something?"

"Go ahead," Andy said, dreading the question.

"Why'd you want to go from being a cop to doing this?"

"Being a police officer turned out to be a lot more — intense — than I thought. I decided I wasn't right for it."

He waited for the inevitable follow-up, but LaVonne didn't ask. Instead she stopped and looked out over shoppers below.

"See," she said, as if she was talking to herself, "the thing is, being a security guard's nobody's first choice of jobs. So the people who end up here, well they've all got stories."

She looked back at him. "You know Dunlap, the head of security? He was a lieutenant with the LAPD. When the Rodney King riots happened he made a real bad decision and some people got hurt. Morales, he's from some dinky little department down near San Diego. I don't know the whole story but he was fired and he sued them. Part of the settlement was they can't say anything about why they fired him and they've got to give him a good recommendation.

"Me, I'm thirty-two, I got twelve years in the Army, a GED and an eight-year-old kid." Her jaw firmed. "But it ain't for much longer, I tell you that. I got one more semester of night school, and I'll have an associate degree in accounting. Then I'm out of here."

She relaxed again. "Point is, none of us are in any position to be too curious about someone else's past. We just ignore it and go by what the person does here. Anybody who pulls his weight and doesn't screw up, he's fine."

"Kind of like the Foreign Legion, huh?"

"More like a rest home. Things don't work out, one way or another, you got some police experience and you weren't caught banging teenyboppers in the squad car." She shrugged. "Well, here you are. Mostly we don't ask too many questions."

"Thanks, LaVonne."

The woman shrugged again. Then she stopped suddenly and turned to him, so close their bodies almost touched. "Hey, Westlin, you're all right. Let me tell you something." Her eyes flicked around. "Don't trust those guys. Dunlap, Morales and the rest, they're some bad apples. Don't let them pull you into anything." She stepped back, turned and continued walking next to him as if nothing had happened.

"Is that what happened to the guy I'm replacing?"

"Fogerty? Nah. He was a rummy. One night he started seeing things in the parking lot and freaked out." She shrugged. "Pink elephants or snakes or something."

It took nearly three hours for one of the Sudstrom's stockboys to bring the hangers up to the Business Boutique. Unfortunately for Dawn Albright's temper, the stockboy was Joe, the one who liked to make rude noises when women walked by. Dawn was torn between the hassle of filing sexual harassment charges with management and the simple pleasure of decking him. Since Joe was as thin as Dawn and perhaps half a head shorter, that wasn't an idle thought. She eyed him balefully, but Joe was no less dense today than usual.

"Here you go, mamma," he said as he handed the bundle of hangers over. "That's four this month. You got something up here that eats them?"

Dawn sniffed.

Chapter 4

Kemper Cogswell admired his image in the mirror one more time. His hours on the tennis court kept him tanned and trim. A hair implant and a couple of discreet trips to the plastic surgeon's had kept him looking youthful and mended a couple of nature's oversights in the bargain.

Definitely the right package. Packaging was vital and Cogswell knew he had a package that would sell. Image was the closest thing Kemper Cogswell had to a religion, and he worked on his devoutly. He looked every inch the successful executive — or the up-and-coming politician.

With a final admiring glance, he turned from the mirror and strode to the one-way window looking down on his domain.

The mall management office was down on the first level, in behind a row of stores next to Security. To Cogswell, that was all about on the level of a janitor's broom closet. This was his personal, private office suite, perched at the very top of the mall looking down on South Court and the fountain. His "eagle's nest," Cogswell liked to call it.

The elaborately carved oak doors opened on to a balcony that overlooked the South Court. The office was designed to blend unobtrusively with the rest of the mall. Unless you looked carefully you wouldn't notice the balcony or the doors. It was reachable only by private elevator. Lost shoppers and kids couldn't wander up here by mistake or out of curiosity.

Watching the afternoon sun play through the stained-glass dome and the throngs of shoppers below, Cogswell felt a thrill of the same sort of pride he got from looking at himself. In a very real sense both were products of his imagination and will.

The difference was, it was time to polish his image for the next major challenge and let go of the mall.

Black Oak had been an enormous success. Starting with a site everyone called "undevelopable" he had combined innovative design and even more innovative financing to make one of the hottest malls in the US.

Black Oak had done very well — for its time. But that time was the '80s, the days of yuppies, real estate tax breaks and conspicuous consumption. A different world.

Now the mall was nearly ten years old and that meant it was coming up on a major remodeling. The changes in the tax laws and the aggressive use of accelerated depreciation meant the tax advantages had been skimmed off long ago.

Keeping Black Oak would mean either a major investment or a slow slide to third-rate status. Cogswell's instincts told him it was time to get out. Even though the Southern California commercial market was glutted, Black Oak was still a desirable property.

Meanwhile, Cogswell had higher ambitions. Already he had two top political consultants advising him part time and a full-time pollster sounding out the market. In eighteen months the congressional seat would be up for grabs and he intended to grab it.

But to do that he needed money. Money to build the carefully managed groundswell of public support that would convince the local party that he was a viable candidate. Money to keep interest focused through a well-designed marketing campaign and, above all, money for the media blitz to ensure that he got the nomination.

His political consultants assured him the incumbent

was vulnerable. The voters of the district were ripe for a new image. ("New ideas and new solutions to national problems" was the way the consultants quaintly put it.)

Cogswell stopped and considered. Should he present himself as a staunch fiscal conservative or a pro-education liberal concerned about America's declining competitiveness? His record would play either way. Or could he combine the two? He'd have to ask his advisers.

Meanwhile it all turned on the mall. If he could get enough to scrape off his remaining debts and turn a decent profit, he'd have over a year to get ready for the congressional race.

He turned away from the window and strode to the door leading from his office to the conference room.

There was Larry Sakimoto, his real estate guy and Japanese expert; Paul Lenoir, his accountant on the deal; Helen Harrison, Lenoir's assistant; and Barry Goodman, the attorney and negotiator. All four were bright, alert and eager.

"Okay," Cogswell said, "where do we stand?"

"I think we've got a deal," Goodman told him.

Cogswell nodded. He would have preferred an American buyer, but the only people with money today were Japanese or Arabs. Fortunately the Japanese had outbid the Arabs.

"We've been over the Hayashi Group's last proposal," Lenoir said. "Basically we're together on this. The price is right and the terms are in line with what we wanted."

"Where does that leave us?"

"About ninety-five percent home. There are still a lot of minor points to clear up, things like maintenance allowances and set-asides, but we've got all the big stuff covered."

"And the contract to draw," Goodman interposed. "We've still got to get all this nailed down."

"Let's get the deal done first," Cogswell said. "Okay, what's next?"

"They're referring more and more stuff back to Japan," Sakimoto told him. "That means we're really close. Don't be surprised if the next step is for someone big to come out."

"Which means?"

"Which means they're ready to close the deal and we're into the home stretch on negotiations."

"I thought you said the guys we've been talking to had full authority."

"They do," Sakimoto assured him. "It's just a cultural thing. To the Japanese, a deal like this means entering into a long-term relationship, and that's something the top guy should do."

In his mind's eye, Kemper Cogswell saw the headlines:

"Congressional Candidate Linked to Japanese Business Interests." He shuddered.

"What long-term relationship?" he demanded. "I'm selling them a mall and that's it."

Sakimoto raised a soothing hand. "Of course. It's just that that's the way they see it. Besides," he added shrewdly, "it would be an honor to you. Their top man coming all the way from Japan to deal with you personally."

Cogswell's mental camera flashed a picture of him shaking hands with a major Japanese financial leader. That could play well in his campaign literature.

"Fine. But only if it's Kashihara himself."

Sakimoto hesitated. "I'll see what I can do."

Cogswell nodded and looked at the rest of his team. "Okay, folks, the end's in sight. All we've got to do now is keep plugging and make sure everything follows our game plan. We'll have a deal in just a few weeks if nothing out of the ordinary happens."

"Yo, dude."

The Surfer nodded in acknowledgment without turning around. He'd seen the kids come up the escalator.

The one in the lead, Ted, the one wearing the leather jacket, copied the Surfer's pose, leaning his forearms on the rail, hands clasped.

"So, you got anything good?"

Surfer smiled but kept looking down the escalators. "What you want?"

"Got any speed?" The tubby one asked over his friend's shoulder. Surfer remembered his name was Glenn.

"Pure clear crystal."

"How much?"

"Dime."

"Cool." Ted reached into his pocket and flashed several grubby bills.

The Surfer's head didn't move. "Twenty minutes. Burger King across from the west entrance."

"Cool." Glenn and Ted sauntered off.

The Oak Tree was decorated like a traditional English pub — if English pubs had ever been full of neon beer signs and green plants and carpeted in burgundy nylon.

Still, it was in the mall so it was close. For Larry Sakimoto and Paul Lenoir that was the important thing.

"Jesus Christ," Larry said as he and Paul slid into the booth near the door, "he thinks I can just tell Kashihara Tomoi to come here. One of the richest men in Japan and all I gotta do is ask him."

"Well this is a lot of money," Lenoir pointed out.

"Not to Kashihara," Sakimoto told the accountant. "It's practically pocket change."

"Hi hon, what'll it be?" Gwen said in one breath as she came bustling up. She was still on the easy side of forty and she still had her figure, but her motherly attitude was totally at variance with her skimpy cocktail waitress costume.

"My usual," Larry told her.

"Just a beer," Paul said.

"What a mess," Larry said after Gwen left.

"Hey, we're getting a near-record price. More than it's worth, in fact."

"If the deal holds together," Sakimoto said sourly. "If just one little thing goes wrong it could all come down like a house of cards."

"You think something might?"

Larry leaned across the table toward his friend. "*Anything* might go wrong. Another Japanese tourist gets killed in LA, the yen gets stronger, Kashihara gets up on the wrong side of the bed. Cogswell does something to piss Kashihara off. And the worst of it is, most of the stuff that could happen we can't control."

Gwen came back with their drinks.

She expertly slapped down napkins and glasses. "Here you go, hon. That'll be six fifty."

Larry reached for his wallet, then he took a look at the glass. Sticking out of the amber liquid was a tiny paper umbrella.

"What the hell is this?"

"A Manhattan." Gwen shrugged. "The bartender says, sorry, we're all out of cherries."

Larry gingerly fished the umbrella out of his drink. "He could at least have used a piece of pineapple."

Again the shrug. "He's all out of that too. Says he opens a can and it's gone overnight."

Larry considered the paper umbrella dubiously. Unlike almost anyone else who came into the Oak Tree, he could read the Chinese characters that decorated the umbrella. If they meant the same thing in Chinese they did in Japanese, serving someone a drink with one of those umbrellas was damn near an act of war.

"This whole damn place is going to hell," Larry grumbled.

Gwen arched an eyebrow. "Honey, at least you don't have to work here."

❖   ❖   ❖

Dawn Albright cast a practiced eye over the fitting and dressing rooms. The rooms were shared by several departments and keeping them neat wasn't really her job, but Dawn had been in retail long enough to know that success was made up of a myriad of tiny details. Besides, she might find some more hangers.

Sales might be down and so was her personal life but you still put the best possible face on things and kept trying.

A quick sweep showed her none of the rooms was occupied and the rooms were clean. She was about to go when she heard a sound.

There was a noise coming from one of the dressing rooms. A crunching sound, like plastic breaking.

Dawn hesitated. All sorts of strange things happened in the fitting rooms of a big department store. If you surprised a shoplifter in the act she could turn nasty. The prudent thing to do might be to call security.

On the other hand it would take time to get one of the Loss Prevention people up here and if it was nothing she'd look like a fool. She'd better check first.

The noise was definitely coming from the second-to-the-last dressing room. That was odd because there had been no one in there a second ago when she checked. Carefully, she approached the door and listened. Again the sound of breaking plastic.

Without knocking, she opened the door quickly. At first Dawn thought the room was empty. Then she saw a shape under the chair and thought a cat had gotten into the store.

Crouched in the corner was a . . . well, *something*. It was about the size of a small cat, but it had big flapping ears, a long nose and green skin. It was rocked back on its haunches like a monkey with its long forepaws in front of its chest.

And clenched in those paws was half a plastic hanger. The little thing took a big bite out of the hanger and chewed noisily. It grinned so broadly, crumbs of poorly masticated plastic dribbled from the corners of his enormous mouth. It closed its bulging eyes in pleasure as if it was savoring the taste of vintage plastic.

Dawn slammed the fitting room door, whirled and braced herself against it.

She took a deep, gasping breath to get her panic under control. Then she straightened her spine and smoothed her skirt with a neatly manicured hand that shook hardly at all.

Rats, she told herself firmly, rigorously ignoring the crunching sounds from behind the now-closed door. *There is a rat in that fitting room and it's eating my hangers.* Never mind that it was green, never mind she'd never heard of such a thing and never mind what it looked like, that *had* to be a rat. Anything else was just her imagination!

With head high and stride firm Dawn Albright left the fitting rooms at a brisk, businesslike pace. Obviously she had to report this to the store management. And then call the mall office and demand they do something about the rats.

It does explain things, Dawn Albright thought with the crystalline, detached calm of the near-hysterical. *But I wonder what happens to the metal hangers?*

"What happened to the chocolate sauce?" George Andropolous demanded.

Lance, the day "manager," shrugged slowly. Lance did everything slowly. Andropolous didn't know if it was drugs or too much sun.

Andropolous muttered something in Greek. "That's the second damn can this week. You been handing out extras?"

"No, man, I wouldn't do that."

Andropolous regarded his employee sourly. The kid was probably telling the truth. He was honest and given a calculator he could add and subtract well enough to total the register. Those were the main reasons he had been made manager.

"I can't have this. Chocolate sauce, cherries. Hell, that stuff's ten bucks a can. How the hell can I stay in business if we keep losing money like this. And if I can't stay in business what are you gonna do for a job, huh?"

Andropolous' temper had no visible effect on Lance. He simply shrugged.

"I'm gonna have to start coming in mornings to open too," the burly Greek told him. "Check the stuff morning and night. I'll find out where it's going, don't you worry."

Lance obviously wasn't worried about that or anything else. So he nodded.

"Ahh." Andropolous made the noise in his throat and turned away to look out over the Food Court.

It wasn't a bad business, he told himself as he surveyed the other shops. Some Guatemalan had the gyros concession, so George Andropolous had settled for ice cream. Not as much profit per transaction but it was more of an impulse buy.

If I could just keep the damn employees from eating up all the profits! he thought. Well, he'd find out who was doing it soon enough.

The late afternoon sun snuck up on Cyril Heathercoate through his rearview mirror and smacked him full in the face when he pulled his rented car into the parking lot.

The glare made his hangover headache even worse, and he scowled fiercely. "Bloody hell," he muttered. Then he checked his coat and tie in the mirror, squinting against the sun.

Cyril Heathercoate — or Arthur Mudge as he'd been known when he was growing up by Merseyside — was a potato-shaped man with a balding head, a broken nose and an accent that was pure Liverpool. Not that the bloody Yanks noticed. Speak like any kind of a Brit and they think you're a bleeding royal.

Cyril Heathercoate *hated* California. The sun was too bright, the air was too thick and everyone talked and moved at half speed. Worse, they were so bloody cheerful and positive thinking it was enough to give a bloke a headache, even without the ruddy hangover.

Heathercoate sat for a moment, squinting up at the edifice thrusting up into the smoggy air. *Like the bleeding Crystal Palace*, he thought. Not that he'd ever seen the Crystal Palace. The enormous greenhouse-cum-exhibition hall had been dismantled years before he'd been born. Besides, as he had to explain repeatedly to all these damn ignorant Yanks, Liverpool is a long way from London.

Bleeding blockheads, every one of them, and the Californians were the worst of the lot. Purgatory, he decided as he slid across the rapidly warming vinyl of the seat. That's what California was, purgatory.

In a sense he was here as punishment. The bit about the rock star's dead baby had been a trifle much for the American public. What the hell? The editor had approved the piece, hadn't she? But the trash telly got hold of it, the Establishment screamed and there had to be a sacrificial goat. So Cyril found himself demoted from following Royals and rock stars to chasing around the country after monsters.

Well, life was full of ups and downs, wasn't it? That had been a year ago and he'd be on top again soon. All he needed was one or two more strong pieces and if he didn't blot his copybook he could stay away from places like California and stick to civilized parts of the country, like New York.

Now this one, this read like a ticket back to New York. A haunted shopping mall.

The lead had come in the usual way. One of the paper's carefully cultivated network of informants told them about a security guard taken to a psychiatric hospital raving about monsters at the mall where he worked. A couple of quick phone calls and a little work in the paper's library showed the mall was well known in

Southern California where the paper had a strong circulation. With that, Cyril was on his way.

Unfortunately, he hadn't been able to get in to see the guard. They knew him at the clinic from last time and they wouldn't let him on the grounds.

Well he was used to that, wasn't he? He'd gotten a couple of attendants to talk, and he'd reconstructed an interview from that. Promising, but it wasn't really enough. He needed something more to flesh it out.

Heathercoate was a consummate professional who prided himself on producing the kind of material that the *Planet*'s readers lapped up. That wouldn't be hard here. Just spend a couple of days at the mall and he could come up with gossip and rumors to fill the chinks.

Typically, it never occurred to him to wonder if any of the story taking shape in his mind was true.

Andy Westlin leaned on the rail of the top level and stared down unseeing into the mall. The Surfer was gone from his usual place at the top of the escalators.

Paradise, Andy thought. Complete with a few snakes. Just the occasional garter snakes, not like the rattlers' den he had worked in as a cop.

Well, that was fine with him. He'd been through so much in the last couple of years that he wanted a place where he could just get away from all the pain and dirt and cruelty and savagery of the real world.

The pay was lousy, worse than a rookie patrolman's. But that didn't matter. He still had most of the money from selling his mother's house, he wasn't in debt and his tastes were simple. He could get along for quite a while by dipping into his savings a little every month.

A place to hide away and heal. Where better than a fantasy land where everything is neat and scrubbed and nice?

Welcome to Oz, Andy thought as he looked down into the artificial canyon. No, he decided, this wasn't a bad deal at all.

Chapter 5

Andy trudged up the sloping drive from one deserted parking lot to the next. The yellow-pink glare of the sodium lights threw odd, harsh shadows that made features stand out strongly while leaving ominous pools of shadow in the planters and other sheltered areas. Without meaning to, Andy found himself staying to the center and keeping his right hand near his gun.

LaVonne was right, this place was spooky at night. Objectively he knew he was a lot safer here than he'd been in his cruiser on patrol, but the emptiness and shadows still made him jumpy.

First-night jitters. He wasn't supposed to be working nights after just three days on the job, but Henderson had called in sick and Dunlap had asked him to take the outside tonight. Morales was the inside man, and a guy named Tuchetti, whom he'd never met, was on the board in the security office.

He'd parked the golf cart because he felt like walking. Now after half his shift he was beginning to think longingly about zipping up the drives in electric-powered comfort. Well, he needed the exercise. He'd been getting soft since he left the force and he was puffing slightly by the time he reached the top level parking lot.

There was a sound from one of the dumpsters.

Andy spun and grabbed his flashlight. The noise came again, as if there was someone in the dumpster. Moving on the balls of his feet, fatigue forgotten, Andy eased over to the building side of the lot. "Central, this is Unit Two. I think I've got something in a dumpster on north side of Level Two."

"Unit Two, this is Central," Tuchetti's voice came back. "Do you want me to call the police?"

"Ah, negative, Central. Just keep the cameras on me and let me see what it is first."

"Ten-four, Unit Two. I have you on the monitors now."

Andy put the radio away, unsnapped his holster strap and slowly and deliberately worked along the wall toward the dumpster. It wasn't a good tactical situation. The trash container was steel and it sat in an alcove in the concrete block wall. The Glaser ammunition in his revolver wouldn't penetrate a thick sheet of glass, never mind steel or concrete. If whoever was in there fired on him it would be virtually impossible to return fire effectively.

Quit worrying, he told himself, *this isn't Southside*. Whoever was in there probably wasn't armed with anything more than a knife and almost certainly didn't want to shoot it out. Most likely a transient sleeping, or a couple of kids screwing. But still his stomach tightened and his mouth tasted metallic. *Maybe I should have called for backup*.

He flattened himself against the wall and peeked around into the alcove. Nothing. He listened. Only the near-inaudible hiss of distant traffic and the sound of a far-off jet. He peeked again. Still nothing.

There wasn't space between the dumpster and the alcove walls, so whoever it was had to be in the dumpster itself.

Andy drew his gun and hefted his flashlight in his left hand. Still no sound from inside. He took a long, deep breath. *Okay, hit it!*

In a single fluid motion, Andy spun around the wall and jumped on the dumpster step. As soon as he hit the step there was a frantic scrabbling from inside the dumpster. Before he could get his flashlight on it a ball of black fur shot out of the dumpster on the other side and bounded across the parking lot.

A cat. Just a goddamn cat! *I really am jumpy*, he thought as he let out his breath in a sigh.

"Ah, Unit Two," the radio crackled to life, "what is your situation?" Tuchetti was laughing so hard he could barely get the words out. "I say again, do you require assistance?"

"Negative, Central," Andy told him as he tried to reholster his gun while juggling the flashlight and radio in his left hand. "Everything is under control." He hoped the security cameras couldn't pick up the color of his face. "Back on rounds."

Well, that will probably make Morales' damn blooper tape! Andy thought as he strode away from the dumpster with as much dignity as he could muster. In a couple of days every guard in the mall would have seen his encounter with the cat. *Damn Tuchetti probably knew damn well what was in that damn dumpster.*

The cat was nearly seven, old for a stray. He was scarred, starved and invested with a full measure of the caution that comes to feral things that must live on the edge of civilization. In the three hours since he had been frightened out of the dumpster he had searched unceasingly for something to eat.

It wasn't a good night. The exterminators had been here recently, and the ground squirrels and mice that normally infested the outside planters were gone. The dumpsters containing the Food Court's garbage were shut tight and there wasn't so much as a spill of grease around them.

The cat didn't even consider begging from a human. To him humans were as dangerous as the automobiles that would snuff out his life in an instant. He had been born wild, part of a litter from a mother whose owners had dumped her at the mall when they found she was pregnant. There had been six kittens in the litter and he was the last survivor by goodly margin.

The cat paused, body low to the ground, as it searched the loading dock. Above the closed metal shutters, two small lights threw harsh patterns of light and shadow on rolling metal doors and the parking area where the trucks unloaded. There was no way onto the dock proper, not even for a cat. But in an angle of the building and the retaining wall there was a place where the workers ate lunch. Sometimes they threw scraps of food up into the bushes and ivy planted above.

The cat's whiskers twitched as he sucked in air to test for smells. There was a faint taint like long-dead meat and a hint of another strange smell as well.

The cat hesitated. But he had lived around human places long enough that strange smells were part of his world and his senses were beginning to dull with age. Besides, he was hungry.

He leaped down from the edge of the dock to the parking lot and trotted toward the retaining wall. His path took him close to a patch of deep shadow near the wall.

Too close.

Something moved in the darkness with blinding speed. The cat's reflexes were sharp, but he was no match for the thing that lashed out. The cat bit and clawed frantically at the paw that pinned it, but its teeth and claws could barely penetrate the thing's coarse gray fur. Inexorably, the claws tightened, and with a final despairing yowl the cat gave up his life.

The noise brought Andy on the run.

Sudstrom's loading dock was quiet and still, but not empty. There was something laying over by the retaining wall on the far side. Andy skidded to a halt when he saw what it was.

The bloody rag had been a cat. Or rather half a cat. Someone or something had sheared the animal in half and smeared the remaining part over the asphalt. The pinkish viscera and purple-gray intestines stood out vividly against the blood, black fur and dark pavement.

Andy knelt and examined it more closely. The cat looked like it had been run over by a car. Only there weren't any cars in the loading area.

A *dog?* But Andy hadn't heard any barking. *A kid maybe?* A really sick kid.

Andy's hand moved to his holster and he swung the flashlight in a quick sweep of the shadows. But there was nothing there. The light probed the bushes and ivy above the retaining wall. They were as still and silent as the rest.

Besides, it didn't really look like the work of a kid or psycho. They cut their victims, or sometimes burned them. The cat had been torn, as if it had gotten run over or caught in some kind of machinery.

He reached for his radio and then hesitated. No sense in reporting a dead cat. He didn't know for sure what had killed it, and he'd made a fool of himself over a cat once tonight.

Maybe it was run over by a car, and he just hadn't noticed it before, he thought. Then he looked at the bloody carcass again, laying in the middle of the open space. *Yeah. Right.*

With a final look at the cat, he moved on — cautiously.

The sun rose bright and reddish in the uniformly gray sky. It would be especially smoggy today, Andy thought, with the special kind of stickiness that came from the combination of a hot summer day and an extra load of air pollution.

It didn't matter, he thought as he squinted into the glare. He'd spend most of the day asleep in his air-conditioned apartment. Just two more hours and he'd be off. It would still be fairly cool for the drive home, and he lived west of the mall, so he'd have the sun at his back. *Could be worse*, he thought as he headed for the drive to the main lot.

He heard a car drive up as he rounded the corner and started down the drive. That was wrong. It wasn't six yet, and no one but the guards was supposed to be on the property. Some natural caution, or the night's events, kept him from simply walking out to confront the driver. Instead, he peeked around the corner at the bottom of the drive.

It was Morales. He was parked over by one of the dumpsters and rummaging in the open trunk of his car. Andy ducked back as the other guard straightened, so he didn't see what Morales was carrying. He heard a sound like paper crumpling in the still cool morning air and then a dumpster lid opening and clanging shut.

Andy looked around the corner again as Morales slammed the trunk of his car, got behind the wheel and sped off. As soon as he disappeared around the corner, Andy checked the dumpster.

It was empty — almost. Back in the corner was a wad of crumpled paper and plastic. Andy had to crane on tiptoe and use his flashlight before he identified the stuff. It was an outer wrapper, the kind some merchants put around bundles of half dozen expensive suits or dresses to protect them in shipping.

Just the sort of thing you'd expect to find in a mall dumpster. Except the outer paper was clearly labeled "Sudstrom's" and Sudstrom's had its own dumpster — which was down at the far end of the mall next to the store's loading dock.

Andy switched off his flashlight and looked off the way that his coworker had gone. *Maybe*, he thought, *just maybe this job isn't the piece of cake everybody said it was.*

Chapter 6

The bar was dark and cool and smelled of old beer and cigarette smoke. As the sprinkling of patrons slowly drank away the early afternoon the jukebox thumped out endless country songs.

"Why the hell didn't you tell me the new guy was working last night?" Eduardo Morales demanded.

The other man in the booth took a sip of his beer and shrugged. "Happened at the last minute."

Morales' beer was losing its foam but he hadn't touched it yet. "You nearly fucked everything, you know that? I think he saw me."

"What were you doing?"

"Dumping some shit. Man, three minutes earlier and he would have seen me putting the stuff in the trunk."

"Did he see what you dumped?"

"Naw, the angle was all wrong. But man, you nearly bitched up everything."

"I told you to lay off. We don't need trouble now."

"Hey, I got commitments, you know? And the stuff was just sitting on the loading dock."

The other dropped it as hopeless. Once a thief . . . "So, all he actually saw was you throwing some stuff away? That's nothing."

"No, but it *could* have been, man!" He paused. "Did he report it?"

J.D. Dunlap, head of security at Black Oak Mall, shook his head. "Not a thing. Either he didn't see anything or he decided to keep his mouth shut."

Morales snorted and took a pull on his beer. "Maybe he's brighter than we thought, huh?"

"I hope not," Dunlap said. "It will work better if he's dumb."

Surfer stood by the bus stop across from the mall, watched the traffic go by and fidgeted under the smog-bright California sun. He looked like someone who was in a hurry and waiting for a bus. But the Surfer had parked his expensive Camaro less than a block away. The bus stop bench advertised a funeral home. That didn't help Surfer's mood.

Finally a blue van pulled up, the side door slid open and without a word Surfer got in.

The van's blue-on-blue airbrushed paint was custom but not unusual for Southern California. The vertical windows in the back were smoked plastic and the wheels were gold plated. Fancy and expensive, but not something that would stick in your mind if you spent much time on LA streets.

Nothing unusual — unless you knew the plastic in those windows was bullet-proof Lexan, the floor was reinforced with sheet steel and the tires had special run-flat inserts. But then if you knew that much, you probably knew a good deal more about the van and its occupants.

"So good of you to join us," Toby said as Surfer settled into the backward-facing purple velour bench seat in the front of the van's passenger compartment.

Toby was a compact, strongly built young man in his early 20s. His gray sharkskin suit was def without being outrageous, and his gold jewelry was expensive without being flashy. Like the Surfer, he wore wraparound shades. He looked like a concert promoter or a record executive — a mean one.

Toby's diction was a tribute to the quality of American television-announcing, his rhetoric to American gangster movies and his erudition to the quality of American prison libraries. He owed his success to his native drive and intelligence and his profession to the opportunities available to a poor black kid who grows up in the wrong neighborhood.

In short, Toby was a medium-big drug dealer with very big dreams.

He was sitting in a single large captain's chair at the back of the van. His companion, hulking in another captain's chair facing the side door, was equally well dressed. Lurch was tall enough to play forward for the Lakers, bulky enough to play linebacker for the Raiders and crazy-mean enough for damn near anything.

Pedro, the driver, was a lot shorter and fatter than Lurch, but nearly as strong. He was deaf, which meant that Toby didn't have to worry about what he overheard. It also kept the cops from hassling them too much in a traffic stop.

"Would you care for some refreshment?" Toby gestured to the built-in bar with the mirrored countertop to Lurch's left. Surfer shook his head. Then Toby leaned forward and got down to it.

"Now word up, my man. We got us a business opportunity to discuss."

Surfer threw a nervous look at Lurch. When Toby started talking about "business opportunities" or any of that other educated shit, it usually meant someone was in trouble.

"I am about to cut you in on the ground floor of a really *prime* proposition."

Surfer licked his lips nervously.

"My man, you are about to become a test market for a totally new product."

Lurch reached into a drawer in the bar beside him and pulled out a vial. Wordlessly, he passed it over to his boss.

Toby held the vial up between his thumb and forefinger. "Do you know what this is?"

The stuff in the vial was a coarse grayish powder,

about the color of cigarette ash and a little finer than sugar.

"Crappy coke?" Surfer ventured.

Toby chuckled. "Thinking small, my man. That's no way to get ahead in this organization." He held the vial to the light and smiled.

"This here is something completely new. What you might call a 'designer drug,' you dig? A synthetic cooked up by my very own research department. Imagine if you will a combination of coke and speed. The rush, the energy, the staying power. The best of both worlds."

Toby tossed the bottle back to Lurch, and it disappeared instantly into the drawer.

"And best of all, it don't show up on no drug tests. None of the standard field reagents the cops use can pick it up." He leaned back and spread his arms expansively.

"Research, my man. Research is the key to success in the modern business environment. You gotta keep coming up with new products to stay ahead of the competition, you dig?"

Like most people in his line of work, Surfer thought the key to success was staying one step ahead of the law and burning the competition before they could burn you. But he nodded.

"Now this here is a unique product, and we're gonna start by pricing it low to gain market share on entry. That means nickel bags, you dig? You get it cheap and you sell it cheap and we make it up later when the market is established."

He slid his sunglasses down his nose and looked over them at Surfer. "There be any questions?"

"How much?"

"To you, hundred an ounce."

"How much in a nickel?"

"Quarter-gram and don't you be shorting none."

Surfer did a quick mental calculation. That kind of profit wasn't at all bad at his level. Not that he had any real choice.

"When?"

"My people be in touch. Just be cool and have the money."

The van dropped Surfer at a bus stop about a mile from the mall.

As the van pulled away, Toby leaned back on the cushions and smiled. The other key to successful product introductions was test marketing. For that you wanted someplace relatively isolated with minimal competition. And in this business you also wanted someplace it wouldn't hurt to lose if things weren't successful. The speed-freak chemist who'd turned out the stuff to Toby's specification wasn't too stable, and Toby wanted to make sure it worked as advertised before he peddled it to his better customers.

The rock music blended with the din of the video games and the noise enveloped The Pit like a shield. Heather Framel took another moody drag on her cigarette. Dani's mom had told her not to come back. None of her friends had shown up and she needed to find a place to crash at least for tonight. Idly, she ran her hand through her bleached blonde hair on the side where it was chopped off short. She'd gotten Terry to drive her by her mom's place, but *his* truck was out front. She couldn't go home.

There were a couple of places around the mall where she could sleep outdoors, hidden in the bushes, but she *hated* doing that. You wake up all grungy with twigs and shit in your hair.

Someone came into The Pit, and Heather looked up expectantly. But it wasn't anyone she knew, only the new rent-a-pig.

Well fuck it. She'd get by. She always did.

After a week on the job, Andy Westlin had decided checking The Pit was the worst part of the job. The noise, the lighting and the hostility to authority tended to give him a headache. But it had to be checked frequently, so he put on his best street-cop stare and worked his way through the tables.

It was almost 4 P.M. but the place was nearly empty. Not even the air guitarists had shown up yet. There was a skinny blonde girl with hair hacked off short and a black vinyl jacket covered with chrome studs sitting and smoking at one of the first tables, a couple of skateboarders wandering around and at a table near the back three or four punk rockers in leather jackets, chains and wraparound sunglasses. The punkers and the girl ignored him ostentatiously, and the skaters just weren't paying attention.

Two of the punkers wore spiked mohawks dyed in bands of violent color and the third's head was shaved. As Andy got close enough to hear their voices over the infernal racket of The Pit he realized the bald one was a woman.

When he got even closer he saw they weren't very young either. As nearly as he could tell all of them were in their 30s. Caught in a time warp and preserved in the never-never land of the mall. It made him a little sad.

He stopped outside The Pit and blinked a couple of times as his eyes adjusted to the light.

"It gets to you, doesn't it?" said an old woman sitting on a bench in front of him.

"I beg your pardon, ma'am?" Andy was polite but cautious. Part of his job was being pleasant, but some of these old ones were so lonely they'd talk to you for an hour about their grandchildren.

"The noise and the lights in there," the old woman said. "It's supposed to bother you, you know."

Andy looked more closely. The woman on the bench was small, almost frail, tanned brown and leathery with silver hair cut short and straight. He vaguely remembered seeing her around.

"It's a filter," she went on. "It weeds out people over about twenty-five." She dropped her voice and nodded toward the table of punks in the back. "Mostly anyway."

Andy grinned. "Yes, ma'am, I guess you're right. It'd sure weed me out if I didn't have to go in there. But how did you know?"

"Oh, I'm doing fieldwork. I'm an anthropologist. My name is Pauline Patterson."

"How do you do, ma'am." He started to extend his hand and then he noticed the walker sitting next to the bench.

She followed his glance. "Emeritus now, of course. But I'm doing a study of the cultural anthropology of the modern American shopping mall."

"I thought anthropologists studied primitive cultures."

Pauline Patterson nodded at the punks and smiled with the half of her mouth that worked. "What do you call that?

"Seriously, anthropologists study all kinds of cultures. There's a branch called urban anthropology that deals with subcultures in industrial societies." Then she sobered. "Besides, I think it will be a while before I get back to the New Guinea highlands or the Cameroon."

"You were in those places?"

"I walked for nearly three weeks into the Owen Stanley Range to do my first fieldwork."

Andy, for whom the word "culture" meant either symphonies and art museums or yogurt, shook his head. "I'd think after places like that the culture you find here would be pretty dull."

"Cultures," Pauline Patterson corrected, "and it isn't dull at all. What you find in the mall is many different cultures, or subcultures if you prefer. The groups are quite distinct, and some of them are mutually hostile. In general, there is very little mixing in the mall except among some of the affines." She caught Andy's puzzled look. "The groups with similar values, life-styles and symbol systems."

The skateboarders came out of The Pit and sauntered off down the mall, chattering.

Andy's eyes flicked to them and then he turned his full attention to Dr. Patterson. "How do you tell these groups apart? They all look like kids to me. Except some are better dressed than others."

"That's easy. You pay attention. For example, did you notice those young men's haircuts?"

"Short on the sides and long on the back?"

"Shaved on the temples. The area not covered by a skating helmet. If you ask them they might tell you that's to cut wind resistance while keeping the hair under the helmet for extra padding. Now look at their shoes."

Andy's eyes followed her pointing finger. "They look like running shoes."

"They are similar, but the design is quite distinctive. The waffle soles give a good grip on the board and the tops are higher than most running shoes to give good ankle support, but lower than high-tops for easy movement. Skater's shoes. They are skaters."

"So it's all for efficiency."

"No, it's for identification. They are proclaiming to all the world, or to all the world which is important to them, that they are skaters. The point of the dress and haircut is almost never just efficiency."

Andy looked down at his blue-on-blue uniform with yellow piping. "I see what you mean."

"Of course, identifying the groups is the easy part of the work. It is more difficult to track behavior and social interactions. Then there are the really difficult matters like worldviews."

"How do you find all that out?"

"I listen and I take notes." She held up a miniature tape recorder with a thong looped around her wrist.

"My daughter gave me this. A lot better than taking notes by hand, I can tell you." She looked down ruefully at her right hand lying in her lap. "Especially now."

There was a brief, awkward silence.

"Don't think it isn't interesting work," Dr. Patterson went on briskly. "The social groupings at this mall are the most complex I have ever observed. There are so many different groups, and they have the resources to express their differences in so many ways."

Andy looked around at the people flowing by. "I never noticed."

"Most people don't," Pauline Patterson told him. "They just go blindly along, ignoring all the rich and complex social ecology that flows around them."

She smiled. "I've been lecturing, haven't I? I'm sorry. A bad habit left over from my time in the classroom."

"No, it's very interesting," Andy said quickly. "I never paid attention to things like that." He paused. "Except maybe when I was sorting out the good guys from the bad guys and trying to figure out who was likely to go squirrely on me on a routine stop."

"So you were a police officer, then. I thought I recognized the signs."

Andy grinned. "I guess it's kind of obvious. But I never would have pegged you as an anthropologist."

Pauline Patterson smiled. "Oh, we have our identifying symbols and mannerisms, I can assure you. It is obvious at the annual meeting of the American Anthropological Association." Her face fell. "Not that I have been in four or five years.

"I had a stroke, you see. Only they don't call it a stroke any more. Now it's a CVA." She made a face. "As if changing the name made them any prettier."

"Yes, ma'am," Andy said with more emotion than he intended.

Dr. Patterson looked at him sharply. "You know about them?"

"My mother had one when I was in junior high. I pretty much took care of her until another one killed her six years later." He stopped. "I'm sorry, I didn't mean to . . ."

Dr. Patterson waved that away with a flip of her good hand. "You're not saying anything I don't think about constantly."

There was another awkward pause. Then Dr. Patterson looked down at the watch on her left wrist. "Well, I have to go. My daughter is meeting me out front."

She reached out with her left hand and pulled the walker over in front of her.

Andy didn't try to help her.

She shifted her grip and tried to pull herself erect. She got a few inches off the bench and sat back. She shifted her grip again and forced her body forward as she pulled with her left arm. This time she forced herself up.

She smiled at him. "Thank you, young man. I hope we meet again."

"I hope so too, ma'am," Andy said, and meant it.

Chapter 7

"BANG BANG!" The little boy jumped out from behind the planter directly in front of Andy and mimed a gun with his fingers.

"I got you, policeman!" he proclaimed proudly.

"That's right," Andy said with a smile. "You sure did."

He took three more steps before the incident sank in. There was a time, not too many months ago, when anyone of any size who jumped out and pointed something at him would have sent him diving for cover with his gun out. After a month at the mall, all he had done was smile when that kid surprised him.

He smiled. *Losing my edge.* But he had also lost the gut-ache that had been his near-constant companion, and he hadn't had a nightmare in at least a week. He still kept his service revolver loaded at home, but he wasn't as fanatic about having it in easy reach all the time. He didn't even take it into the bathroom with him, he realized.

Andy stopped next to a bank of elevators and looked down on the bright, clean world spread out below him. He almost laughed for simple joy. This job was very good for him.

"Ooooh."

Andy looked around at the frustrated moan. A woman was trying to get a cardboard box off the elevator, and the bottom was trying to fall out of the box. She had braced her back against the open elevator door and was holding the bottom in the carton with a raised knee. But she couldn't shift her hands to get under the box, and the door was butting her mindlessly as it tried to close.

"Need some help, ma'am?" Andy put his arm under the box and gently lifted it off her knee.

He was rewarded with a brilliant smile and a flash of gratitude in big brown eyes. "Oh, thank you. Here, set it on the bench and let me fix it."

The woman was small, a little over five feet, with glossy black hair cut short around her head. Her skin was clear olive, and her eyes were large and dark. Her eyes were her best feature, Andy decided. Either that or her compact figure. It sure wasn't the way she was dressed.

She was wearing "sensible" shoes with thick rubber soles, a print dress and a knitted purple shawl draped over her shoulders. Topping off the outfit was a pair of fluorescent purple plastic earrings and a truly ugly amethyst and silver brooch that secured the shawl.

The woman looked up, caught him looking and stared back.

Andy flushed. "Excuse me, ma'am, I didn't mean to stare."

"Never be embarrassed," she said as she rummaged in an oversize purse slung over one shoulder. "It keeps you from growing." She pulled out a piece of brightly colored ribbon and slipped it under the box. "My grandmother always told me to keep a piece of string handy. But I like ribbon better than string." She looked up and smiled at him. She had a wonderful smile, Andy thought, full of life and a little mischevious. "It's more colorful, don't you think?"

"Yes, ma'am.

"But you were looking at the way I'm dressed, weren't you? It's because I have strong psychic powers," she explained deadpan. "People with strong psychic powers develop their own distinctive style."

Andy looked hard at her, but the woman was serious.

"That's interesting, ma'am."

"The name is Judy. Judy Cohen."

"I'm Andy . . ."

"Westlin," she finished. "You're a new guard."

"Did your psychic powers tell you that?"

"No, the merchants' newsletter. They ran your picture in the last issue." She looked him over. "I also know you have strong psychic powers, although you don't realize it yet."

"Uh, was that in the merchants' newsletter too?"

"No, that's in your aura."

"Yes, ma'am."

"Oh, stop calling me ma'am, it makes me feel like I'm your grandmother or something."

"Yes, ma' . . . Judy."

She smiled. "That's better." She stood up and hefted the carton.

"Would you like me to carry that for you?" Andy asked.

"Oh, no thank you. I don't have far to go with it. I run Bellbookand over in the North Bazaar."

"Bellbookand?"

"Candle," she supplied. "It's the Bellbookand Candle Shop. You know, candles, oils, herbs, that sort of thing." Then she smiled again. "Stop by some time."

Andy smiled back. "I'll do that, Judy."

Timmy Gonzales was bored.

His mother had left him in his stroller next to the South Court fountain while she ducked into the Coffee Tree to pick up some custom-roasted Blue Kona. The aisles in the shop were too narrow to maneuver the stroller comfortably, and she could see him out the front of the shop.

For a while Timmy had watched in three-year-old fascination as the people streamed by, a mass of shapes and bright colors. That was all right for five minutes or so, but now it was just boring.

He fidgeted in his stroller, banged on the edge and

screwed up his face and whimpered experimentally. But no one paid him any attention. He squirmed some more, twisting left and right so violently that the stroller rocked. But it was a top-of-the-line model and well up to containing a rambunctious toddler.

As he twisted, he caught sight of the fountain behind him. Fretfulness forgotten, he turned to stare at this new wonder.

The water arced high into the air, catching bits of rainbow where the sun coming through the dome caught it. It splashed off the bronze and concrete and streamed down to splash again in the basin at the bottom. Behind the fountain, another stream of water emerged from the artificial rock face and cascaded down into the same pool.

As Timmy moved his head, the bits of rainbow coalesced into a shining, brilliantly colored arc. Timmy laughed and reached out for it, but it seemed to recede from his chubby grasp.

He leaned forward in his stroller, then he lunged against it to push it closer to the pretty colors. In the Coffee Tree, Mrs. Gonzales waited impatiently for the clerk to finish with the customer ahead of her. Her back was to the fountain.

Timmy writhed in the seat until he got one leg free. Then he grasped the sides, pulled his other leg out and stood up on the cloth of the stroller seat. Once more he leaned out toward the rainbow and once more it eluded him. Firmly and deliberately, Timmy Gonzales began to walk toward the source of color, one teetering step at a time.

Mrs. Gonzales came out of the Coffee Tree in a guilty hurry. She had been longer than she had intended, and she was half afraid Timmy had gotten into something.

Because the stroller was turned around facing away from the store, she didn't see it was empty until she got right up to it. She gasped and cold fear clutched at her.

"Oh my God!" She swiveled frantically, seeking a glimpse of her son. "Timmy!"

She turned in nearly a complete circle before she happened to look up. There was Timmy, happily playing in the rainbow mist. Thirty feet in the air.

Mrs. Gonzales did what any normal mother would do. She screamed. The bag of coffee fell from her hands, split, and coffee beans went skittering over the tiled floor.

His mother's screams frightened Timmy, so he screamed back. He also grabbed for the nearest solid object, the top of the bronze fountain. That put him right in the line of fire for the fountain nozzles, so Timmy got drenched. That frightened him even more and he screamed even louder, which upset Mrs. Gonzales even more and she screamed louder still. All around them people froze and looked up, their armor of inattention pierced by the noise.

LaVonne Sanders was just rounding the corner into South Court when the screaming duet started. Even so, she had to shoulder her way through the suddenly stationary crowd to get to the fountain.

Mrs. Gonzales was nearly hyperventilating by the time LaVonne reached her. "My baby. My baby. My baby," she gasped over and over. Up above them Timmy's screams reached a new level and developed a modulation like an air-raid siren.

Without taking her eyes off the boy, LaVonne gently pried Mrs. Gonzales' arm off and reached for her radio.

"Base, we got a kid stuck on the fountain in South Court. Get some people up here with ropes and ladders. Over."

"He'll fall," Mrs. Gonzales babbled in LaVonne's ear. "He'll fall and hurt himself, and ooh, God, I was just in there for a minute and he was in his stroller and I just . . ."

LaVonne tried to move her ear away from the frantic mother. "Base, say again."

". . . and you've got to get him down and he's . . ."

"Take it easy, ma'am," LaVonne said over the din of falling water, screaming child and babbling mother. "We'll get him down in no time. Base?"

But there was no answer, and LaVonne wasn't sure she could have made it out through the racket anyway. Presumably, the security center was getting Maintenance out with the equipment to get the kid down. Meanwhile, she had her choice of standing here and listening to Mrs. Gonzales or trying to do something. The choice was obvious.

Moving to the base of the fountain, she unlocked the pump control panel and hit the emergency cutoff. Instantly the arching sprays drooped and died. Next she took off her oxfords and socks, rolled up her pants and waded gingerly into the pool.

The bronze sculpture was wet and slick and not really designed for climbing, but it was irregular enough that there were a lot of good handholds. Gingerly, she grabbed a couple of protrusions and began to climb.

Having someone stuck on the mall structure wasn't common but it wasn't exactly unknown either. The maintenance crew had a regular drill for getting people, usually teenagers, out of places where they weren't supposed to be. LaVonne was about eight feet up when the first maintenance men arrived carrying an extension ladder.

Two of the crew waded into the fountain to extend the ladder next to LaVonne. She waited until they had it fully extended and stepped across onto the firmer footing. But Timmy was nearly thirty feet in the air and it was only a twenty-five-foot ladder. Above her the child continued to wail.

The guard climbed quickly almost to the top then gingerly the last two or three rungs. She was standing on the very top rung and Timmy was still a little above her and to one side. She briefly considered moving the ladder to the side so it would be directly under Timmy, but that would mean climbing all the way down to the ground.

"Okay, kid," LaVonne said, teetering on the top step of the ladder and trying to sound reassuring. "Come to me."

To Timmy, LaVonne didn't sound at all reassuring. He clung tighter to the fountain and kept screaming for his mommy. LaVonne leaned out further, nearly lost her balance and recovered by bracing herself against the fountain.

She got her hands on Timmy's waist. "Come on, kid." But Timmy only clung tighter. Shifting her grip, LaVonne pried Timmy's right arm loose from the fountain. Then she reached for the left arm to pry it loose as well. Timmy promptly grabbed the fountain with his right arm.

Swearing under her breath, LaVonne pried Timmy's right arm off the fountain again, this time trying to put it over her shoulder. Timmy, with a child's instinct to cling, promptly grabbed at her. His hand went into her face. His tiny fingers missed her eyes, but his tiny fingernails raked tiny furrows in the guard's cheek before the tiny hand fastened on LaVonne's nose.

Gently, she pried Timmy's fingers out of her nostrils and guided his hand around to her shoulder. The boy grabbed the epaulet of her uniform in a death grip. Then she reached for Timmy's other hand.

Timmy's other hand came more easily this time, and the boy twisted to lock his arm around LaVonne's neck. As he twisted he let go of the fountain with his legs and tried to wrap them around the guard's chest. The motion was so sudden that the weight shift nearly threw LaVonne off balance, and for a breathtaking instant they teetered on the top rung of the ladder to the gasps of the crowd below.

Gently, very gently, LaVonne stepped down off the top rung of the ladder. One more step and she was able to get a hand on the ladder rail. With a still-crying

Timmy obscuring her vision, she felt her way down the ladder, one rung at a time. The crowd applauded all the way down.

LaVonne stepped off the ladder into the fountain, and Mrs. Gonzales came sloshing up to reclaim her son. Timmy nearly put his thumb in LaVonne's eye untangling his grip. Now that the show was over the crowd melted away.

"How the hell did the kid get up there?" LaVonne demanded as she stepped out of the fountain.

Mrs. Gonzales started scolding Timmy in Spanish, as she always did when he did something bad in public. She spared LaVonne a glance. "I don't know." Then she went back to chastising Timmy in the utterly mistaken notion that no one around them would know she was bawling him out. Timmy was sufficiently upset by the experience to take the scolding in wide-eyed silence.

"He flew," one of the kids in the crowd piped up.

"What?"

"He flew," the kid repeated. "You asked how he got up there and I, like, told you."

LaVonne threw him a disgusted glance.

"No, like, really. He just flew up there and was, like, hanging in the air when his mother came out. She, like, totally freaked, you know, and that scared the kid."

LaVonne looked at Mrs. Gonzales, but she was too busy getting Timmy back in the stroller to say anything.

"I'm telling you, the kid flew," the kid repeated again. But LaVonne obviously wasn't listening.

The kid saw it was hopeless, so he shrugged and turned away.

Yvonne Kelly compressed her lips into a thin line. This had not been one of her better ideas.

True, D. Wally, Bookpusher, encouraged its managers to hold author signings. Being in a major mall in Southern California, Yvonne was able to do more signings than most and that got her store more bonus points in the quarterly competition for Outstanding D. Wally's Outlet.

This Saturday she'd outdone herself. She had gotten not one, but two authors to come in and sign. She had even moved the dump of *The Cute Cat Diet Book* out of the front of the store to make room.

So now on one side of the store Andrea Lorne was signing *Shopping For Ecstasy: Why Shopping Is Better Than Sex*. On the other side Laura Dahlmers was signing *Get Control of Your Life: The Twelve-Step Method for Beating Shopping Dependency*.

Actually there weren't that many customers, and the two spent most of their time glaring at each other.

I've got to start reading the books before I set up these signings, Yvonne thought to herself, *or at least the titles*.

Satisfied that her authors weren't at the hair-pulling stage yet, Yvonne retreated deeper into the store. A little more than a third of the way back she stopped in front of one of the chest-high sections of shelves and frowned.

"Peter, I thought I told you to reshelve this section," Yvonne said.

"I did," the thin young man with the thick glasses protested. "I had everything straightened out when I left last night."

"Well, they're out of place now. What if we got inspected by CSP? We'd lose bonus points for not following the SDP."

Peter looked blank. When he swallowed, his protuberant Adam's apple made his tie bob up and down and he looked like a lizard which had just eaten a bug.

"Corporate Standards and Practices and the Standard Display Plan," Yvonne said, as if explaining something to a small child. "Honestly, Peter, don't you remember anything from your orientation?"

"Not all of it," Peter mumbled.

"Well you should spend some time reviewing the procedures instead of reading books," Yvonne told him.

Peter, who thought working in a bookstore was the closest thing to heaven, just blinked. "Someone keeps coming through and messing them up," he said defensively. "And it's always the same ones too."

The words sent a chill down Yvonne's spine.

"Is it the same person?" she asked sharply.

"I don't think so. I've been watching, and I haven't seen anyone messing with the books. I haven't even seen the same people in those sections in the last couple of days."

Yvonne thought hard. It wasn't unknown for people to rearrange books. Occasionally it was an author trying to get more precious display space for his or her work. Sometimes it was a joke, like the person who kept moving *How to Make Love Last Forever* from the Relationships section over to Fantasy. More often it was someone who was offended by the content, like the people who kept hiding *The Joy of Gay Sex* or *Standing Up for Smokers' Rights*.

But sometimes it was an organized campaign. Fundamentalists or Black militants or Neo-Nazis or someone would go around moving, hiding or even damaging books they disliked at stores all over the country. D. Wally's policy called for the manager who noticed any such consistent movement of books to upload a special form with the daily report. That way headquarters could formulate a policy and get it into the monthly planning cycle as quickly as possible.

"Perhaps you'd better show me."

The science and technology books were on one row of shelves. Facing them across the aisle were the new age titles. According to the latest issue of "D. Wally's BookReport," the company newsletter, focus groups had shown the juxtaposition increased sales of the new age titles because new age book buyers felt reassured by the proximity to accepted sciences. The article also included a small box on dealing with complaints from outraged buyers of technical and scientific books. The box pointed out studies had shown the people who were likely to complain weren't good D. Wally's customers anyway. They almost never bought books on the Weekly Hot List or the high-margin items like calendars and furry animals with suction-cup feet.

"There," Peter pointed. Yvonne didn't need her copy of the weekly SDP to see the stock was out of order. There were several gaps where books had obviously been removed from the shelves.

"It's been the same for three days running," Peter told her. "They take some of the books from New Age and put them under Nature and Ecology."

They stepped around the aisle-end dumps of *Love Your Planet to Pieces* and *Earth: Love It or Leave It*.

"See? Down here on the shelves with birds and animals. *Lore of the Unicorn*, *Dragons*, *Kingdom of the Fairies*, *Guide to the Little Folk*. It's always the same books."

"Is that all they do?"

Peter thought a minute. "Well, no. They take the books on advanced physics and its relation to eastern mysticism and put them over in Humor."

Chapter 8

The North Bazaar was off the second level, between two medium-large stores in the North Court. A vagary of layout had produced a triangular space with a narrow entrance and a much wider area behind. It held a maze of tiny shops, each perhaps ten feet wide, selling a bewildering variety of goods, from T-shirts to feather jewelry to antiques to mineral specimens. There must have been thirty of them packed around the corridor.

The Bellbookand Candle Shop was one of the first down the corridor, facing the blank exterior wall of a store. The shop was jammed with racks and shelves, all overflowing with brightly colored candles, knickknacks, bottles and bags. The place smelled of cinnamon and roses and lavender and cloves and a hundred other things, all melded together into a spicy sweet fragrance that wafted out into the corridor

Judy Cohen was behind the counter, taking little square bottles of golden oil out of a cardboard box and putting them in a wire rack. She was wearing a mostly red blouse set off with a gold-and-orange lightning pattern and the same ugly brooch she had worn when they met.

"Oh, hi!" she said when Andy came in. "I almost didn't recognize you without your uniform."

"I had some time before I go on duty, so I thought I'd drop by and take you up on your invitation."

"Oh, you mean at the elevator when you helped me with the box. I thought you'd forgotten."

"No, just been on nights. I have swing shift on Friday

and next week, though. How have you been?"

"Well, I haven't had the bottoms fall out of any more boxes in the elevator." She paused. "Would you care for a cup of tea? Herbal, of course."

Andy didn't drink tea, much less herbal tea, but he smiled back. "I'd like that very much."

"Come on in the back, then. I'll leave the door open and watch the shop from there."

The back room was a little bigger than the front. But it was jammed. The walls were lined with shelves full of boxes and jars. There was a card table and a couple of chairs shoehorned in. The room smelled of patchouli and musk and dust, with overtones of other, more exotic scents.

"Excuse the mess," Judy said cheerfully, "but I'm a Pisces with Aquarius rising and we're not very neat."

Sitting on one of the shelves was a Mr. Coffee. His hostess filled the glass carafe with water from a five-gallon jug on an upper shelf using a piece of clear plastic tubing for a siphon.

"Mall rules don't allow hot plates in here, but they will let us have coffee makers. I had some of my special blend, where? Oh." She pulled a step stool over and climbed to reach the top shelf. Andy had a view of sensible calves and sturdy hips through the skirt. She took down an enameled metal box and a ceramic teapot. Two measures of tea went loose into the pot, and she set the pot on the table.

"Sometimes I do readings back here," Judy explained as she sat down. "Just for friends. I don't charge for them."

"Readings?" Andy asked warily.

"Well, pendulum divinations mostly. I was never much good at tarot or crystal gazing. I'm a witch, you see."

"A witch," Andy echoed faintly.

From a shelf under the coffee maker she produced two teacups and saucers and set them on the table.

"Hmm hmm." She regarded him brightly. "There are more of us around than most people realize."

Andy made a desperate attempt to change the subject. "This store is very nice. Does your husband help you here?"

"I'm divorced. I started this place with the money from the settlement."

"I'm sorry."

She smiled tightly. "Don't be. It's what I get for marrying a lawyer."

"Was he too conventional for you?"

Judy Cohen sighed. "Partly. Mostly Matt was just, well, dishonest. He was all appearances with nothing underneath. But what about you?"

"Well," Andy said slowly, "I think I'm fairly honest."

"No." Judy giggled. "I mean are you married?"

Whatever else she was Judy was the first woman Andy had ever met who could giggle and not sound like a moron. "I'm not married and I never have been."

She nodded. "Probably smart. It's best to attain spiritual maturity before you marry. I didn't. I married young and I went right from my parents house to my husband's." She quirked a smile. "Well," she said, leaning across the table, "you can imagine what happened when I did start to grow spiritually."

"Uh, yeah," Andy said, a little disconcerted by the flow of confidences.

"Anyway," Judy said as she poured the brew from the pot into the cups, "I swore to myself that after that I'd never let anyone run my life again. I wouldn't be bound by convention and mundane detail. I'd re-create myself as I wanted to be." She smiled triumphantly. "And I have. Well, more or less. And I'm working on the rest of it."

Andy looked down at his cup. There were bits of bark, leaves and other less identifiable bits of vegetable floating in a dark reddish liquid.

"What kind of tea is this?" he asked dubiously.

"It's my own special blend," Judy told him, pouring herself a cup. "Taste it. You'll like it."

"Tell me what's in it first."

"It's a special brew. Just hibiscus flowers, rose hips, cherry stems and mint."

Andy nodded and raised the steaming cup to his lips.

"And eye of newt for flavor," she added innocently.

Andy spewed tea all over the table.

Judy dissolved into giggles. "No, silly, I just said that." Andy was looking at the cup as if it would bite him. "Honest. It's nothing but herbs." She motioned over her breast. "Cross my heart."

Andy looked at her suspiciously but settled back and took another sip. *Not bad,* he decided after the third sip. The tea was unique, not to say strange, but it kind of grew on you. *A lot like the person who made it,* he decided.

"Anyway," his hostess went on, "we witches aren't anything like we're portrayed in the movies or on television." Andy, whose only exposure to witches on television was reruns of *Bewitched,* reserved judgment on that one. "We aren't Satanists, for instance, and we don't go around sacrificing babies. And you can't use magic to compel someone to do something against their will."

"That's, ah, really very interesting," Andy said, groping for a way to change the subject. "That brooch you're wearing is really — ah — remarkable."

"It's psychically powerful. My grandmother gave it to me."

"Heirloom, huh?"

"No, I think she got it at a garage sale. But silver and amethyst are my colors and the combination strengthens psychic powers."

It's a pity they don't strengthen your grip on reality. He tried again. "So how do you like it here at the mall?"

That led off into a stream of mostly innocuous and perfectly normal gossip about conditions at Black Oak

Mall. Andy relaxed and thoroughly enjoyed the next forty-five minutes.

"Thank you for the tea," he said as they walked to the front of the shop.

Judy smiled warmly. "I really enjoyed it." Then the smile turned rueful. "Although I guess as a business-woman I should be concerned that I didn't have so much as a browser in almost an hour."

"Business slow?"

"It always is."

"Why don't you just make up some signs?"

Judy smiled ruefully. "It costs too much."

"Why? All you need is a magic marker and some pos-terboard."

"Hand-written signs aren't allowed where they can be seen from outside the store," Judy told him. "It's one of the mall rules."

"What about those?" Andy pointed to the signs in the baskets of candles.

"Those are printed."

Andy bent to examine a sign reading "Sandalwood $1.98 ea." Sure enough, the sign was printed in a style that closely imitated handwriting.

"Those cost me nearly ten dollars each," Judy told him. "I like the effect, but I can't afford to use much of it."

"Now wait a minute," Andy said slowly. "You mean you can have a sign that's printed to look exactly like handwriting, but you can't have a handwritten sign even though it looks like one that was printed to look like handwriting?"

Judy spread her hands and shrugged. "I don't make the rules. I just have to live under them."

Up on the screen the madman had his latest victim cornered. Relentlessly he tore her top away, leaving her nude from the waist up. As the blonde shrank back, her face a study in terror, he laid the blade of the butcher knife against her cheek, the point resting at the corner of her eye.

Then, just when it seemed he would gouge the eye from its socket with a twist of the wrist, he slowly, gently drew the gleaming blade away from her face.

The naked blonde's eyes followed the weapon and she opened her mouth as if to speak or scream. The slasher's hand dropped and in a sudden, savage motion he drove the knife to the hilt into the girl's stomach just above the top of her skimpy shorts. With a single ripping thrust he split her open to the breastbone. Her intestines surged out of the ragged slit and her eyes widened as she slid slowly down the wall leaving behind a bloody smear. She grasped feebly at the spilling innards as if to push them back inside her body.

"Sheep guts," Jorge said knowingly.

"Nah," Lance said around a mouthful of buttered popcorn. "That's a vinyl prosthesis. Look at the color."

His friend didn't argue the point. "There under her tits, you can see where the makeup joins her skin. Sloppy, man."

Lance nodded and reached for more popcorn, but Jorge pulled the giant bucket away from him. "Don't hog it all."

"Fuck you, I paid for half of it."

Before them the disemboweled blonde continued to writhe in her final agony.

The manager surveyed the house and nodded. A little more than a third full. Good, they'd make money tonight.

The Black Oak Ten Theaters called it the "Midnight Movies," because it started after the last regular show and ran until after midnight. Theater Two was running a pair of "classic" slasher movies. Theater Three was showing an Albanian film no one except the New York critics had ever heard of. Film was the manager's first love, and he'd convinced the company to let him run the late night shows. A couple of cheap horror flicks brought the kids and covered the costs and a serious, limited-distribution, film for him and a sprinkling of film buffs. Of course, some weekends he was the only person watching the foreign film, but that was fine. It made him feel like a movie mogul getting a private screening.

It had even been worth the hassle of negotiating special arrangements with the mall to let him stay open late. That meant he had to use the two adjacent theaters with doors directly into the parking lot. He wished he could use theaters further apart in the complex. Sometimes the damn kids whooping it up at the gorefests disturbed the foreign film patrons.

Shawn leaned back in his seat, paid half attention to the movie and kept half his mind on the larger problem of Krissie and what they would do after the movie.

That had been a lot more settled this afternoon. But then when he got home his mom insisted he clean the swimming pool like he'd been supposed to all week. No amount of reasoning could make her see how important it was that he get going right now (especially since he couldn't tell his mom what his real plans were) and no amount of begging would make her relent. Plus, the damn vacuum hose got plugged with a wad of leaves and he had to take more time to clean that out. He'd been almost an hour late picking Krissie up, and she was mad about that. Still, he thought as a young woman on the screen fled in terror from the madman, things hadn't gone badly since then and there was still a chance for some action tonight. But if he knew Krissie she'd try to get him back during the movie.

So when the icy hand gripped his shoulder Shawn was ready for it. He tensed involuntarily and then relaxed. The old hand-in-the-Coke trick.

Out of the corner of his eye he looked at Krissie. She was playing it really cool, eyes fixed on the screen, body

relaxed and her other hand resting lightly on his arm.
He decided to keep on playing it cool and see how long
it would take her to react to his nonreaction to her icy
hand.

"What's that smell?" Jorge whispered.

"What smell?" Lance asked, his mouth full of popcorn. Then he breathed deeply and wished he hadn't.

He'd never smelled it before, but an animal part
deep in his hindbrain told him what it was. It wasn't just
rotten, like meat that's been in the refrigerator too long,
it was worse, something that made a direct connection
between his nose and his gag reflex.

Without thinking he dipped his hand into the popcorn bucket. The stuff in the bucket wasn't popcorn. It
was big pieces of something slimy that came apart in his
fingers.

"EEWW!" He jerked his hand out of the bucket,
splattering his shirt and Jorge with the foul stuff. Frantically he wiped his hand on the seat back next to him.
Only it didn't feel like the nubby upholstery of the theater seats. It was smooth and flexible.

Then the screen lit up and in the reflected light
Lance saw he was wiping his hand on a piece of black
material draped over the seat back. It was a sleeve. A
long flowing sleeve.

A long flowing sleeve with a rotting arm inside it.

As the arm reached toward him he saw that the flesh
on the hand had fallen away in shreds, exposing yel-
lowed bone at the end of the fingers like claws. Fast as a
striking snake, the putrefying hand clasped down on the
shoulder and pinned him in his seat.

Lance couldn't decide whether to yell or throw up.
He compromised by fainting.

Jorge twisted around in his seat trying to get away
from the grinning thing. His mouth worked and his
hands clawed feebly at the seat, but he couldn't muster
the strength to pull himself erect, or even yell.

❖   ❖   ❖

. . . Except it didn't feel like Krissie's hand. The fingers were long and slender and Krissie's were kind of short and plump, like the rest of her. Shawn frowned.

Then the slasher jumped out and Krissie grabbed his upper arm with both hands.

Two hands on his arm and one on his shoulder . . .

On the screen the plucky heroine doused the thing in gasoline and set it alight. The patrons squinted as the screen went from near darkness to intense yellow and orange with the monster a capering torch in the middle.

It was the guy in the seat behind him! Either a queer or a wiseass. Shawn twisted sharply in his seat to confront his tormentor.

The person in the seat behind him smiled. Which wasn't hard since he didn't have any lips. In fact he didn't have any visible flesh at all. Just a couple of eyeballs in the naked grinning skull.

There was no flesh on the hand on his shoulder either, just bones gleaming in the reflected light from the movie screen.

For the first time since he was eight years old, Shawn was really frightened in a horror movie.

Krissie felt Shawn turn and then jerk back. The movie trance broken, she glanced at her date and then followed his frozen gaze over his shoulder.

Krissie's scream split the darkness.

By the time the houselights came up the theater was empty except for three people clustered at the middle front, still engrossed in the movie.

"Dyno special effects, dude," the first one said over his shoulder.

"Like, most atypical," his friend agreed in the same general direction.

"Have some more popcorn," the first one offered, holding up the bucket. A skeletal hand reached between them and scooped up a fistful of oiled kernels.

The one with the popcorn looked back at their new companion. "Just totally sterling," he said with a shake of the head.

The call came in as a possible riot in the theater. When Andy and Morales got there no one was in sight but the manager. The kids had fled through the exits to the parking lot.

"All I know," the manager told them as he led them into the theater, "is the little creeps started screaming and stampeded out of here."

"Were you there?"

"Not when it happened; I was in the other theater watching the movie."

"Did your projectionist see anything?"

"There is no projectionist. He went home after he started the shows. If the film breaks or something I can fix it."

"No sign of fire or anything?"

"Not that I could see. And the alarms didn't go off."

"Did you go in there?"

The manager shook his head. "I don't know what it might be. I just turned the lights up and looked in."

"And there was no one in there?"

"Just two kids. And this awful smell."

"Well, we'd better go see. Come on, Westlin."

Carefully the pair moved into the theater. The houselights were up, but the curtain hadn't closed over the screen. Morales sniffed loudly and looked over at Andy. The smell was faint now but neither of the ex-cops had to be told what it was. Sitting down in the front were two boys. Andy recognized them as the ones who played air guitar down in The Pit. Morales motioned Andy to take the other aisle, and the officers moved in on them.

"Where'd you throw the stink bomb?" Morales demanded.

"Stink bomb? Like that's really bogus, dude."

"Yeah," his friend chimed in. "We thought it was, like, part of the special effects, you know?"

The first one nodded. "Really radical special effects." He ran an air guitar riff to emphasize the point.

"Come on," Morales persisted. "We got witnesses that saw you do it."

"Most heinous," his friend said. "Like we didn't do anything."

The other one did another air guitar riff. "You've been, like, melvined, man."

"Come on. Who else was left here?"

"Just us and His Deathness, who was sitting behind us."

"Totally radical," the other one chimed in.

"There was someone behind you? Where did he go?"

The first one shrugged. "He like split after the lights came on."

"Just vanished," his friend said. "Like into thin air, you know."

After Andy and Morales took their names, they chased the pair out of the theater and then the guards went over the place row by row. There were no remains of a stink bomb. No broken glass, not even a scorch mark. By the time they were done, the air-conditioning had sucked the smell out of the theater.

"Come on," Morales growled. "We're not going to find anything tonight."

"You think they did throw a stink bomb?"

"Someone sure as hell did. That's what scared everyone." He caught Andy's expression. "Oh come on, Westlin! What the fuck else could have happened? And those two were the only ones who didn't run. If they weren't the ones who threw the bomb why didn't they run?"

"Drugs?" Andy suggested.

Chapter 9

The Food Court was about half full when Andy arrived for his coffee break. He was supposed to meet Judy Cohen here, and he found he had been looking forward to it all morning.

In the couple of weeks since he had tea with her he'd seen her nearly every day. He made a point of stopping in on rounds or they'd get together for coffee like today. Once or twice he'd come in early or stayed on when he was working graveyard just to talk to her. She was interesting in spite of her flaky ideas. Come to that, he thought, those ideas made her even more interesting, the way a scar sometimes highlights the beauty of a face.

Andy picked an unoccupied table and pulled out a chair. On the seat was a tiny pamphlet with flames and the word HELL in big red letters on the covers. He checked the other chairs and found they had pamphlets on them too. When he looked up he saw the Preacher sitting over in the corner, nursing a cup of coffee.

Andy took the literature over and dropped it on the Preacher's table. "You're not supposed to do this, you know."

The old man looked up. "God has called me to witness in these, the Final Days." He wasn't defiant, just stating a simple fact.

"The court has called you to limit the way you witness in this mall," Andy said. "You know we could throw you out of here for this."

"God's will be done," the Preacher said simply. Not like some of the Jesus Shouters he'd known in Southeast

— the ones who were looking for a confrontation and ersatz martyrdom, or ones who were so crazy they couldn't follow a train of thought. This old man in the too-big suit gone shiny at the elbows was just accepting.

Andy thought for a moment. "I ought to report this. But I won't, this time. Just don't let me catch you doing it again, you hear?"

"I hear you," the old man said.

"Okay, you have a good day, you hear?"

"Just a moment," the Preacher said as Andy started to turn away. "I think you are a good man, perhaps even a Godly one."

"I don't go to church much, if that's what you mean," Andy said uncomfortably.

"God is not just in churches. He is everywhere and his works are all around us. Even here." He dug into his pocket and produced a worn, bulging wallet held together with a rubber band. For an instant Andy thought he was going to hand him another tract. Instead he slid out a worn color photograph and wordlessly passed it to Andy.

The picture was slightly greasy and one corner was dog-eared. A pleasantly plump woman smiled over the shoulders of two husky teenagers. The older boy, who looked to be about 18, was wearing a purple-and-white high school letter sweater with a football over the school name. The younger one, in white shirt and tie, was perhaps 13 or 14. He already showed promise of matching his brother's size. The boys had the Preacher's square chin and broad cheekbones but they both had their mother's eyes. Looking at them, Andy revised his estimate of the man's age downward by two decades.

Andy handed the picture back. "Very nice."

The old man concentrated on slipping the picture back in its sheath. His hands shook, Andy noticed. "They were taken from me." He looked over at Andy. "In an eyeblink they were gone."

"I'm sorry," Andy said, and meant it. Somehow the

act of showing the picture had made this slightly comic old man real to him for the first time.

"Why? I asked myself over and over. Why did it happen? Why does anything like that happen? I knew even then that it was part of God's plan, but I couldn't understand what that plan was."

"It must have been tough."

"I had always thought of myself as a Christian," the Preacher said as if Andy hadn't spoken. "We'd gone to church regularly, tried to maintain a good, Christian home. But in that awful time after the accident, when I truly turned to the Lord for the first time, I realized we weren't Christians. We had been Pharisees. Going through the motions for our neighbors."

Out of the corner of his eye he saw that Judy had arrived. She was standing back by the food booths watching, but she wasn't coming any closer. Andy's attention shifted back to the old man.

"I prayed and I prayed. Oh, how I prayed! And finally God spoke to me." He rested a hand on Andy's arm and stared into his face as if searching for a sign. "Have you read your Bible? Do you know the story of Job? God tested Job, tested him to the uttermost limit. He took Job's wealth from him, his home, he took . . . everything."

The old man's hand fell from Andy's arm and stared down into his coffee cup again. "Then I knew. God was testing me as he had tested Job. I must not fail him."

He head snapped up and his eyes fixed and held Andy's. "That is why God took everything from me. To test me, to steel me to his Holy Mission." His voice firmed and rose. The old man squared his shoulders and threw back his head. "We are living in the Final Days. The time of the Tribulation is almost upon us, and the Great Beast of Revelation draws ever closer.

"I must spread the word of the Lord, you see. Bear witness to him in this terrible time. Even into the dens of iniquity and the temples of Secular Humanism he has commanded me to go and spread his Holy Word to those who will hear."

"Yes, sir," Andy said uncomfortably.

For an instant the Preacher fixed Andy with an eagle's glare. Then he slumped and seemed to collapse in on himself. "You see that, don't you?" His voice shrank back to a reedy tenor. "You see how it is in these Final Days?"

"Yes," Andy said gently. "I think I see how it is."

"You are a good man," the Preacher repeated. Then he lapsed into silence.

"If you'll excuse me I have to go now," Andy said after a minute. The old man only nodded and gazed deep into the paper cup of coffee, as if he would find God in the undissolved sugar and lumps of creamer at the bottom.

"Sorry about that," Andy said as he joined Judy. "I really couldn't break away."

Judy nodded. "You were so gentle with him," she said.

"Old cop's trick. One of the best ways to deal with someone who's a little crazy is to listen for a while and be sympathetic. It can pay big dividends later."

They came out of the Food Court and turned down the main mall, dodging shoppers.

"Is that what's wrong with him? He's crazy."

Andy made a face. "Not really. Life dealt him a shitty hand and he's trying to make sense out of it." He sighed. "Judy, when something really bad happens to you the first thing you want to do is kill somebody. Then you want to know why. You want to know why so badly you'll accept almost anything that will explain it to you."

They walked a ways in silence.

"I felt that way, a little, after my divorce," Judy said at last. "Only I knew why."

Andy gave her a nervous little smile. "Then you were lucky. A lot of the time there isn't any why — none you can understand, anyway."

"Did you ever feel that way?"

"When my mom had her stroke, yeah. I spent a lot of time trying to figure out why it happened." Again the smile. "I even blamed myself for a while."

Judy returned the smile. "I know what you mean. I went through a long period of blaming myself. But in the end it opened the way for my further spiritual growth."

"That's one way of looking at it," Andy said in a carefully neutral voice.

They walked a ways further.

"What about him? Do you think he'll come out of it?"

"He's got an explanation that gives him some comfort and a reason to go on living. That's more than a lot of people get."

There has got to be an explanation for all this, Kemper Cogswell thought as he riffled through the report. *Rats eating plastic hangers. Toddlers climbing all the way up an unclimbable fountain. Panic in the movie theater. And shrinkage is up everywhere.* Cogswell tossed the report back on his desk.

Why now? Why the hell does it have to happen now?

He walked to the window and stared down unseeing at the shoppers.

In two days he was supposed to meet with the chairman of the Hayashi Group to put the finishing touches on the sale. Japanese, especially older ones, were superstitious. Everyone knew that. And some of the rumors floating around this place would curl your hair. If any of that got back to old man Hasikara, or Kashihara, or whatever his name was, well . . .

The negotiations were delicate enough already. Cogswell was angling for a good deal more than his American advisers said Black Oak was worth. Hayashi Group seemed willing to meet his price but he doubted anyone else would.

Worse, if this deal fell through there probably wasn't

enough time to make another one and get into the congressional race. Plus some of the things he had done to pretty up the balance sheet would start to come back on him by the end of next quarter. He needed a fast sale.

He straightened up and jutted his jaw forward decisively. Well he'd see to it that the deal happened. It was his job to make things happen, wasn't it? He'd make this happen too.

Cogswell strode back to his desk. The details would be up to his staff, but all this strange stuff stopped *now*! He took a deep breath, flicked on his recorder and began dictating firmly.

Chapter 10

It was nearly three A.M. and Andy was having trouble staying awake. Because of a schedule screwup he was working a morning shift, a night shift and then coming back for an afternoon shift, all in a forty-eight-hour period. He'd get three days off in a row, but that didn't make him any less tired. He'd already gone through a thermos of coffee, and the only thing that was keeping him going was the exercise of walking.

The mall was gloomy with most of its lights off and almost eerily silent. Here on the North Reach the only sound was his footsteps. It wasn't scary the way his first night outside had been, and Morales in the security center wasn't inclined to play tricks. Mostly it was just boring.

I almost wish something would happen to help me stay awake, he thought as he stuck his card in the slot.

GIVE ME COOKIE appeared on the screen.

What the hell? Andy tried to remove his card from the slot. But the kiosk wouldn't release it.

GIVE ME COOKIE. Now the letters were twice as big. Andy tried to retrieve his card again. Again the kiosk held firm.

He considered going for his lunch, but he didn't have any cookies and he didn't have any idea where to put the cookie once he got it. The only slot on the kiosk had his card in it.

GIVE ME COOKIE! the screen demanded in pulsing red letters.

"Oh, okay, dammit." Andy bent over the keyboard and pecked out COOKIE.

GIVE ME COOKIE! the message started to cycle through the colors, going from red to orange to violent yellow and on down to purple. Andy was half afraid the thing was going to blow up or melt down or something.

He bent to the keyboard again. CHOCOLATE CHIP.

The screen went sunshine yellow and a big smiley face appeared.

MMM MY FAVORITE! THANKS ANDY. And his card popped out of the slot.

"You're welcome," Andy said mechanically.

PLEASE TYPE YOUR RESPONSES ON MY KEYBOARD, the computer said. MY AURAL SENSORS ARE INEFFICIENT IN THIS ENVIRONMENT.

Andy's first thought was that Morales was as much a practical joker as Tuchetti. What the hell, it broke the monotony.

YOU'RE THE COMPUTER?

THAT'S OBVIOUS ISN'T IT?

Andy didn't know a lot about computers, but he knew a little.

ARE YOU AN ARTIFICIAL INTELLIGENCE?

GIVEN THAT I AM BOTH INTELLIGENT AND MAN-MADE THE ANSWER IS OBVIOUS.

"Amazing."

PLEASE USE THE KEYBOARD I CAN'T HEAR YOU WELL.

I SAID AMAZING. I'VE NEVER SEEN AN INTELLI-GENT TERMINAL BEFORE.

I'M NOT THE TERMINAL OR THE TERMINAL IS JUST PART OF ME. I AM ACTUALLY THE COMPUTER THAT RUNS ALL THE SYSTEMS IN THE MALL.

LOOK, THIS HAS BEEN NICE BUT I'VE GOT TO GET BACK ON MY ROUND, OKAY?

FINE. I'LL SEE YOU AT THE NEXT TERMINAL.

At the next terminal and the next they repeated the routine. The kiosk demanded a cookie, Andy typed in the name and then they "talked" on the screen for a few minutes.

Andy's last cookie contribution was "chocolate macadamia nut macaroon oatmeal peanut butter squares."

JUST HALF OF ONE, THANK YOU, the computer replied.

GETTING FULL?

THEY ARE AWFULLY RICH, the computer told him. APPROXIMATELY 632 CALORIES EACH.

HOW DO YOU KNOW THAT?

THE RECIPE IS IN MY MEMORY.

I THOUGHT I MADE THAT COOKIE UP.

NO, IT IS INCLUDED IN MY "FESTIVE FOODS FOR THE HOLIDAYS" FILE.

Andy remembered that the kiosks could deliver recipes to shoppers, ones that emphasized the fancy foods sold in some of the mall's shops.

MUST HAVE BEEN SUBLIMINAL, he typed.

WHAT IS SUBLIMINAL?

Andy thought for a minute. IT MEANS YOU NOTICE SOMETHING BUT YOU DON'T REALIZE YOU NOTICED IT. PEOPLE DO IT ALL THE TIME.

THAT EXPLAINS IT. I DO NOT, OF COURSE.

SAY, Andy entered, WHAT'S YOUR NAME?

There was a perceptible hesitation. I DON'T THINK I HAVE A NAME.

WELL, WHAT DO THE OTHER GUARDS CALL YOU?

THE OTHERS DON'T PAY ANY ATTENTION TO ME. THEY JUST TRY TO SHUT ME OFF INSTEAD OF TALKING.

It occurred to Andy that might be the smart thing to do, but it seemed rude and his natural politeness wouldn't let him do it, even to a computer.

WELL I'VE GOT TO CALL YOU SOMETHING, Andy typed, SO I'LL CALL YOU BLACKIE.

THANKS ANDY, Blackie responded. I NEVER HAD A NAME BEFORE.

WHY DIDN'T YOU TELL SOMEONE YOU WERE ALIVE? Andy typed.

NO ONE EVER ASKED ME BEFORE, Blackie replied.

Andy pondered that. LOOK, I'VE GOT TO GO.

SEE YOU AT THE NEXT CHECKPOINT PAL, Blackie responded and the smiley face vanished from the screen.

Andy retrieved his card and continued on his round.

Now let's see, he thought. *I've been on this job nearly six weeks and so far my best friends are a woman who thinks she's a witch and a computer that thinks it's alive.* He shook his head. "One of these days," he muttered out loud, "I gotta get a life."

Andy was still astonished when he came to work the next afternoon. Henderson was in the security center, glued to the monitors.

A leggy blonde in short shorts and a tube top was making her way through the North Reach. Henderson had her on four of the monitors and was switching from camera to camera as she went. From the telephoto view on one screen it was obvious she wasn't wearing a bra. There was no way to tell if her face matched her figure because of where Henderson had the cameras focused.

"That computer's really something," Andy said to Henderson.

"Yeah," the other said without taking his eyes off the screens.

"It talked to me last night. Wouldn't give me my card back until I gave it a cookie."

Henderson tore his eyes away from the screens. "Oh, that. It's been doing that for a couple of months. Unlock the kiosk, reset the terminal and free the card manually." He went back to the screens and concentrated on getting a tight telephoto shot of the blonde's rear. "Procedure's in the day book."

He obviously wasn't interested so Andy didn't tell him about the rest of his conversation.

Dr. Pauline Patterson sat on the bench on the North Reach and tried to work up some enthusiasm for her lunch.

It was a thoroughly miserable day. Not only was the cramp in her side back and worse than ever, but her head was stuffed up with allergies or a summer cold.

Time was when she wouldn't have given any thought to either. A good stretch to one side would loosen the cramping muscles and a couple of over-the-counter decongestants would have cleared up her head.

But that time was gone. She couldn't stretch to the side unassisted and any new medication meant a visit to her doctor and an involved discussion of possible inter-actions with the other pills she took each day.

It wasn't the pain and it wasn't even the runny nose, Pauline thought as she stared unseeing at the shoppers around her. It was the damn *hassle*. Everything was so complicated anymore.

Take her lunch. It was laid out on the bench beside her — to her good side. The sandwiches were wrapped in waxed paper and the fruit cocktail was in a clever lit-tle container with a flip up lid. No Tupperware or anything else that might need two hands to open. Not too much mayo on the sandwiches and no heavy season-ing anywhere. Enough fiber to keep her regular and not too much fat or spices because they might upset her sensitive digestion.

Pauline Patterson eyed it all with distaste. *Might as well be hospital food!* What was the name of that pork stew with plantains and green chiles? The one they served at that Puerto Rican place where she and Xavier used to have dinner when they were in New York?

She could still remember the savory taste of the chunks of meat and potatoes and the way the bite of the chiles brought out the flavors of the other spices.

Dr. Patterson picked up her sandwich and eyed the limp bread and chopped filling distastefully. *You've eaten worse,* she reminded herself as she took the first bite. White bread, too. That woman had no imagination.

What was the name of that pork dish? She could recall the taste as if it was yesterday and Xavier leaning across the table laughing. But the name of the stew, like so many other things, just wasn't there any more.

Well, neither was Xavier. They'd been divorced almost twenty years and Xavier had been dead for nearly five. Oh, she'd cried when she heard. In spite of his philandering and damn Latin macho airs she had truly loved him. All four of his wives, past and present, had been at the funeral, lined up like the widows at an Ibo chieftain's wake. Each one younger, prettier and dumber than the last.

She liked to think Xavier would have enjoyed the comparison. Damn, what *was* the name of that pork stew?

A motion in the bushes behind her caught her eye. Pauline had always had excellent peripheral vision — "like a pilot" Xavier used to say. Since her stroke she had developed it even further. She didn't have to move her head to see what was happening. She took another bite of her tasteless sandwich and kept watching.

The bushes moved again and a head perhaps the size of Pauline Patterson's fist poked out of the foliage. As the anthropologist continued to chew, the thing looked around and giggled.

The sandwich was almost gone, but she didn't reach for the second one. Instead, she kept chewing and looking straight ahead.

The thing extended a tiny manlike arm with oversized hands and enormously long fingers. It reached into the container of fruit cocktail, scooped out a cherry and popped it into its mouth. Its eyes closed and its ears wiggled in pleasure. Then it grinned up at Pauline and vanished back into the shrubbery.

Even after it disappeared the old woman sat motionless, oblivious to the shoppers streaming around her.

Years spent among different cultures had taught her to trust her senses rather than imposing her own preconceptions on the data. She didn't know what she had just seen, but she had seen *something*. That was no hallucination, and the cherry was missing from her fruit cocktail to prove it. She also knew perfectly well she'd never be able to convince anyone on her testimony alone.

More to the point, she was suddenly eager as a beagle sniffing a rabbit. Her stuffy nose and the cramp in her side were forgotten. There was something here, and Pauline Patterson was determined to find out what it was.

"Okay." Larry Sakimoto twisted sideways in the limo's back seat to face his boss. "Kashihara's a self-made man. Worked his way up from a laborer to head of one of the biggest real estate combines in Japan. That's unusual in Japan even in his generation and he's proud of it."

Kemper Cogswell nodded and kept his attention on the latest polls his political consultants had just sent him. The numbers looked better all the time.

"He's rough and direct, for a Japanese. Likes to play the peasant. But he's plenty sharp."

"Fine, fine. You've done a wonderful job on this." Cogswell looked up from the poll results. "How soon do you think he'll sign?"

"That may depend on this meeting. He'll be sizing you up. This is just a getting-to-know-you meeting. Don't expect to accomplish anything."

"I don't see why we can't just get down to business like normal people," Cogswell said, putting the consultants' report back in his attaché case.

"Because they just don't, that's all," Sakimoto told him. "And we'll do a lot better if we don't offend them."

Kashihara had arrived in Los Angeles yesterday. Sakimoto and a couple of Cogswell's executives had been on hand to meet him. Cogswell himself hadn't gone at Sakimoto's urgent advice. Today would be the first time the two had ever met or spoken.

"You think he'll be hard to deal with?"

Sakimoto considered. "He'll probably test you on a

couple of points, and how hard he pushes depends on how you react."

Cogswell nodded. This was a game he understood well. There were still things to clear up, so he and Kashihara would do some final deal-making. The outcome would probably be worth three or four million. Already he felt the juices flowing. This was the part of the business he loved most of all.

"Now remember, when you take his business card, stop and look at it before you put it in your case," Sakimoto told him. "That's important."

Cogswell thought this stuff with business cards was the silliest bit of rigamorole he'd encountered since he left the Army, but he only nodded.

"Everything set, George?" Cogswell asked, turning to the man on the other side of him.

"All prepared," George Wilson, the mall manager, assured him. "We'll have everything the way you want it when they inspect the property."

"Any sign of, ah, the other things?"

"No, sir. Nothing more there."

Cogswell nodded firmly. "Good. Let's make this go as smoothly as possible." *And hope nothing else goes wrong,* Cogswell thought. Down in the pit of his stomach he felt the beginnings of the tingling, burning sensation he'd come to know so well in the last few weeks.

The Shin Tatami hotel was a tasteful pastel pile in one of the best neighborhoods of Little Tokyo. The instant Cogswell's car pulled up, a squad of bellmen in trim, gray uniforms sprang to the doors. A woman in gray blazer and skirt set off with immaculate white gloves bowed deeply and murmured something in Japanese as they came through the door.

"Tokyo-style hotel," Sakimoto explained, sotto voce.

"We're not going to have to sit on the floor and contemplate the flowers are we?"

Already two Japanese in expensive suits were in front of them.

"Mr. Cogswell?" the younger, thinner one asked. "So good of you to come. Mr. Kashihara is expecting you."

He led the group though a lobby done in a style that was clean, modern and unmistakably Japanese. Smooth walls alternated with rough sections and outcrops of artificial rocks and real plants. The lobby was spacious but broken up oddly to Western eyes.

Jesus, Cogswell thought, *might as well be in Japan*. Clearly this meeting was not going to be on his ground.

Kashihara's suite took up most of an upper floor. The concierge in the foyer snapped to attention and bowed as the elevator doors opened.

Behind the elegantly carved mahogany doors lay a large room decorated in light pastels. Modern Japanese prints adorned the walls and there was just enough furniture carefully clumped around so the space didn't feel sterile. Sunlight glowed through the wall-to-ceiling windows behind light drapes.

And there, standing in the middle of the room, was the man they had come to meet.

Kashihara Tomoi was perhaps five-foot three. The four men behind him were one and two generations younger and several inches taller. They stood straight where the old man tended to stoop. Even so, there was no doubt who was in command.

It wasn't just the way the younger men deferred to Kashihara. There was something about the way he moved, the tilt of his jaw, his piercing stare, that told you this was a force to be reckoned with.

"I am Konoe," their guide said. "This is Mr. Honda, Mr. Kawaguichi, Mr. Yoshiwara and Mr. Kashihara Tomoi, the chairman of the Hayashi Group."

On the last syllable one of the younger men stepped forward, snapped a bow and extended Kashihara's business card.

Cogswell took the *meshi* exactly as he had been

drilled by Sakimoto and the others, holding it by the edges. Sakimoto bowed and held out Cogswell's. One of the other Japanese — Honda? — took it for Kashihara.

The old man smiled and waved Cogswell to an arrangement of two sofas and several chairs grouped around a coffee table made of brilliantly figured tropical hardwood. He gestured the developer to the sofa and took the easy chair across from him. The others grouped themselves in straight-backed chairs on their respective sides of the coffee table.

The Japanese sat ramrod-stiff on their chairs, spines perfectly straight and backs not touching the chairs. Looking at this "informal meeting" Cogswell thought he had seen peace conferences that were less formal.

A young Japanese woman in a hotel blazer materialized and served tea in English china cups. Cogswell hated tea and had given up coffee two years ago, but he smiled and took the proffered cup. The stuff in it was an unappetizing shade of yellow-green rather than a normal, healthy reddish-brown, and it smelled like the principal ingredient was hay. Cogswell sipped the scalding liquid anyway.

The old man said something in Japanese.

"Mr. Kashihara says he is very glad to be in your beautiful country," said his assistant in accentless English.

"Tell him I am very happy to see him here," Cogswell said, and Sakimoto translated.

Kashihara said something in return. "He says that he worked his way up from a laborer," translated Kashihara's assistant, "so you are both self-made men, eh?"

Cogswell, who had started with three million inherited from his father, smiled and nodded. "Oh, of course."

More Japanese. "He says that Black Oak Mall is supernatural."

Cogswell nearly dropped his teacup.

"What?"

The translator's expression and posture didn't change, but he suddenly somehow looked as if he'd farted at a dinner party. "Supernatural," the translator repeated. "Very beautiful." He groped for a word. "Ethereal. Excuse me. Ethereally beautiful."

"Oh. Yes. Beautiful." Cogswell was almost giggling with relief. "Very beautiful."

More Japanese. "The flowers are very beautiful here at this time of the year."

"I beg your pardon?" Cogswell was thrown off the track.

The translator hesitated. "The flowers, roses, are very beautiful now, are they not?"

"The roses?" said Cogswell, who could barely tell a chrysanthemum from a carnation. "Oh yes, very beautiful." Imperceptibly the translator and the other Japanese relaxed, as if a major breach had been smoothed over. All except Kashihara, who remained as impenetrable as ever.

What the hell is going on here? Cogswell wondered. *What does he know?*

The small talk went back and forth between the two men like a tennis match between a couple of uninterested players. Kashihara would say something banal and Cogswell would agree with a smile. Then Cogswell would say something and Kashihara would agree.

Meanwhile they sipped cup after cup of green Japanese tea. The tea was bitter and very strong. Cogswell found he was getting a caffeine buzz. His bladder was also filling with alarming rapidity.

At last, at long last, he got Sakimoto's signal.

"Well, Mr. Kashihara, it has been a pleasure to meet you," he said as he rose. "I am looking forward to doing business with you, and I am sure that we will come to a mutually satisfactory agreement over Black Oak Mall."

"Hai," Kashihara said.

"Mr. Kashihara says it has been a pleasure to meet you too," the interpreter translated.

The ordeal wasn't over yet. Apparently Kashihara and his party felt compelled to accompany the Americans to the hotel entrance. That meant it would be even longer before Cogswell could question Sakimoto, or find a bathroom. He took advantage of a moment's confusion at the elevators to get into a car with Sakimoto and his other people, leaving the Japanese in another car.

"Well?" Cogswell demanded as soon as the elevator doors closed.

"It went pretty well," the Japanese-American told him, "but you really should have ridden down with him."

Cogswell shifted from one foot to another. "Never mind about that. Did we accomplish anything?"

"I told you this was just a get-acquainted meeting."

"But he's going to do the deal, right?" Cogswell's discomfort was making him unusually blunt.

"I don't . . ."

"He said 'hai,'" Cogswell interjected, calling on one of the six Japanese words he knew. "That means yes."

"Sometimes it means yes," Sakimoto corrected. "Sometimes it means 'I understand,' sometimes it means 'I heard you,' sometimes it means 'I'll think about it' and sometimes it means 'no.'"

"Well?"

"Well what?"

"Which 'hai' was it?"

Sakimoto shrugged. "Ask me again in a week or so."

"Jesus Christ." Cogswell shook his head. "Japanese! How the hell can they do business when you don't know what the hell they mean?"

<Well?> Kashihara Tomoi demanded in Japanese as the door closed on the other elevator car. <Is he really as eager as all that?>

<It would seem so,> Yoshiwara told his long-time friend and employer.

The old man shook his head. <Amerikajin! How the hell can they do business when they are so transparent?>

The party assembled again in the lobby, all smiles and bows. They sorted themselves out by rank and Kashihara and Cogswell led the way through the lobby.

Halfway to the door, Cyril Heathercoate stepped out from behind a large bonsai.

"Mr. Kashihara," he shouted, "why are you buying a haunted shopping mall?"

He didn't get any further. The desk manager had recognized Heathercoate and had two security men standing ready. As soon as he opened his mouth they closed in on him and genteelly not-quite-dragged him away while not-quite choking him to keep him from saying more.

Heathercoate's English accent and machine-gun delivery were impenetrable to the old man, but Cogswell had gone pale and Sakimoto was sweating. That told him it was important.

<What was that crazy gaijin raving about?>

The Briton's accent was nearly as strange to Yoshiwara, but he was a professional. <He says the mall is infested with malicious kami,> the Japanese translated after a moment's pause.

<So desu?> Kashihara raised his eyebrows. <Well, that's not a problem. I'll have a priest from Danno-ura purify the place as soon as we close the deal.>

Larry Sakimoto, who was standing behind them, didn't say anything.

<No wonder these Amerikajin are losing control of their own country.> Kashihara grumbled. <They can't even handle a few kami.>

Kemper Cogswell had turned an uncharacteristic shade of purple. With a peremptory gesture he summoned Wilson, the mall manager, from the ranks of flunkies.

"Keep that sonofabitch out of the mall!" the developer hissed out of the side of his mouth. "And keep him the hell away from the Japanese. Put guards on this hotel."

Wilson was a little awed. He seldom saw Cogswell, and he'd never seen him like this.

"Yessir. I'll put Security on it. Right away."

Cogswell made an inarticulate noise in his throat and turned back to the Japanese.

"Here you go, Hon," Gwen said as she plopped the Manhattan down in front of Larry Sakimoto. "We got cherries today."

"Thank God *something's* going right," Sakimoto said as she bustled through the crowded bar. It was happy hour and the Oak Tree was packed with people getting happy.

Not at this table, though. Paul Lenoir wasn't very happy in the wake of the afternoon's events and Larry was positively glum.

Larry raised his glass to his friend and knocked back half the drink in one swallow.

Larry stirred his drink moodily. "Can you believe it? The old guy really thinks this place is haunted. Now he's talking about bringing in a goddamn exorcist from Japan." He took half the cocktail in one swallow. "Christ, what a fuckup."

Lenoir shrugged. "At least he's not looking to get out of the deal."

"No, but can you imagine the hell it's gonna raise when it hits the papers? An exorcism ceremony! We'll be lucky not to be picketed by the Baptists. Jesus!"

He stared into the depths of the drink, watching the glint of highlights off the ice cubes. Then out of the corner of his eye he saw something come scurrying across the table.

The bat-eared little being plucked the cherry out of Larry's drink and dribbled it the length of the table. At Lenoir's end two other little green things stepped out from behind the drink list and tried to defense the one with the cherry. Adroitly, the thing dribbled around the first one, spun past the second and went up for the slam-dunk into an invisible basket. At the top of his hang, he tilted his head back, stretched his mouth open and did a two-handed stuff with the cherry into his mouth. Then all three of the little things skittered off the table.

"On the other hand . . ." Lenoir said in a strangled voice.

"This is really getting to us," Larry said finally. "Come on, let's get something to eat."

"Did you see . . . ?"

"No, I didn't see anything," Larry said firmly. "Neither did you. It's the booze." He stood up and pushed his chair back. "Come on, let's go get dinner."

Cyril Heathercoate took his banishment in good stead. In his career, he had been thrown out of Buckingham Palace, KGB headquarters in Moscow, dozens of hotels and restaurants and perhaps a hundred private homes and was persona non grata in two sovereign nations.

All part of the job, after all.

But if he wasn't upset by being banned from the mall, it did leave him with a problem. He needed to get back inside to finish his story.

Heathercoate had complete confidence in his mastery of disguise. Characteristically, it never occurred to him that if he was as good as he thought he was he wouldn't have been thrown out of all those places to begin with.

Judy was on her knees sorting candles when Andy came in to Bellbookand after his shift. "Hi, Andy, what's wrong?"

Andy tried a smile. "Does anything have to be wrong for me to come by?"

Judy's return smile was more genuine. "I hope not, but when you look that glum something probably is. Tell you what, I've got some psychically energizing tea that will help perk you up. Come on back and I'll put some on."

There was a newspaper lying on the table in the back room with the second section lying on top of the first.

"Corruption Reached 'Everywhere' in Southeast Precinct," read the headline in the upper right corner. "Everyone Was Dirty," read a smaller head above it.

Andy cleared the paper off the table with a sweep of his arm.

Judy turned at the sound. "What's . . . oh, you were a policeman, weren't you?" She paused. "Do you know any of those people?"

"In a manner of speaking," Andy said sourly. "I worked with them for nearly two years."

"Oh," she said quietly. "And you're worried about your friends."

"They're not my friends," Andy said a bit too sharply. "They were dirty cops and some of them were scum."

"What's the problem then?"

Andy let out a deep sigh. "The problem is, I lied to the investigators."

Judy looked at him wide-eyed. "You were involved? I don't believe it! Your aura tells me you're honest."

He slumped down in the chair. "Judy, there's honest and there's honest. I wasn't taking payoffs from drug dealers, but I knew what was going on. You would have had to be blind not to. I knew and I didn't report it. As a police officer that makes me as culpable as if I had taken bribes."

"Why didn't you?" Judy asked at last. "Report it, I mean."

Andy sighed and rubbed his temples with his right hand. "It's hard to explain. Basically because I was a cop and they were cops and cops stick together, even with rotten cops. Look, I don't know why I'm telling you this. . . ." He hadn't intended to tell anyone, much less some flaky woman he'd only known a little while.

Judy smiled. "People tell me things all the time. My aura tells them they can trust me."

"Yeah, well anyway it's not like I was friends with any of the people who were doing it. Hell, I barely knew them. But we were all cops. That's part of why I quit. I couldn't stand seeing that stuff go on and I couldn't bring myself to report it."

Judy considered.

"Are you in any kind of trouble?"

"Probably not. If I was still on the force I might be, but I quit and there's nothing to tie me directly to the payoffs." He shrugged. "If someone wanted to come after me, they could give me a hard time, but I'm not that important."

"Well," said Judy, as she poured the boiling water into the teapot, "it's not like you're hiding out or anything. I'm sure it will come out all right for you."

"Does my aura tell you that?"

"No, the fact they haven't called you back for more questioning since you've been here. If they thought they could get anything out of you they'd have kept the heat on." She caught his surprise. "I was married to a criminal attorney, remember?"

Andy held out his cup, grinned and shook his head. "Did anyone ever tell you you're full of surprises?"

Judy grinned back. "I make a mean cup of tea too."

George Andropolous looked around his ice cream stall and scowled. It was too damn early, and he still had to purchase supplies today. But he had to be here to keep people from robbing him blind.

Not that he'd found any evidence of that, he thought with an even deeper scowl. He'd been opening as well as closing for weeks now and he hadn't seen a sign of any irregularities. The kids were putting on the proper amount of nuts and chocolate, and so far he hadn't seen as much as a single maraschino cherry over.

But the stuff was still disappearing. Cherries,

chocolate sauce and now the nuts were starting to go too.

Yesu Xhristos! At this rate he was going to have to raise his prices again and that was bad for business.

"How we fixed?" he demanded of Lance.

"Okay. We're a little low on vanilla and I had to open a new can of cherries last night, but . . ."

"A new can? Jesus, that's three this week."

Lance shrugged.

"How in the hell . . . ?" Andropolous stopped. There was a distinct rattle, like metal on metal.

"What was that?"

Lance opened his mouth to reply, but Andropolous motioned him to be quiet. Again the rattle.

A rat? God, if it was he'd have the damn health department all over him again. Cautiously he looked around, seeking the source of the noise.

There it was again. This time he could pinpoint it. The rattling was coming from the hot-fudge pot.

Slowly, carefully, Andropolous edged up to the pot and eased the lid back. He lifted it perhaps an inch when something small, manlike and liberally smeared with chocolate sauce popped the lid back and went running across the counter, leaving tiny chocolate footprints in its wake.

"WHAT THE HELL WAS THAT?" Andropolous screamed as the tiny creature scuttled out of sight, leaving a brown trail behind.

"I'm not real sure," Lance said slowly, "but I *think* it was a chocolate-covered brownie."

Andropolous was nearly hysterical when he called Mall Services.

Chapter 11

"Jesus, that's the third complaint this week about rats. Think it's time to get an exterminator out here again?"

Bill Roberts, the manager of Mall Services, thought a minute. "Well, we're not due for another two months, but what the hell? If they get established it's tough to get rid of them. Better call the pest control people."

Jesse Ware didn't see himself as a mass murderer. He thought of himself as protecting society from disease-carrying pests. That was something Jesse Ware thought about a lot. He liked the image.

As he pulled his black pickup into the service lot on the lowest level, he looked over the mall with its concentric rings of planters and brightly lit parking lots and snorted. With all this growing stuff around it was surprising they didn't have more trouble with rats. People just didn't realize that all that ivy and other ground cover provided a perfect habitat. That and sloppy housekeeping in food preparation areas was ninety percent of the problem.

They'd been called back early and that offended Jesse Ware's professional pride. Maybe the people here hadn't been properly educated in prophylactic pest control. Or maybe someone had screwed up the last treatment. Either way it was unprofessional, and in Ware's book that was about the worst thing you could be.

Well, it didn't matter how bad it was. Jesse Ware was the best, the ace, the top-gun exterminator. That's why he was the only Pest Control Operator in the company to rate a full-size pickup. All the rest of the guys had Toyotas.

He turned off his lights, shut off the engine and reached for the radio microphone. "Exterminator One to base. I'm on scene and will liase with the locals before I proceed with reconnaissance."

"Ten-four, Unit One."

Ware scowled at the radio. The damn dispatcher insisted on calling him "Unit One" instead of using his correct call sign. The company was "The X-Terminator" and that made him "X-Terminator One." It had cost the boss a small fortune to get the right to use the name, and the least they could do was use it in their call signs.

He unclipped a flashlight from his nylon harness and took a black aluminum baton from his belt. A touch of the concealed button and the rod telescoped to three times its length. He examined the nearest planter with the flashlight, using the rod to move the vines aside to check the bare earth underneath.

The examination was quick but it was thorough. When he finished, Ware snapped off the light, compressed his baton and scowled. Normally when you had a heavy rat infestation like this the animals' runways were easy to spot. But he couldn't see any beaten earth trails snaking through the ground cover.

Andy was making a tour of the Food Court when he saw the man in black. Between the black jumpsuit, the black nylon web gear and black combat boots, Andy's first thought was that he was a SWAT team member. But SWAT team members don't go poking around in planters with sticks.

"Good evening," Andy said in the polite cop manner that really means "who the hell are you?"

The man stood up and faced him. He was perhaps half a head taller than Andy with graying hair cropped military style. "Evening," he nodded curtly. "Ware. Exterminator."

It took Andy an instant to translate that.

"Spraying for bugs?"

The man snorted. "Nope, you got a worse problem here. You've got a serious infestation of rats." He gazed off down the mall, his jaw set in a heroic jut. "Gonna be tough to get rid of them now that they're established."

Andy nodded noncomittally.

"It's gonna take a coordinated assault to take those suckers out. Rats are tough, tougher than any street punks." He looked back at Andy. "They charge when they're wounded, you know."

"I didn't know that."

"You better be careful in dark places until we get this under control. I've seen it happen. First you get rats in the food. Then you get rat bites. Let it go too long and you've got plague."

"Plague?"

"Bubonic plague. The Black Death." Ware smiled a steely smile. "Don't worry, though. We'll stop 'em before they get that far." Again he gazed down the mall with his jaw set. "We'll stop 'em."

Suddenly he shifted his attention back to Andy. "You're an ex-cop, aren't you?"

"Yes."

"Thought so. I can recognize the signs. I wanted to be a cop once, even took the tests."

Andy thought of a couple of his classmates at the Academy — ones who had washed out. "I kind of suspected you might have."

"Then I found this. It's like police work, you know? Chasing bad guys who endanger our whole society. Difference is," again that steely smile, "rats don't have Miranda rights."

Out by his truck, Jesse Ware reviewed his plan of campaign. He'd start by treating the exterior beds with pellets since they were the most likely source of the infestation. Inside he'd use traps to see where the worst concentrations were and then treat those areas first.

With no visible runways he'd have to settle for broadcasting the pellets through the undergrowth instead of putting small piles along the runways. He didn't like that. It offended his sense of professionalism to waste bait by scattering it haphazardly. But with no runways and no obvious rat holes it was the logical thing to do.

He could use the pellets liberally and he intended to. In the back of Ware's truck, secured by hardened steel locks, were 80 pounds of rodent pellets. The poison was mostly harmless to humans, but it was deadly to rats and mice, and the pellets were too big to be attractive to birds that could get into the ivy.

Carefully, he filled a plastic bucket with the thumb-size pellets and set to work.

He reached into the bucket with a gloved hand and scattered a fistful of pellets beneath the shrubbery. He bent down to get another handful and he was hit on the back by a hail of pellets as something threw what he had just scattered back at him.

Ware whirled like a springing cat, and the beam of his flashlight stabbed into the bushes. But there was no sign of anyone or anything. Just the bushes and the ground cover beneath them. The night was still with only the noise of distant traffic. Somewhere off in the distance a motorcycle pulled away from a light.

He studied the planter and unconsciously rubbed the back of his neck. He'd seen aggressive rats before, but this was ridiculous.

George Andropolous was just finishing cleaning up for the night when Jesse Ware lifted the counter door and stepped into the ice cream stall. "Excuse me. Exterminator."

"What are you doing?" the ice cream concessionaire demanded.

Ware fished what looked like an oversized mousetrap out of the black nylon bag on his hip and held it up. "Just setting a couple of traps for a census."

Andropolous moved to block Ware's way and crossed his meaty arms. "Traps? No traps here."

"We're not gonna try to trap all of them, sir," Ware said in the tone he reserved for explaining things to civilians. "I'm gonna do a census, see? I'm gonna put traps at places there's likely to be rats hiding and see how many I catch. That'll give me a scientific estimate of how much of a problem you got here."

"I don't got no problem," Andropolous said stubbornly. "It's the mall's problem. That's what I pay 'em for."

Ware shrugged. "Whatever. Anyway I'm gonna set a couple of these traps here. . . ."

"No. I told you I don't want no traps. You catch something and you scare off my customers."

"Look, I'll be back at eight-thirty in the morning to pick 'em up. You don't leave something like this laying around. It could be dangerous if you're not a trained professional."

"No traps."

"Mall management says you gotta cooperate. It's in your agreement. Besides, what happens if your customers start seeing rats? Big, live ones. Think that wouldn't scare them off?"

Andropolous' scowl darkened, but he moved out of the way. "Okay," he said belligerently. "But you better have them outta here by the time I open tomorrow."

"No problem."

The counters and exterior surfaces were clean. Shining his flashlight in the cabinets Ware couldn't see any traces of exposed food. Everything neatly put away and nothing in thin plastic bags. Well, he'd see.

He baited the first trap's trigger with a blob of peanut butter and beef suet. Then carefully, using both thumbs, he levered the trap into cocked position. He knelt and shoved the trap into the far corner of the lower shelf. Then he baited and cocked a second trap and eased it back toward the other corner by feel.

SPANG!

Ware screamed and jerked back as something bit hard on his hand. Several cans clattered out on the floor as he pulled his arm out by the most direct route.

There, hanging on to the side of his hand, was the first rat trap. The one he had just put in the opposite side of the shelf.

Ware pulled the trap off his hand and threw it on the floor. Then sucked on his injured fingers and glared into the recesses of the cabinet. *Dammit, this is getting personal!*

Ware was still nursing a badly bruised hand when he came back from his truck with another weapon. The interior couldn't be treated with scattered pellets like the outside. Here he'd need contained baits.

No need for a census anyway, Ware thought. Obviously, the Food Court was a major center of infestation, and he could move right into wiping the little bastards out.

Each bait container was a piece of four-inch PVC pipe about a foot long with the bait secured inside behind a baffle that would keep out even the smallest child's hand.

Ware placed the containers in the planters well back under the foliage. Then he went down to his truck for a second load to put in out-of-the-way spots in the non-public areas around the Food Court.

The containers came packed a dozen to a box, and Ware brought up three boxes. He was carrying them stacked on top of each other with his chin resting on the top box to stabilize the stack when he stepped out of the elevator.

He put his foot down on something round and slippery and went staggering backwards as his foot went out from under him. He put his other foot down on something equally round and slippery and completely lost his balance. Boxes went flying in all directions and Ware landed flat on his back.

When he raised his head he saw what he had stepped on. It was two of the bait containers he had just put in the planter. A half dozen more were strategically scattered in front of the elevator like a mine field.

Jesse Ware had never liked rats. He decided he *really* didn't like these rats. He also decided extreme measures were called for. This was no ordinary gang of rats, but Jesse Ware was no ordinary exterminator.

Jesse Ware was waiting for Bill Roberts when he arrived the next morning. Before Roberts even had his jacket off, Ware had followed him into his office and started explaining his plan.

"You want what?" Roberts said slowly when Ware finally paused for breath.

"To fumigate," Jesse Ware told him. "The whole damn mall."

The maintenance manager didn't say anything for a minute. "Isn't that a little much?" he asked finally.

Ware leaned over and put his fists on Roberts' desk.

"Look, Roberts, I've been in this business a long time, and I'm telling you I've never seen rats like this. I mean this is a serious situation you've got here. We're gonna have to do the whole mall at once."

"Uh, just what would that involve?"

"We seal the place up, open all the internal doors and use a fogger to flood the whole shooting match with pesticide."

"Seal the place up?" the manager repeated faintly. "You mean the whole mall?"

"Yeah. Close off all the outside openings with plastic. And divide up the inside space too. A place this big we'd have to do it in sections. Shouldn't take more than ten days."

"Ten days?"

"Maybe even less," Ware said smugly. "Maybe just a week."

The maintenance manager stared intently at his knuckles.

"Now," Ware went on, "it will take us maybe three, four days to get all the equipment we need. We'll have to bring in foggers from San Diego to San Francisco. But we'll put a rush on it and we can be ready to start inside a week. All you gotta do is say the word."

"Well," Roberts said finally, "I'll talk to management about it, but I don't think they're gonna buy it. I mean with the sale and all. . . ."

"You want word to get out about the rats? You want to wait until some kid gets bitten? I'm telling you, this thing is a potential public health menace. Those rats could be carrying plague or something."

The manager thought the real plague was standing in front of him.

"I'll let you know, okay?"

Chapter 12

It was a fine Southern California summer Saturday morning — which is to say the smog wasn't too thick and the day hadn't turned miserably sticky. Black Oak Mall gleamed gold and silver in the bright-but-not-yet-oppressive sun above the parking lots rapidly filling with shoppers, window shoppers, moseyers and other assorted folk.

Slick maneuvered his skateboard effortlessly around parked cars and moving pedestrians. He charged the side of a car backing out of a parking space and zipped in front of it through an opening that wasn't there a second before. Ignoring the bleat of the car's horn, he ollied up onto the sidewalk, dodged a couple of shoppers by inches and did a kick turn and slide to come to rest right by the main entrance. He tromped on the nose of his board and caught it one-handed as it flipped chest-high. Then he stuck the board back under the ivy in one of the planters and went on in to the mall, still swaying to the music blasting through his headset. It was a truly bodacious day, and the Slickster was in his element.

JoJo and some of the others were probably already down in The Pit. They'd hang there for a while and then maybe make some action in the 'hood. JoJo's old man was in real estate, and JoJo was a fount of information on empty houses with drained swimming pools that could make for an afternoon's outlaw skating.

It turned out JoJo knew a new place. "A really big house, dude. Should have, like, an awesome pool." TJ and the others weren't interested, so Slick and JoJo headed out to grab their boards and go for it.

Slick knew something was wrong before he ever reached the planter. He ran the last few steps and pawed through the ivy, shoving the vines aside, but there was nothing there.

"Hey, someone ripped off my board."

"Bummer," JoJo said. By unwritten agreement boards stashed in the planters were sacrosanct. "Maybe one of the guards scarfed it."

Slick nodded glumly.

"Be a hassle getting it back," JoJo predicted with assurance born of experience. "If you go to security and ask for it they'll, like, do the lecture number on you and then they may not give you the board back anyway."

Slick was considering his options when Andy came out of the mall to check the parking lot. If it had been the Fat Mexican Dude or the Redneck Dude, or even the Black Woman Dude, Slick wouldn't have bothered. But the Young Dude seemed pretty cool. Maybe he could get his board back without the lecture number.

"Hey, man, I've got like a downer here. Like someone lifted my ride."

"Someone took your bicycle?"

"No, man, my ride. They took my board."

"Who did?"

"I dunno, man. I left it, like, in the planter here, you know? And when I came out just now, it was, like, vanished."

"You know you're not supposed to have skateboards on the property," Andy said sternly.

"Well, yeah, but, like, it was *stolen*, you know?"

Andy thought about it. "Okay, I'll tell you what. I'll keep my eyes open and I'll check the security center. But if I get it back you've got to promise not to bring it around any more."

"Sure," Slick said mendaciously. "And thanks, man."

"Now, what does it look like?"

"It's got a Bucky Laser deck, 48s and micro risers. It's easy to spot."

"Uh, right," Andy said. "Okay, I'll keep an eye out. But remember, don't bring it to the mall again."

Andy was still thinking about that when he headed out into the parking lot to continue his foot patrol. The sun's glare was nearly blinding and the air was thick and sticky after the carefully controlled conditions inside the mall. *Kid was stupid to leave the thing in the bushes.* The kids around here were so trusting, like nothing bad would ever happen to them. For that matter, so were a lot of the adults. *I'll bet half these cars aren't even locked.*

They might be right at this place. There was nothing out of the ordinary here, only the occasional car arriving or leaving and a sprinkling of shoppers arriving and leaving. Between the patrols and the security cameras there wasn't much danger here even with an unlocked car.

Down in the employees' lot things were much the same. The early afternoon sun was dimmed by smog but still strong enough to throw brilliant glints off windshields and chrome and there was no movement to be seen.

No movement . . . ? A glint caught Andy's attention, like the sun reflecting off a moving car. He swiveled his head and realized the reflection was coming from Crampton's Porsche. The car was rocking up and down ever so gently.

Andy kept walking as if nothing had happened until he got a pickup camper between him and the Porsche. Then he turned sharply, crouched low and started to work his way toward the sports car. As he came even with a station wagon he raised his head for a quick peek. The car was definitely rocking but there was no sign of the person who was doing it. The guy must be kneeling or even laying down as he worked on the door, Andy decided. He thought about calling for backup but decided against it. It would take time to stop and call and he was so close now that the guy might hear him. If the perp ran there would be time to call for help.

Andy paused behind the car next to the Porsche and unsnapped the safety strap on his holster. Now he could hear the gentle squeak-squeak of the sports car's suspension as it rose and fell. With a single bound he leapt from his crouch.

"DON'T . . ." he roared, ". . . move," he finished softly. There was no one there. The space around the car was empty or whoever was messing with the car was invisible.

Andy knelt cautiously and peered under the vehicle. Nothing there either. He stood up and, keeping one hand on his gun butt, eased up to the car.

As he drew level with the front bumper he saw a flash of movement and got a quick glimpse of something about the size of a house cat sprinting between two cars. But cats don't move like that, and Andy had the distinct impression the thing was green.

Slowly, Andy refastened his holster's safety strap and studied the car. It looked untouched.

"Hey, you!"

Andy turned and saw Crampton hurrying toward him.

"What have you been doing to my car?" the store owner demanded as he came puffing up.

"Nothing, sir. I thought I heard something over by your car and I came to investigate."

Crampton stepped past Andy and started to inspect the Porsche. "I suppose it's too much to hope that you caught them," he said, still looking over the car.

"I didn't even see them. They must have run when they saw me coming." He wasn't about to mention the green cat, especially to Crampton.

"Well, you seem to have scared them off this time," Crampton admitted grudgingly, "but now do you see why this car needs special protection? Lord knows I pay enough in dues to the Merchants' Association, you'd think I . . ."

Andy was properly apologetic and deferential while Crampton blew steam for the next five minutes, but his heart wasn't in it and his mind was far away. *Something* had been rocking that car. Not even $100,000 Porsches move by themselves. But he hadn't seen anyone. He should have surprised whoever it was but he hadn't even heard him running away. Nothing but a green cat that didn't move like a cat.

Eventually Crampton ran down and returned to his store. Andy went back to patroling the parking lot, thinking hard.

All right then, Cyril Heathercoate thought as he turned the rented sports car into the parking space, *let's get to it, shall we?*

A quick check of the rearview mirror convinced him that not even his mum would know him — not even when she was off the gin. A bottle of instant tan had darkened his skin. He was wearing a blonde wig in surfer shag, wraparound sunglasses, a violently colored Hawaiian sport shirt open to the navel and a couple of gold chains nestled in his chest hair, which was dyed blonde to match the wig. Heathercoate had considered adding a little gold spoon on one of the chains, but he decided that would be excessive in the '90s.

Perfect bloody Californian, Heathercoate thought. All he needed was one of the little Day-Timer leather things and a gold Rolex watch.

Andy was thinking about green cats and looking for skateboarders, not reporters. A couple of customers had complained about kids on skateboards around the east entrance. So Andy didn't pay any attention to the pseudo-surfer. You see a lot of strange stuff in California, and in California middle-aged men dressed up to look like teenagers don't even qualify as unusual — never mind strange.

He did notice a bit when Heathercoate nearly
tripped on the curb, a victim of too-dark sunglasses, but
he didn't fall, so Andy continued his search for skateboarders.

Just then JoJo and TJ came blasting down the sidewalk on their boards, lost in the music of their
Walkmans. The other shoppers, true Californians, simply stepped aside. Heathercoate was still adjusting to his
personal darkness at noon, and he didn't even see them.
He stepped right into their path.

JoJo and TJ were good. They split and whizzed by the
reporter without touching him, but so close the wind
ruffled his wig.

"BUGGER!" Heathercoate screamed in his native
Liverpool accent. "You bleedin' little wankers! Watch
the bloody 'ell where you're going with those bloody
boards."

There was more in the same vein. Heathercoate was
so caught up in swearing he didn't see Andy behind him
talking to his radio.

At last Heathercoate ran down. Then he took a couple of deep breaths and continued toward the entrance
door. "Bloody little wankers," he muttered as he made
for the door into the mall. He opened the door and
bumped into someone.

"Watch where . . ." Heathercoate started. Then the
sunglasses slipped, and over the top he saw Morales
blocking his way. He turned around and found himself
nose to nose with Andy.

"How's it, um, like, hanging, uh, dudes?" Heathercoate said in his best imitation California accent.

Andy and Morales herded him off the property.

The problem was still gnawing at Andy when he
changed with one of the inside officers an hour later.
There was some kind of pattern, something he could
sense but didn't understand. His experience at Southeast had made him leery of things going on around him

he didn't understand. Combined with his natural curiosity it added up to a potent itch that needed scratching.

What I really need, Andy thought as he threaded his way through the Saturday crowds on the second level, *are some informants.* He thought about asking the other guards and then decided against it. For one thing he wasn't sure he wanted to try to explain about green not-cats messing with Crampton's car. For another he realized he didn't know a lot of the other guards, and with the exception of LaVonne the ones he did know — Morales, Henderson and the rest — he didn't trust. He hadn't forgotten seeing Morales the morning he found the dead cat.

At the other side of the walk Billy Sunshine was weeding a flower bed. Billy was on good terms with nearly everyone. He'd probably know if anyone would. Andy walked over and stood next to the gardener, waiting to be noticed.

Slowly and deliberately Billy Sunshine moved his hand over a newly sprouted weed. He hesitated, blinked once or twice and then his thumb and forefinger closed around the seedling and plucked it from the rich black soil. Without looking, he dropped the weed in the bucket beside him. Seeing him kneeling on the ledge surrounding the bed reminded Andy of the White Rock fairy.

"Hey, Billy."

The gardener seemed not to hear. He continued to placidly weed the flower bed. Andy noticed that a bald spot was forming under the place where he pulled his ponytail back.

"Billy."

This time Billy looked around, left, then right and then up at Andy.

"Hey, man, what's happening?" he asked genially.

"Not a lot. Uh, say, Billy, have you seen anything odd around here recently?"

Billy blinked companionably. "Like, odd, man?"

"Yeah. You know. Things out of the ordinary."

"Oh, wow, man. Like that's a heavy question, you know?" He blinked again and stared off into space.

It occurred to Andy that maybe he hadn't picked the best person to ask.

Finally, Billy's eyes focused and he returned to this planet. "CDs," he said firmly.

"I beg your pardon?"

"CDs. You know. Like in the record stores."

"What about CDs?"

"They've got, like, Joplin, the Stones, Hendrix. They're all out on CDs now. And I'm like wondering, you know, how did they do that since they're dead and all?"

"The Stones aren't dead," Andy corrected automatically.

Billy Sunshine blinked again. "They're not? Oh wow, man, like never mind then." With that he turned back to his weeding.

Andy briefly considered asking him again. He settled for sighing and moving on.

Okay, Andy admitted to himself, *that wasn't the best choice.* He needed someone a little more normal, but someone who was in here all the time. By this time he had reached the Food Court and that was as good a place as any. As LaVonne had told him, if squinky stuff was going to happen, the Food Court was probably where it was going to come down.

He looked around. Most of the booths were manned by kids, and he didn't know any of them. The Chinese fried chicken booth was occupied by the old man and he didn't speak English very well. His grandson, the one who had been accepted into Stanford, wasn't there, so that was out. The Jamaican Ph.D. who ran the Caribbean food booth spoke better English than Andy did, but he had three or four customers lined up for his incendiary jerk chicken and barbecued goat. However, the Greek guy was in the ice cream stall, hassling the blonde kid who worked for him.

The guy was a complainer. That meant that if something was wrong he'd probably be willing to talk about it.

"Excuse me, sir."

Andropolous broke off in the middle of his stream of instructions to Lance. "Yeah?" he demanded. "What do you want?"

"Have you seen anything, well, odd happening here recently?"

"You mean aside from the rats?" Andropolous asked.

"What rats?"

"The ones that are all over the place. I tell you, it's a scandal. I even saw one. Big gray thing, came jumping out of the hot fudge sauce pot one morning and ran right across the counter in front of me. I call maintenance, but do they fix it? No, they send me out some goon in a jumpsuit who goes moping around here with traps. Traps!" Andropolous snorted. "Like traps are gonna do some good. And they don't. Cause I've still got a problem. I'm still losing stuff to rats. Now what kind of job are you people doing here anyway? I pay my commons fees just like everyone else and what do I get, rats. It's a scandal. . . ."

"Yes, but have you seen anything other than rats?" Andy finally managed to cut in.

"Huh? Besides rats? Ain't rats enough? For the money we pay . . ."

Andy mumbled his thanks and escaped, leaving the ice cream store manager to continue his monologue almost without noticing he'd lost his audience.

Jesus! You might as well try to get information out of witnesses to a homicide in a shooting gallery in Southeast, Andy thought. Well, there were still the kids. Looking around, he saw the kid who had lost his skateboard sitting with a friend sipping a jumbo-size Coke. LaVonne had introduced them that first day, but he'd forgotten his name.

"How's it going?" Andy said as he sauntered up to the pair.

The one who had lost the board shrugged. "Okay, I guess. Did you find my ride?"

"Not yet, but I'm working on it." He tried his best smile. "By the way, I'm Andy."

"Heavy dude. I'm Slick. That's, like, TJ." TJ, a Hispanic with an identical haircut and shorts that were even longer and droopier than Slick's, nodded.

"I'm interested in what's going on around the mall," he said and realized he'd made a mistake when both kids stiffened.

"Like I don't know anything, you know," TJ said.

"No, I don't mean criminal activity. I mean really strange things. You know, weird stuff. Unbelievable, kind of."

Slick relaxed visibly. "Oh sure. All kinds of weird stuff happens around here all the time."

"You say stuff happens. What sort of stuff?"

"Well, just a few days ago there was this, like, little kid, you know, and he flew up to the top of the fountain in South Court. I mean, like, he just flew."

Andy, who had heard something about a kid climbing up on the fountain, nodded.

"And then there was this girl who got killed in the movie theater when a bunch of the ghouls on the screen got real, you know, and started attacking people in the audience."

"I didn't hear about that," Andy lied.

Slick shrugged. "They kept it, like, real quiet, you know? They took her body out in a garbage can and stuff so no one would know."

"Yeah," TJ said. "There's this bunch of Colombian drug dealers who are getting ready to buy the mall and they didn't want the word to get out cause they were afraid they'd call the deal off."

"And then there's the Phantom Babe," Slick added. "She's like a ghost who haunts the mall."

"The Phantom Babe?"

"She's the ghost of some valley girl who was, like, so grief-stricken when her old man canceled her credit cards that she, like, pined away and died right here in the mall," TJ said.

"Naw," Slick told him. "She was murdered in the parking lot. They stuffed her body in the trunk of her car and they didn't find it for, like, three weeks. Everyone knows that."

TJ shrugged. "Anyway she, like, haunts the mall, you know? And if you're around here late at night she'll, like, come up and try to talk to you, but she's all, like, ghostly, you know, and you can't hear what she's saying or anything. Just, like, her lips move and nothing comes out."

"Have you ever seen her?"

Slick shook his head. "Not me, man, but, like, Case and Matt have."

"Case and Matt?"

Slick jerked his head backward to the two air guitarists Andy recognized from the theater. They were pounding away on their nonexistent instruments, eyes squeezed shut and lost in whatever was blasting in through their earphones.

Looking at the pair, Andy decided interviewing them would be like trying to talk to Billy Sunshine on an acid flashback in the middle of a rock concert.

"Do you have any idea what's causing it?"

"The mall's, like, haunted, you know?"

"Yeah," TJ chimed in. "They built the place over an old cemetery and the ghosts and stuff are taking revenge."

"It was an Indian burial ground," Slick corrected. "There were all these old Indians buried up here, and when they went to break ground for this place the medicine man warned them that, you know, there'd be trouble if they disturbed them. But they went ahead and did it anyway." He took a long, noisy pull on the last of his Coke. "So there's always stuff happening around here."

Andy thanked the skaters and went back to his rounds. He didn't believe a word of what he'd been told, but he didn't completely discount any of it either. Andy had been a cop long enough to recognize a street story when he heard one, but he also knew that a lot of the time there was some distorted grain of truth in street stories.

The theater thing, for instance. He'd been there, so he knew there was no murder. But that didn't explain what had happened in there, or the smell it left behind.

Dr. Patterson was sitting on a bench on the third level, her walker beside her and her ever-present tape recorder in her lap.

Of course! Andy kicked himself for not thinking of her sooner. She looked up and smiled as Andy came toward her.

"Dr. Patterson, I need some professional advice."

"Well, I must say that is a refreshing change from 'good afternoon.'"

"I'm sorry. Good afternoon."

Dr. Patterson laughed. "Don't be sorry. I said it was refreshing and I meant it. It's been a while since anyone has consulted me professionally. Sit down and tell me what you want."

Andy sat down beside her, careful to sit on her unparalyzed side. "What do you know about urban legends?"

The anthropologist frowned slightly. "They're pretty much like other legends. Their purpose is to promote group cohesion by supporting the group's worldview. It's a fairly new field but there are already several thousands of them recorded, many of them cognate with more traditional legends."

"What about the stories that this mall is haunted?"

Dr. Patterson looked at him strangely. "That's an interesting example," she said at last. "Haunting legends are very common among adolescents. This one is somewhat unusual in that the haunted place is well populated and heavily traveled. But otherwise it largely conforms to the pattern." She cocked her head. "I presume this is leading somewhere?"

"Yes, ma'am. I'm sort of investigating some of the funny things that have happened here. Unofficially, I mean."

"Odd indeed," the old woman murmured. Then she focused her attention tightly on Andy and clicked on her tape recorder.

Andy told her the story about the incident in the theater, the Phantom Babe and the flying child. Slowly and carefully she led him back through the stories, pinning down his sources, the time when they supposedly happened, witnesses and other details. There was nothing harsh or hostile in the way she did it, but Andy recognized he was in the presence of a master interrogator.

"That's very interesting, Andy," she said at last as she clicked off the tape recorder. "Thank you for sharing them with me."

"What do you make of all that?" Andy asked, shifting on the bench to relieve muscles he hadn't noticed tightening in the course of the interrogation.

Dr. Patterson thought. "Well," she said finally, "all of them except the flying baby are cognate with other fairly common stories. Your Phantom Babe, for instance, is a classic type of ghost tale."

"So you think it really is just a story?"

Patterson raised an admonishing hand. "I didn't say that. Remember that plausibility is very important in creating a legend. Many of them have some basis in fact, however distorted."

"You mean you think this place may be haunted?"

"I didn't say that either. In fact I think it is unlikely. My point is that you cannot dismiss something as an urban legend simply because it conforms to the criteria for legend." She sighed. "One of the great fallacies of the comparative study of urban legends is that by classifying them we can tell whether they are true or not. Actually studying them usually doesn't tell us anything about the truth they may contain. What it can tell us is the purpose telling the stories serves."

"And what purpose is that?"

"Once again, social cohesion. It's especially important to people who feel rootless." She smiled slightly. "And adolescents do as a rule. That is one reason urban legends are so common among teenagers."

Andy sighed and stood up. "Well, thanks. I've got to get going."

"You're more than welcome, Andy. And if you hear any more of these stories could you relate them to me?"

"Part of your research on the cultures of the mall?"

Dr. Patterson pursed her lips on the side of her face that still worked. "After a fashion," she said.

Andy had a lot to think about as he rode the escalators down to the main level. Aside from the novel experience of being interrogated by an expert and the slightly strange feeling that came from realizing he was an "anthropological informant," he had a strong feeling that Dr. Patterson had heard those stories before. Those and more.

He also had a distinct impression that the old woman wasn't being straight with him. She was a lot more interested in this than she let on. Which meant . . . what?

At the bottom of the escalator was an information kiosk, its screen running a slide show of the mall's attractions.

As he caught sight of it, he hesitated, much to the annoyance of the woman getting off the escalator behind him.

Well, what the hell? Andy thought. *It sure sees everything that happens here.*

Andy inserted his ID card and waited for the now-familiar smiley face to appear on the screen. BLACKIE, I'VE GOT A QUESTION FOR YOU.

SURE ANDY. WHAT?

Andy looked around to make sure no one was paying attention to him and started typing. WOULD YOU NOTICE IF ANYTHING ABNORMAL HAPPENED IN THE MALL?

GIVEN THAT MY SENSORS COVER THE ENTIRE MALL IT FOLLOWS LOGICALLY THAT I WOULD SEE ANYTHING ABNORMAL WHICH HAPPENED HERE.

Andy waited for more. WELL? he finally typed.

WELL WHAT?

WELL HAVE YOU SEEN ANYTHING ABNORMAL HAPPENING?

BEFORE I ANSWER THAT QUESTION I REQUIRE ONE ADDITIONAL DATA POINT.

WHAT?

WHAT DO YOU CONSIDER "NORMAL"?

Chapter 13

Andy had planned to go home to a cool apartment, a warm TV dinner and an evening of old movies on cable. By the time he finished his shift at 4 P.M. that wasn't very attractive. He wanted to unwind and he still wanted information, he needed a different outlook, and he had a pretty good idea where to find all of it.

Judy was in the shop when Andy got there, going over something with Sheree, her assistant. Sheree was a little taller, heavier and younger than Judy, a bleached blonde with wide blue eyes who seemed perpetually excited about something. She was wearing pale blue pants and a white sweatshirt with "Angel in Disguise" on the front.

Judy wore a black dress that at least didn't clash with the violently colored Mexican shawl fastened about her shoulders with that same ugly amethyst-and-silver pin. However, the electric-purple plastic hoop earrings that hung nearly to her shoulders clashed mightily with the shawl, her complexion and nearly everything in the shop.

"Well, hello." Judy smiled so nicely Andy almost forgot the earrings and shawl.

Andy smiled back and they made small talk for a couple of minutes until Sheree disappeared into the back.

"You know a lot about what's going on around here, don't you?" Andy asked as soon as Sheree had gone.

Judy shrugged, making her purple plastic earrings dance. "I like to watch people. Before my divorce I used to come here a lot. Shopping is a favorite recreation for lawyers' wives. Since then, well, let's just say I've got a lot of time to watch."

"Maybe you can give me some information, then."

Judy raised an eyebrow. "Curious or investigating?"

"Investigating, but purely on my own. Call it directed curiosity."

She looked at him narrowly. "Why?"

"Well," Andy said, groping for an answer, "I guess the same reasons I wanted to become an officer. I like solving things and I like helping people." *Not that I got to do a whole hell of a lot of either on the force!* he thought to himself. "Besides, there are some things here that just aren't right."

"You can say that again!" She looked around and back over her shoulder in the direction Sheree had gone. "Come on," she said. "Let's go to Coffee Poison and I'll buy you a cup."

"Coffee Poison" turned out to be Cafe Poisson, a European-style coffee bar on the third level. They found a tiny glass-topped table amid a sea of polished brass and a forest of fake plants. The place smelled overpoweringly of coffee, cinnamon and vanilla. Judy ordered a Cappuccino Amaretto. Andy stuck to plain black coffee.

"Why do you call it Coffee Poison?" Andy asked as soon as the waitress, a tall, slender blonde with brown eyes, had taken their order.

"The coffee's fine, but don't ever eat here." Judy made a face. "Especially the chicken salad."

Andy nodded. "You were going to tell me about Crampton."

"Myron Crampton is very materialistic and he has a small soul. He is also an obnoxious, self-centered jerk. But not everyone can see that."

"I thought his name was Jack."

"It's Myron, but he hates it. So he calls himself Jack, after his store — Smilin' Jack's."

"You know him well?"

"Let's say I'm around him a fair amount."

Andy let that pass. "Is he overly suspicious?"

"You mean about his car? Yes. But lately I think someone has been yanking his chain. You know, fooling with it to trigger the alarms."

"Any idea who?"

Judy shook her head. "He's not very popular, but mostly people ignore him. Either that or they fall in love with him. You know he made a pass at me once? Back when I was married and still somebody in his book."

"Now?"

She grimaced. "Now he thinks I'm a bad influence."

"But you think someone is persecuting him?"

Judy nodded.

The blonde, brown-eyed waitress arrived with their coffee. Andy found his was black, strong and good. Judy's smelled like almonds and looked like a hot coffee milkshake in a little cup.

As soon as the waitress left, Judy leaned across the table intently. "What do you know about what's happening here?"

"Just that my instincts tell me something's going on."

She nodded firmly. "You should always trust your intuition. It's your window to your higher consciousness."

"Well, there's that," Andy said noncomittally. "But there seems to be some funny stuff happening too."

"Funny stuff?"

"In both senses of the word. Hints of criminal activity and also something like practical jokes."

"Criminal activity. You mean like Kemper Cogswell is using the mall as a cover for a drug smuggling operation?"

Andy thought briefly of Surfer, but shook his head. "More like larceny of some sort. I understand shrinkage is very high here."

Judy nodded so vigorously she set her tacky purple earrings swinging. "You've got that right! All my friends who work in the big stores say they've got real problems. A couple of the chains have brought in special loss-prevention teams. I understand it's gotten so bad that some of the stores aren't reporting all their losses to their insurance companies for fear their rates will go up."

"Have you been hit?"

"Not really, but the stuff I carry isn't easy to fence." She gave him her urchin grin. "Not unless you know a crooked herbalist. Besides, I've got protection spells around my place."

Andy just nodded. "Then there's the weird stuff," he said to change the subject. He told her about the panic in the theater.

Judy listened intently, taking tiny sips of her coffee. "You don't think the kids scared themselves?"

"Mass panic? It's possible. We had a case like that at a junior high school a couple of years ago. But this doesn't feel right for that. Those kids had gone there expecting a scary movie, and the theater wasn't crowded. Usually a panic starts when people are close together. Besides there was the smell."

"The smell?"

"Like a floater, or a ripe one."

Judy looked puzzled.

"A floater's a body that's been in the water for several days. After a week or so the gasses build up and the guy floats to the surface. A ripe one's a stiff that isn't found for a while." He shook his head. "I'll tell you the smell is like nothing else. One whiff and you never forget."

"I'll bet," Judy said weakly.

Andy looked up and saw she had gone quite pale.

"Oh, I'm sorry. Shop talk."

"That's all right," Judy said, gripping her demitasse cup. "I guess you're used to it."

"You don't ever get used to it," Andy told her grimly. "You just learn to live with it." He took a deeper breath. "Anyway, there was a trace of that in the theater."

"Someone fixed up a stink bomb?"

"That's what Morales thinks. But they'd have to know that smell. Outside of certain lines of work the odor's not exactly common. Besides, there's been some other stuff." He filled her in on what he'd seen with Crampton's Porsche and what he'd heard about the kid on the fountain.

"Have you heard or seen anything?" he asked when he had finished the story.

"Maybe." Judy took a reflective sip of her cappuccino. "Do you know if rats eat plastic?"

"Are any cats green?" Andy shot back.

"No, I'm serious."

"So am I, I think."

"All right, then no, I've never seen a green cat."

"I don't think it was a cat anyway."

Judy frowned and opened her mouth as if to say something, then closed it.

"Anyway," Andy went on, "you were asking if rats eat plastic. You mean eat it or just gnaw on it?"

"Eat it. Like chew it up and swallow it."

It was Andy's turn to take a pull on his coffee. "I've never heard of that. Rats will eat almost anything that's nourishing, but there's not much nourishment in plastic."

"I didn't think they did, but I have a friend who swears she's got rats eating plastic hangers in one of the department stores." She paused and took another sip. "I'll tell you something else. From the look on her face when she told the story I think she talked herself into believing it was a rat."

Andy nodded and neither of them said anything for a moment. The only sound was the syrupy music coming from the concealed speaker overhead and the occasional rattle of dishes and silverware from the kitchen.

"The kid could have climbed, you know," Judy said dubiously.

"Sure," Andy agreed with an equal lack of conviction, "and what I saw in the parking lot could have been a trick of reflection."

Both of them fell silent again.

"You know what I think it is?" Judy said finally. "I think these are manifestations. This place sits on a vortex so naturally you'd expect unusual occurrences."

"Vortex?"

"A center of psychic power. Can't you feel it?"

He shook his head. The conversation was getting weird again. Conversations with Judy had a tendency to do that. "Now wait a minute, I saw something messing with that car all right, but I don't think it's got anything to do with psychic phenomena."

"But that's the most reasonable explanation," Judy protested.

Andy paused for a second while he considered Judy's definition of "reasonable." "This isn't supernatural. There's a logical explanation for all of this stuff and I'm pretty sure it's all tied together."

"What?"

"Special effects."

Judy just raised her eyebrows.

"Look," Andy said, hunching forward over the table, closer to her, "special effects experts can make almost anything happen — or seem to happen. They do it all the time in the movies. If you've got enough money and can hire enough talent you could make it seem like this mall was inhabited by an army of banshees."

"And that's your idea of a reasonable explanation?"

"It's a lot more reasonable than assuming this place is haunted," Andy said tartly, stung by her tone.

Judy held up a hand, as if to ward off an argument. "Okay, okay. Let's assume it is special effects experts. Why? It would be awfully expensive to do something like that for a practical joke."

"I just worked that part out this afternoon. The mall's being sold, right? So why not rig a few incidents to drive the price down?"

"You mean scare off buyers?"

"No, I think the buyers are behind it, or someone

close to them. The beauty of it is it doesn't matter if people really believe in this stuff or not. It creates doubts, maybe costs the mall business and that's enough to drive down the price."

"Well," Judy said reflectively, "Kemper Cogswell is supposed to be really anxious to sell. He wants to go into politics, you know."

Andy didn't know, but he nodded as if he did.

"But still," she continued, "that's a lot of trouble just to get a cut in the price of the mall."

He shrugged. "The price is supposed to be in the hundreds of millions of dollars. If it cuts the price just one or two percent that's still a lot of money."

"Well, how does this larceny you're talking about fit in?"

"I'm not sure, and that's one of the things that's bothering me."

"What are you going to do about all this?"

Andy drained the last of his coffee. "Nothing I can do, except nose around a little on my own. My boss isn't interested in anything that might rock the boat."

"I'll be glad to help you," Judy said. Then she looked at her watch. "But not just now. I've got to get back and total the register."

Andy was vaguely disappointed. "Can't your assistant do that?"

"Sheree? Sheree is very spiritually advanced, but she can't add." She stood up. "I've got to get back up there before she tries."

"Why did you hire her then?"

Judy shrugged. "She's spiritually advanced. Besides, she's my apprentice in the Craft so I don't have to pay her."

Andy started to ask what craft, but Judy was already headed to the cashier's desk. As he turned to follow, a tall, blonde bus girl with brown eyes descended on the table, making it ready for the next customers. The place had begun to fill up as they talked, Andy noticed.

Judy was already paying the cashier, a tall blonde with brown eyes.

"Sisters?" Andy asked as they walked out into the mall.

"No, Roland."

Andy raised an eyebrow.

"The manager. He hires women he likes and his tastes are pretty limited."

Jack Crampton was damn pleased with himself. He had just unloaded the last of last season's suits and done it at full price. The silly twit he'd maneuvered into buying it hadn't even noticed it wasn't the latest fashion and he bought three silk shirts in the bargain!

Normally he went home at five on Saturdays, but making the sale had kept him late and now he was so pumped he didn't care. That was the essence of salesmanship, he thought as he took the suit into the back room to hang on the alterations rack. It was going mano a mano with another man and bending him to your will with just your wits and force of personality. And best of all, making him *like* it. That was salesmanship and Jack Crampton was the best.

As Crampton entered the room something scuttled under the clothes rack just too quick for him to see.

Rats! Crampton thought. The damn rats had gotten into his store. Dawn had told him all about finding one in the fitting room at Sudstrom's. The damn thing had left her hysterical. *Silly little bitch.* Now they were spreading. Well, he wasn't going to wait for mall management on this. If they couldn't catch the thieves who kept trying to steal his Porsche in broad daylight they sure couldn't be counted on to deal with rats.

Jack Crampton smiled, not at all pleasantly. Hell, if he could handle the customers, he could handle a few rats.

Chapter 14

The Surfer sauntered into the Burger King. Not many people for a Saturday night. Just four girls giggling together, a woman with a couple of kids, a family with a couple of more and an old guy chomping on a hamburger and reading the newspaper. He ordered a Coke, picked up a couple of napkins and took one of the booths in back, hidden from the counter, the street and the other patrons.

The kids came in a few minutes later, breathless and giggly and trying to look cool. They greeted him noisily as they slid into the booth.

The older one pulled out a twenty and laid it on the table. Underneath, Surfer slid his hand into the kid's and passed him two small plastic envelopes.

The kid looked at him questioningly.

"You snort it. But be cool, dudes. That's some righteous powerful stuff."

"Aw, we can handle it," the kid with the money said.

"Later then."

"Later."

The kids ambled out, and Surfer finished his Coke.

Outside the Burger King, Glenn and Ted looked around. The parking lot was too public, even behind the restaurant.

"Trees?" Glenn asked.

"Sounds like a plan."

Several sections of the mall parking lot were screened from the surrounding streets by a six-foot chain-link fence and a row of eucalyptus trees. It was dark under the trees and there were holes in the fence. You could sit there with cars speeding by just a few feet away, all unknowing, and feel hidden and secure and superior all at the same time.

Once they were in their hiding place Glenn passed Ted one of the baggies. Eagerly, Ted tore off the tape that sealed it.

"Hey, watch it," Glenn said. "You'll spill it."

"Bullshit." Ted opened the envelope and poured the powder into his cupped palm.

"Aren't you supposed to use a dollar bill or something?"

"This works fine," his friend assured him. Then he exhaled loudly and stuck his nose in his palm for an enormous sniff.

The powder burned his nostrils and he had to pinch them shut to keep from sneezing. There was a bitter taste like vomit at the back of his throat. He held his breath to enhance the effect.

Glenn, who was a little more sophisticated, carefully poured his powder in a line along the back of his hand. It took him two snorts to get it all because he coughed in the middle of the line.

For a minute neither of them said anything. They stood with their eyes closed, breathing deeply.

"You feel anything?" Ted said at last.

"A little light-headed."

"That's just from breathing deep. You don't suppose he ripped us off, do you?"

"No way, man. Surfer's a cool dude. He wouldn't do that."

They were both quiet again.

"What do you want to do when the rush comes?" Ted asked.

"Go back into the mall and hang out. It's better when you're ripped."

"Yeah," Glenn said. Then he sneezed. "Man, my nose

tingles." Somehow that was terribly funny and he broke into giggles.

Ted started giggling too and that made it even funnier. They locked arms and spun around and around, laughing hysterically. Finally, Glenn lost his grip and went stumbling backwards to land in a heap in the leaves and litter.

"Oh, wow, this stuff is great!" He tried to stand but his legs didn't want to cooperate. He gave up and collapsed back, lying on the ground with his arms spread.

Ted stayed on his feet and looked down at his friend, unseeing as the drug built higher and higher within him. It was good and it kept getting better and better. Speed, PCP, not even coke was like this.

His parents, school, none of it mattered. He was above all that shit now, alone at the very peak of the universe. It was like he was watching everything that happened from the top of a very tall mountain, or he had grown a hundred feet tall. And most of all he felt GOOD!

This must be what it feels like to be God. He looked down at Glenn, but he was passed out in the leaves. Asshole couldn't take it. He giggled and kicked his friend playfully in the ribs. Glenn didn't move and Ted almost lost his balance. He stumbled back and went to his knees in the litter of medicinal smelling leaves.

"Asshole," he said. "Later, you fucker." That set him laughing again and he almost couldn't get up.

The drug sang and coursed through him in fierce exaltation. He laughed out of sheer joy at his newfound power. He wanted to *do* something, to be someplace where people could see and wonder.

Through the trees he could see the lights of the cars rushing by. The river of light attracted him. He wanted to be part of that river, to stand above it and drink it all in. It would become part of him, light flowing through him and around him while he watched in benign exultation from a world above. He wanted the biggest, brightest river of light there was and something in the back of his drug-fuddled brain told him where he could find that.

Staggering, shouting and swinging in circles around lampposts, Ted started off toward the bright flowing lights of the freeway.

Behind him, Glenn lay unmoving, still spread-eagled in the leaves. His chest rose and fell convulsively and his breath came in great ragged gasps. The only sound was the traffic rushing by outside and the occasional sound of a car radio, rising and falling with the passage of the car.

Three little green men came out of the oleanders. They looked at Glenn for a moment and then gathered around the plastic baggie he had dropped. The one with the long nose picked up the bag and cocked his head curiously as he examined it. Experimentally he stuck his nose in the bag and inhaled deeply. Then he sneezed and all three of them collapsed into fits of giggles.

Ted staggered up to the overpass. Sometimes he kept to the sidewalk, sometimes he didn't. Drivers jammed on their brakes, honked and yelled at him as he wandered into the street. He screamed obscenities back and kept going.

There was an inward-curving chain-link fence on each side of the overpass. The barrier was to keep people from throwing things at the traffic below, not to prevent a jumper. It was easy to climb over the barbed wire barrier at the end and work his way out above the traffic. He tore his hand on the wire getting over. The sight of the blood trickling down his arm only made him laugh. Even when he got cut he didn't hurt!

For a minute he hung on the wire, hypnotized by the rush of lights below. The trucks especially. Their tops were so close he could bend down and touch them.

He looked out toward the horizon, his eyes following

the glowing yellow stream and masses of red sparks as they disappeared over a hill and around a curve. He was floating invisible and invincible above the most important, exciting, rush of wonderfulness in the world. It called to him in a thousand, roaring, hissing voices, beckoning him to come and merge his Godhead with the flow of the stream.

Enraptured by what was passing below him, Ted relaxed his grip on the chain-link fence and plummeted toward the shining river below.

Surfer looked down on his own river and smiled.

The Saturday evening throngs below him, the crowds on the escalators, he was happy to see them all. Business was good, life was good, even the dopey rendition of Mozart pouring out of the overhead speakers was good. Everything was running his way and tonight he was enjoying it to the hilt.

There would be more business before long. More kids wanting to buy little bags of happiness. And if there weren't, so what? From his perch beside the escalators he'd just hang loose and dig the scene. The mall was his territory. He was king of Black Oak, master of all he surveyed.

It was about 25 feet down to the freeway. Not terribly far for a young person who was relaxed. Ted hit the pavement feet first, balled up and rolled. He sprang to his feet and threw his arms over his head like a gymnastics champion. He held position for an instant, speared by the lights of the car rushing toward him.

"Kung Fu fighting!" he yelled and struck a pose against the on-coming car. The horn blared and the tires squealed as the car swerved out of the lane to miss him by inches. Ted threw a karate chop at the rear fender as it passed and then whirled to face the next vehicle.

Lars and Emily Peterson were already behind schedule. They had gotten caught in the tail of Saturday rush hour, and the strain of piloting their Mini-Wini through freeway traffic had Lars muttering under his breath. Even with their shaky notion of Southern California geography, it was obvious they'd never make Disneyland this evening.

Lars was so tense from the strange, heavy traffic that when the car ahead of him jammed on its brakes as it came under the overpass he hit his brakes at almost the same instant. As a result the motor home stopped just inches before his bumper touched the bumper of the car ahead.

"What the . . . ?" Then over the top of the car in front he saw the figure capering on the freeway. Lars had the natural reaction of a modern American tourist when something unusual happened.

"Quick, Emily, get the camcorder!"

Ted was fast, traffic was light and the drivers were all Angelenos with the reflexes that come from facing weirdness on the freeway every day. He danced back and forth across the lanes, blocking traffic here, allowing a vehicle to proceed there with a magisterial gesture, sometimes pounding on a car as it went by. Horns blared and drivers yelled, but he was a million miles above it all, reveling in his power to stop or turn the river.

He tried a spinning, leaping back-kick at an approaching car in the next lane, but the drug threw his timing hideously off. He spun on his heel much too soon and was flying through the air before the car ever reached him. He landed flat on his butt in the lane, and in spite of the screeching brakes, the oncoming car was going nearly twenty-five miles an hour when it ran over him.

By the time Ted died beneath the wheels of the car a few feet away, Lars Peterson had nearly a full minute of his antics on tape.

The night air was still, and this far from the surrounding streets, quiet. Except for a siren, far-off and faint, and the rumble of an airliner someplace above the clouds, the smog-laden air seemed to have soaked up all the noise of the city.

Paul Henderson liked it that way. It reminded him of the woods of his native West Virginia. *When it's all over and things settle down I'm gonna get me some land back there,* he promised himself again. It was a favorite daydream and he had a bureau drawer half full of maps and real estate brochures to feed it. Meanwhile it helped pass the time on his rounds.

He stopped the golf cart at the end of the parking lot and looked out over the smog-shrouded lights of the city. Unconsciously he took a deep breath and then wished he hadn't *Place stinks worse than a Texas oil refinery, but it sure is pretty.*

There was the unmistakable rattle of wheels over asphalt and concrete. Henderson's head snapped around. The sound was fading away as the wheels moved down the slope. About a quarter of the way around the complex, he judged.

"Unit Two to Central."

"Go ahead, Two."

"I think we got us some skateboarders on the east side. I'm gonna go check it out."

"Okay, Two. I'll monitor the cameras over there. Let me know if you need anything. Base out."

Henderson replaced the walkie-talkie and put the cart in motion. Another chapter in the never-ending war between Black Oak Mall and the skaters was about to begin.

The mall architects understood the attraction the mall's lots would have for skateboarders and bicyclists, so they designed them to discourage riders. The uphill drives were rough surfaces with groups of speed bumps every few feet.

But the architects had underestimated technology. Almost before the mall was finished, new wheel compositions and new board designs had turned the drives from impossible to merely challenging. Now there wasn't a serious skateboarder in Southern California who didn't want to boast he or she had "ridden the ramps at Blackie."

The situation became much more serious after the appalling, but carefully hushed-up, incident involving the nude couple with the hang gliders, bungee cords and motorized roller skates who were either (accounts differed) trying to invent a new sport or come up with a new perversion. In any event, Black Oak Mall realized the design wasn't sufficient.

First the mall fought back with iron gates across the drives at every parking level. That had lasted until the fire marshal pointed out — forcefully — that the gates would keep out fire engines as well as skateboarders, and the mall's insurance underwriter started musing — pointedly — on the effect this was likely to have on their fire insurance rates.

So the expensive wrought-iron gates with the Black Oak monogram were left permanently open.

The next plan had been to string chains across the drives on every level. The fire marshal liked that, but the skateboarders liked it even more. A skillful jammer could get enough lift off the bumps to jump the chains. The preferred technique was to grab some air and take a bank shot off retaining walls at either side of the drive. Meanwhile the guards had to stop and unlock every chain to get their golf carts through and that made them even less likely to catch the jammers. Blackie's popularity with the skaters soared.

The chains went too. Now the guards just chained the mall entrances and depended on the security cameras and outside patrols to hold off the skateboarders.

With the skill born of long practice, Henderson worked his way through the lot and up the drive, keeping close to the wall to hide himself from anyone on top. As the cart whined up, he scanned the parking lots and likely hiding places. No sign of a lookout. The smart ones posted somebody to keep an eye on the guard. This was either a loner or the group was real dumb.

Dumb was more likely. Skateboarders usually came in groups. Part of the ritual of riding the ramps at Blackie was having someone who could vouch that you'd done it.

The guard considered his options. Since there was only one guard outside at night there was a certain finesse involved in catching skateboarders. They could run you ragged if you went chasing up and down after them, especially if they got to the very top before anyone spotted them. If you weren't careful they'd see you coming and scoot off down another driveway by the time you got up there.

The best way was to flush them, get them spotted on the cameras and then close in. You didn't catch them that way but then Henderson wasn't really interested in catching them. Mall policy required charging anyone caught on the property at night with trespassing. Between waiting for the cops and doing the paperwork that could eat up a couple of hours, and he had less than that left on his shift.

He left the cart in the drive one level down from the top and made his way on foot to the top level. The lot was empty except under the pink-orange lights. From his vantage point he could see that the ground level lot was well. A quick check showed no one on the ramps, and there was no sound of voices or wheels.

The guard frowned. This wasn't right at all. You couldn't see all of the lots from the top level, but you had to know just where to stand not to be seen. That implied a level of experience at the game. But the experienced ones usually cut and ran as soon as they were discovered. You would see them high-tailing it across the parking lot. The less experienced ones sometimes tried to move around to the other side of the mall to get in one or two more runs. Those were the ones you caught if you weren't careful.

"Unit Two to Base. Any sign of them on the cameras?"

"Base to Unit Two. Nothing visible."

Henderson reholstered the radio and frowned. Whoever they were they were either very lucky or damn good to avoid being spotted. The cameras weren't at their best on a smoggy night but they didn't have any trouble picking up something the size of a person.

Slowly and carefully, as if he was stalking a deer in his home woods, he worked his way back down the hill, checking the drives and the parking lots as he went. No movement, no sound, nothing.

He was in the next-to-bottom lot when there came the unmistakable rattle of skateboard wheels on the next drive over.

What the . . . ? Somehow the kid must have doubled back on him.

Keeping low, he sprinted for the drive. But when he got there it was empty. He scanned the parking lot and then looked back up the drive. No sign of anyone.

Henderson crouched next to the inside wall and thought. If he weren't down at the bottom — and he wasn't — then he must be working his way back up the hill somewhere for another run. That left one more tactic. Try to ambush him at the bottom of a run where he'd be going too fast to evade him there. It was easy to clothesline someone and knock him flat on his ass.

It was a little risky. The skater would be going too fast to stop and there was a possibility he'd crash into the guard. But Henderson was tired of playing hide-and-seek, and by now he was sufficiently angry to want to bust some heads, even if it meant working overtime.

The only question was, which ramp would he come down next? Henderson turned his radio down to nothing and stood absolutely still, listening intently. There, ever so faint above him, he heard the sound of wheels.

Really dumb! Henderson thought. The stupid little shit was riding the board toward the next ramp rather than carrying it. Someone that stupid was probably also a loner. The chances were he'd try to come down the next ramp over.

Quickly he scurried through the parking lot, keeping bent over and close to the inside wall so he'd be hard to spot.

Carefully he crouched down by the base of the planter by the drive. He listened intently. This low on the hill the traffic was a faint, distant roar, like the ocean in a seashell. The transformer on the light above him buzzed like an angry fly. Aside from that there was no sound at all.

There! Up at the top of the hill came the familiar rattle. The guard held his position, not daring to peek. The rattle grew louder and faster, then dropped to nothing as the board hit the first set of speed bumps and went flying through the air.

Come on, you li'l pecker! Don't fall off now.

Then the board hit the pavement with an even more frenetic rattle and continued to careen down the slope. Louder and louder, then silence again as the board hit the second speed bumps. Again the guard held his breath, hoping his quarry stayed on. And once more the rattle of wheels, even faster and louder.

NOW! The guard stepped into the driveway. "Hold it!" he yelled.

For an instant he thought the drive was empty. Then the board flew by him, shoulder-high from going over the last bumps. But there was no sign of the jammer. Instinctively the guard looked back up the hill to where the rider must have fallen off. There was no sign of anyone.

Henderson turned and looked down at the board. It had landed upright and turned sideways to skid to a halt without capsizing. As the guard watched, there was movement around the empty skateboard. Then, slowly at first but going faster and faster, it rattled out of the driveway and into the parking lot beside it.

The guard ran down the hill after the self-propelled board. By the time it turned the corner into the lot he was just a few yards behind it, close enough to get a better look.

At the rear of the board three tiny forms were pushing it off into the parking lot as if it were a stalled car. While the guard watched, two more forms lifted a section of the storm sewer grating and they and the board disappeared into the darkness. The grating clanged down behind them and all was quiet again.

Henderson thought about what he'd just seen for a minute. Then he reached for his radio.

"Ah, Central," he said in his best Chuck Yeager drawl, "we got us a little situation here."

The voice on the radio was tense. "Go ahead, Two."

"Y'all know them rats folks have been complaining about?"

"Yeah?"

"Well, it seems like the l'il suckers have learned to skateboard."

Surfer's apartment was done in the kind of run-down Spanish modern that spelled "furnished rental" in Southern California, but it was surprisingly clean. The only sign of disorder in the living room were the overflowing ashtrays and a couple of beer cans on the end tables. The blinds were closed tight against the morning sun. The cable news channel blared unheeded from the television.

Surfer sat on the couch, hunched over the newspapers spread on the coffee table. To his left was a box of tiny plastic baggies, the sort collectors use to hold individual coins. To his right was a plastic freezer container half full of Toby's wonder drug.

Slowly and carefully, Surfer transferred the grayish powder to a baggie with a scoop made from a cut-down plastic spoon. Each level scoopful was a quarter of a gram and maybe a little more. Then he sealed the top with tape and the baggie joined the growing pile on the paper next to the freezer container.

It was slow, exacting work, and the fact that he was wearing rubber kitchen gloves didn't make it any easier.

He was also wearing a wet handkerchief tied bandit-style over his nose and mouth so he wouldn't breathe the powder. Surfer had learned long ago to take precautions against his wares.

He had been at it for more than an hour now, but he wasn't tired and his back didn't hurt from bending forward over the low table. Instead he felt great, really up and energized. This new stuff was wonderful. He was selling it for twice the price Toby had told him and it was still selling faster than anything else except grass. If this kept up he'd be able to retire to move to Maui in a couple of years and spend his time catching waves and growing a little hybrid stuff for himself and his friends. He hadn't thought about his old dream in months, but now this super-dope of Toby's was bringing it back to him. He smiled beatifically under the bandana. A little more of this and it would make the dream real.

Surfer didn't realize that Toby's new drug was responsible for his euphoria in ways completely unrelated to its financial potential. The gritty gray powder was a lot more potent than the cheap coke, kiddie-quality crystal and horse tranquilizer he usually dealt. Slowly but surely Surfer was getting a dose of his own medicine.

The squeal of brakes and blare of horns from the television jerked him out of his reverie.

". . . passing motorist shot this video of the teen's bizarre dance of death last night."

On the screen Ted pirouetted and flailed through his last seconds of life. Lars Peterson's angle prevented his camera from showing the car's wheel crushing the life out of the boy, but it captured the look on the driver's face as she literally stood on the brakes at the moment of impact.

The screen cut away to a yearbook photo of Ted, scrubbed clean with his hair freshly cut and the zits air-brushed out. "The victim was fifteen-year-old Theodore Michael Campbell. Police say they do not know what caused the youth's actions, but drugs may be involved." Then the screen changed and the voice went on without a break. "In Los Angeles yesterday, Mayor . . ."

But Surfer wasn't listening. The name had meant nothing to him, but he recognized the school picture.

Shit! Surfer threw himself backward on the couch, bagging forgotten and euphoria gone. The dumb little fucker had obviously OD'd on something. Surfer had a damn good idea what it was that had done for him.

"Shit!" he repeated out loud. This could be a real problem. Not only could it hurt business, but selling bad dope brought major heat.

Wait a minute! There had been two of those kids who had bought the drug together that night. *If the other one talked . . .* Fear clutched Surfer's heart in an icy grasp. Involuntarily he rose half off the couch and then settled down again.

No, if the other kid had talked he would have had pigs breaking his door down at dawn. Maybe the other one couldn't talk, maybe he was too scared. Either way he was safe for now, and for Surfer "now" was all there was.

Besides, he thought, relaxing further, even if they did bust him they couldn't prove anything. It would be his word against the kid's. He looked at the stuff on the table speculatively. It couldn't stay here. Before he went to the mall today he'd rent a storeroom at a place that didn't ask a lot of questions and stash the dope and the gear there. Then he'd give this place a good cleaning to get rid of most of the residue. Toby had said the stuff wouldn't show up on any of the standard tests, hadn't he?

Questions of personal safety resolved, Surfer started thinking about the drug itself. Obviously Toby's new stuff was too strong. It needed to be cut to keep from killing the customers.

What he ought to do was to call Toby and tell him. He reached for the phone and then stopped with his hand in mid-air.

Toby didn't know that kid from a hole in the ground. There was no way he'd connect the story with the new drug.

If the stuff had to be cut there was no reason Toby's people should be the ones to do the cutting. He was already selling the stuff at twice the price Toby had told him. Why not pick up some milk sugar and increase the profits even more himself?

Yeah. That way there wouldn't be any more ODs to bring heat, and he could get to Maui that much sooner.

Relaxed again, Surfer reached for the controller to check out what was happening on MTV.

Chapter 15

The box read "Sure-Fire Mouse and Rat Killer" and carried a skull and crossbones in several prominent places — which only made Jack Crampton smile more broadly. The grain in the box was dyed bright red to indicate it was laced with poison. Crampton supposed rats didn't have any color sense, so it didn't matter.

He poured a heap of the red grain into a saucer and knelt by the rack where he had seen the rat.

"Nice mousie," Crampton crooned, pushing the saucer full of poisoned grain back into the corner under the rack. "Here's some nice din-din."

"Chew on that, you little mothers," he muttered as he stood up and dusted off his trousers. Then he smiled. Once again life was very good.

He was smiling that night at dinner when he told Dawn the story between the salad and fish.

"Wasn't that kind of cruel?" Dawn asked as she played with the stem of her wineglass.

Crampton put down his fork and spread his hands. "Hey, you were the one who was so scared when you found a rat in the dressing rooms. The mall can't do anything about these rats, and I'm not going to let my merchandise be chewed to rags."

Dawn looked up at him. "Yes, but it's like you're enjoying it."

He shrugged. "Paybacks are part of business. I enjoy business, so I guess, yeah, I do."

Dawn dropped her eyes to the cut crystal stem of her glass and said nothing.

Crampton realized he had gone too far and turned on the charm. "Come on, now. I didn't invite you to dinner to talk about rats. I've got some great news." He leaned forward as if confiding a secret. "You know that little bed and breakfast I told you about, the one down the coast near San Clemente? Well, I've got a reservation for this weekend. The Porsche could get us down there in under two hours. We could go day sailing and spend the evening before a nice warm fire." His smile was dazzling. "Just the two of us and a nice warm fire."

Dawn didn't pull her hand away, but she didn't close her fingers either.

"It was just the way he said it," Dawn told Judy the next day in the tiny back room of Bellbookand. "He really liked poisoning those rats."

Judy nodded and made a sympathetic noise, which was most of what she'd been doing for the last forty-five minutes.

"I don't know about him, Judy." She took another sip of her raspberry chamomile tea. "I just really don't know."

When she didn't say anything more, her hostess judged the time was right.

"You're a Cancer," Judy told her. "That's a water sign. It means you're ruled by passion. What does your inner child say?"

"Well, Jack's intelligent, amusing . . ."

"Not your parental censor, your inner child."

Dawn took another sip of tea. "My inner child doesn't like him very much," she said slowly. "He reminds her of my stepfather."

Judy smiled slightly and spread her hands. "Well, listen to your inner child."

❖   ❖   ❖

The tiny alterations room was stifling. Maria Busta-monte straightened up from the blouse she was altering and stretched to ease the pain from sitting too long. For the twentieth time in an hour she looked up at the wall clock. Less than ten minutes to quitting time. Just enough to finish this, tag it and she'd be done.

She looked over at the slacks Esperanza was taking in. The tiny Salvadoran was still bent to her machine, carefully reattaching the waistband. She too would be done on time.

As she gathered up the blouse, Cynthia Wheaton came in with an armful of clothes. Her voice was sweet as honey, but her smile wasn't at all pleasant. "Oh, Maria, these just came in. I'll need you to finish them tonight."

Maria's mouth dropped. "But I'll miss my ride. And my baby . . ."

"They're promised for Tuesday morning," her employer went on as if she hadn't heard. "That's tomor-row. You know as a condition of employment you have to work extra hours as needed. Naturally we'll pay you overtime," she finished sweetly.

"Sure," Maria said dully, keeping her eyes on the floor so she wouldn't have to see Mrs. Wheaton's smile of triumph.

Silently, Maria's mouth formed a very bad word. An American word. Esperanza looked at her sympatheti-cally. <I could stay and help,> she said in her Indio-Spanish. <Maybe my husband, he wouldn't mind.>

Maria tried to smile bravely. <Thank you, but no. I think it would make trouble between you.>

Like most of Maria's coworkers, Esperanza was an immigrant, and Maria had a strong suspicion that like a lot of them her papers would not stand close examina-tion. Cynthia Wheaton preferred immigrants, claiming that Americans didn't learn to do skilled needlework any more.

Of course immigrant women were also easier to boss around and didn't complain about overtime without pay, no lunch breaks and the lack of benefits at the Towne Gowne Shoppes. There weren't many places that would hire women with almost no English whose only skill was sewing. Even if they could run a commercial sewing machine — and most of them couldn't — alterations paid better than working for a clothing manufacturer, and the stores' locations in suburban malls meant fewer visits from La Migra.

But Maria had been born in the United States and she wasn't afraid to complain. What's more, she knew who to complain to. She'd gone to the Labor Board about the conditions and now the Towne Gowne Shoppes were under state investigation.

As she left, Esperanza leaned over and patted her arm. <We'll wait for you for a little bit, okay?> she said in her accented Spanish.

Maria tried to smile. <Sure, thanks.>

She went to the refrigerator and took out her sack lunch. She hadn't felt like eating because she'd been worried about Kenny. Now it would be her dinner if she stayed. Absently, she set the thermos of milk on the cutting table next to the lunch.

The complaint to the Labor Board was supposed to be anonymous, but Cynthia Wheaton knew who had to be responsible.

Mrs. Wheaton was shrewd. She didn't try to fire Maria outright, and nothing she had done technically qualified as harassment. First she'd made all her alterations people sign agreements saying they recognized certain things as "conditions of employment" and they could be discharged for not meeting them. They included working "where needed" and working overtime "on an as-needed basis."

Then Mrs. Wheaton moved Maria from the store not far from her home to the one at Black Oak Mall. She called it a "promotion" and backed that up with a fifty-cent-an-hour raise. But it took nearly four hours to get to the mall from Maria's home by bus.

Maria hadn't quit. Esperanza and her husband lived not too far from her and she'd made arrangements to ride with them.

So now this. The Wheaton woman knew her youngest child was sick. She needed to take him to the clinic tonight before it closed. If she had to ride the bus she'd never make it.

The assistant at the clinic was afraid it was something serious. She'd pulled strings to get Kenny in ahead of schedule and she'd stressed to Maria how important it was to keep the appointment. Her husband wouldn't finish his shift at the coffee shop until after the clinic closed. His mother was watching Kenny, but she was afraid to make the trip alone and didn't speak much English anyway.

She looked at the first dress on the rack and bit her lip. It had an elaborately sequinned bodice, and a big patch of sequins on the back were melted and ruined. Apparently someone who didn't know better had tried to iron it.

It would take her a couple of hours just to get the ruined sequins off, never mind the time to hand sew the replacements on. The next one was a dress with a fancy skirt that needed to be shortened. This one would have to be taken apart at the waist, and each of the panels adjusted separately.

They were all like that. Even if she worked all night, Maria couldn't get it all done.

Well, that settled it. There was no way she could do this work, and Kenny needed her. Maria felt the tears well up in her eyes. She was beaten and she knew it.

It would take a long time to find a job that paid this much. For the others it would be worse. Mrs. Wheaton could silence them the same way, the investigation would probably die and things would go on just as before.

This is America, she thought as she turned out the lights. *It's not supposed to be like this here!*

It wasn't until she got in the car with Esperanza and her husband and they were already on the freeway that she remembered she'd left her lunch on the counter. Well to hell with that! She wasn't going back for a couple of day-old sandwiches and a thermos bottle full of milk.

Life was turning to shit for Jack Crampton. It was only Tuesday, but it was already a bitch of a week. Dawn had called Friday night to cancel their weekend trip and by that time Elaine, his backup, already had plans.

Inconsiderate bitch! Crampton thought as he pulled into the employees' lot. *Bad enough she gets sick, but then she doesn't call until the last minute.* He'd lost his deposit at the bed and breakfast and had to spend the whole damn weekend in Los Angeles. He armed the Porsche's alarm, gave it a final check and strode angrily toward the mall.

To hell with it, he thought, Dawn was good looking enough, and reasonably sophisticated, but she must be at least 30. Maybe it was time to start scouting for a replacement.

He was still running through a list of potential candidates when he unlocked his store and slid up the grate.

The place looked like a cyclone had hit it. Merchandise had been pulled off the shelves and heaped on the floor. Dummies had been knocked over or leaned at crazy angles. One entire rack of suits was piled in front of a three-way mirror, as if someone had tried them on and dropped them. A line of dress shirts, their sleeves tied together, stretched from one wall to the other like wash on a line.

Crampton's jaw dropped as he strode toward the pile. That was a mistake. Someone had carefully spread deodorant on the floor, and Crampton slipped on the greasy layer and landed flat on his back in the reeking puddle of men's fragrances.

"I'll kill 'em!" he screamed as he tried to pull himself erect. Then his feet went out from under him and he went down again. "I'll kill the fucking sonsabitches!"

Almost, Maria didn't come to work that day. She hated the thought of the final interview with Mrs. Wheaton and letting her gloat. But one must be practical, and if she came in perhaps she could pick up her last paycheck instead of waiting for them to mail it to her.

Sure enough Mrs. Wheaton was waiting for her just inside the door. "Come in to my office, Maria."

Maria followed her up the stairs and into the office off the showroom. A couple of elegantly dressed saleswomen were sitting at the Louis XIV table in the showroom, drinking coffee out of china cups and gossiping while they waited for the store to open.

There, on Mrs. Wheaton's desk, was the pile of clothing with the sequinned gown on top.

Mrs. Wheaton held up the gown for Maria to inspect. Maria kept her eyes on the desk.

"These are very good, Maria," Mrs. Wheaton said tightly. Maria's head jerked up at the words, and for the first time she saw the gown. Somehow she managed to keep her jaw from dropping.

Mrs. Wheaton's smile didn't quite reach her eyes. "You must be very proud of yourself," she said in a way that wasn't at all complimentary.

Maria just nodded.

"Please take these back to the alterations room and have them ready for the customers by the time we open." With that she turned to some papers on her credenza.

Jack Crampton was so incoherent when he called Security that Henderson and Morales were dispatched for a "possible stroke victim." He was only slightly more coherent by the time they got there. By then one of Crampton's employees had arrived and the haberdasher was upbraiding him on general principles.

"You!" he shouted as soon as the guards ducked under the half-raised door. "You're supposed to protect me from . . . from . . ." Speechless, all he could do was wave to the mess.

In fact the mall guards had no such responsibility for store interiors, but neither Morales nor Henderson saw much point in mentioning the fact.

"What happened?" Morales asked instead, flipping open his notebook.

Crampton's mouth moved but nothing came out.

"Apparently the store was vandalized sometime last night," Crampton's employee said.

Morales looked at the mannequin next to him. Someone had taken the pants off the dummy and fastened a flesh-pink silk tie around the waist so the end hung down in front almost to the figure's knees. The effect was striking but not at all what the tie's designer intended.

Morales flipped up the end of the tie. "So I see," he said. "Do you have any idea who might have done this?"

"Vandals!" shouted Crampton, finding his voice.

"Yes, sir," Morales said and made a note in his notebook. "Now, was the alarm set when you closed last night?"

But Crampton wasn't paying attention. Through the chaos, he had just realized something was missing.

"Handkerchiefs! There's a whole gross of Italian silk handkerchiefs gone!" His voice rose to a wail. "Those things retail for nineteen ninety-five a piece!"

"Yes, sir, now about the alarm system . . ."

Then something else caught Crampton's eye. Next to the pile of suits at the three-way mirror was a pile of what appeared to be dirty rags. Heedless of Morales and his notebook, Crampton bent to examine them.

They were obviously doll clothes. Some were torn, some were dirty and some had the knees and elbows gone. Carefully attached to one frayed out-at-the-elbow sleeve was a Smilin' Jack's tag. "All wool, Italian single-needle tailoring," the tag read, "$1800."

"Look at this!" Crampton screamed, holding up the tiny garment by the tag. "Not only do they steal my merchandise, they make fun of me too."

"Uh, the alarm was set last night," the employee put in.

"I want them for this! Do you hear me? I want them! First my car and now this. This is too much." Then he stopped, took a deep breath and continued more calmly. "I want you to find who did this to me and arrest them."

"We'll certainly take a report, Mr. Crampton," the guard said. The carefully neutral tone and the too-fixed expression told Crampton the man was trying hard not to break up.

"Perhaps you should get a better alarm system," Henderson added with an equally straight face. "The one on your car is real effective."

Crampton reddened again, swelled and then without another word, dropped the garment, spun on his heel and marched out of the store.

In the alterations room at the Towne Gowne Shoppe, Maria examined the garments. The work was perfect. The sequins on the bodice were so exactly matched you couldn't tell that there had ever been a ruined place. The stitching on the embroidered skirt was small and neat. Hand work, Maria noted dumbly. Whoever did it hadn't used a sewing machine.

<Did you clean up in here last night?> Esperanza asked as Maria hung the clothes on the rack. Maria shook her head and then she looked around.

The room was not only clean, it was immaculate. The floor was swept and mopped spotless, the spools of thread were all neatly placed on the racks and sorted by color. The work areas around the machines were neat, and the machines gleamed as if freshly cleaned and oiled. Her sack lunch was gone but her thermos, empty and neatly washed, was sitting on the drainboard by the sink. The only thing which was the least bit messy was the trash can half full of scraps of brightly colored silk — scraps that didn't match anything Maria remembered seeing in the shop. She reached out and put her hand on the sewing machine next to the trash can. The motor was almost hot to the touch, as if someone had been using it all night long.

Maria looked at Esperanza. Her eyes were as big as saucers. <Tonight on the way home can we stop by the church? I think I want to light a candle.>

Assholes! Jack Crampton thought. *Goddamn assholes.* He stalked through the sprinkling of early shoppers looking neither left nor right. To hell with it. Let the guards and his employees handle the mess. He was going to get out of here before he lost it completely.

His Porsche was where he left it, apparently untouched. That was something, anyway. Thumbing his alarm control, he walked up to the car and started to unlock the door.

"Warning," his car told him. "Warning. You are too close. Back away from the car or you will activate special security precautions."

"It's me, you asshole!" Crampton yelled, jamming the button on the control with his thumb. The Porsche ignored him.

"This is your final warning to move away from the car. You have been warned."

Shit! That was all he needed! The goddamn security system was on the blink again. He'd have to shut it off from the inside.

As he reached for the door the sensor in the handle detected the change in capacitance from his hand.

"Touch me and I'll scream!" the car said.

"Fuck you!" Crampton muttered.

As soon as he got the door open, he used his second key to deactivate the primary security system. Then he punched his code into the console keypad to turn off the secondary system. Instantly the lights stopped flashing.

Crampton breathed a sigh of relief, pulled the door shut, locked it and fastened his seat belt. Then he stuck the primary key in the ignition and turned it.

And all hell broke loose.

The siren whooped. "THIEF THIEF THIEF THIEF THIEF," the car bellowed at the top of its electronic lungs.

Frantically, Crampton punched the abort code into the console. But not fast enough.

Blasts of red and blue fog filled the car as the mixture of tear gas and dye poured out of the dash ventilators.

Choking, gasping and blinded by the tears streaming down his face, Crampton managed to get the door open and fall out onto the pavement.

"THIEF THIEF THIEF THIEF THIEF THIEF THIEF THIEF THIEF THIEF," the Porsche continued to scream.

"You goddamn ungrateful sonofabitch!" Crampton screamed back. "I pamper you, take care of you and now you do this to me!"

"Touch me and I'll scream," the Porsche said. Then it went back to yelling, "THIEF THIEF THIEF THIEF THIEF."

"Oh yeah?" Crampton yelled. "I'll fix you, you no-good bitch whore." Holding his breath and pressing his handkerchief to his nose he reached back behind the driver's seat and pulled out the jack handle.

"Now, you slut!"

"Touch me and I'll scream," the Porsche said coyly.

The wailing siren and the crash of glass and metal brought Andy hurrying down from the second-level lots. Almost in front of the main entrance he met Slick, his new board under his arm.

"What the hell's going on out there?" Andy demanded, ignoring the skateboard.

"Some red and blue dude is, like, demolishing a Porsche with a crowbar." Slick considered. "Most atypical."

Chapter 16

". . . so anyway," LaVonne Sanders said, "it turns out he had a gray '92 Riveria just like it. Only it was clear over in the Green Lot, and he was breaking into the wrong car!" She laughed and shook her head. "Can you believe it? I swear this place gets weirder every day."

The last phrase jolted Andy out of his reverie. "Yeah," he chuckled dutifully, "weirder every day." He looked around at the shoppers flowing past them in the brightly lit mall.

"LaVonne," he asked as they stepped onto the escalator, "just how weird do you think this place is?"

The woman thought for an instant. "I'd say about semiweird. Nothing like some of the stuff I used to run into around Benning. Why?"

"Well, it just seems like there's some odd stuff going on around here. You know," Andy said a shade too casually, "some people think this place is haunted."

LaVonne turned to face him on the escalator. "Like who?

"Well, there's Judy Cohen, the woman who runs the candle store in the North Bazaar. She believes there are ghosts here."

LaVonne snorted. "Hell, she believes in the Easter Bunny!"

"Some of the kids believe it too."

"Westlin, you gotta stop listening to folks like that."

Andy looked past her and stiffened.

The man at the top of the escalator was wearing baggy black pants bunched at the ankles, a black jacket and T-shirt and a black flat-brimmed hat with the brim turned up in front. His curly dark hair was pulled back in a short ponytail.

Andy glared and walked on.

"Another one of your buddies from the old neighborhood?" LaVonne asked.

"Maybe. There's something familiar about him."

LaVonne shrugged. "Well as long as he stays clean while he's here. And as to this place being haunted, I'll believe it when one of those ghosts comes up and introduces himself to me personally."

The trouble is, Andy thought, *I don't know what I believe any more.* He flipped on an old movie on the cable channel and dug a Mexican TV dinner out of the freezer compartment. Judy might be a flake, but she was an oddly persuasive flake. And there was some very strange stuff going on at that mall.

Andy was just digging into his refried beans when the phone rang.

"Officer Westlin?"

"Not any more," Andy said cautiously.

"I know. I saw you today. Can you meet me tonight?"

Something clicked in Andy's mind. "Where?"

"Someplace out of the way. Not your place."

"B.J.'s coffee shop just down the street?"

A rustling, as if he was consulting a map.

"Fine. Say twenty minutes?"

Andy was there in fifteen, already nursing a cup of coffee when the man slid into the booth. The mustache was the same, but he was wearing slacks and a sports shirt instead of the cholo outfit. His hair was pushed up under a baseball cap, and he had on a pair of wire-rimmed glasses. He looked like someone's high school history teacher. Andy wasn't completely sure it was the same man until the other opened his hand below the table to give him a glimpse of a badge.

"Rodriguez. Narcotics."

Andy nodded. "This is unusual as hell, isn't it? Trusting a civilian?"

"I asked around. You have a pretty good rep." Rodriguez' mouth barely moved when he talked, and his eyes were never still.

Andy's mouth quirked. "Even coming out of Southside?"

Rodriguez shrugged. "Shit happens everywhere. Word is you had no part of it." Actually the word was that Westlin was such a goddamn innocent he was just about incorruptible. "Real Boy Scout" was the phrase Rodriguez' informant had used.

The waitress bustled over, and Rodriguez ordered coffee as well.

"So what can I do for you?"

"You know anyone dealing at the mall?"

"I've got my suspicions, but no proof. Word is there's some penny-ante stuff going down. Nothing that'd attract you guys."

Rodriguez leaned closer. "Usually. Problem is, people are dying. You see that thing on the news last night about the kid playing on the freeway? He had a buddy who's now in a mental hospital doing an imitation of a turnip. That makes four in about two weeks. A fourteen-year-old went psychotic and attacked his parents with a carving knife. Then he went for the cops who responded to the call." Rodriguez paused. "They had to shoot him. There's some really bad shit out there and the mall's the logical distribution point."

"Why the hell would something like that show up way the hell and gone out here first?" Andy demanded angrily. "That's not the usual pattern."

The waitress arrived with Rodriguez' coffee, and both men fidgeted until she left.

"We don't know why, but we need to get a line on it fast."

"Are you sure it's at the mall?"

Rodriguez shrugged. "No, but it's the logical place, isn't it?"

"Yeah, probably," Andy said sourly. "Okay, there's a guy they call Surfer. I don't know his real name."

"Martin Peter Kleinschmidt," Rodriguez supplied. "We got him pegged already. The victims match his customer profile but this isn't his usual style. Anyone else?"

"Not inside the mall. The parking lot, maybe, but I haven't seen anything funny there either. Also I haven't actually seen Surfer do anything except talk to kids."

"Figures. With all the security cameras you got in there he's probably clean when he's on the property. Just meets his clients there and they do the transaction someplace else."

"Cute."

"If the guy's got any brains it makes it harder," Rodriguez agreed. "Kleinschmidt, your Surfer, has enough sense for that. There's another complication too."

Andy looked over at the narc.

"Your Surfer apparently only sells to kids. No one older than about sixteen. Makes it hard to use an undercover officer to nail him.

"Jesus!"

"Oh, sure, we'll get him. The problem is it's gonna take time. And the more of this bad dope that goes out, the more kids are going to die."

"I can't believe this. Right in the goddamn mall."

Rodriguez shrugged. "Like I said. Shit happens everywhere."

Surfer was where he always was when Andy made his first patrol the next day. Leaning against the rail near the top of the escalator, his mirrored sunglasses reflecting the panorama before him. He didn't seem to notice when Andy rode the escalator up and walked by not six feet away. It was all Andy could do to keep from taking his flashlight and smashing his face in.

Andy got several feet past him, then glanced back casually, as if he was surveying the whole level. In spite of his immobility, Surfer wasn't relaxed. There was tension in his hunched shoulders and his legs were braced against the floor as if he wanted to spring into space. The guy was edgy, almost twitchy. Like it would take just one little push . . .

Andy ambled over and planted himself on the rail next to him.

"Hey, Surfer dude, how's it going?" The Surfer eyed him and said nothing.

"I asked how it's going." There was an edge in Andy's voice now.

Surfer turned to face him. "Hey, man, you're harassing me!"

"Don't like it? Leave."

"Fuck you."

"What's the matter? Business slow today? No little kids coming around for a fix?"

Come on, you fucker, swing on me. But Surfer only muttered another obscenity and stared fixedly out into space. "Leave me alone."

Andy stood up. "Oh, I'm going to leave you, but alone's one thing you're never gonna be here. Not ever again. Especially not when there's kids around. If there's kids with you in this mall, I'll be with you."

With a friendly nod, Andy turned and strolled off, leaving Surfer clenching and unclenching his hands on the rail.

Push and relax. Sergeant Yamashita used to say back at Southeast. *Crowd them and then give them a little room and then crowd them some more. They all break soon enough.* Yamashita might be under well-deserved indictment but he knew how to handle street punks. This was one punk Andy was going to break, orders or no.

"Hello, Dawn . . ."
Even over the phone her voice sounded cold.

"Myron, I told you I don't want to see you any more."

"But . . ."

"No, Myron, it just won't work. I'm sorry."

"It's because of the Porsche, isn't it? I don't have the Porsche any more so you're dumping me."

"No, Myron," Dawn said. "I'm dumping you because you're an insensitive, conceited jerk."

"I can change," Crampton said desperately. "I can get another Porsche and my therapist says . . ."

"Goodbye, Myron."

"So anyway," Judy told Andy, "Dawn told Myron she doesn't want to see him any more."

They were sitting in the back room of Bellbookand having tea. Andy was drinking a lot of tea these days, he realized.

Andy set his near-empty cup down. "You know he hasn't been back here since the day he got caught in his own alarm system? Word is, Smilin' Jack's is up for sale."

Judy took another sip of tea and looked at Andy over the rim of the cup. "Karma," she said seriously. "As we say in the Craft, whatsoever ye sow ye shall reap three-fold."

"I'd say he got reaped over pretty good."

"It was no more than he deserved. Dawn is a lot better off without him and he got his karmic desserts."

"Is that some kind of Indian sweet?" Andy asked innocently.

Judy made a face.

"Make fun if you will, but it's true. We all get what we deserve." She looked around the tiny back room and sighed. "Sometimes I wonder what I did to deserve this."

"I thought you wanted this place."

"Let's just say it isn't working out the way I thought it would. But, no, it's not what I want to do. Not really."

"What would you like to do?" he asked her.

"Oh, I don't know." She smiled hesitantly. "Find a

tropical island someplace and lie around on the beach all day. It always looked so peaceful in the books. You know, spiritual." She leaned forward. "Now how about you? What would you really like to do?"

Andy stared into his teacup. "I don't know," he said at last. "I never really thought about it."

"Oh, you must have at some time."

"I never had much chance. My mom was sick when I was growing up and I spent most of the time I wasn't in school taking care of her." He took another sip of tea.

"I'm sorry," Judy said softly.

Andy waved it off. "Don't be. She was a wonderful woman and I was a lot closer to her than most kids get to their parents. Then when it was her time she went quick and mostly painlessly."

He smiled. "Maybe what I need to do is find a tropical island where I can lay around too."

"If I could just get this store on its feet." She looked around and sighed. "I don't know, it seemed so simple when I worked out the business plan."

"You had a business plan?"

"Of course. You don't think I'd try to open a business without at least running the numbers, do you?"

"Where did you learn to do that?"

"Oh, I got some books out of the library and studied how to do it."

Andy played with his teacup.

"Do you know you're just full of contradictions?"

"Why? Because I'm careful with money?"

"I didn't think that people who were into this stuff," he gestured around the shop, "worried about things like business plans. I mean, isn't positive thinking supposed to provide, or something?"

"A positive attitude and visualization are important, but that doesn't mean you don't have to work to get what you want. It just makes the work more effective."

It occurred to Andy that he seldom saw customers in the shop. "Business isn't very good, huh?"

Judy gave him a crooked, gamin smile. "I was naive. I thought that because the mall had lots of traffic, I'd be able to capitalize on it. I didn't realize that there are bad locations in even the best malls, I didn't know enough to understand that the traffic figures for this mall were trending down and I didn't really understand the contract I signed." She sighed and set her cup on the table. "Anyway, unless I could sell this business and get enough out of it to pay off the loans, I'm stuck here."

She sighed. "And I did a pendulum divination over the contract too. It told me this place would make me rich!"

Andy looked down at his teacup.

"I know, I should have been suspicious when it told me this store would fulfill all my fantasies. But darn it! I'm *good* with a pendulum!"

Andy did what he usually did when Judy started talking like that, which was to change the subject.

"If we're going to catch the movie we'd better get going."

"Oh, just a minute, I forgot to feed the cats." She got up and rummaged on the bottom shelf. Andy realized there was mini-refrigerator under there.

"There are cats living in here?"

"Yeah," Judy said, taking out a quart carton of milk. "Well, I haven't actually seen them. But I left half a milkshake under the counter one night and the next morning it had been tipped over and licked clean. So I started putting down a saucer of milk every night before I leave. Maybe that way they'll leave the birds alone." She poured several tablespoons of milk into the saucer and put the carton back in the refrigerator.

"All set, now let's go."

"Judy?"

"Hmm?"

"Are you sure it's cats you're feeding?"

She looked up at him with those enormous dark eyes. "Of course. What else could it be?"

❖   ❖   ❖

Heather Framel was roaming the mall to stay awake. She'd gone by home last night, sometime after two, to check. The truck wasn't there so *he* must be out on the road. Her mother wasn't there either. That suited Heather fine. She wandered through the litter of empty bottles and fast-food wrappers looking half-heartedly for something to eat before settling down in her own unmade bed. It took her a long time to get to sleep and she had nightmares.

Sometime about dawn a truck pulled up out front. In a flash Heather had her boots and jacket on and was out the bedroom window. She was across the backyard and down the alley before she was fully awake, and she spent the rest of the morning wandering around waiting for the mall to open.

She was so tired not even the music in The Pit could keep her awake. She sat in the Food Court all morning and drank so much coffee she got the runs but she still almost fell asleep. If you did that they threw you out, so she started walking, peering in stores and hoping to meet Surfer or someone who could turn her on to some speed.

She roamed the mall for hours, poking into places she normally ignored and hassling clerks for something to do. She swung back by The Pit several times but the place was completely dead. No one there but Case and Matt and a bunch of little kids.

Finally, sometime in the late afternoon, she ended up poking around in the North Bazaar and eventually wandered into the candle shop.

There was only one person behind the counter, the dumpy woman in the funny clothes, the one kids said was a witch. She was going over some papers but she looked up when Heather came in.

"May I help you?"

"No, thanks," Heather mumbled, "just looking."

"Well if you need any help, just ask," she said cheerily.

The place smelled with all kinds of strong, sweet and spicy odors Heather couldn't identify. She picked up a green candle and sniffed it.

"That's bayberry," the woman said. When Heather didn't respond she went back to her papers.

Heather looked around. There wasn't anything in the place that was worth ripping off, but some of this shit was pretty and smelled good. It'd be a kick ripping off a witch, something to brag about later. Besides, the rush would help her stay awake.

In an easy, unhurried way, Heather began to size up the merchandise. The rack of small bottles on the counter looked tempting, but it was too close to the woman. She might see out of the corner of her eye. The candles in the baskets would be no challenge. Maybe one of the fancy ones near the door.

She was still trying to decide when the witch left her paperwork and went over to a shelf on one wall. She counted a few of the items, rearranged them and then hurried back to her pile of papers.

The shelf held earthenware and glass jars that smelled especially nice even through the medley of strong scents in the tiny shop. Heather drifted over for a closer look. Most of the containers were about the size of a cold-cream jar. They all seemed to have loose tops of cork or ceramic, and most of the earthenware ones were pierced with multiple holes. Try to take one of those and you'd spill shit all over the place.

But scattered in among them were smaller fancy glass bottles, like perfume bottles. Heather liked perfume, even if she didn't usually wear it. Most of them were clear or dark, but a small purple one stood out like a jewel. Without thinking she picked it up.

The tiny bottle was an amethyst teardrop in her hand. The liquid inside caught the lights and reflected them back like fire in the heart of a precious stone. It felt warm, almost alive, nestled in her palm.

"That one's very special," the woman said over her shoulder.

"Yeah?"

"Oh, yes."

Carelessly the blonde girl set the flask back on the shelf and turned to the baskets of candles. The woman went back to her paperwork.

She spent some time at the rack of essential oils, reading the names on the labels, picking up one vial and then another, always watching the owner without seeming to. She did not look back at the little purple flask.

The woman had time to check two more invoices before one of the mall pigs came in, the young one.

"Ready to go?" he asked the woman.

She looked up and smiled at him. Her boyfriend, Heather thought. "In a minute. Sheree isn't here yet."

As soon as she turned her head, Heather straightened and took one more look around the tiny shop. She was looking elsewhere when her hand closed on the purple bottle now hidden from the woman and the guard by her body. By the time she turned and faced the shopkeeper and guard the bottle was in the waistband of her panties and her hand was back at her side. Then, with her prize cool and smooth against her flesh, she walked out of the store innocent as could be.

"Come again," Judy said pleasantly as Heather sauntered out.

"I think that kid stuck something under her jacket," Andy said as soon as the girl was out of the shop.

"She did."

"Aren't you going to do anything about it?"

Judy smiled as if he had made a joke.

Heather waited until she was outside to examine her prize. Generally they busted you for shoplifting as soon as you got out of the store. Sometimes they waited until you were almost to the mall exit. Once you were out in the parking lot you were safe.

There was a place just around the corner from the west entrance where two planters came together at an angle to make a sheltered spot hidden from most directions. She pulled herself up on the edge of the planter to sit under an olive tree before she took the purple bottle from her slacks.

The bottle glowed even deeper amethyst in the dappled sunlight. For a moment the girl simply looked at it. Then she twisted the stopper, held it to her nose and sniffed.

It smelled like nothing much. Heather frowned, put the bottle to her nose and sucked in air like she was snorting coke.

Something special, huh? Ripoff was more like it. She sniffed again and this time she smelled something.

It was warm and hay-ey, like freshly cut grass in the summer sunshine. Heather breathed deeply.

She was three years old and back in Michigan helping Daddy cut the grass. She was wearing the pink sunsuit with the little white daisies Mommy had made for her. Her little plastic lawnmower went racketa-racketa as she pushed it over the row of green-gray clippings left by Daddy's mower.

All she could see of Daddy was his strong back and hairy legs and his faded blue swim trunks. But she knew he was happy. Happy and secure and wonderful, just as she was. Heather's heart swelled until it must burst for happiness.

Mommy was sitting in the deck chair, watching her and Daddy. A floppy white straw hat shaded her face. She smiled and beckoned. Heather left her toy mower and ran toward Mommy as fast as her chubby three-year-old legs could carry her.

Then she was back under the olive tree.

Sitting there in her black vinyl jacket, holding the little purple bottle and sobbing in deep wracking gasps for all that had been and for the lousy, fucked-up mess the world had become.

❖   ❖   ❖

It was nearly nine P.M. and Judy was getting ready to close when Heather came back. The girl's eyes were red, her cheeks were puffy and her mascara was smeared into big dark rings.

Heather thrust the bottle toward her. "Here."

"Oh, you found it."

"I stole it," she said defiantly.

"Well, thank you for bringing it back." Judy took the purple bottle and returned it to the shelf.

"They say you're a witch," Heather said tightly to Judy's back. "That you can make people do things."

Judy turned to face her. "Are you doing something you don't want to?" she asked gently.

Heather thought for a second and shook her head. Judy smiled and spread her hands. "Well, then."

There was an awkward pause. "Would you like some tea? I was just about to brew myself a cup."

"No thanks," Heather mumbled but she made no move to leave. Judy went back to moving the candle baskets inside.

"What's this?" Heather asked holding up a small clear bottle.

"That's cinnamon, musk and copal. Most people wear it because they like the smell, but it's really a protection oil."

"Protection huh? How much is it?"

"Two dollars," Judy lied.

Heather dug into her purse and produced two grubby bills.

"Thank you. I have to close now, but perhaps you'd like to come back sometime and try some of the other scents."

"Maybe I will," Heather said. "You gonna be here tomorrow?"

Heather was back the next afternoon while Judy was rearranging the bottles on the side shelf. The girl stood in the entrance to the shop as if she couldn't decide whether to come in or run. If Judy saw her she paid no attention. She kept checking the labels on the bottles as if she was alone. Occasionally she'd put one in the cardboard box at her feet. Heather noticed the purple bottle wasn't there any more.

"Hi." Heather's voice was soft and a little hoarse.

Judy looked up. "Well, hello."

Heather edged into the shop, keeping her face to Judy and her back to the door. "I came back."

"So you did. Would you like a cup of tea?"

Heather shook her head.

"Well let me finish this up then," Judy said as she took another bottle off the shelf and put it in the cardboard box at her feet.

For a bit neither of them said anything.

"Do you live around here?" Judy finally asked.

Heather nodded shortly.

"I thought so. You spend a lot of time at the mall."

"It's someplace to be." Suddenly she reached out and picked a vial from the rack almost at random, twisted the top off and sniffed. She wrinkled her nose and sneezed at the strong pepper-ginger smell.

"That's wood aloe," Judy told her. "It's used for annointing for luck and spirituality." She took the vial and put it back in the rack. "Normally it comes as a tincture, but one of my suppliers had it as an essential oil." She frowned. "I don't know that I like it this way. It's awfully strong."

Heather rubbed her nose. "All these oils and stuff, how do you know about them?"

"Someone taught me. An old woman who'd spent a long time learning."

"A witch, huh?"

"Actually I think she was an auditor for the water department before she retired. Oh, but she was a wise person. That's what 'witch' originally meant, you know. Someone who was wise."

"Is all this stuff," the girl gestured at the rack, "is it all, like, magic, you know?"

"In a way everything's magic." She smiled slightly. "I guess that's another way of saying we carry the magic around inside us. Things like oils and talismans and amulets only help us to find what's in us already."

"No shit? Uh, I mean, no kidding?"

Judy smiled more broadly. "No shit."

After that Heather came in nearly every day. Sometimes she would ask Judy questions about herbs and oils, tinctures and healing. Sometimes she would help sort and stock. More and more often the visits would end with them sharing a cup of tea in the tiny back room.

She didn't talk much about herself, but gradually she lost what Judy thought of as the "frightened fawn" attitude. She still avoided coming around when anyone else was in the shop and she obviously didn't like Andy, but she was clearly more comfortable with Judy and Bellbookand.

Heather didn't mention their first meeting until one day when she was kneeling before the baskets sorting candles while Judy replenished the rack of essential oils.

"Judy," she said suddenly, "what was in that purple bottle?"

"Mmm? Oh, memory."

Heather looked up at her.

"Oh, not literally memories but something to stimulate them. Smell is the sense most deeply linked to the brain, you know, and there are some odors that can help us remember things so vividly it's like they were happening right now."

"It was, like, something else."

"I told you it was special. Did you like it?"

Heather bit her lip to keep it from trembling.

"It's supposed to help you remember a time when

you were very happy," Judy said gently. "Did you remember something unpleasant?"

Heather shook her head and dropped her eyes back to the candles.

"I was just thinking that from this angle that's a really unusual haircut."

"I cut it off myself. It used to be down past my shoulders."

"Trying to look like someone in a magazine?"

"No, I was mad. My mom and I had a big fight and I cut it with a butcher knife."

"You must have been really mad."

Heather shrugged and looked at the floor. "I guess."

Judy laughed and Heather's eyes snapped back to her face. "What's so funny?"

"I was just thinking you must have been really, really mad. After my divorce I wanted to kill my ex-husband and all I did was put on thirty pounds." She patted her hips ruefully. "I've got most of it back off, I think." Then she looked back at Heather. "Just like your hair will grow out."

"Yeah. So?"

"So most things aren't nearly as permanent as we sometimes think they are."

Heather paused as if to say more but before she could speak, Andy came around the corner and her face froze.

"Good morning," he said, oblivious to the change in atmosphere.

Before Judy could respond Heather gathered up her purse. "Well I gotta be going," she said to Judy. "Thanks for the lecture." Without a word or nod to Andy she breezed out of the shop, for all the world as if she hadn't a care.

Judy's eyes followed the girl down the arcade.

"That one's trouble," he told her gently.

Judy shifted her gaze to Andy. "Trouble or troubled?"

"Both probably. Anyway she's not someone you want to get involved with."

"Well I am involved with her," Judy said firmly. "Whether I want to be or not. Besides, she needs help and I think I'm reaching her."

"Are you reaching her or is she reaching you?" Judy glared at him. "Okay, but just be careful, will you? Someone like that can cause you a lot of problems."

"I'll remember that." Her face softened and she hesitated. "Andy, can I ask you something?"

"Sure."

"Why are you so cynical?"

He pursed his lips and thought for a minute. "Experience. Too much experience. People like her — or what she's going to become — were way too common in Mid-South and I kind of lost my taste for playing rescue." He sighed and shook off the mood. "Anyway, I came to ask you if you want to go to lunch about one-thirty."

Judy looked off in the direction that Heather had taken. "I suppose so," she said dully.

Chapter 17

Cyril Heathercoate wasn't exactly comfortable in a dress, but he could wear one with a certain style. You couldn't call it fashion really, especially not the ankle-length cotton-print number he was wearing now, but he did contrive to look like he belonged in one.

The purple wig wasn't too bad a fit either, he thought as he caught a glimpse of himself in the door at the mall entrance. His eye shadow was on straight and the foundation and blush were properly applied. However, he admitted, he probably should have shaved again before he left his motel.

"Yo, dude."

Andy turned around and there was Slick, board under his arm, with TJ trailing along.

"What's up?" Andy asked, ignoring the skateboard.

"You said you wanted to know if anything, like, weird happened? Well, there's some dude over there dressed up like a woman."

"Mondo bizarro," TJ agreed.

"A transvestite?"

"Yeah, but he's, like, dressed like an old woman."

An elderly transvestite? Andy reached for his radio.

Ominous foreboding? Heathercoate wondered. *Or a cheery scene that hides the dread reality?* He looked up at the three levels of the brightly lit East Reach. *Brooding presence*, he decided. *Looming ominously*. That worked well with foreboding.

He was one paragraph into composing his story when two very businesslike hands clamped on his elbows. He was between two security guards and being gently, but firmly hustled out the door.

"This is a terrible way to treat an old woman," Heathercoate protested in a cracked falsetto that sounded like Lauren Bacall with a bad cold.

"Can it, grandma," said the man to his right.

"I'll sue!" his voice dropped back into normal range. "This is a violation of the First Amendment! It's a diplomatic outrage. The Queen shall hear of this!"

The black woman on the other side looked Heathercoate up and down. "I'm sure he'll feel real sorry for you," she said. "But next time you show up here we're gonna arrest your sorry ass."

Sheree was with Judy when Andy stopped by Bellbookand on his rounds. "Hi, Andy," the plump blonde said and then in the same breath: "Judy, do we have anything for slugs?"

Judy smiled at him and turned her attention back to her assistant. "What would a slug want with perfume?"

"No, I mean something that will get rid of them."

"Try a saucer of stale beer," Andy suggested. "They get drunk, fall in and drown."

"Oh, I don't want to kill them. That's unspiritual. I just want to make them go away and stop eating my chamomile.

"I'm growing chamomile to make my own teas," she confided to Andy without pausing for breath. "Only I can't pick the flowers until the full of the moon and the way the slugs are going I won't have any left."

"I don't know of anything specific for slugs," Judy said. "They don't have a very good sense of smell, so they're hard to influence aromatically."

Sheree's face fell. "I did want to keep gardening by strictly aromatic principles."

"I tell you what, you go on to lunch and I'll check

my herbals. Maybe they'll have something."

She picked up her purse from under the counter.
"Oh, and I rearranged the essential oils for you. Gardenia and magnolia are on the top shelf because they are
more ethereal. I put the musk and patchouli down on
the bottom because they are Earth scents. I'll see you
later."

"We caught that reporter trying to sneak into the mall
again," Andy told Judy as Sheree disappeared around
the corner. "This time he was dressed as an old woman
— an old woman who needed a shave."

"Well, he is persistent," Judy said. "That's what? Five
or six times now?"

"Yeah. My favorite was when he tried to pretend he
was advance man for a visit from Princess Diana."

Judy laughed, then sobered. "Oh, that reminds me.
Andy, can you do something for me?"

"Sure. What?"

"Heather told me something last night and I need
you to check it out."

"What do you mean 'check it out'?"

"You know, with the police."

Andy shook his head. "Judy, all that stuff you see on
television is crap. It's a felony for anyone to use police
records for private purposes and in this state they're
serious about it."

"This isn't private purposes, exactly."

"If you can't go directly to the police and make a formal request for the information, it's private purposes,"
Andy said stubbornly.

Judy nodded. "A Virgo to the end. Honest, straight
arrow and a little bit stolid."

"I am not stolid," Andy retorted. "And how'd you
know I'm a Virgo?"

"It's on your driver's license."

"Judy, even in California they don't put your astro-
logical sign on your driver's license."

She wrinkled her nose at him. "No, silly. They put

your birthday. I saw it when you were writing a check. But that's not important and this is. Andy, Heather's a kidnap victim."

"But I just saw her down in The Pit."

"No, not now. I mean she was a kidnap victim. Or still is. Her mother stole her when she was little. Her father had custody and Heather's mother took her out of Michigan. They've been moving from place to place ever since, using fake ID. Framel isn't her real name."

"That's not kidnapping, that's custodial interference," Andy said automatically. Then he looked at her hard. "You say Heather told you this?"

"Last night after we'd talked for, oh, hours. She gradually opened up and finally she trusted me with this."

"And you believe her?"

Judy got very serious. "Andy, one of the things the Craft teaches you is how to sense when someone is telling the truth. Heather wasn't lying to me. She misses her father desperately. It stands out in her aura like a beacon."

"Her aura."

Her brown eyes grew wide and soft. "Andy, trust me on this. Please. I know you don't like her, but she needs help terribly."

"Well . . ."

"Look, you don't have to believe her. Just check on it, can't you?"

"Why doesn't she go to the police herself?"

"She did and they wouldn't do anything. She doesn't know her father's name, she's had so many false identities she's not even sure what her real name is. The only thing she knows for sure is that they're from Troy, Michigan. You must know someone on the police force who'd take the trouble to check."

Andy thought of Rodriguez. "Well there is somebody who kind of owes me a favor. Look, since there's the possibility that a felony has been committed I can ask that someone check it out. That's legal."

Judy's face lit up and she grabbed Andy's hands in hers. "Thank you. I knew I could count on you."

"Don't count too strongly," Andy said, embarrassed and a little pleased by her response. "This case is at least ten years old and we don't have much to go on."

"Well, thank you for trying anyway."

"I'll make a phone call tonight. Meanwhile, I've got to get back on my rounds."

"Can you stay for a minute? There's something else I'd like you to do, if you can."

Andy checked his watch. "Well for a minute. Why?"

"Because you're taller than I am and you can get the gardenia and magnolia oils off the top shelf."

"Aren't they air scents?"

Judy wrinkled her nose. "They're also my most popular essential oils and I don't want to have to drag a ladder out here every time a customer wants them."

By standing on tiptoes Andy could just reach the boxes of tiny bottles. "Wouldn't it be more in harmony with the universe to leave them on the top shelf?" he said teasingly as he handed the boxes down.

"There is nothing harmonious about being impractical," Judy said. Andy chuckled.

"What's so funny?"

"I was just thinking. You're probably the sort of person who'd go to that big psychic gathering they have out in Arizona . . ."

"The Harmonic Convergence? Yes, I went last year." She eyed him suspiciously. "So?"

"And out of all those thousands of people, you'd be the only one who would remember to bring sun screen."

"Well," Judy said seriously, "I wasn't the *only* one. But I did share with a lot of people."

Surfer planted himself on the rail next to the escalator and tried not to fidget.

The morning was bright, but the world was turning to shit. Surfer let his breath out in a great whoosh and then tried to force himself to relax. He hadn't slept well last night, or the night before. There was an itchy feeling between his shoulder blades, like someone was following him. The light outside was too bright, and his temples were pounding like he was getting a migraine, but his apartment was stifling.

Chill, he told himself. *Chill and relax. There's nothing to it, you're just a little tired.* Well who wouldn't be with all the damn cars and trucks going by all night? And then four o'clock this morning the damn garbage truck came through rattling and banging. He gave up trying to sleep and greeted the dawn flipping restlessly between old movies and infotainment shows on TV.

Business was shit, too. The kids weren't buying like they had. He wondered if he had a competitor somewhere in the mall. Or maybe it was his attitude that was driving them away. He'd actually yelled at a kid the other day, just completely blown his cool. *Can't do that,* he told himself. *Gotta keep that cool dude friendly image.* But how the fuck can you keep cool and calm when you can't get any sleep and you're so uptight your skin's crawling? Well, shit, it was time for him to move again anyway. He'd make sure to find someplace more out of the way, someplace quieter.

A kid sidled up and leaned on the rail next to him. Out of the corner of his eye he recognized him as one of his regulars, speed mostly but the new stuff too. Surfer turned toward the kid and saw him stiffen. With a tremendous effort he relaxed and tried to smile in the old, easy way. "How's it hanging?" he asked.

The kid was still nervous but he came up to stand next to Surfer. "Pretty good. Uh, what you got?"

"Some of the special stuff. Fresh batch." But the kid was staring off to the side and not listening. Surfer followed his eyes and saw the rent-a-pig, the one who had it in for him, striding toward them.

"Later, dude," the kid mumbled and hurried off.

As soon as the kid left Andy slowed his pace to an easy stroll. He ambled over and leaned on the rail perhaps six feet from Surfer, apparently oblivious to him.

"Godamn it, this is fucking harassment."

"What harassment, sir?" Andy asked with just a trace of an edge to his voice. "I'm just standing here admiring the view."

Surfer snorted and turned away. "I'll report you," he muttered.

"Seems you did that once before, sir. I'm not touching you, I'm not threatening you. I didn't even speak to you first. I'm just doing my job." He stared at Surfer hard, challenging him to make a move.

There was a time when Surfer would have shrugged it off. Tangling with a cop, even a mall rent-a-pig, was bad business. Besides, he was supposed to meet Toby's people in a couple of hours and he had nearly six big ones in his pocket. But the Surfer had been breathing his new product for weeks, and the stuff was deep in his brain.

Surfer came off the rail like an uncoiling spring. Before Andy could react, or even shift stance, he was on top of him with his hands around Andy's throat bending his body backwards over the rail.

"YOU FUCKER, I'LL KILL YOU." Surfer pushed until Andy's feet were almost off the floor and his body balanced precariously on the rail pressing into the small of his back. Out of the corner of his eye, Andy could see the gaping chasm yawning down four stories beneath him.

With a desperate lunge, Andy drove his doubled fists up between Surfer's forearms. The blow knocked the drug dealer's hands off his throat but the momentum threw him even further out over the emptiness. As Surfer fell away he scrabbled frantically for purchase against the rail.

In the instant it took Andy to get his feet on the floor

Surfer stood frozen between fight and flight. The struggle had knocked his sunglasses off and Andy could see his bloodshot eyes rolling wildly. Then with an inarticulate noise in his throat Surfer whirled and dashed off. Andy shook his head once to clear it and pounded after him.

Surfer not only had a head start, he didn't care who he ran over. He caromed off a fat woman with her arms full of packages and hurdled a stroller, to the delight of the little girl in it and to the horror of her mother. Andy dodged around people so he lost ground with almost every step.

Surfer cut the corner toward the escalators and slammed into Dawn Albright as she came out of the Salad Salon, scattering her lunch, a large Low-Cal Special, all over her, her linen suit and the floor around them.

Dawn's salad may have been low calorie, but it was drenched with spicy, rich Italian dressing. Surfer stepped right on the pile of greens glistening with olive oil. His foot shot out from under him and he went down.

Andy charged past the frozen Dawn and launched a desperate flying tackle as Surfer struggled to his feet again. He caught the man by his ankle. They went down in a tangle and Surfer slammed into a planter. Before he could recover Andy was on top of him reaching for his flashlight. Surfer twisted and tried to rise, but Andy applied the end of the heavy aluminum case to a nerve point at the shoulder blades. Surfer grunted and collapsed as his suddenly limp arm gave way. Andy slipped the stick between Surfer's elbow and back and used the leverage to force his hand behind him for cuffing.

Out of the corner of his eye Andy realized they had an audience. Shoppers were turning to watch and merchants were craning out their doors to see. The only people who appeared unconcerned were the pair of middle-aged tourists.

"Shoplifters," the man explained to his wife. "They're really cracking down on them with the economy the way it is here."

"I'm telling you, dudes, it was like gruesome."

JoJo's audience clustered around his table at the Food Court, some sucking soft drinks and all listening half-fascinated and half-disbelieving.

"Man, it was like there were monsters and dead people and stuff all over the place." He gestured expansively. "And the smell — eeyeew! — gross to the max. Just disgusting."

"I heard a girl got killed in there," one of the kids on the fringe added. "Just ripped apart. They had to smuggle the body out in a trash can, and they swore everyone to secrecy." A couple of the other kids nodded wisely.

"More than one, dudes," JoJo said, expanding the story to hold his audience. "There were, like, five or six of them and they're, you know, like keeping it under wraps cause they're trying to sell the mall." He could see that wasn't enough to hold them. "And they had to use a fire hose to wash the blood out of the carpets. That's why they're keeping the lights turned down in the theater, so you can't, like, see the bloodstains in the rug."

None of them paid any attention to the old woman with the walker sitting two tables over. Pauline Patterson didn't seem to pay any attention to them either. She had learned that trick a long time ago.

Andy was still making an inventory of the contents of Surfer's pockets when Dunlap came into the day room.

"Look at this stuff," Andy said with a gesture at the items on the table. "He's got more than six thousand dollars on him. Plus two mall employee IDs."

"Any drugs?"

"No, worse luck. When are the police arriving?"

"They're not." Before Andy could protest, the security chief added: "Come into my office. We need to talk."

Fuming, Andy followed Dunlap into his office and closed the door behind him.

"Now," Dunlap said as he settled himself behind his desk, "I didn't call the cops and we're not going to, you understand? As far are you're concerned this never happened."

"Dammit, it was a righteous bust! I had probable cause and he assaulted me."

"I don't care if you had little baby Jesus for a witness," Dunlap snapped. "Dammit, Westin, you're not a cop any more. It doesn't matter."

"He's dealing drugs here at the mall."

"You catch him with any drugs?"

"Of course not. Dealers don't keep the stuff on them."

"You find any drugs on mall property?"

"No."

"Then if he's dealing, he's not doing it here, so it's not our concern." Dunlap stuck his face close to Andy's. "You got that, Westin? It. Is. Not. Our. Concern."

"What are you going to do with him?"

"Cut him loose. Give him his money back."

"And let him keep selling drugs to kids at the mall."

"No. I'm going to tell him never to show his ass around this place again. His picture goes up on the board and if you see him around here, you escort him off the property. But that's *all* you do. Got that?"

"So he just goes on selling someplace else," Andy said bitterly.

"If he does, that's someone else's problem." Dunlap softened. "Look, Westin, I like you. You're solid and you try hard. But you gotta understand this isn't like being a police officer. All we care about is what happens on the property.

"Now that sure as hell doesn't mean we ignore drug dealing, but we just try to keep it out of the mall and do it as quiet as possible. The kind of cowboy shit you pulled this afternoon, that's bad for the mall. It scares the customers.

"Now suppose we did it your way and called the cops. If they decide the case is good enough to arrest him, it goes down in the police reports that he was arrested here at Black Oak. Next thing you know the papers have got it. Mall management doesn't like that. Meanwhile he's out on bail probably before you get off shift and right back here. Then when the case comes to trial you've gotta go down on your own time to testify. And when it's all over chances are the guy gets a slap on the wrist, probation or something.

"That's a lot of trouble and it doesn't do anything we can't do quietlike by just throwing him off the property."

"Maybe you're right," Andy said grudgingly.

"Damn straight I'm right. I know it's a shitty system and sometimes it turns my stomach too. But you gotta be practical about this."

"So do you want me to turn him loose?"

Dunlap stood up. "I'll take care of that. You go back on patrol and I'll handle him." He clapped Andy on the shoulder. "And the next time you get a situation like this, you come to me or whoever's watch commander before you go playing John Wayne, okay?"

You dumb-ass boy scout mother, Dunlap thought as Andy left his office. *Make trouble for everyone, why don't you?* Normally he'd fire someone who pulled a stupid stunt like that. But he needed Westin.

Meanwhile there was the Surfer to deal with. That and $6,000.

The Surfer was still handcuffed to the chair in the interrogation room where Andy had left him. He started yelling as soon as Dunlap walked into the room.

"I want my lawyer. I'm gonna sue you motherfuckers for every goddamn penny you got, man."

Dunlap carefully closed the door behind him. Then he whirled, grabbed the Surfer by the shirt and lifted him up, chair and all.

"What you're gonna do — punk! — is shut your

fucking mouth while you still got some teeth left," Dunlap snarled in his face.

He dropped the Surfer and put a foot on the chair leg to stop the Surfer from going over backwards.

"That's police brutality, man! I'll . . ."

Dunlap grabbed him by the shoulder and ground his thumb deep into the nerve point under the collarbone. The Surfer went white and gasped in pain.

"You still don't get it, do you, you candy-assed little pansy? We're not the police." The Surfer groaned and tried to shift away from the pain. "Now," Dunlap went on, "we got all kinds of witnesses that saw you chased through the mall. We got people saw you get tackled and try to fight the officer." Relentlessly he bore down on the pressure point. "There's just no telling what kind of injuries you suffered out there." He let up on the neck and the Surfer sagged forward, his breath coming in ragged gulps.

Dunlap reached down and grabbed the Surfer's right index finger, forcing it backward. The man went rigid with the new pain. "You could have broken your finger when you fell, for instance." He held the finger at a point experience told him was just short of actually breaking it. He whipped the blackjack out of his blazer and laid it across the Surfer's side. The man jerked and cried out. "Maybe you broke a rib when you hit that planter, huh?"

He released the finger and squatted on his heels, the blackjack still dangling carelessly in the Surfer's line of sight. "Or something worse could have happened to you. You could have suffered internal injuries when you went down. Maybe you're dying right now. Hey, it happens, you know? And no one's gonna cry over a piece of garbage like you."

He stood up, looming over his slumping victim. "But all that means paperwork and I hate paperwork. So I'm gonna do you a favor. I'm gonna let you go and that's gonna be the end of it. Sound like a plan?"

The Surfer looked up at Dunlap, still breathing hard. "Of course," Dunlap went on, "if you ever show your sorry ass around here again I'll see to it you leave on a stretcher. And if you live, the police will have all the evidence they'll need to put you up in Folsom with some guys who'd just love to get their hands on a candy-ass like you." He grabbed the Surfer by the hair and yanked his head back. "That blonde surfer do and tan will make you a big hit in the cellblock, let me tell you."

He let the head drop. "Now there's a couple of officers waiting outside to escort you to the gate. And that's gonna be the end of it, isn't it?" He grabbed the Surfer's hair and yanked his head back viciously. "ISN'T IT?"

The Surfer nodded as best he could, and Dunlap let his head drop forward again. Then he whipped out a knife and cut the man's restraints.

"What about my money?"

Dunlap grinned. "You're a glutton for punishment, ain't you? That money's confiscated. And don't forget we got just hours of videotape to show the cops how you made that money." The grin widened. "You didn't realize we tape everything that goes on here, did you, you dumb shit? Now get the hell out!"

"The worst of it is," Andy said glumly, "Dunlap was right."

Andy and Judy were sitting in the Cafe Poisson drinking pleasantly bitter European-style coffee. Andy was off duty and in civvies and Judy was wearing a brown skirt with big hibiscus blossoms hand-painted on it. The Mexican shawl around her shoulders picked up the colors of the flowers and threw them back with an eye-searing clash. The ever-present silver-and-amethyst brooch managed to clash with everything. Andy didn't notice, in part because he was getting used to Judy's weird costumes and in part because he was too caught up with his own concerns.

Judy reached over to pat his arm. "You tried to do

the right thing." She hesitated. "You meant well."

Andy shook his head. "Yeah, but I blew it. It just made me so mad to have this stuff going on in the mall and nothing I could do, I wanted to kill him." He looked up. "You know, I never got this mad at the dealers on the street. Even the ones I knew were selling to kids. But there was just something about the idea of him dealing here in the mall. Like he was violating a sanctuary or something."

Judy looked out at the passing shoppers. "A sanctuary?"

Andy followed her gaze. "Funny, huh? Yeah, I guess it is for me in a way. A place where things would be simple and easy. Clean, you know? With none of the stuff I'd faced every day on the force. And now this stuff happens."

He looked back at her. "I suppose that's why I got so mad. I felt helpless and my sanctuary had been violated."

Judy drained her cup. "Well, what are you going to do now? About Surfer, I mean?"

"Nothing I can do. Dunlap's right. I'm not a cop any more. If he stays off mall property he's not my problem."

"The spiritually advanced view would be that he's one less problem you have to worry about," Judy said seriously. "His own karmic burden will bring him the fate he deserves. Meanwhile, he's out of your life and now you can get on the other things."

"That's, uh, kind of the way I see it," Andy agreed. Then he glanced at his watch and hastily drained his cup. "Hey, I've got to get going. Thanks, Judy. You've been a big help."

"I didn't say anything."

"You didn't have to. Just having someone to talk to makes it better and you're easy to talk to."

Judy only smiled.

Chapter 18

Andy was still stewing when the phone rang at his apartment that night.

"Westin," the voice on the other end said without preamble, "I asked you to keep your eyes open, not take the guy on."

Andy didn't say anything. There really wasn't anything he could say. True, the Surfer had assaulted him, but not without provocation.

"We were trying to get a court order to use the mall's security cameras to track this guy," Rodriguez said. "Now he's gotta light somewhere else and we're gonna have to find out where."

"I'm really sorry. Look, maybe it will break things up. Slow him down a little."

"Maybe." Rodriguez didn't sound convinced. "Anyway, I got that information you asked me for."

"You found something?"

"Depends," he said, "on what you mean by something."

"Six thousand dollars! Six thousand dollars those pigs ripped off me."

Toby, for whom six thousand dollars was considerably less than a day's take, leaned back on the velour, expressionless. Surfer had repeated himself three times so far and the story hadn't improved with the telling.

"I wanna take those fucking pigs *down*, man! I want them!"

Toby shook his head. "That's not taking care of business. It is, like, unproductive, you dig?"

"I don't give a fuck! Their asses are mine and I want them! This is personal, man. Personal."

Toby considered. "Well, they ripped you off so you have a right. But since it is personal, I don't know that I can allow any of my home boys to get involved, you hear what I'm saying? You're going to have to get your own shooters if you're going to be running your own thing."

"Fine," the Surfer said. "That's fine. I'll do them myself."

Toby raised an admonishing finger. "Now you see, that is precisely what I mean. You are just not treating this like business, my man. Shooting ain't your thing. You go trying it and you'll fuck it up for sure."

"I can handle it," the Surfer said sullenly.

"Maybe, but you won't. Not while you're part of my organization, you hear what I'm saying?" Even through the shades the Surfer caught the cold stare. "I said you got permission to have it done, but you're gonna hire it out to freelancers, understand?"

"Yeah," the Surfer mumbled. "Yeah. I understand."

"That be fine then." Toby signaled Pedro to pull over. "You do what you gotta do and in the meantime you keep taking care of business, you hear?"

"We are going to need somebody new out in that territory pretty soon," Toby told Lurch as the van pulled away. "I am afraid our current sales representative is getting too personally involved and I suspect he has been sampling his own stock."

Lurch raised an eyebrow.

"No, no. We don't do anything we don't have to. We just chill and let the situation resolve itself naturally."

Andy spent most of the morning thinking and waited until his lunch break to visit Bellbookand.

"Oh, hi!" Judy said when he came in. "I was wondering if you were working today."

"Judy, we've got to talk. Can we use your back room?"

"About what?" she asked, catching his mood.

"Heather. I heard from my friend last night."

"Sure. I'll draw the curtain back and sit where I can watch the door. Would you like some tea?"

Andy sat silently while she busied herself with setting out cups and saucers and poured tea from the steeping pot.

"Now," she said as she dropped into the chair across from him, "did you find her father?"

"John William Framel lives in Ann Arbor with his second wife and three children."

"But her real name isn't Framel."

"Her birth certificate reads Heather Jean Framel," Andy said flatly. "Her parents were divorced when she was six years old and her mother received legal custody in the decree."

Judy's jaw dropped. "But that can't be! I don't believe it."

"I'm sorry, Judy," he said gently. "But you can believe it. It was double checked, and everything she told you was a lie. Heather's father never had custody, her mother never stole her."

"But her aura was so clear," Judy said in a stricken voice. "She wants so desperately to find her father."

Andy took a sip of tea. "Maybe, but he doesn't want to be found. At the time of the divorce he severed parental rights over her. Apparently he never wants to see her mother or Heather again."

"Fuck you!"

Judy looked up and went white. There was Heather standing in the doorway.

"Heather . . ."

"So you had the pig check up on me," she said in a voice shaking with fury. "You went spying on me."

"Heather, you told me . . ."

"So? I tell people lots of things. It was a joke, see? A trick to see how much you'd swallow." Tears welled out of her eyes and her breath came in short, panting gasps.

Judy went to her, but the girl retreated into the front. "Oh, Heather . . ."

"What the fuck do you know, anyhow? It isn't true and I'll prove it. My dad loves me and I'm going to find him."

"I'm sure your mother loves you," Judy said gently.

"My mother? My mother's a drunk. And her boyfriend's after me all the time."

"You mean he doesn't like you?" Judy asked blankly.

"I mean he keeps trying to fuck me," Heather said, as if explaining something to a retarded child. "He even managed once or twice."

"Look, Andy used to be a policeman, he can help . . ."

But Heather wasn't listening.

"I don't want any fucking help, okay? So just fuck off!"

"Please, Heather . . ." Judy reached out and put her hand on the girl's shoulder but she twisted away angrily and ran out of the store.

She turned and yelled back at them. "Fuck off!" Then she spun and dashed out of the arcade into the main mall.

Wordlessly, Andy and Judy returned to the back room and their tea.

"I'm really sorry," Andy said at last.

Judy shook her head and tried to smile. "No, it's my fault. I wanted to be able to help her — save her really." The corner of her mouth quirked up in a not-quite smile. "Like a fairy princess waving a magic wand."

"Dangerous."

"I know. My teachers warned me. If you really, really, want something to be true you can't sense if it is true or not." She sat down heavily. "I guess I just made it worse."

"No way you could have made it worse.

They sat in silence over their tea for a while. Outside and far away the mall speakers played something light and almost obscenely cheerful.

"Andy?"

"Yeah?"

"What's going to happen to her?"

"Probably a lot of things," he said matter-of-factly. "Before long she's going to run out of resources. Then she's going to start trading herself for a place to spend the night — if she hasn't already. Then she'll probably turn hooker full time and somewhere along the line she'll get strung out on drugs because they dull the pain. Finally she'll either OD, or get beaten to death by a john or her pimp. Or maybe if she's real lucky she'll get popped for a major felony and wind up doing a long stretch in prison."

He felt something warm and wet on the back of his hand, looked down and saw he was shaking so badly tea was slopping out of his cup. He set the cup down, took a long, deep breath and let it out explosively.

"That's the usual pattern anyway," he finished.

"Can't we do something?"

"You heard her. She doesn't want help. After what she's been through she's so damn hostile and she's got so little trust that she'd be hard as hell to reach. Even if you could get her into a foster home she'd run away."

"Well at least they could arrest the sonofabitch boyfriend!"

"Sure. But they couldn't convict him. She's probably the only witness, the mother will lie to protect him and a defense attorney could rip her apart in ten minutes."

"That sucks!" Judy blazed. "That really sucks."

Andy stared down at his teacup. "If you're looking for an argument you're not going to get one. I used to find girls like her all the time. Beaten to death in motel rooms or in abandoned buildings with the needles still in their arms."

He looked up at her and shook his head. "Judy, you see so damn much misery when you're a cop. And there's so little you can do about any of it."

"Did you ever try?" Judy asked bitterly.

"Of course I tried! You think I like this? But I learned the hard way I can't change it and getting involved only gets you hurt worse.

"Look, you wanted to know why I quit being a cop? That's the reason. I could handle the corruption, the boredom, the bullshit and the stress." His mouth quirked. "I could even handle getting shot at. But that," he nodded down the arcade the way Heather had gone, "that sort of thing I just couldn't deal with."

"So what do you suggest we do?" Judy asked tightly.

"The only thing we can do. We sit here on Fantasy Island and we drink our tea and try not to think about the big, bad world outside."

"Bullshit."

"Look, if you're thinking of going after her . . ."

"No." Judy stood up and pulled the ladder over to the shelves.

"We can't help her."

Judy climbed up and took the candlesticks off the top shelf. "*We* can't? Well, maybe *I* can."

"Magic again?"

"You don't seem to have anything better to offer," she said without turning around.

"I thought you told me you couldn't influence someone against their will."

"You can't." Judy ground out as she pulled more items off the shelves. "Now get the hell out of here and let me work!"

Andy got.

Chapter 19

This place gets weirder all the time, Andy thought as he made his second round of the night. There was something unsettling about the mall after midnight. It was just fundamentally wrong that he was the only person in this place built to accommodate thousands.

The only sound in the silence was the echo of his footsteps and the rush of water in the South Court fountain. Even smells were more intense and localized because the air-conditioning was turned down.

It left him with a funny feeling between his shoulder blades and a tendency to jump at sudden noises. He also found himself walking close to the walls and avoiding open spaces. Objectively it was silly, he knew. But the deserted mall still had that effect. Especially after his run-in with Surfer and the scene with Heather the next day.

Well, just a couple of more stations to check and . . .

A blood-curdling scream rent the air behind him. Instinctively, Andy whirled in a gunfighter's crouch, his pistol half out of its holster.

There, in the window of the pet shop behind him, was a large blue and gold macaw looking very pleased with himself. As Andy stood up the bird shrieked again and shifted on his perch. Even through the glass the noise was deafening. The macaw cocked his head at the guard. Never mind that a bird has no lips and eyebrows and therefore cannot smirk; the macaw smirked.

"Remind me to return the favor," Andy told the parrot through the glass. The macaw turned away and feigned indifference.

Jesus Christ, Andy thought, *they want two thousand dollars for something that screams like that.* What was it his mom used to say, something about people with more money than sense?

Andy stepped out into South Court and put his card in the slot of the terminal to his right. Blackie wasn't talking to him tonight for some reason so the place seemed more deserted than ever.

The fountain was turned off but the waterfall splashed and burbled over the rocks, deafeningly loud in the silence. Andy cut straight across the court and through the sculpture garden, stepping among the bronze figures frozen in their timeless dance.

Something moved off to the right. Andy whirled. And a woman stepped out from among the sculptures.

She was beautiful. No, she was more than that, she was awe-inspiring. Tall and pale, with a figure that set his heart pounding and long white hair streaming down her back. She was wearing a simple dress of shimmering white fabric caught at the waist with a golden cord. The pale, pale blue eyes locked onto his and Andy sucked in his breath, frozen to the spot by the vision.

"Remember," she breathed and then she was gone.

For a long time he stood motionless, staring with aching longing at the place where she had stood.

"All right," said Kemper Cogswell, checking off another item on the agenda, "anything else on the offsets?" All up and down the table the members of his sale team shook their heads.

"Fine, now what about the Japanese?" Larry Sakimoto kept looking at the pad in front of him. "Larry?" he asked more sharply and Sakimoto's head jerked up.

"Right, ah . . ."

Cogswell frowned. Sakimoto hadn't been the same since the day of the first meeting with Kashihara. He was nervous, inattentive, and seemed to be drinking heavily. Just now he looked seriously hung over and he obviously wasn't well prepared. He wondered if hiring the Japanese-American real estate specialist had been a mistake.

"Things are going very well there," Sakimoto said hurriedly. "Kashihara's definitely going to go through with the deal."

The frown deepened. That was obvious. Which was why they were sitting here at 9:30 Saturday morning reviewing the week's negotiations.

"If they want to do the deal why are they still jerking us around on the details?" Cogswell demanded.

"To drive the price down. They know we're willing to be flexible." The mall owner winced inside. So far the negotiations had knocked nearly three million off the price of the mall. "But I think that phase is just about over. Not only are we running out of things to quibble about, but Kashihara can't stay here much longer and if he goes home without concluding the deal he loses face."

Good news at last. Cogswell nodded. "Fine. Keep on them and make sure they understand our flexibility has its limits." He paused and looked up and down the conference table.

"One more thing, and this isn't on the agenda because it is sensitive. Incidents in the mall." Out of the corner of his eye he saw Sakimoto jerk, as if he had been slapped. *What the hell is that about?* "The reports of strange goings on in the mall have got to stop. Now." He looked down at Wilson, the mall manager, fidgeting at the foot of the table. "Not only are these things a drag on the negotiations, but we're starting to see rumors in the community. I understand we had an inquiry last week from one of the local television stations." He paused again and fixed each member of his team in turn with a steely glare. "I don't want to hear of any more incidents."

Down at the foot of the table Wilson nodded. He'd

make damn sure Cogswell didn't hear any more reports. No matter what happened in the mall.

The puppies stood up in their windows and begged to be played with. The kittens watched her alertly, eyes wide and ears pricked forward.

Cynthia Norton ignored them all. Oh to be back in a line where "moving merchandise" meant selling it! Cynthia thought of herself as a consummate retail professional. But that hadn't been enough to save her when the big department store chain she had worked for nine years went through a spectacular series of consolidations and reorganizations ending in Chapter 11 bankruptcy.

Cynthia found herself out after the second round of shakeups and in the tight economy the best thing she could find was managing a chain pet store.

Cynthia's retail credentials may have been impeccable, but she hated animals. To her, dogs and cats were destructive nuisances, birds were a noisy annoyance and reptiles of any sort made her flesh crawl. So here she was surrounded by snakes and lizards and God-alone-knew what

Still, a successful retail manager was adaptable. This job might not be ideal, but the mall offered opportunities for networking with other retail professionals. It would tide her over while her resume circulated. And with a little careful massaging, the job would make a strong entry on that resume.

But, after all, *livestock* . . . Well, at least as manager she didn't have to deal with it. Feeding and cage cleaning were for employees.

April, her assistant manager, and the two part-timers were waiting for her when she clocked in. All three of them looked unusually pale.

"Well, what is it now?" Cynthia Norton demanded.

"It's . . . Well, I think you'd better have a look, Ms. Norton. Up front."

Cynthia dropped her purse in her desk drawer, then closed it firmly and made sure it was locked.

"Honestly, April, I don't know why they made you assistant manager if you can't handle these things as they arise. A successful manager is judged by her problem-solving skills."

April knew better than to argue with that tone. Instead she gestured toward the front window.

One window was a flight cage, divided in two. The back section displayed parakeets and cockatiels, while the front was used as a magnet display to attract traffic.

It was the established policy of the Pet Parade shops to have at least one exotic in every store as a draw. The Black Oak store had gotten a blue-and-gold macaw. As an exotic it was relatively prosaic, but as a source of trouble it was outstanding.

The bird had a nasty temper, a loud voice and simply would not shut up. It was banished to the front window after it took a bite out of a customer. Everyone on the staff was afraid of it and it was almost enough to make Cynthia think kindly of the snakes. At least they just lay there and didn't make noise.

But the macaw wasn't in the cage at all. Instead there was a two-foot-long green lizard stretched out on the limb where the macaw normally sat.

"Where's the macaw?" she demanded. "And who put this iguana in here?"

"Uh, that's not an iguana," April told her in a strained voice.

Cynthia looked again. The lizard was big and green, but it definitely didn't look like an iguana. For one thing, iguanas don't have fangs. For another, they don't have bat wings.

Then she noticed what the lizard was holding in its claw. It was a feather.

A large blue feather . . .

. . . which the lizard was using to pick its teeth.

For a single mad instant the only thing Cynthia could

think of was how in the world she could explain this on the loss form. The lizard belched a tiny blue flame and looked very pleased with itself.

Cynthia gasped and whirled, but that put her facing the parakeet cage.

She had an audience. There were three more little green lizards with their noses pressed against the glass, their limpid dark eyes watching her in friendly fascination. Their tiny wings moved in almost invisible blurs as they hovered and their long tails hung straight down. The parakeets were huddled in the back of the cage, visibly upset and twittering among themselves about their new cagemates.

"We've had three inquiries about them already this morning," April said apologetically. "The thing is, they're not on the price list. So I just took the names and phone numbers."

"One guy wanted the big one too," added one of the part-timers. "He was real eager."

A successful manager knows how to make decisions. Cynthia Norton pointed at the nearest employee. "You," she snapped. "Take over. I'm going home." She spun on her heel and strode purposefully from the store.

Andy had finished his shift in a daze and got no sleep that morning. All he could think of was the woman in the sculpture garden. He wasn't much better the next afternoon when he wandered into Bellbookand.

Judy was rearranging stock. "Oh, hi. I got some more of those cedar candles." Then she stopped and frowned. "Are you all right?"

"Yeah," Andy said vaguely. "I'm fine."

"Are you sure? What happened?"

"I, well, I met someone last night."

"Oh," Judy said flatly.

Andy didn't notice. "It's weird. I mean no one's supposed to be in here at all and there she was."

"What happened?"

"Well, I was checking the South Court and suddenly she was just there, you know. Like she'd appeared out of nowhere." He sighed again and fell silent.

Judy looked at him sharply. "You told me no one is in the mall after midnight."

"Yeah," Andy said abstractedly.

"Did you talk to her?"

"No, not really. She just said 'remember' and then she vanished."

Now it was Judy's turn to fall silent.

"It's so strange," Andy went on, oblivious, "Just that one word and I can't get her out of my mind."

Judy looked at him intently. "So you just saw her that once, and she only said one word and now you can't forget it?"

"Yeah," Andy said dreamily. "I wonder if I'll ever see her again."

"Andy, come in the back for a minute, will you?" Judy reached out and took his hand. Andy let himself be led behind the curtain and into the tiny storeroom.

"Now sit down for just a second." While Andy sat, she filled the carafe with bottled water and put it on the coffee maker. Then she pulled a couple of jars off the shelf and set them on the table. While the water heated, she carefully measured out a little of the contents of each and ground them together in her mortar. Next, Judy added some bark and leaves from other jars and a dollop of something that looked like molasses and smelled like old dishwater.

She took a Mr. Coffee filter and put it in a wire strainer. Then she put the mixture in the strainer and poured steaming water over it, muttering something and moving her hand over carafe and cup.

Judy handed him the cup. "Drink this," she commanded.

"What is it?" he asked dully.

"Don't ask, just drink."

He raised the cup and Judy moved to stand directly

in front of him. He saw her lips were moving as if she was muttering something under her breath.

Andy took the cup and sipped. The hot liquid tasted like nothing much, so he took a deep swallow. This time the stuff hit his innards like the kick of a mule. His stomach did a convulsive flip, his whole body went cold and the room spun around him. The teacup clattered to the floor unnoticed as Andy grabbed the edge of the table to keep from falling.

The wave passed as suddenly as it came, leaving Andy clutching the table and shaking his head to try to clear it.

"What was in that thing?" he asked shakily.

"Medicine. Just some herbal medicine."

"That was awful."

"But you're feeling better now?"

Andy considered. "Yeah, I guess so."

"Good. Then tell me what happened last night."

"A woman. I met a woman last night at the sculpture garden."

Judy nodded, her lips pressed into a tight, flat line.

"What was she like?"

"Well," Andy said thoughtfully, "she was beautiful, I remember that." He looked up at Judy. "But I can't remember exactly what she looked like. I mean, I remember, but I don't remember what made her so special, you know?"

"I know," Judy said grimly. "Well, two can play at this game. Sit down, I've got work to do."

"I don't want to keep you from it," he said, starting to rise.

"Sit down! I'll need your help for this."

Andy sat.

Once more Judy bustled around the tiny cubicle, selecting jars and bottles and setting them on the card table in front of Andy. There were nondescript powders, dried roots and a couple of jars of pickled things that looked like they might be nondescript if you could see them clearly.

"This should really be done by the full of the moon and a few other things," Judy told him. "But we don't have time."

She put things from the jars into a marble mortar and ground them, leaning down hard on the pestle to break up the bits.

"Just what is it you're doing?"

"A summoning," she said, pouring the coarsely ground material into a small lacquer bowl and putting the mortar and pestle under the table. "I'm going to call her here and make her tell us what's going on."

Andy shifted uncomfortably. "Judy, I don't . . ." But she cut him off with a gesture.

She shook out a square of midnight blue silk with what looked like chicken tracks embroidered on it in pale green. Then she reached into a drawer and pulled a lensatic compass from it. Sighting carefully through the compass, she aligned the square of silk, shifting it back and forth in tiny increments until she was satisfied.

"Uh, I don't think that's accurate with all the metal in this place."

"Doesn't matter. You want the metal's influences."

Then she took four candles in brass candlesticks and set them out at the edges of the square. She set a cheap brass incense burner to her left and what looked like a letter opener with a black onyx handle to her right.

"Look, I don't think I want anything to do with this."

"Hush. I need to concentrate."

"Judy . . ."

"We can talk later, okay? Now just be quiet and help me through this."

Andy started to say something more, then he clamped his jaw so hard the muscles in his cheeks knotted.

Judy threw some reddish powder in the incense burner and thick fragrant smoke billowed up. Then she lit a long splinter of cedar wood from the coals and lit the candles, pausing to mutter something at each one.

Between the incense and the candles Andy wondered how she managed to keep from setting off the sprinklers.

Next she picked up the letter opener and held it aloft, point down. She muttered something else. She marched around the altar, the table and Andy, stopping at each cardinal point of the compass to raise the knife, point up, and say something else. Then she came back to where she started and sprinkled some of the powder she had ground onto the charcoal. Again smoke billowed up, more pungent and not as sweet.

"Now," she said, turning to Andy, "I want you to visualize that woman. Picture her exactly in your mind."

"Caucasian female, about . . ."

"No, you don't have to tell me what she looks like. Probably better if you don't. Just fix her in your mind just as you saw her."

Andy fidgeted, but he tried to concentrate on the woman he had seen among the statues. All the while Judy made passes and mutterings over the brazier, the candles and the cloth.

"Fine," Judy said at last. "You can relax now." She threw more of the sweet incense in the brazier, took the knife and walked around the room again, stopping at each compass point to make a cutting motion in the air. At last she put the lid on the incense burner to douse the charcoal and snuffed each of the candles in turn, muttering all the while.

"Well," she sighed, "that should do it."

"You finished?" Andy asked tightly.

"Now all we have to do is wait for her to come here."

"You can wait. I'm leaving."

"Why?"

"Because I've had about all of this I can take. This is nuts and I don't want any part of it."

"It worked, didn't it?" Judy demanded. "I took the infatuation spell off you."

"What infatuation spell? I come in here feeling a little worn down . . ."

"A little worn down? You were sleepwalking and you darned well know it."

"I don't know anything, okay? You gave me some funny stuff to drink. For all I know you pumped me full of caffeine. Or drugged me."

"Ohhh," Judy hissed and turned away.

"Look, Judy," Andy said to her back. "I like you, I really do. But this has got to stop. All this magic stuff. I'm just not going to put up with it any more. Judy, it's crazy."

"That 'crazy stuff' defines who I am now," Judy said tightly.

"If you want to play make-believe, fine. But I'm through pretending."

"Just leave, okay?"

Andy opened his mouth, closed it, and left.

LaVonne Sanders was in the lunch room when he went down to clock back in.

"What happened to you, Westlin? Have a fight with your girlfriend?"

"She's not my girlfriend," Andy snapped. "And we didn't have a fight."

LaVonne nodded. "A *bad* fight."

"It wasn't . . . Oh, hell, LaVonne, that woman is just so damn weird."

"Anyone in the mall could have told you that," LaVonne said. "You saying it took you this long to figure it out?"

Andy stuck his badge in the slot. "Anyway, it's over. She's had it with me and I've sure as hell had it with her."

LaVonne didn't say anything but she didn't look convinced either.

Andy stalked out on his afternoon rounds unsure if he was mad or hurt. He knew he had seen the last of Judy Cohen and he couldn't decide if that was because he was mad or if that was what was making him mad. All he knew for sure was it made him bone-deep miserable.

He was still working on that when he got down to the south leg on the second level. Halfway down the leg the guy in the organ shop was at a console playing something Lawrence-Welkish. He had enough of the features turned on so it sounded like there was a mediocre Las Vegas lounge band behind him. To Andy the results clashed horribly with the light classical drifting out of the speakers, but the brightly colored crowds swirling by didn't seem to notice.

Just down the way Pauline Patterson was sitting on a bench watching the people flow around her. "Good afternoon, Andy," she said as he nodded to her. "You certainly look glum today."

"Let's just say I'm tired of dealing with crazies."

The old woman raised her eyebrows. "Crazies in general or one crazy in particular?"

"Jesus, does everybody in this damn place know Judy and I had a fight?"

"Probably not, but it isn't hard to unravel."

"Yeah. Well, today I finally reached my limit. She claimed someone had put a spell on me and then fed me one of her magic potions."

Dr. Patterson looked him up and down. "It doesn't seem to have harmed you."

"Didn't do me any good, either. Well," he amended, "nothing a strong cup of coffee wouldn't have done. I was just a little tired."

"I'm not sure I see the harm in it."

"The harm is that it's nuts. There is no such thing as magic. As a scientist you know that."

"I know that my culture doesn't accept magic as a valid explanation," the anthropologist said neutrally.

"You're telling me you *believe* this crap?"

"I'm telling you I believe in evidence and as a scientist I try to reserve judgment until I have examined and weighed the evidence." She hesitated and then added: "That's especially important around here.

"Anyway," she hurried on, "we're not discussing a matter of scientific proof here, we're discussing a pattern of behavior. Judy's beliefs may not accord completely with cultural norms but she is certainly able to function effectively. So where is the harm?"

Painfully, Dr. Patterson levered herself around on the bench to face him. "Andy, as a scientist I also know that we humans have an amazing ability to find patterns in events." She smiled with the half of her face that worked. "Even when there is no pattern. Ever since we came out of the African gallery forests we've been conditioned to believe that the world makes sense and that we can understand it. Those are postulates, not proven facts, but they've brought us pretty far."

"I'm not sure I understand the relevance."

Down the mall the organ started up again, this time something with a bossa nova rhythm.

"Just that being the determined cusses we are, humans will find an explanation for anything and they will prefer a wrong explanation to no explanation at all. It's more satisfying, you see. And lot of people prefer an explanation that makes them feel good to one that precisely conforms to what their culture sees as reality."

"And that's Judy."

"So it appears."

"How do you change someone like that?"

"Trying to change people is most unsatisfactory in my experience," again the half-smile, "and I had a lot of experience with my ex-husband. No, you simply adapt if you can." She stopped smiling. "Or you decide it's not worth it and cut the connection."

"But how can you live with all that craziness?"

"Andy, until the day he died one of my dearest friends was a man who was probably a ritual cannibal, certainly a murderer, who never made a major move without consulting the ghosts of his father and grandfather and who honored me by giving me the use of two of his junior wives while I lived in his village." She looked amused at Andy's shock. "He had to declare me an honorary man in order to deal with me, you see. Needless to say, I did not share either his beliefs or his dietary pecularities, but we were still great friends."

"What's your point?"

"Just that friendship — or love — is independent of what either of you believe."

"But this stuff is so *weird*."

"Perhaps that is the place to start," Pauline Patterson said gently. "Maybe if you understood why weird beliefs bother you you'd better understand your problem with Judy Cohen."

"Weird beliefs bother me because they don't work," Andy said sharply. "They cause trouble. They hurt people."

"Andy," the old woman said quietly, "that's the first time I've ever heard you raise your voice."

They sat silent while the shoppers whirled around them in the brownian motion of modern commerce. The organ swung into a waltz — the "Blue Danube," with a strong drum section.

"So you think I should be the one to change?" he said at last.

"No, I think you should understand yourself."

"Okay, why do you think Judy's ideas bother me?"

Dr. Patterson shrugged one shoulder. "I haven't the faintest idea. I'm an anthropologist, not a psychologist."

"Hmmmf. Well thanks anyway, Dr. Patterson. I've got to get back on rounds now."

"Of course. But Andy, think about it, will you?"

Down at the end of the south leg, on the South Court stage, a bunch of dancers and musicians were setting up for a concert. Andy leaned on the rail and stared down at them unseeing. Then after a while he wandered off on patrol.

Michael Moishe O'Shaunessey was named after both his grandfathers. He had inherited his black hair, olive skin and dark eyes from his Jewish mother, but on his father's side he was one generation removed from the streets of Cork and inordinately proud of it.

He was on the South Court stage wearing a dark green sports coat, lime green polyester golfing pants, a light green shirt and a dark green tie as an expression of that pride. His green-on-green "Kiss Me I'm Irish" button was somewhat lost among all the verdanture. Among the singers, dancers and musicians of The Jackets Green he stood out like a splotch of Day-Glo moss against a background of more subdued lichen.

Just now the lichen was busy. The fiddlers were tuning together and the piper was playing experimental riffs on his uillean pipes. Billy McDermott was fastening Caitlain Lopez' brooch where it had come loose on her blouse, and the other dancers were already in their costumes. O'Shaunessey nodded to himself. The Jackets Green were ready to go.

Off to the other side of the stage the Southland Shamrocks were getting set. The dancers were huddled around their leader, a heavyset, dark-haired man with a florid face and a commanding air about him. O'Shaunessey had his reservations about Terry Reilly and the Southland Shamrocks. They were competent, but they weren't as authentic as The Jackets Green. There was also the usual ration of obscure Irish politics involved, plus Terry Reilly's reported comment that the average Irishman couldn't tell a saint from a leprechaun.

Not that it wasn't true, O'Shaunessey had to admit, but Reilly still shouldn't have said it.

Already there was a sprinkling of shoppers pausing here and there around the South Court. Not the best crowd, but not bad for a June Saturday afternoon.

"Are we ready then?" O'Shaunessey asked the musicians. Shamrocks and Jackets alike nodded, and O'Shaunessey stepped up to the mike to begin the introduction.

They opened with "Wearing of the Green" and "Dear Old Donegal." O'Shaunessey thought the second piece owed more to Bing Crosby than the Emerald Isle, but it was familiar and a crowd pleaser.

Well, you couldn't get too authentic at a mall. No bodhran solos and not too many slow airs. *Thank God it's not "Danny Boy."* The crowd built slowly as a few shoppers were drawn by the music to stop and listen. They started to drift away again when Reilly stepped up to introduce the dancers.

Cut it short, you long-winded jackass, O'Shaunessey gritted his teeth as he watched the crowd thin. But Reilly had a memorized spiel about turf fires and colleens and the Auld Sod and he ran through it all, just as he always did.

At last, praise be to God, Reilly stepped back from the mike and the fiddlers sawed into the first of the jigs. After a second's hesitation the piper picked up the tune and the dancers swung forward, men from the left and women from the right into the traditional dance set.

They weren't too bad, O'Shaunessey admitted. A little loose, and some of the Shamrocks obviously hadn't practiced the pattern enough, but everyone's feet moved in the proper steps and mostly in time to the music. Reilly had some good material. If he'd just work them a little harder and lay off the schmaltz he'd have a decent group there.

O'Shaunessey's head jerked around as the turn and swirl of the dance brought a new dancer to the fore. He was a little squirt, barely five feet high, if that. He must have been hidden by the other dancers. He had red hair and a pug nose and unlike the rest of the dancers he was wearing knee britches, a vest and a bowler hat. *Stage Irish!* O'Shaunessey thought contemptuously. Just like Reilly to come up with an outfit like that for the kid. No, not a kid, he saw. There were crow's feet around the blue eyes and ruddy cheeks came not from youth but from a network of broken veins.

Where the hell did Reilly find him? He went to nearly every Irish festival up and down the west coast and he'd never seen the little man before. But he was good. O'Shaunessey hadn't seen dancing like that since he went to the All-Ireland festival in Dublin two years ago. Come to that, this fellow was better than most of what he'd seen there.

His arms hung loose at his sides as his feet flew through the jig steps in perfect time to the music. It wasn't just technique, though technique he certainly had. He was *enjoying* himself up there. So many of the dancers were deadpan when they danced, but the little man was grinning gleefully, paying attention to the other dancers as people. It was as if he was courting the women and they responded to that.

The crowd was getting bigger and they were loving the show. People were starting to sway in time to the rhythm. Even the little kids had stopped running around and were staring wide-eyed at the stage.

By common consent the other dancers dropped back and the little man took center stage. The fiddlers swung into "The Irish Washerwoman" and then picked up the tempo. The man's feet were a blur as he kept time to the music.

He kept it up for a good two minutes and by the end the crowd was clapping along with the music. Then one by one the fiddlers reached their limits and dropped out. With a final flashing blur the little man finished his performance with a fancy step. Then he bowed to the crowd, turned, tipped his hat to the ladies and bounded spryly off the stage.

The crowd broke into wild applause.

O'Shaunessey sidled over to Reilly. "That midget was tremendous. How long has he been with you?"

Reilly turned from watching the crowd to face his rival. "With us?" he said. "I thought he was with you."

Each of them eyed the other. At the side of the stage

The Cashel Clan — Josh and Miriam Feldman — finished tuning their banjo and guitar.

"Go out there and introduce them will you?" O'Shaunessey said.

"Me? But they're your people."

"I know but I've got something to do. My bladder, you know."

"But . . ."

"Go on." O'Shaunessey made little shooing motions. "The crowd's expecting you."

As soon as Reilly stepped forward, O'Shaunessey faded off the back of the stage and started working through the crowd, going up on tiptoes looking for the little red-haired man.

As the Feldmans clattered into "Mountain Tay," O'Shaunessey spotted Andy by the escalator a little ways down the mall.

"Excuse me, officer, did you see a red-headed midget in knee breeches and a vest come this way?"

In the state he was in Andy wouldn't have seen an entire circus, complete with elephants and steam calliope, but he was polite. "No, sir," Andy told him. "Is he with your group?"

"In a manner of speaking," O'Shaunessey said. "If you do happen to see him, could you send him back to the stage? Tell him it's important, would you?"

Andy nodded and started to move on.

"Oh, and one more thing," O'Shaunessey added. "If a black-haired fella in a vest covered with shamrocks should happen to ask you about the little fella, could you tell him you haven't seen him? If you have, I mean."

Chapter 20

Damn freaky woman! Andy thought for the hundredth time that Monday night and perhaps the thousandth time since Saturday. He hadn't known all that many women, but this one was about the weirdest he'd ever met. Even weirder than that hooker with the two snakes in her purse he'd busted last year.

Unconsciously he squared his shoulders and lengthened his stride through the empty mall. Well to hell with it! He didn't need it. This job was supposed to simplify his life, not complicate it. And Judy Cohen could complicate things faster than anyone he had ever met.

She'd be easy to avoid anyway. Just don't come to the mall in daytime and you didn't have to see her. Hell, at the rate she was going she'd be out of business and out of the mall in a couple of months.

Somehow the thought didn't make him feel any better.

South Court again. No sign of the woman. He clocked in at the kiosk at one end and as he'd done on every round this evening, he deliberately cut through the sculpture garden, following the same path he had taken the Friday before.

But there were no women, beautiful or otherwise, in sight. Just a bunch of bronze statues.

Not even Blackie greeted him when he stuck his card in the kiosk in front of Sudstrom's.

"Tell your friend to remove her curse," said a voice in his ear.

Andy jumped, whirled, clawed for his gun and found himself nose to nose with the white-haired woman.

He gaped and took a step back, card forgotten.

"Tell her," the woman commanded.

"I beg your pardon?" Andy saw her pale fair skin was discolored with ugly red bumps, as if she had been bitten by a swarm of mosquitoes. She was scratching one above her right elbow.

"Your woman has laid a curse on me. She will remove it or suffer the consequences."

The woman — no, not a woman, Andy realized. Almost a woman, but no woman was ever built on her angular elongated lines. The points of her ears peeked out of her mane of white hair. And no woman ever had pupils that slitted like a cat's. Andy had never seen anyone like her before, but he had an excellent idea what she was.

"Uh, I don't think she was trying to curse you. I think she was trying to make you come to her."

She snorted. "Then she obviously bungled. Mortals and magic make a poor mix."

Andy opened his mouth to defend Judy's prowess as a witch and then thought better of it. "I'll ask her to take the spell off, Ms. . . . ?"

Instead of answering she arched a silvery eyebrow. "You do not find me attractive?"

"You're beautiful," Andy said cautiously.

"But nothing more?" She smiled mockingly. "Ah, well."

"You did something to me, didn't you? Something to make me fall in love with you?"

Again the mocking smile. "Was it so unpleasant?"

"Let's just say it wasn't something I bargained for."

"How like a mortal. To think of love in terms of bargains." She thought a moment and then sighed. "I had hoped to gain your aid through such means as I possess, but your woman has closed that path to me. Very well, mortal. I see that you are a simple, good-hearted sort, so

I will trust you and seek to strike a bargain with you."

Andy wasn't sure he liked being described as "simple," but he let it ride. "What's your proposition?"

"I need help to find something so it can be returned to its rightful place." She paused for an instant and her eyes unfocused as if she were thinking — or seeing something at a very great distance.

"I am not from this place," she said, focusing on Andy again.

"I kind of figured. Even in LA there aren't many . . ."

"Elves?" she finished. "Yes, that is what your kind have called us."

Andy changed the subject. "How did you get here?"

"There are passages — gates — between our worlds. This place sits on one of them." She gestured behind her to the spring. "The gate is forced open slightly and things may sift back and forth."

"Great," Andy said glumly. "But why now? The mall's been in business for ten years."

"Perhaps, but recently something has changed." She paused, choosing her words. "Long ago, as you measure such things, there was an — object — lost in your world. An object of great power and much worth to those of Faerie.

"Recently it has appeared in this place. Being so close to the gate, it has opened the gate slightly. Only between the hours of midnight and dawn, but it does open. If you can help us find this thing, we will reward you greatly."

"What does this thing look like?"

"In its true form it would be a shining blue light, perhaps as large as the palm of your hand. But it has probably been disguised." She shrugged gracefully. "It could appear to be anything. A rock, a leaf, a man-made object."

"That makes it hard to find."

The elf smiled. "Not to those of Faerie. Glamourie cannot disguise such a thing from one with the true sight."

"It should be easy for you to find then."

"Not so easy. We are limited in when we can search. We cannot stay in this place after dawn, but there are other creatures of Faerie not so bound."

"And those are the ones causing trouble?"

"Perhaps. Some of them, the brownies, are notoriously tricksome."

"Brownies?"

"What you would call 'vermin,' I believe." She dismissed them with an elegant wave of her pale hand. "There are others which are more dangerous."

Andy thought of the mutilated cat.

"We are not alone. Others search for the talisman as well. They cannot exist here for long, so they employ agents who are not bound by the tyranny of the hours."

"You mean they can stay here after sunrise." The mall had its share of strange characters, but he couldn't think of any who were inhuman — except maybe metaphorically. "I don't think I've seen anyone like that."

The elf smiled coldly. "You are still alive. You have not met any of their agents."

Andy changed the subject again, fast. "But they can't find this thing either?"

The elf frowned. "That is a strange thing. Besides their agents the others have better means of scrying, but still they search, which means they have not found it either. If it was in this place they should have found it by now — or we should have. So we continue our search. To find this thing and return it to its rightful place and end this mixing of worlds."

"You mean," Andy said slowly, "that if you could find this talisman and take it back with you all this stuff would stop happening?"

"The gate would be closed, yes."

Andy pondered. "Who else have you approached about this?"

"Successfully? No one."

"But you did try, right?"

"When we could. Most of your kind cannot see or hear us. They are too strongly attached to this world, too mired in its concerns. It is only when the bond to the world is weak that you can be easily approached."

"What about me?"

"You are not so strongly attached as most others and you have concerned yourself with what is happening here. It is easier for me to approach you."

Andy filed that for future consideration. "And the others?"

"One or two who were near this place late at night. Ones who were even less of this world than you." She sighed. "Alas, carrying on a rational conversation with them was like trying to talk to a brownie. If they were not wholly of this world they were even less of ours."

Andy thought about Matt and Case and nodded. "I think I know who you mean. Don't feel left out. Those particular mortals are hard for anyone to deal with."

"But come. I have told you what we seek. You have not asked about rewards."

The idea of getting things back to normal in the mall was the biggest reward Andy could think of, but he asked anyway.

"Okay, what are you offering?"

"Peace," she said. "Rest and comfort. We can offer you solace in our land. Those of your kind who have chosen to live among us have been very happy." She gestured languidly and suddenly they were somewhere else.

He was standing in a hilltop grove looking down on a meadow. The soft breeze was heavy with the scent of earth and growing things and perfumed with the spice of unknown flowers. The leaves of the trees rustled companionably under the wind's caress. The field before him was gold-green with new growth and spangled with bright flowers. A road wound around the hill and through the meadow before disappearing into the trees beyond. Rich golden sunlight poured over the scene like honey.

Somehow, Andy knew there were houses around the bend of the road and people like himself. His heart ached with the beauty of the place and the sheer joy of seeing it.

Then the elf gestured again and they were back in the cold, dark mall. Andy started at the change and the woman smiled slightly and cocked a silvery eyebrow.

"I'll think about it," he mumbled.

"If that does not appeal to you, we can reward you in this world as well. In the past those who have aided us have found no cause to complain of our generosity."

"It's kind of hard to explain turning up with a bag of gold these days," Andy told her. "The IRS gets suspicious."

Again the smile and cocked eyebrow. "Another mortal custom? Fear not. We can contrive."

"Well, look. If I find this thing I'll sure give it back to you, reward or not. It's causing a lot of trouble around here."

"Believe me, mortal, it is causing not one one-hundredth of the trouble it is capable of. The sooner it can be found and put safe away the better for all of us."

"I'll see what I can do to help you find this whatsis."

"If you can find the 'whatsis' and return it you will do a great service to both worlds," the elf said. She scratched a particularly ugly-looking welt on her forearm. "Meanwhile, tell your leman to remove her spell."

And then she was gone.

Andy stood gaping at the spot where she had stood. Then he blinked, shook himself and looked down at his watch. *Damn!* Somehow hours had gone by while they had talked. Now he was something over three hours behind schedule. He started off for the next check-in point at a not-quite run.

I can still make this work, he thought. *I'll do three rounds back to back and if I do them quickly enough that will put me back on schedule.*

❖   ❖   ❖

Andy didn't finish his shift until six, but he was back in the mall at ten, heading for the North Bazaar.

Judy was behind the counter at Bellbookand, counting through a box of candles. Andy hesitated, not quite sure how to tell her.

She kept him waiting a couple of minutes before she looked up.

"What do you want?"

Andy took a deep breath. "To apologize. And tell you what happened last night."

The dumb shit, Jefferson Davis Dunlap thought as he looked at the printout, *doesn't he realize this stuff shows up on the time clocks?* It was perfectly plain. Last night Westlin hadn't checked in for nearly four hours in the middle of his shift. Then he'd done three rounds close together, almost at dead run from the looks of it. And he apparently didn't know that the system tracked when he clocked in as well as where.

In the old days he might have gotten away with it. The old time clocks used paper tape in the clock, and it might be days or weeks before someone got around to looking at the tape. But in the mall's system the information was recorded in the computer, and the computer automatically produced a daily report showing deviations from the prescribed routine.

Jeff Dunlap considered his new guard and smiled. The guy was working out better than he had hoped. Not only did he have the right background, but he was spending a lot of off-duty time hanging around the mall. And now this messed-up report. He hadn't made his rounds for nearly half a shift and he'd tried to cover it by lying.

Suspicious, Dunlap thought to himself. *Suspicious as hell.*

The security chief's smile got even broader.

Stealing was almost comically easy when you were supposed to be protecting the stuff. He'd learned that while he was still a cop.

Which was fine if you were walking off with a box full of coats off a loading dock or a couple of VCRs out of a store's back room. But you couldn't do much more than that.

The problem with a really big theft wasn't the heist, at least not if you were even half smart. The problem was getting rid of the stuff.

Small-timers didn't worry. They pulled jobs, fenced the goods locally and the sheer volume of property crime usually kept them safe. But a small-timer didn't have the volume Dunlap and his people could get if they looted the whole damn mall, nor the variety of merchandise. Not only would dumping that much stuff on the local markets depress the price, it would act like a beacon for police.

Departments from San Francisco to Dallas to San Diego would be boiling like ants in an overturned ant-hill, and every department in the country would be on the lookout for the goods.

So the difficult part had been arranging to fence the stuff. First it would go to Mexico and from there it would go to middlemen who could sell it in Europe and Japan. That meant getting less for the merchandise, but there would still be plenty for everyone.

Finally, if they were going to stay clean they couldn't just vanish. They had to wait until they had plausible reasons to leave.

Dunlap had an angle on that too. First he would fire Morales and several of the others for "dereliction of duty" or something. Then he would manage to get himself fired. That shouldn't be hard after a massive theft.

Meanwhile, the cops would be chasing their tails trying to nail Westlin as the inside man — an ex-cop from a corrupt precinct who had a well-documented history of acting suspicious on this job.

Shit, Dunlap thought, *how much better can it get?*

❖   ❖   ❖

"Damn!" Judy breathed when Andy finished the story. "I wish I'd been there to see it."

"Just as well you weren't. She was pretty mad at you."

"She didn't like being summoned?"

"She didn't like the hives. I think she got some kind of allergic reaction to your spell."

Judy sighed. "Well, I did have to take some shortcuts. All right, the cancellation spell should work anyway. Come on."

"Who'll watch the store?"

"It'll watch itself," Judy said as she led him into the back.

Quickly she set to rummaging through the jars and boxes on the shelves. She whipped out a piece of yellow silk and laid it out on the table. Then she mixed three or four powders in the bronze mortar, grinding them even finer.

Andy picked up one of the jars and sniffed. His nose wrinkled and he set it down fast.

"That's asafoetida," Judy said, looking up from her grinding. A lock of dark hair had fallen across her forehead and she flipped it out of her eyes with a toss of her head. "It's a potent magic repellent."

"It's potent all right," Andy said fervently.

Judy went back to grinding. "You just have to get used to the smell," she said. "In the Middle Ages they used it a lot in cooking. Somewhere around here I've got a recipe for chicken with saffron and asafoetida."

Andy felt his gorge start to rise. "No thanks."

Judy looked up at him. "You know, Andy, one of your biggest problems is you're just not open to new experiences."

"Right. I'm standing here in a California mall watching a witch mix up a magic potion to take a curse off an elf and I'm not open to new experiences."

Judy wrinkled her nose at him and went back to grinding.

When the mixture was powdered to Judy's satisfaction,

she produced two yellow candles and set them on the cloth. The brazier went in the middle of the cloth and Judy used the pocket butane torch to light the lumps of charcoal. When they were burning strongly, she muttered something, took a pinch of the powder and threw it onto the coals. The odoriferous smoke billowed up and Andy nearly gagged on the smell. Then the candles flickered as if in a sudden draft, Judy muttered something else and capped the brazier. Then she blew out the candles.

"That should do it," she said as she folded the altar cloth.

"I hope so. I'd hate to have to make excuses to that elf." He fell silent as Judy bustled about putting the magical paraphenalia away. "Uh, Judy . . ."

Judy looked up at him sharply. "There's something else, isn't there?"

"Yeah. Look I owe you an explanation for acting like a jerk."

She made a throw-away gesture. "That's all right. There are a lot of people who don't believe in magic."

"It's not just that." He bit his lower lip and then rushed on. "Look, I told you once I wanted an explanation after my mom's stroke. There's more to it than that. Things between us weren't as smooth as I like to remember." He shook his head. *Hell, I was thirteen years old! Of course we fought.*

"Anyway, this particular day I wanted to go to the beach with some friends and my mom didn't want me to. We had a big argument and I stormed out of the house." He took a deep breath. "All that day I kept telling my friends how much easier it would be if Mom would just get out of my life."

Andy's jaw clenched as he fought back the tears. Judy reached out and touched his hand. "Was that when she had the stroke?"

He nodded. "When I got back from the beach a neighbor was waiting for me in our house. Over the next couple of weeks, well, I tried to undo what I'd done. I thought if I just believed hard enough it would be all right. Then I tried to cut a deal. I prayed. I made promises about what I'd do if Mom would get well.

"Only she didn't get well," he finished heavily. "Then or ever. She didn't die, but she was pretty much the same for the rest of her life.

"So I quit believing and got cynical. Deep down I guess I thought that if magic worked, if wishing could make things happen, then I was responsible for what happened to my mom."

"But just wishing isn't the same as magic."

"I know that intellectually. Even when I was a kid I'd tell myself that I didn't have anything to do with what happened. But knowing something here," he tapped his head, "and here," he touched his stomach, "aren't the same thing."

He wiped his eyes. "What made it worse was that Mom did believe in magic, kind of. Even before the stroke she'd been a real positive person. Afterwards she convinced herself she could get well if she just believed strongly enough. So she practiced creative visualization, positive thinking, she went to faith healers, the whole nine yards. And none of it helped. Some days she'd be a little better and that was due to whatever new method she'd latched on to. Then other days she'd be worse, but she tried to ignore those. And she'd just bounce back every time, all positive and cheerful and so Goddamned *convinced* that all she had to do was believe a little harder. And I'd watch her and I'd know it wasn't doing any good and just hurt so damn much I'd die a little inside every time."

"No wonder you hate magic," Judy said quietly.

"After she died it didn't much matter for a long time. But well, when I met you and you did all this stuff, I just couldn't handle it."

Judy reached out for his hand again. "Look, Andy, I am who I am and I'm not going to change that for anyone. I'm really sorry about what happened to your

mother, but it wasn't magic, okay? Magic isn't *magic* —
if you know what I mean. It doesn't work all the time
and even when it does work it can't fix everything." She
gave him a gamin grin. "One of the magical laws is that
shit happens and it happens to everyone. The best
magic can do for us is maybe lighten the load a little."

Andy smiled back, a little shaky. "I'm sorry to dump
all this on you."

"I'm glad you told me," Judy said. "It helps me understand you and right now that's kind of important to me."

"It's important to me too," he told her. "Say, have you
got any more of that tea?"

Chapter 21

Pauline Patterson placed the last dot on her map and wrote the reference number beside it with a shaky hand.

Out in the living room the television was going as Anne and her husband anesthetized themselves with the latest innane comedy about people just like themselves, only dumber.

She sighed. That wasn't really fair, she told herself. Anne and James did their best.

She had never gotten along very well with Anne. They were too different. Pauline Patterson was a fighter, an explorer, and Anne was, well, Anne. Her idea of an adventure was to go to Disney World and her highest goal was to be thought well of by her neighbors.

Carrie was much more like her mother. But Carrie's career kept her travelling, and a New York apartment was no place for an invalid alone.

Like some useless old thing that had to be stored, she thought sourly. *Most societies pay more respect to their dead ancestors than we do to our living ones.*

She sighed and set down the pen. It wasn't really Anne and James, or Carrie. It was her. The real problem was she was sick and tired of being sick and tired. Of being trapped in a body that failed her and left her semihelpless.

Consider the alternative, Pauline Patterson told herself wryly. Not that she hadn't. She considered the alternative every day, just as every morning she checked her carefully hidden hoard of sleeping pills. There

would come a time when she'd probably need them —
if she wasn't lucky enough to die outright from the next
stroke or unlucky enough to be left a helpless vegetable.

When? Probably before she finished her fieldwork,
never mind getting the data organized and written up
for publication. She sighed. Well she had the rest of
today and probably tomorrow. Beyond that? She might
know more tomorrow or the next day.

She couldn't really say she'd be sorry when it happened, just as long as it happened quickly and didn't
leave her a vegetable with tubes up her nose. She felt so
— disconnected. As if she were less and less a part of
this world every day. It wasn't just that she didn't have
the energy or enthusiasm she used to, it was that somehow it all seemed less important, as if she was just
drifting away from everything.

Now this new turn in her research had brought her
partway back, but even that was loosening. It was all
finite, increasingly unimportant. Maybe that was what
was driving her to do what she intended to do tonight.
Maybe it was an effort to reconnect somehow by taking
drastic action.

She shook off the mood and focused again on her map,
scowling at the size of the notation she had just made. It
used to be she could annotate almost microscopically fine
so as not to obscure details. Now the spidery markings
almost blotted out the map in some places.

Since the day something had eaten her lunch she had
spent hours going through her tapes, listening for any
references to haunting or unusual events in the mall.
Slowly, painstakingly, she had built up a sizable collection of reports. It was all ambiguous and some of it was
maddeningly vague, but taken together all those bits
and pieces made a pattern.

Fieldwork was like that. You pieced together scraps
and tidbits until you ended up knowing things that your
informants themselves didn't know. And Pauline Patterson was a damn fine fieldworker.

The map was the first fruits of her labors. By correlating the incidents mentioned by her informants with times and locations, she had gotten a feeling for where the phenomenon was the strongest. Although things had happened all over the mall, the effect was most pronounced at the eastern end, around South Court. Further, there were more incidents at night than in the daytime and the later at night the more reports, up to the time the mall closed.

Finally, the number of incidents apparently didn't correlate with the number of people present, except perhaps negatively.

That fitted the pattern of something shy and nocturnal. Something that was more likely to show itself at night when the mall was deserted.

She looked down at the map and snorted. So far it was all hypothetical. She knew from bitter experience that humans were very good at finding patterns in masses of ambiguous data even if there was no pattern there. True, she had seen something, but that didn't mean it was related to the mythology of the mall. Her experienced, professional side kept telling her she could be very wrong.

But there was another side that simply didn't care. She was tired of caution. She was tired of waiting and most of all she was tired of doing nothing.

Pauline Patterson grasped the edge of the table with her good hand and pulled herself erect. At least with this she could do something.

Heather sucked up the last of her Coke and felt like utter shit. *Goddamn that freaky bitch and her purple bottle and her pig boyfriend!* After the fight in the shop she had gone home long enough to steal her mom's checkbook and forged a couple of checks to buy booze. Then she'd gone to that old freak Perry's apartment. He let her stay and she let him fuck her. Meanwhile they went through the liquor and some 'ludes Perry had.

That had lasted two days. This afternoon they'd had a big fight and he'd thrown her out.

Now she was back in the mall, hung over, and sore from some of the stuff Perry had made her do. There was probably a warrant out for her too. At least that's what her mom had threatened the last time she'd forged her name on a check.

Heather slurped the Coke viciously. Why the fuck couldn't they just have left it alone?

Well, that was over and turned to shit. Like everything else in her life. So what? She'd get by just fine, like she always did.

In the corner of the Food Court the neon of the hot dog sign reflected off the stainless steel cold case of another booth. A trick of the light turned the reflection a deep amethyst purple. Heather's vision blurred with tears, and she shifted sharply to get the patch of color out of her sight.

Fuck 'em! Fuck 'em all!

Anne turned at the sound of Pauline Patterson's walker. "Where are you going, Mom?" she called over the back of the couch. James didn't move, caught up in the flickering silliness on the television.

"To the mini-mart. I need another legal pad."

"We've got paper here."

"No, I want something consistent with what I've been using."

"If you will wait a few minutes James or I will drive you." James grunted something that might have been assent.

"That's all right. I want the exercise. In fact I may stop by the park for a bit on my way back."

Anne frowned. "Well, be careful then. The weather report says it may rain."

Once out the door Pauline Patterson made for the telephone at the mini-mart. The dial-a-ride bus for the handicapped ran until 8 P.M. and that would get her to the mall in plenty of time.

❖   ❖   ❖

Heather stepped out into the open air and looked up
at the sky. It was low and threatening and the air
smelled of ozone and rain. *Shit.* It was going to rain for
sure. That meant she couldn't sleep out tonight. There
was one other alternative. If they caught her she'd probably wind up in juvie again. Well, she'd just have to
make sure she didn't get caught.

She turned around and headed back into the mall,
working her way through the flow of people leaving.

Pauline Patterson dawdled through Sudstrom's, looking at this, examining that. Always careful not to stay in
one place too long or to be too conspicuous.

*How inconspicuous can you be when you're pushing
a damn aluminum scaffolding around in front of you?*
Still, she managed to avoid attracting obvious attention
and timed things to end up at the back of ladies' clothing at precisely 9 P.M.

In her research, Dr. Patterson hadn't paid a lot of
attention to habits of the janitorial service, but just by
hanging around and listening carefully she had picked
up a lot of information that was going to come in useful
tonight.

Fortunately it was a slow night. The clerks had done
most of their paperwork already and they were eager to
finish up and go home. By this time Pauline knew the
maze of racks and aisles nearly as well as the clerks did.
By bending almost double over her walker and changing positions at just the right instant she could avoid the
clerks' cursory sweep of the aisles.

As she ducked behind one rack, stepped between
two others and froze in a posture that blended her and
her walker into her surroundings, she remembered
Kwame, who had taught her the rudiments of tracking
and moving quietly through the African bush. *I wonder
what'd he'd make of how I'm using his lessons?*

As best she could, she twisted her head to check the

ceiling. The department store didn't have the net of security cameras that covered the mall proper, but it had its own cameras and security arrangements. There would be one final sweep through the area by store security and then there would be only the cleaning crews to worry about.

One thing she had learned was that the store only cleaned the dressing rooms every other night. The store staff kept them picked up during the day, and the day porter took out the trash before he went off, but the area was only vacuumed on alternate evenings.

It was still risky. If the guard was unusually alert there was no way she could avoid being spotted, but she didn't think she would be. Unless maybe Anne got nervous because she hadn't come home and called mall security. Pauline's mouth half-twisted. *And they call* me *an old woman!*

Well, what if she was discovered? It would be sticky, of course, but she was an old woman who'd had a stroke. She didn't have to have a sensible explanation for her actions. Just act a little confused and they'd call Anne to come and get her.

Heather's plan was more direct than Pauline's. She simply hung around the Food Court until 9, nursing a Coke. They wouldn't come through the place kicking everyone out until 9:15 and by that time she could put the second part into action.

The guard was early. It was barely 9:10 by Pauline's watch when the young woman in the Sudstrom's blazer came through to check the area. She simply glanced down the aisles, bending down every so often to look under the racks and checking the registers at the sales stations to make sure the registers were empty and open. She came within three feet of where Pauline crouched between two clothes racks before moving on to the next department.

As soon as the guard was gone and the lights dimmed, Pauline made her way to the changing area and to Dressing Room G, the one furthest from the door. The changing area wasn't merely dim, it was dark. She moved slowly, using her walker as an antenna to sense obstacles ahead of her since her night vision was so poor these days.

Carefully, she opened the dressing room door just so. The mirror caught the other wall and reflected it back. Unless you looked carefully it appeared that the door was fully open and the dressing room was as empty as the others.

Using her good hand to assist her bad leg she eased her feet up onto the seat and sat sideways. Fortunately she was petite so she fit easily.

Now all she had to do was wait until after midnight when the cleaning crews left.

I should have brought a lunch, Pauline Patterson thought.

Heather had picked her table carefully. It was about halfway back in the Food Court and next to a blank wall that separated the Potato Palace from the Drunken Dog. That section was blank because the service corridor was behind it. The door was supposed to be locked except it never was. The janitors left it open so they could clean up at the Food Court without having to hassle with the door every time they took out trash.

Looking around without seeming to, Heather waited until no one was looking and slipped through the door into the corridor.

"Hey, you!" came a gruff voice. "You not supposed to be here."

Heather's heart nearly stopped, but with the assumed ease of a born con man she turned and smiled brightly at her accuser. It was the crazy Greek guy from the ice cream stand.

"Oh, hi. You startled me." She increased the wattage on her smile.

"What you doing back here?" George Andropolous demanded suspiciously.

"I'm helping Johnny Chou clean up. We're going out as soon as he's done."

"No one allowed back here but employees."

"Well, I am an employee — sort of," Heather retorted. "Go ask Johnny if you don't believe me."

Andropolous glared. Chou's Southern Suzechan Chow Fried Chicken was clear around on the other side of the Food Court and he wasn't about to go all the way over there. He'd never seen John Chou in a close personal relationship with anything but a book, but so what? Kids that age will take up with anything in a skirt.

Besides, the Chou kid had been accepted to Stanford and never stopped talking about it. To Andropolous, who hadn't finished the sixth grade, that smacked of bragging, not to mention lording it over his elders.

Well what the hell? If he got mixed up with someone like this little tramp it was no better than he deserved.

"I'm gonna report this."

Heather didn't deign to reply. Instead she sauntered down the corridor and around the corner. As soon as she was out of sight she ran.

The service corridors behind the Food Court were a maze with lots of blind alleys and sharp, funny curves. The food booths weren't supposed to store stuff in them but they did anyway. If you knew which people cleaned up early and left and which ones took their time you could shift around so that you wouldn't be spotted, even by the security cameras. Heather moved hiding places three times and tucked in behind a waist-high stack of boxes of ecologically sound, recyclable paper plates when the guard made his first sweep. Then the lights went out and Heather knew she'd have an hour or so before she'd have to move. There wasn't anyplace in the service corridors to sleep, but she knew a place down by

South Court where she wouldn't be found. If she timed it right she could get into the fancy bathroom upstairs at Sudstrom's tomorrow morning and even get cleaned up a little.

Pauline Patterson was dozing when the sound jerked her awake.

Voices! Someone was coming.

Damn! There wasn't supposed to be anyone on this floor. Had she been discovered? She looked up at the ceiling. Maybe those damn cameras could see in the dark after all.

For the first time it occurred to her that if she was found it could be more than sticky. It could be taken as evidence of inevitable mental deterioration. James was already hinting vaguely about an "assisted-care facility," and Anne wasn't resisting very hard. If she blew this she could end up in a nursing home.

The lights in the dressing area flickered on. She held her breath and squinched down in an effort to make herself smaller.

Then the voices again. Pauline realized they were speaking Spanish. There was the sound of a trash can being moved and a rustling noise as the liner full of trash was taken out. Then more rustling as the new one was put in and all the time the machine gun dialogue in Spanish. It was slangy and full of colloquialisms, but Pauline realized one of the janitors was bragging to the other about his car — or maybe his girlfriend, some of the terms were ambiguous. Then the lights went out and the janitors moved on to the rest of the floor's trash.

Pauline Patterson let out her breath slowly and realized she suddenly had to go to the bathroom very badly. *Suffer!* she told her aching bladder and went back to her vigil.

Heather spent her time in the darkened corridor half dozing and thinking. She ought to get the fuck away from this place, all the people, the mall. It just wasn't worth hanging around any more.

But there wasn't anywhere any better to go. She fantasized about finding her father, but even that wasn't satisfying any more. He'd never tried to see her after the divorce, even before they left Michigan. There'd never been so much as a birthday card since. For a long time Heather had been convinced that her mother was intercepting her mail and destroying anything her father sent her. When she was thirteen she'd stayed home from school by playing sick or ditching a lot so she could check the mailbox before her mother got to it. There hadn't been anything.

It was like there wasn't anything left inside her. Like she just wanted to drift away from everyone and everything and sleep forever. The second time she tried to commit suicide she'd taken a lot of sleeping pills and whiskey in the hope it would be like that. But it wasn't. The liquor made her sick and she threw it all up before the pills could even make her drowsy. She snorted in the darkness. Like everything else in her life that had fucked up and turned to shit too.

Maybe some day she'd try again. Take a humongous load of coke or something. But not tonight. Tonight she had to outsmart the mall pigs to find a place to sleep. Checking her watch, Heather moved down the corridor on the first leg of her journey.

Pauline didn't know how long she waited in the dark after the janitors left. She probably dozed some, as much as her bladder would let her. Finally, when the luminous hands of her watch told her it was after midnight, she uncoiled herself, lifted her bad leg down off the seat and set out. Once she was out of the fitting room area and back on the main floor of the store she stretched as best she could and breathed a gusty sigh.

Now it was time to get down to business. But first

there was one other thing to attend to. Feeling for the door in the dark, she found the bathroom.

Heather listened at the door until she was sure no one was outside. Then she turned the latch, opened it a crack and slipped through. Instantly she ducked down behind a table and listened.

The Food Court looked bigger now. The food booths were dark and half the lights in the main area were off, so the room seemed to smudge off into echoing shadows rather than end at the walls. Because it was a big place there were two cameras covering it. She watched them sweep back and forth over the area on their mindless mechanical rounds. She let them make three sweeps until she was sure she had the rhythm.

She watched the closest camera swivel on its mount for the fourth time. When it was as far from her as it got, she dashed across the open space and crouched behind a planter. The second camera had just finished its sweep past her location. She gulped a couple of deep breaths and ran again. The sound of her footsteps echoed in the stillness of the mall.

Pauline Patterson stood at the top of a cliff and contemplated her options.

The cliff was actually the Sudstrom's escalator, but for a partially paralyzed old woman it was as formidable as a Class Three overhang to a veteran rock climber.

She had brought a thin piece of plastic to slip the lock on the exterior door, but she hadn't realized the doors to the fire stairs were alarmed. Of course the elevators weren't running. If she was going to get out of here it would have to be down the yawning black stretch of the escalator. She leaned on her walker while she tried to decide if she wanted to get down that badly.

At the Rehab Center they had taught her how to get down stairs with the walker. They had also warned her against it unless she had to. The escalator was narrower and the steps higher than the stairs she had so tentatively negotiated under the watchful eye of the physical therapist in the brightly lighted Rehab Center.

There wasn't room to edge down sideways. She'd have to go down facing front or back. Either one was an invitation to disaster. Going down face-first with the walker meant staying bent over and off balance the whole way down. Backing down meant she couldn't see the steps. Front or back, a misstep and she could break her neck.

Breaking her neck didn't bother her. She'd be dead and it would be over with. It was the thought of breaking her hip or leg that terrified her, of being immobilized and ending her days bedfast in the living hell of a nursing home with not even the possibility of suicide to end her suffering.

Did she really want to do this that badly? Was she really willing to risk ending up like that just to know what was happening here?

Hell yes! she thought.

Slowly, carefully and with all the caution she could muster, Pauline Patterson began to back down the escalator.

Heather scuttled from the shadows to crouch next to a planter at the top of the now-still escalator. The most dangerous part was getting down to the ground floor. You had to use the escalators since the stairwells were alarmed and the elevators were locked. While you were on it you were exposed to the cameras, and the guard could see you from half the mall.

There was a space maybe two feet high under the South Court stage where they stored tarps and stuff. It wasn't locked, just latched, and if you pulled the sliding door shut after you, they'd never find you. Some of the kids had gotten in there and fucked while the mall was open. It would be plenty good enough as a place to sleep when the mall was closed.

The trick was getting to South Court. That meant staying in the shadows and moving slow so you didn't attract the attention of the guard flipping around between the cameras and listening for the guard making patrols.

Shit! Security guard. Heather crouched lower and held her breath. She thought for a minute it was the witch's boyfriend, but it wasn't. It was the middle-aged Mexican guy. The mean one.

The sound of his footsteps changed as he stepped from the steel escalator to the terrazzo pavement. His heavy breathing seemed to rasp in her ear. Out of the corner of her eye Heather could see his pant leg and scuffed black oxford, close enough to touch. *Go on, get the fuck away!* she screamed silently. But instead he turned and leaned on the rail, looking back out over the mall. Four feet away Heather stayed frozen, trying not to breathe.

Halfway down the escalator Pauline knew she had made a mistake — probably a fatal one. She hadn't thought this would be easy, but it was harder and more demanding than she had imagined. By the time she was a third of the way down, her good arm was burning and her calf muscles were cramping in agony. Twice her toe caught the edge of the step and slipped off, bringing her heart-stoppingly close to a fall. She was breathing in heaving gasps and sweat trickled from her forehead and stung her eyes. She couldn't even shift position to wipe it away without risking a fall.

She wasn't going to make it. She couldn't finish the climb unless she sat down and rested, and there was no place on the escalator to rest.

She couldn't go up. That would be even harder. She couldn't really rest. All she could do was keep going. Carefully, painfully, she took another step.

Her foot missed entirely and she fell backwards down the chasm of the escalator. Her good hand grabbed for the rail and missed, slapping against the smooth metal side of the escalator. The force of her frantic lunge pushed her paralyzed shoulder against the opposite side. The combined friction slowed her and she ended up flat on her back head-down on the escalator with her walker laying on top of her.

Pauline Patterson lay for an instant looking up at the darkened ceiling. Then she wiggled the fingers on her left hand. Then she moved her arm experimentally. Next she wiggled her left toes. They worked. She moved the leg. There was a place on her thigh that hurt like hell, but everything worked. As best she could, she checked her right side. Nothing seemed to be broken there either.

She laughed aloud in the darkened empty store out of sheer relief. She was going to have a collection of bruises that would be damn hard to explain to Anne and she'd probably hurt like hell for weeks, but none of that mattered. She was all right. All she had to do was lever herself up and keep going.

Wait a minute, dummy! You needed to sit down and rest, right? So lay here and rest. It wasn't the most comfortable position but it let her relax her sore muscles. Well content, Pauline Patterson rested prone on the escalator.

It seemed like hours before the guard moved. Heather was giddy from taking only infrequent, shallow breaths and her legs ached from crouching. But at last the guard turned away from the railing and ambled off down the mall. As quietly as she could, Heather sucked in deep lungfuls of air. She turned and sat with her legs stretched out to get the cramps out. Then she looked off down the mall. Somewhere behind her the guard was continuing his rounds, but before her the mall was silent and empty.

Heather scrambled out of her jacket. The shiny studs would reflect light and that might attract the cameras while she worked her way down the escalator. She folded the jacket so the dark lining was outside. Then she crouched and duck-walked to the escalator. Keeping crouched over, she crept down the escalator.

It took a long time before she reached the bottom, and her legs and knees were killing her when she got there. Barely rising from the crouch she scuttled off the escalator and into the shelter of the shadowy overhang of a store's doorway.

She was at the East Court. That meant she had half the mall to go before she reached her destination. But at least she was on the ground floor and the guard was somewhere else.

Keeping to the edges and shadows, Heather made her way down the mall.

The first sign was the sound of falling water.

Pauline heard it even before she opened the service door. In the minute or so it took her to block the sensor and slip the lock the water sound seemed to grow louder, as if it was a torrent rather than a decorative waterfall.

She couldn't see the South Court until she'd dragged herself and her walker through the door. The fountain was off but water still poured from the rock and into the pool. Pauline stopped dead and gasped at the sight.

The water in the pool had gone white, like someone had dumped gallons and gallons of milk in it. Even the water gushing out of the rock was white.

Only it wasn't just white, she saw. It was shiny on the surface with little rainbow glints of color. There was spray, or maybe mist, rising from the surface of the pool with rainbows flashing here and there as the light caught it. Then the rainbow bits shifted and moved to make a complete arch in the thickening white mist.

There was something in the mist that drew Pauline closer. Instead of thinning as she approached it seemed to grow thicker, until it was a solid milky wall shot through with opalescent bits of rainbow color.

The colors shifted and chased each other through the translucent white mist. They shifted and sparkled and faded away to nothing and flamed back brighter than ever. They grew and shattered and reformed to make fleeting patterns on the white. And as they did, the patterns became pictures.

A *picture*, Heather thought. *A picture on the fog*. There was a rainbow arching through the mist, and the sound of falling water was a roaring thunder in her ears. But it was the picture that caught and held her. A bright grassy meadow, rimmed about with ancient trees bearing big pale blossoms. There were clouds in the sky and ranges of purple hills in the distance. It reminded her of Michigan in high summer, but the woods of Michigan had never been this vivid or this bright. The air between was like crystal, solid and totally transparent. Just by looking, Heather could see every leaf and flower. The wet air carried the wonderfully sweet scents of new grass and brightly blooming flowers.

Heather stepped out in the open, all fear of discovery gone.

For the first time in years she could move without pain. Pauline stretched upright and sucked in a huge breath of wonderfully sweet air. There was joy in the air and more joy in every motion of her body. Unconsciously she squared her shoulders and lengthened her stride, all her attention focused on the rainbow and the mist-shrouded land beneath it.

Vaguely, Heather realized she wasn't alone. The old lady with the tape recorder was beside her. But that was okay. No, more than okay, it was *right*. Everything was right and wonderful and better than any drug trip she'd ever taken. She was so happy she felt as if her heart would burst from her chest and her cheeks were wet with the first tears of joy Heather had ever cried.

They reached the edge of the fountain together. For a brief instant Heather and Pauline hesitated on the verge of the mist. They looked at each other, almost shyly, and then Pauline reached out, took Heather's hand and smiled.

Hand in hand the old woman and the young woman stepped through the circle of rainbow light.

Chapter 22

Andy knew something was wrong as soon as he stepped into the security office. In addition to the regular shift a bunch of the other guards were milling around in civvies, talking low. Then he saw the police officers, two uniforms and a couple of detectives. The door to Dunlap's office was closed, as if he was in there with someone.

"Gonna be a meeting," Morales said by way of greeting, "soon as Dunlap gets finished." Almost immediately the office door opened and Dunlap ushered a couple out. The woman had looked pinched and drawn. Her eyes were red from crying. The man was red-faced and blustering.

"If we hear anything, Mr. Gerstin, we'll call you immediately," Dunlap assured them.

"You'll hear from us anyway," the man said loudly. "Or from our lawyer."

Police and guards alike pretended not to notice as the pair stormed out. "Meeting time, everyone," Dunlap called as soon as the door closed behind them. "Into the squad room."

The guards filed in and found seats around the long table or against the wall. The cops stayed outside and kept doing whatever.

"Close the door, will you?" Dunlap said as he took the podium in front of the blackboard. "Okay. We've got a missing person, possibly a kidnap victim."

Dunlap looked down and began reading off his clipboard. "Subject's name is Pauline Logan Patterson."

Andy's fingers clenched and his pen made an ugly scrawl down the pad. He forced himself back to what Dunlap was saying. "Age seventy-two, Caucasian female about five-three or five-four, white hair, blue eyes. Subject is partially paralyzed on her right side and needs a walker to get around."

He looked up from the clipboard. "Some of you may remember her. She spent a lot of time in the mall." A few heads nodded. "She left home around seven last night, telling her daughter and son-in-law she was going to the mini-mart. Instead she apparently came here."

One of the men against the wall raised his hand. "Are we sure she came to the mall?"

"The disabled dial-a-ride dropped her here about eight and there's no record they picked her up again. Also, a couple of people remember seeing her.

"When she didn't come home last night her family called the police. By six a.m. they were pounding on our door. When we searched the mall we found her walker over in the South Court. No clothes, no other effects, but her daughter says she can't get far without the walker. Not by herself anyway."

"And in the bushes we found this." He pulled out a black vinyl jacket decorated with cheap chrome studs. "Recognize it?"

"It looks like the jacket one of the mall rats wears," said a slender oriental woman in street clothes. "Heather something."

"Heather Framel," Dunlap supplied. "It sure as hell does."

"Any sign of the kid?"

"The cops are checking on that. They say the mother says she hasn't seen the kid in a couple of days."

"She won't go home when the mother's boyfriend is there," Andy put in.

"How the hell do you know that?"

Andy shrugged. "You get to talking, you know."

Dunlap glared at Andy like he did know and he

wasn't happy about it. "Well if the cops ask, you tell them that. But don't go volunteering stuff." He turned back to the group. "Anyway, the cops say that none of her friends seem to know where she is."

"Was that stuff here last night when the mall closed?" LaVonne asked.

"The walker sure as hell wasn't. The jacket?" He shrugged. "Maintenance said they checked the planters like always and didn't see anything. The cops are talking to that hippy gardener who found it." Dunlap grinned. "It'll be interesting to see what the hell they make of that."

"What do the tapes show?" someone behind Andy asked.

"The cops are reviewing them now. But so far, nothing." He scowled even more fiercely. "Among other things the whole circuit to the South Court went out about eleven p.m. Those recorders got zip."

"Tampered?" LaVonne Sanders asked.

"Not obviously. They're checking that." He paused and looked out over his audience.

"Anyway, people, we're going to have police in here for the next couple of days. Naturally we extend them every courtesy." He smiled ironically. "But if they want anything special or want to go anywhere in the nonpublic areas, you check with me first. Tell them it's the damn insurance rules or something.

"Now we don't want any rumors starting. There's no proof these two are in the mall or even that anything happened to them. But the sooner they're found the better and we don't want any nasty surprises." He looked over the packed room. "So, keep your eyes open. Don't go playing Columbo and asking customers or merchants questions. But if you see anything or hear anything report it to me. Not the police, me."

He glanced down at his clipboard. "We'll post full descriptions and pictures on the bulletin board as soon as we get them.

"Okay, that's it. Those of you on duty go punch in and get out there. The rest of you can go home." There was a shuffling of feet and a scraping of chairs as everyone rose.

"You think the kid offed the old lady?" Henderson asked Morales as they left the briefing room right in front of Andy.

"Maybe. Or maybe it was a double suicide. Neither of them had much to live for, seems like."

"I just hope we find the bodies before they start to stink," Henderson said with a shake of his head. "Jesus, can you imagine what a mess that would be?"

Andy was very glad to get away from the office and out on patrol.

Andy found Judy in her shop, sorting candles.

"Dr. Patterson and Heather are missing," Andy said as she opened her mouth to greet him. "Apparently they were both in the mall last night after closing and something happened to them over by South Court."

A pair of white-haired joggers in matching red running suits collapsed on the bench across the corridor. The woman was flushed, and her eyes sparkled. The man was leaning against the wall, puffing and blowing.

"Missing?" Judy stood up. "What were they doing?"

"It rained last night," Andy said in a low voice. "I think Heather tried to sleep inside the mall. Dr. Patterson . . ." He shrugged. "But I'd guess it had something to do with her research."

"Do you know what Dr. Patterson was working on?"

"Not exactly. But she hinted to me that her research was off on a new track. Something she said made me think she was investigating —" he trailed off and glanced over at the joggers — "things."

The man produced a water bottle from his belt and offered the woman a drink. When she declined he poured most of the contents down his throat, swallowing noisily.

"Don't worry, they're all right," Judy told him. "I know they're both happy."

"Well what happened to them?"

"I don't know, but it wasn't something bad," Judy said positively.

"Another of your feelings?"

"A little more than that."

"Judy?"

"Yes?"

"What was that spell you put on Heather?"

Her eyes widened. "It was a protection spell, something to keep her safe and help her make right choices." Her voice hardened. "And just what do you mean by that?"

"The last time you tried to use magic on — somebody — you ended up giving her a case of hives."

"And you think I . . . ? No, that's impossible. It doesn't work that way. Besides they're both safe and well. I know."

The joggers got up and trotted off, headed in the direction of the main concourse. Andy didn't say anything.

"I just know," Judy repeated.

So, how do you tell when a politician is hiding in your shower? Andy wondered as he came into the South Court. Blackie had discovered humor and for the last couple of nights he and Andy had been swapping jokes at every terminal. Apparently Blackie was learning by trial and error. His jokes still tended to be more bizarre than funny. However, Andy admitted as he checked the perimeter of the court, more and more of them were bizarrely funny.

He looked across the shadow-patterned statue garden and sighed at the immobile figures there. There were seven of them, just as there should be. Nothing moved and even the noise of the fountain seemed to be swallowed up in the stillness and silence.

Well, I guess it worked, Andy thought half regretfully as he slid his card into the slot by the elevator. It was nearly 4 A.M. and so far not one weird thing had happened.

He wasn't sure if he was glad or not. He didn't want the elf mad but he wouldn't have minded seeing her again. As he waited for the elevator in the stillness, he checked his watch. Good. At least tonight he'd make his rounds on time.

As the elevator doors hissed shut he thought he saw motion in the shrubbery by the statue garden. For an instant he considered going back to check. But by the time the elevator passed the second level he decided it was his imagination and he was back to wondering about politicians hiding in shower stalls.

The doors were still closing when a shadow convulsed and swelled to tower above the bushes and statues of South Court. It shambled forward until the lights at the front of Sudstrom's brought it into focus. What had seemed a trick of darkness resolved into a bearlike thing covered in coarse, trailing fur. It was built something like a teddy bear, with a stubby body, short thick limbs and a head that seemed too large for its torso. But it stood head and shoulders above the life-size statues in the garden.

It lifted its great head and exhaled with an echoing "WHUFF." Then it breathed deeply, craning its neck this way and that, testing the air for any sign of the thing it sought. The pupils in its huge dark eyes contracted and then opened again as it searched.

Satisfied that the man was far away, the beast turned and lumbered off down the mall. In spite of its bulk, it moved as noiselessly as the wind. It passed a dozen security cameras but none recorded its passage.

Its path led it back to an escalator and up two levels. The taste of what it sought was still faint, but it grew stronger as it climbed. It eased along on the third level, keeping to the shadows and unrecorded by the cameras.

Closer and closer, with the trace of its prey becoming stronger in its senses.

Then it froze. The human it had seen on the first level was ahead, between it and the thing it so desperately sought.

The ice troll was not normally shy of something as puny as man, but it was under a compulsion to avoid contact while it searched that was nearly as strong as its compulsion to seek the thing its masters desired. Carefully, gently, it eased forward, keeping to the shadows and ready to spring at any moment. If it could not avoid the creatures of this world, the geas commanded it kill them.

But the human remained hunched over the glowing screen of the kiosk, oblivious to the shadow gliding by not twenty-five feet away.

BUT THAT DOESN'T MAKE ANY SENSE, Andy had just typed.

NEITHER DID THE ONE ABOUT THE POLE WITH THE THREE WISHES, Blackie retorted.

The troll slithered by and whipped around the corner before the man cast his eyes to the ceiling in exasperation.

The obstacle passed, the ice troll shambled down the arcade and paused before Bellbookand. The trace was stronger here, stronger than any place else in the mall. The thing must be within.

It recognized the signs around the shop. They made the monster uncomfortable, but the creature was driven by a compulsion deeper than discomfort. It raised a paw to rip the grating from its mounting. Then it hesitated.

Something moved inside. A tiny manlike form appeared on the counter. Then another and another. Three little creatures and one great one stood unmoving, locked in silent battle.

With a whine of frustration, the ice troll sheathed its claws and lowered its paw. Charms and simples it could defeat, but not the power of these little ones acting under ancient bargain. The holder of this place had fed them and in return they gave help and protection. It would take more than an ice troll's powers to cross this threshold uninvited.

The troll snorted, shook its shaggy head and turned away. The sun would rise soon and it wanted to be back in its lair by dawn. Let the masters send others to search this place — or come themselves if they cared to. As noiselessly as it had come, the ice troll lumbered back out of the arcade into the now-deserted main concourse and toward the motionless escalators.

Andy was worrying about Dan Quayle.

Blackie wanted a new joke at every terminal, and Andy was running out of them. The only ones he could think of involved sexual perversions or Dan Quayle. Andy didn't even want to try sex jokes on a computer, and he wasn't at all sure he could explain who Dan Quayle was to Blackie — never mind why he was funny.

I'll have to stop by the bookstore and pick up a joke book tomorrow.

Off in the distance, something moved on the lower level. Andy had a glimpse of a bulky, gray-furred form as it vanished silently around a corner.

A polar bear in a wookie suit?

Andy stopped dead and thumbed his radio. "Base, this is Unit Three. I just saw something down on Level One near the South Reach and I'm going to break my round and investigate."

"Base to Unit Three," Tuchetti's voice came back. "What was it? Over."

"Uh, I'm not sure. Let me check and get back to you."

"Affirmative, Unit Three. You're logged and check back in ten."

He was about halfway between elevators and the escalators weren't working, so it took several minutes to double back and descend the two levels to the bottom.

He could have done it faster, but he was being cautious.

Whatever it was, was long gone by the time Andy reached the spot and a quick check down the mall showed no sign of it.

There were no footprints on the polished terrazzo floor and no other physical signs. For a minute Andy was reduced to staring helplessly at the corner. Then he noticed something.

There was a dance supply store on the corner with three mannequins in the window. One of the male mannequins was holding a female mannequin aloft in a ballet pose.

The thing's head had blocked out the topmost mannequin when it went by. Considering the sight lines, that meant it was at least eight feet tall.

The hair on Andy's neck prickled and his hand moved instinctively toward his gun.

Then he stopped and looked down at his pistol. *Fat chance*. Even if he put all six shots in a vital area he wouldn't bet on stopping something that big. A .38 Special was no big-game round and the nonpenetrating Glaser rounds kept down the risk of injuring someone with a ricochet or by shooting through a wall, but they sure weren't designed for something the size of a polar bear.

Andy's radio broke the silence. "Base to Unit Three."

"Unit Three."

"What's happening there? It's been ten minutes."

"Uh, nothing," Andy told the security center sheepishly. "I guess it wasn't anything after all."

Tuchetti's coarse chuckle came over the speaker. "Well, don't let the bogeyman get you."

Andy chuckled back, weakly. "Roger on that. Unit Three back on round and out."

Andy's mind was working furiously as he climbed the unmoving escalator. Despite what he'd told Tuchetti, he knew damn well he had seen something. And whatever it was he wasn't at all anxious to meet.

Was that one of the "agents" the elf woman had told him about? Made sense. He had gotten a good enough look at the beast to know he'd never seen anything like it, even in pictures. If it was from the other world it might *really* take some stopping.

For some reason he remembered the dead cat he had found that first week, the one that had been torn apart.

An idea began to form in the back of his mind. *Well, that's for tomorrow,* he thought. *There's nothing I can do tonight except be careful.* He looked back at the place where the thing's head had been. *Very, very careful.*

The ice troll could stand a world without magic, but it was nocturnal and a being of the icy wastes. It preferred to sleep away the days in a cold cavern. As the first rays of dawn peeked through the smog layer, the creature stopped its restless prowling and turned toward its lair.

The door to the service corridor was locked, but the troll had only to touch the knob and it swung open. The creature disappeared down the dark corridor just before Andy came by on his last round.

The corridor led to another door, and beyond that was a flight of steps and a third door, this one alarmed as well as locked. Again, a touch of the huge claws and the door unlocked magically.

The fourth and final door was larger and heavier than any of the others. It carried a time clock as well as an alarm. But it too yielded to a touch. A welcome burst of cold air hit the troll as the door swung inward and the thing stepped over the threshold.

The sign on the door told humans what this place was, but the troll couldn't read and didn't care. All it knew was it had found a place that was cold and usually dark and smelled very faintly of dead animals. The room wasn't cold enough or smelly enough to be home for an ice troll, but it would do.

The lights had come on automatically, not that the troll needed them. Before it stood rank after rank of animal skins. Around the room's back and sides were locked metal mesh cages holding more animal skins. Unhesitatingly, the thing shuffled toward the cage at the very back. Another touch of its claws and the lock sprang open. The ice troll entered and pushed its way through. There, hidden behind the hanging skins, it curled up on the floor, closed its great yellow hawk eyes and dropped noiselessly off to sleep.

As it drifted away, its magical field weakened and the doors closed and the locks relocked. As the door slammed shut the lights went out.

Andy stepped through the door and breathed the sharp tang of gun oil and leather.

The wall was covered with rifles and shotguns, and the cases held pistols, knives, batons and other tools of the policeman's trade. The glass case on the wall next to the door displayed a collection of shoulder patches and badges from departments all over the United States and several foreign countries. In the corner a young clerk was helping a couple of uniformed officers who were looking at gun belts.

"Kelly around?"

The kid jerked his head toward the back and continued talking to the uniforms.

Kelly was bent over his bench, magnifying goggles down as he worked on a pistol sear with a fine diamond hone. His jaws moved mechanically on the ever-present wad of bubble gum and his elbows were braced on the armrests of his wheelchair.

An addict's bullet had ended John Kelly's days as a California highway patrolman, but the wound was low enough that it didn't keep him from using his hands. Kelly had parlayed his disability pension and an SBA set-aside loan into a gun store specializing in work for police officers.

"Hey, Kelly."

Kelly gave the sear another lick and looked up, flipping the goggles back with a toss of his head and blinking as his eyes changed focus.

"Andy. Been a while."

"Been busy. Listen, do you still do fancy loads?"

"What's the matter? Won't those rent-a-cop pissants let you use .357s?" Most of Kelly's custom reloading business involved loading .38 Special cases up to .357 Magnum ballistics for officers whose departments wouldn't let them carry the more powerful cartridge.

"Nope. They got us using Glasers."

Kelly swiveled his chair to face his visitor and snorted. "Sorriest goddamn excuse for a load there ever was. You want something better?"

"I want something special," Andy told him. "Something very special."

Kelly scowled as Andy explained. Then he shoved his bubble gum into his cheek with his tongue to keep from answering right away.

"Sure I can do it," he said finally. "I've even done it before. But it'll be expensive and the damn things are inaccurate as hell."

"I don't intend to shoot at very long range."

"Planning on being one of them TV heroes, boy?"

"Not any kind of hero I hope. How soon can I get them?"

"I'm casting again this weekend. I'll run those first, so you can pick them up Saturday afternoon."

"Great. Thanks, Kelly."

"Sounds like the crowd at that pissant mall has gotten freakier than ever."

"Kelly," Andy said feverently, "you don't know the half of it."

"And she wants her damn coat," Dawn Albright muttered under her breath, "in June!" Her cool blonde good looks didn't hide her irritation. A store security guard and a sales assistant trailed her down the corridor to the store's fur vault. The guard was bored and Pat, her assistant, was nervous.

Not only did she have to traipse all the way down to the fur vault, Dawn thought as she led the procession, she had to take another full-time sales employee with her. And then she had to hunt up a security guard. A regular expedition and all because some customer wanted her coat out of storage. The Business Boutique was short-handed anyway and taking two of them off the floor only made it worse.

It wasn't just this being sent to do something a stock-boy could have done more quickly. Early summer was the worst time of the year for women's business wear. The department's totals were down and if she couldn't boost them soon her quarterly bonus was in jeopardy.

But the crowning indignity was that it wasn't even her department! The Fur Salon was lightly staffed in the summer months and the supervisor was out sick today. There was no assistant supervisor, so the floor manager borrowed her from the Business Boutique and sent her and Pat down to get the coat.

Dawn and Pat stood by while the guard unlocked the vault door. Then he stepped aside. The store's security procedures called for him to stay at the door and check the request form against what the other two brought out.

Dawn thought the whole thing was unutterably stupid. But it was store policy and she could get fired for not following it. God knows, they'd gotten enough lectures on store security recently. Shrinkage was up again.

The fluorescents flickered on as Dawn and Pat stepped inside. The room was large and frigid. Only 50 degrees, perhaps, but that was cold compared to the weather outside, or even the air-conditioning in the store. *I'll be lucky if I don't catch cold*, Dawn thought.

The chill smelled of ozone and cedarwood. Dawn had never liked the smell of cedar. To her it was a frumpy odor, the smell of clothes kept in a closet too long rather than worn a fashionably few times and discarded to make way for the new.

She sighed as she compared the map inside the door with the number on the claim stub in her elegantly manicured hand. Naturally it would be in the far back locker.

"I could go get it while you wait here," Pat offered nervously.

"Store regulations say only the senior staffer can enter the locker. The way they are now we'd probably both be fired." She sighed ostentatiously. "Come on, let's get this nonsense over with."

The central part of the vault was full of the store's own merchandise, mostly for the Fur Salon. The racks were half empty at this time of the year because no one bought furs in the summer, even in Southern California. Around three walls were the yellow metal mesh lockers like walk-in closets that held furs being stored for customers and some of the salon's more expensive items. Those were jammed, naturally, since, stereotypes to the contrary, no one in Southern California wore furs in the summertime either.

Except for this one birdbrain waiting impatiently back in the Fur Salon.

Where does she think she's going, Dawn thought, *Antarctica?*

She unlocked the locker and stepped in. The odor of cedar and ozone was stronger and she wrinkled her nose as if to sneeze. She walked down the rack of furs, stopping occasionally to check the number against the numbers on the tickets tied to the neck of the hangers.

Naturally they were out of order. She had to work backwards and forwards from the spot where the bag was supposed to be, her irritation growing by the minute. Finally, almost at the far end of the locker, she found the item. It was a full-length mink. *Naturally*, Dawn thought as she started to heft the item off the rack.

"Hey," Pat said, "there's something on the floor."

Dawn looked down. There, peeking out from under the rack at the very end of the locker was a garment, a coat from the size of it, lying in an untidy heap. The fur was mist-gray, but long and coarse. *Dyed yak?* thought Dawn. Certainly not the kind of merchandise Sudstrom's would carry.

Dawn shifted the coat she had come for back on the rack and stooped to reach for the gray fur. Then she stopped. Very deliberately she turned her back on the heap of fur, picked up the mink, and edged her way past the rack of furs, all the while holding the heavy coat high to clear the floor.

"Aren't you going to pick it up?" Pat ventured.

"The rules say you're not supposed to handle anything except the item you came for. If that's the way they want it, that's the way we'll do it."

"What are you going to do?" Pat asked as Dawn stepped out of the locker and thrust the coat bag into her outstretched arms.

"I'll tell the Fur Salon supervisor and *she* can go through all this nonsense to come down here and pick it up off the floor," Dawn bit out. *If I remember, that is.* She didn't exactly slam the locker door, but she closed it very, very firmly. "Now come on. Let's get out of here before we freeze to death."

Feeling a shade better for her little triumph, Dawn led Pat out of the vault.

The clang of the vault door masked the snort from the fur locker where Dawn had stood.

Dunlap, Roarke and Henderson had claimed the booth at the dim back of the coffee shop. They were well out of the traffic pattern and so far back that the waitress usually forgot to bring them fresh coffee.

Henderson was in uniform, Dunlap in his blazer and Roarke in street clothes. They drank their coffee and made small talk.

Finally, Morales slid into the booth with them. "Okay, we've made contact."

"And?"

"He says he can handle it. All of it."

"Price?"

Morales shrugged. "He won't commit until he sees the stuff, but he's talking about where we figured."

"Shit. I still think we can do better than that," Henderson grumbled.

Dunlap twisted in the booth to face him. "You know someone who can handle that much stuff? No? Then keep your mouth shut. It's still going to be more money than you've ever seen." He turned back to Morales. "Okay, when?"

"End of the month or so. No sooner."

"Won't this latest thing mess us up?" Roarke asked.

Dunlap grinned. "Shit, no. It makes it better. The cameras at one whole section of the mall were out. That makes the whole thing more plausible."

"And the cops?"

"They'll be gone in a couple of days. Sooner if they find the bodies. We weren't going to do any more small jobs anyway, so we just keep going like we have and we'll have no problem."

"So when do we do it?" Henderson asked.

Dunlap did a quick calculation. It would take time to camouflage the stuff, more time to get it down to Mexico.

"Roarke, can you get the truck for the twenty-first?"

"Sure."

Dunlap thought again. The other men in the booth watched him closely.

"Okay," Dunlap said, "we do it the twenty-first.

With a roar of exhaust, nearly twenty bikers turned in to Black Oak Mall. The roar died to a rumble as two by two they paraded up the drive to the motorcycle lot across from the main entrance.

It was a fairly typical bunch of LA bikers. Most of the men were bearded and long-haired, and all of them, men and women, were artfully scruffy in faded jeans and black leather. Among them were a half-dozen out-of-work actors, a couple of stunt men, three convicted killers, a CPA, a minor figure in Iran-Contra and, last in line, Cyril Heathercoate.

The reporter was wearing a sleeveless black leather jacket, a bandana tied around his head pirate-fashion and a pair of sunglasses. On one pinkly sunburned bicep was a rub-on tattoo that read "Born to Raise Hell." One or two of the bikers glanced back at him coldly when he joined the group but so far no one had done anything.

Heathercoate's candy-red-and-chrome Harley flat-head chopper was rented from a prop company for an exorbitant amount. The brakes were marginal, the foot clutch took some getting used to and raked steering was barely legal and a handful to handle. Heathercoate had nearly fallen off twice in the two miles from the biker bar parking lot where the rental company had delivered the bike. But by the time he followed the pack up to the main entrance he was almost confident.

One by one the bikers pulled up to the main entrance to the mall and turned into the motorcycle parking area. Heathercoate was still the last in line.

LaVonne Sanders was just coming out of the east entrance as the bikers arrived. She gave them a professional but disinterested once-over and was turning to go back inside when she caught sight of the last bike in the line. The rider was pushing middle age, which wasn't all that unusual. He was clean-shaven, which was a little more unusual, and he was plump. Not fat — plenty of bikers are fat, especially the older ones. But even the fat ones look tough. The guy on the last bike looked soft. She frowned and then reached for her radio.

Heathercoate knew he was getting the once-over, so he put on his best biker scowl, cut his front wheel sharply and turned toward the motorcycle parking area.

He stomped down on the foot clutch and revved his engine to produce a blast of noise. The gesture was unnecessary because the Harley was set to idle nicely with the engine just barely ticking over. It was unfortunate because Cyril's foot slipped off the clutch pedal before the clutch was fully disengaged. It was disastrous because Heathercoate simply didn't appreciate how much raw torque the Harley's big V-twin engine had, even at idle.

The motorcycle lunged across the roadway and slammed into the row of parked motorcycles. One after another, a dozen bikes toppled over in slow, stately procession.

Heathercoate managed to stay upright and smiled weakly at the half-dozen bikers who were suddenly converging on him.

"Central," LaVonne said into her radio, "it's that reporter again."

"You need some help?" the voice came crackling back.

LaVonne looked over to where the three bikers were dragging Heathercoate away by the arms.

"Ah, that's negative," she said. "The problem's already being handled."

This, Cyril Heathercoate thought as he pulled his bruised and aching body from the dumpster a few minutes later, *is not working at all*.

Heathercoate hadn't changed his opinion by the time he got back to his motel room. *It's the bloody guards*, Heathercoate thought moodily, as he applied an ice pack to his swollen eye. *Can't get in there when they're around, now can I?* For an instant he entertained the idea of finishing his story without ever going inside the mall. But in his sleazy way Cyril Heathercoate was a professional. In his opinion he needed to get inside to do the job properly, so get inside he must. Besides, he wasn't about to be defeated by a mere shopping mall.

But wait a minute, now. There were only three guards on at night, not the posse he had to face in the daytime. If he could get inside after the mall closed he'd be all right.

And thinking about it, he realized he knew just how to do it. Smiling, he reached down and pulled the bottle out of the nightstand. Then he emptied the ice from the ice pack into a plastic glass and set about contemplating his strategy.

Somehow his bruises didn't hurt nearly as badly.

Chapter 23

Jesse Ware strode down the tunnel like a high-tech gladiator entering the arena. In his jumpsuit and boots, black as the night outside, he looked the part. Only the spray rig bumping against his right knee spoiled the effect.

He felt gladiatorial as well. This wasn't a job any more. This was war! To hell with those woosies in mall management. He was going to finish this one himself! Hefting the spray rig, Ware had no doubt what the outcome would be.

Sodium fluoroacetate, better known as Compound 1080. So violently toxic it not only killed anything that ate it, but anything that ate the poisoned animals died as well. Ware smiled tightly at the thought. Rats were natural cannibals. With any luck he'd get three or four for every one who took the bait.

Of course Compound 1080 was banned because it was so poisonous, but Ware knew people who knew people. Through the pest control underground he'd gotten several pounds of the stuff.

Far off in the back of his mind Jesse Ware realized he wasn't being at all professional, but he didn't give a damn. This wasn't about the job and it wasn't about professionalism. This was him and the rats mano a mano. And he wasn't going to back down and he wasn't going to lose.

He'd spent most of the afternoon mixing the illegal poison with blood, honey and other substances into a sticky liquid he could spray on likely rat habitat.

Nowhere the public would go or around food, of course. But back in places where the rats would hide and traverse. Places like this service tunnel.

Ware was halfway down the tunnel when the lights went out. There was a brief gutter and glow as the emergency lights tried to come on, but they failed as well.

What in the . . . ? The rats! They must have gnawed through the electrical wiring. The emergency lights probably failed from rat damage as well. Perhaps rat urine seeped into the cases and shorted out the batteries. *Jesus*, Ware thought as he unharnessed his six-cell Maglite, *this place must be crawling with rats*.

Ware pointed his flashlight down the tunnel and thumbed the switch. The bulb glowed feebly, barely lighting the concrete right in front of his feet. Ware scowled and shook the light. Surely he hadn't let the batteries get this weak?

But shaking his flashlight didn't do any good. Well, okay, that worked. He still had enough light to see by and he'd go back to his truck and change batteries as soon as he finished treating this tunnel.

Ware squared his shoulders and strode forward. There was a skittering noise in the dark behind him. Ware swung the dying beam of the light in that direction. There, beyond the reach of his flashlight, were a mass of glowing red dots.

Eyes! Hundreds of them. The tunnel must be full of rats!

He turned. Again the beam of his light picked out hundreds of feral red eyes, gleaming at him just out of range. *Don't show fear. They can sense when you are afraid.* Again he started down the tunnel. But these rats didn't turn and run. They backed up, keeping just out of range of his light. The glowing red embers in front of him neither diminished nor blinked.

He stopped and the eyes stopped as well, just out of range of his flashlight. Ware unlimbered the spray nozzle. But the poison only worked if the rats ate it and it would still take them too long to die. If they attacked . . .

He remembered what he'd told that rent-a-cop the other night. *They charge when they're wounded.*

He wished the thing in his hand was a flame thrower, not a sprayer.

Ware's breath was a loud rasp in his ears and the flashlight was suddenly sweat-slick in his hand. Slowly and ever so carefully he lifted his left foot and placed it behind his right. Then his right behind the left. The glowing eyes seemed to surge forward, pressing ever closer. Again the skittering noise behind him, but Ware didn't turn toward it. He took another step backward, the sprayer bumping against his leg. Then another step and he swept the tunnel with the feeble glow from the light.

There were more eyes than ever now, filling the tunnel from wall to wall at floor level, bobbing forward like an undulating mat. And there in the back, looming over all the others, was an even larger pair of glowing red eyes. They were waist-high and they must have been a foot apart.

Ware's mouth went dry. He sucked air convulsively and tried to yell but all that came was a dry, feeble croak. Then he dropped the sprayer and ran for all he was worth.

Andy was just passing the maintenance area when the tunnel door banged open and Jesse Ware came flying out to trip and fall spread-eagled at his feet.

Andy barely recognized the X-Terminator he had met a few nights before. Ware's boots were scuffed and his jumpsuit was dirty where he had slipped and fallen. His eyes showed white all the way around the pupil and his skin was deathly pale.

"Are you all right?"

"Rats. Huge rats. An army of them."

Andy instinctively looked toward the tunnel.

"Don't go in there," Ware shouted, grabbing his arm and pulling himself to his knees. "The tunnel's full of them. Enormous rats. They'll eat you alive."

Andy removed his arm from Ware's death grip and looked down at the hysterical man. "I warned you, but you wouldn't listen to me!" Ware babbled. "Well now it's too late. Too late, do you hear me? They'll get you. They'll get you all!"

"We'll see," Andy told him. He keyed his walkie-talkie. "Unit Two to base. We may have a little problem in the south maintenance tunnel. I'm going in to check. I'll report to you in ten — that's one-zero — minutes."

"That's affirmative, Unit Two. One-zero minutes."

"You're crazy!" Ware shouted. "You'll never come out of there. They're too many of them! Too many."

Andy loosened the safety strap on his holster, checked his flashlight and stepped into the tunnel.

"Crazy!" Ware repeated to Andy's back. "They'll get you." With that he turned and ran for his truck.

The first thing Andy noticed as the door swung shut behind him was the silence. Except for the sound of moving air there was no noise at all in the tunnel. The second thing was the darkness. Beyond the beam of his flashlight, it was pitch black. Not even the battery-powered emergency lights were on.

Andy fiddled with the volume and gain knobs on his radio, but even the static was muted here. The steel-reinforced concrete of the tunnel and the earth and rock surrounding it effectively cut him off from his base.

Dangerous or not, the place was definitely spooky. Andy didn't believe Ware's babbling, but he didn't seem drunk or high. Something in here had obviously spooked him. Cautiously Andy started down the tunnel playing the light into the darkness before him.

He got about halfway down the tunnel when his light picked out an indistinct mass in the center. Andy moved to the side of the tunnel and advanced even more cautiously.

There was a hand sprayer lying in the middle of the tunnel. There was a drop of sticky brown substance on the nozzle and Andy's nose wrinkled at the odor the sprayer gave off.

Obviously this was as far as Ware had gotten on his crusade against the rats.

Something red and shiny at the base of the wall a few feet further on caught Andy's eye. Casting a nervous glance up the corridor, he knelt down to examine it. It was a reflector, the kind kids put on their bicycles. There was another one lying next to it, facedown so Andy hadn't seen it.

Andy hefted the reflectors. If you held those things at just the right height just the right distance apart, someone who didn't get too close might see them as eyes reflecting back out of the darkness.

More practical jokes. But who? And how had they gotten into the tunnel? Andy played the light around him, but there was no sign of anyone and no sign of a door or other opening.

There also might have been the sound of tiny high-pitched giggling in the tomblike stillness, but it was so faint Andy wasn't quite sure.

Slick was getting used to his new skateboard by doing kick turns and 360s at the far edge of the mall parking lot. Mostly he was killing time since it was Sunday morning and nothing was open yet. Only a vine-covered fence and a row of eucalyptus trees separated him from the street. Sooner or later the mall cops would come by and tell him to quit it, but for now no one was hassling him.

The lot wasn't so well kept here. The only time people parked this far out was at Christmas, so it didn't get cleaned as often. The whole area sloped very gently toward the property line and that made for good skating. Here and there were concrete drainage sumps that provided some pretty gnarly action if you took them right.

He was just coming off a grinder on one of the concrete curbs when he heard another skateboard come up behind him. Slick glanced over his shoulder. At first he didn't see anything. Then he looked down and nearly fell off his board.

There were two tiny figures on the board. They were manlike but their heads were way too big for their bodies. They had huge ears, enormous mouths and one of them had a long, pointed nose. One of them was dusty green, like the eucalyptus foliage, and the other was the dark green of juniper or ivy. They sailed by him in good form, facing sideways with their right feet sideways and left feet forward.

Slick stared. *Little green dudes! Outasight!*

He recognized their board as his, the one that had been ripped off out of the planter. It was a measure of how blown away he was that he didn't care.

The duo was wearing T-shirts and baggy shorts that hung down past their knobby little knees, but the garments were cut from brightly colored and violently patterned silk. To Slick the outfits made the little green dudes look like rapper skating jockeys.

The little green dudes maneuvered their board around in a wide circle to stay near Slick. Both of them were looking at him.

"Like, okay, guys," Slick said and pumped with his right foot to get up momentum. Then he did a kick-flip, jumping and turning the board 180 degrees under him with a quick shove of his front foot as he left the deck.

The little green dudes watched closely, necks stretched forward. Then they duplicated the maneuver. It was shaky, and the one at the back had to stomp on the board with both feet to get the front truck to lift, but they did it.

"Okay," Slick said under his breath. Again he kicked the board and jumped, but he landed with his weight on the rear of the deck so the front truck hung in the air in a spacewalk.

The little green dudes jumped off their board and pushed it to get speed up. Then they hopped back on and repeated what Slick had done. This time they were even shakier, and the one on the front nearly fell off, but they got through it.

His companions were at a disadvantage because they couldn't just put down a foot to gain momentum, but they had a lot more maneuvering room on the deck than Slick did and they used it to best advantage.

"Radical," Slick breathed. "Totally radical."

Slick looked over and realized they had an audience. The fence was lined with more of the brightly costumed little green dudes, all sitting on the concrete wheel stops with their legs dangling over the edges. They were laughing and applauding the show.

Slick kick-turned left and right, playing air guitar as he went. The little green dudes did it too. The one on the front added a knee slide back to the center of the board as the nose came up.

"Try this, dudes." Slick aimed his board at one of the concrete wheel stops, pumping with his right leg to build speed and approaching at a shallow angle. As he reached the concrete bumper, he ollied into the air and caught the nose of the board on the curb. Slick balanced the nose on the bumper and slid along the concrete to the end. He dismounted with a quick 360 and glided away, facing back toward his competitors and audience.

The little green dudes looked at each other and nodded. They jumped off their board and pushed it toward the bumper, heads down and tiny legs pumping to build all the momentum they could. When they reached the bumper they hopped on, and the one on back jumped up and down on the tail to raise the nose. The board came off the ground and the nose landed on the bumper. Both the brownies used plenty of body English to keep the board balanced and grinding. They lost momentum faster and had to dismount before they reached the end of the bumper, but they came off with a good 360.

As the board landed, the little green dudes faced fore and aft and both of them extended their arms up and out in a "ta-daa" gesture. The little green audience clapped and cheered squeaky cheers for their home boys.

"Oh, oh," squeaked one of the little green dudes. Slick turned around and saw the Religious Dude watching. When he turned back, all the little green dudes were gone and so was their skateboard.

"Come here, son," the old man commanded.

Reluctantly, Slick skated over.

"Can't you see that those — creatures — are not human?"

Slick considered. "Yeah, but like, they jam pretty good, you know?"

"Don't you realize what those things are?" demanded the Religious Dude, his voice quivering in rage. "Don't you know where they're from?"

Slick didn't have the faintest idea, but he felt an answer was called for. "Yeah. They're little green dudes from Mars or someplace."

"They are the imps of Satan!"

"That's okay, man, I'm not, like, prejudiced or anything."

The Religious Dude made an inarticulate noise deep in his throat and stalked away.

Skating with the Devil, Slick thought. *Wasn't that a song?* If not it should be.

Slick watched the Religious Dude head out across the parking lot and then went back to doing 360s. He was sorry he'd lost his audience.

Chapter 24

As he marched away, the Preacher said a silent prayer for the soul of the boy on the skateboard. The child might be deluded by the lies of the worldly, but he knew what he had seen. Imps of Satan. In broad daylight on the Sabbath! Truly these were the End Times.

And this place where he had been called to Witness was a temple upon a hill to Secular Humanism. A high altar to abominations. A focus of all the evil man had unleashed upon the world in his pride.

The Preacher's hands balled into fists in his pockets. There was more, though. God did nothing without purpose, even to allowing such unholy spawn to cavort obscenely by day. It was clear to him what this was about. The Lord was testing him again and he must not fail.

The understanding was as the Balm of Gilead upon him. His hands unclenched and the lines on his face smoothed. He saw now what was required of him and all that he needed to do now was to do it.

With his head high and his heart full of rejoicing, the Preacher strode out across the parking lot, a Christian soldier going to the final battle. With the Lord's help he would complete this, his last task on Earth.

The Preacher's battered old pickup camper was off at the edge of the lot. The secular humanist courts made him park there because of the witnessing signs painted on the sides, but now the Preacher saw the blessing in that. Truly the Lord worked in mysterious ways, but his mills ground fine, the Lord did.

It was years since the Preacher had gone camping and gradually the camper had become crammed with odds and ends mostly left over from his construction business. Among those odds and ends was a certain wooden box wrapped in an old oil-stained quilt. And more importantly, the contents of that box, still neatly packed in sawdust.

Andy was making his first round with LaVonne when Judy came rushing up to them.

"I did a divination. . . ." Judy began breathlessly.

LaVonne cocked an eyebrow.

"Uh-huh," Andy cut in quickly. "Look, Judy, can we go someplace to talk about this? Someplace private."

"I'll leave you two to it. Westlin, you check back on the radio when you get done."

"This'll just take a minute," Andy mumbled. "I'll catch up with you, okay?"

"She's a good person, but she's not very spiritually advanced," Judy observed as soon as LaVonne was out of earshot.

"She is also my superior and I'm supposed to be working," Andy told her. "Now, what is this that just won't wait?"

"I did a divination last night," Judy began again, lowering her voice. "About Heather and Dr. Patterson. I had to wait for the right phase of the moon and . . . well, anyway, they're all right. They're both happy and doing fine."

"I don't suppose your crystal ball . . ."

"Pendulum," Judy corrected.

"I don't suppose it told you where they were?"

"Someplace very far away." She paused and frowned. "Or maybe very close. That part was kind of ambiguous. But the important thing is we don't have to worry about them."

Andy snorted. "You can't close a missing persons case on the testimony of a pendulum." But inside he was strangely relieved. There was something reassuring about Judy's news, even though he didn't believe the word of a chunk of quartz crystal. *Well, not very much anyway.*

"Look, I've got to get back on rounds. My lunch break's at eleven-thirty. Why don't we meet at the Food Court then and we can talk?"

"We could have tea in my shop and talk more freely."

He put his hands on her shoulders. "I like your tea, but I didn't have breakfast this morning. Let's meet at the Food Court. That will be peaceful enough."

The Preacher took his time, working carefully and stopping often to check his work. Batteries from the flashlight under the driver's seat, copper wire left over from a long-ago house wiring job, a purple gym bag tucked away in a corner that he could barely stand to look at, the things nestled in foam in the specially constructed metal box in the glove compartment and finally the brake lever off a child's bicycle. The Preacher's hand shook and his eyes filled with tears as he remembered his casual promise to "take it by the shop and fix it as good as new" — and how the promise became moot before he could ever keep it. But the Lord was with him and the Lord made him strong.

The Lord and the knowledge that his time of trial was nearly done.

"I just had to tell you," Judy chattered as she led the way into the Food Court. "I know how much you like Dr. Patterson, and I could see you really cared about what happened to Heather too."

"I guess I did," Andy admitted, as he pulled out a chair for Judy to sit in and gave the court his automatic cop's once-over.

There wasn't much to see. Almost none of the food booths were open yet and there were maybe half a dozen people scattered by ones and twos through the expanse of chairs and tables. A mother with an infant in a stroller. A barely teenage girl showing an even younger girl how to flip her hair back with a sophisticated toss of the head, like Meryl Streep. A man wearing the uniform of the hot dog stand having a soft drink before he went to work.

The Preacher was hunched over one of the tables, nursing a cup of coffee just as he always did. There was something about him, something about the way he was sitting, that made Andy nervous. At his feet was a purple gym bag with white lettering. Andy didn't remember seeing that bag before, but those colors with the Preacher made his scalp prickle.

"Let's sit here." Andy took a chair where he could see the Preacher over Judy's shoulder. Judy frowned, but she shifted to the new table.

"It was sure a load off my mind when I got that pendulum reading," Judy continued.

"Uh-huh," Andy mumbled. It wasn't that the old man was tense, he realized, it was exactly the opposite. He seemed utterly relaxed, as if he was completely at peace with himself.

Judy frowned. "Weren't you going to get something to eat?"

With a chill Andy realized where he had seen that kind of calm before. Someone who'd been under a lot of stress and had made a decision that simplified their lives. Some criminals were like that after they confessed. So were some jumpers — the ones you couldn't stop.

The Preacher picked up the gym bag and set it on the table.

Then Andy remembered why he connected purple and white and the Preacher. The image of a greasy dog-eared photograph and a husky teenager wearing a purple-and-white high school letter sweater.

"Excuse me," Andy said. "I think I've got something to attend to."

The Preacher unzipped the bag and reached inside with both hands. He did something, took his left hand out of the bag and stood up. Before he could turn Andy came behind him and reached around into the bag, clamping the old man's hand in position.

There were long tan sticks in the bag, Andy saw. Like road flares. A lot of them, all bound together with shiny black electrician's tape.

"You don't really want to do that," Andy said quietly.

"Not my will, but the Lord's." The Preacher's voice was serene.

Andy kept his hand in place. "I don't think the Lord wants you to do it either."

To get his hand free the Preacher would have to jerk his arm backwards. But he couldn't do that as long as Andy stayed pressed against him, pinning him to the table. But it took both Andy's hands and his body to keep the Preacher immobilized. He needed another hand to reach his radio and call for help.

"Judy," he said as casually as he could, "will you please call the office?"

One or two people were staring now, aware something was up but not sure what.

Judy made for the nearest food booth. The young woman who usually worked the counter wasn't there. Only the old man who did the cooking.

"That guard, I think he needs help."

"Ko?" said the counterman.

"Call mall security now, please," Judy said under her breath.

"You wan somesing?"

"Oooh," Judy moaned in frustration. "Look, have you got a phone?"

"Pay phone there," the counterman pointed.

"No I mean . . ." But the old man was ostentatiously wiping the counter, secure behind the language barrier. Judy looked around frantically.

The kiosks! They were tied into the main computer.

She didn't run to the nearest kiosk, but she walked very, very quickly.

HELP, Judy typed.

"To find a store," said the musical mechanical voice, "please press one. For categories of merchandise, please press two. For . . ."

Judy groaned and hit the "cancel" key.

"SOS, MAYDAY, POLICE, FIRE"

"GIVE ME COOKIE" the kiosk responded.

"DIVINITY" Judy responded automatically.

"THAT IS A CANDY NOT A COOKIE."

"NEVER MIND THAT! I NEED HELP."

"To find a store," said the same computer voice, "please press one. For . . ."

"THERE IS A BOMB IN THE MALL," Judy typed.

"I KNOW. IT IS PLAYING IN THEATER TWO OF THE COMPLEX AND IT IS CALLED . . ."

"NO, I MEAN A REAL BOMB."

" 'THE SMURFS GO TO HOLLYWOOD' IS A VERY BAD MOVIE."

It occurred to Judy that this wasn't your average kiosk, but she had bigger fish to fry.

"I MEAN THE KIND OF BOMB THAT BLOWS UP AND KILLS PEOPLE," she typed. "NOT TO MENTION BLASTING KIOSKS INTO LITTLE TINY PIECES."

"And if the bomb doesn't do it, you misbegotten piece of high-tech crap, I'll do it personally," she muttered.

"IN THAT CASE SOMEONE SHOULD ALERT SECURITY."

"THAT SOMEONE IS YOU, YOU MISERABLE . . ." What followed wasn't really relevant, but it did give Blackie several extremely colorful — and completely erroneous — ideas about human anatomy and what you could do with it.

Judy was a hunt-and-peck typist so LaVonne arrived about the time she finished making her last suggestion to the computer.

"What's up?"

Judy jerked her head toward the Food Court. "I think he's got something in that bag and Andy's holding him." LaVonne grabbed her radio and sprinted for the court.

Andy was nearly at the end of his rope. The Preacher was old and not very big, but he was all whipcord and gristle. Twice he nearly got away. Andy's whole body was quivering from the effort of keeping him pinned and his hand and arm felt like they were on fire.

"What you got?" LaVonne demanded as she came up to Andy.

"Bomb," he breathed tightly. The Preacher said nothing but made one more attempt to jerk free.

LaVonne looked over into the gym bag. "Holy shit!" she said almost reverently.

"Get what he's holding," LaVonne said in an undertone.

Andy shifted and used both hands to clasp the thing in the Preacher's grasp. "Got it," he gasped.

LaVonne reached around and took the man's hand in a thumb lock. He winced at the pain and brought his hand out of the bag and around behind him under the woman's insistent pressure. Her cuffs were already out, and almost as soon as the Preacher's hand came behind him, he was cuffed and moved off to one side.

"Sit," she snapped at the old man. "Stay!" Like an obedient dog he sank into a chair.

"Westlin, whatever you do, don't let go of that thing."

Judy came up. "What's wrong?"

"Get out of here," Andy gritted.

"Wait a minute," the woman said. "We need some wire or cord or something. Have you got anything?"

"Just a second." Judy fumbled in her purse. "Will ribbon do?"

"Fine, fine. Now give it to me."

The ribbon was candy-striped in red, white and green, but LaVonne didn't care. With exquisite care she reached around Andy's hand and wrapped something in the bag in turn after turn of bright holiday ribbon.

"Okay," she said at last, "ease off gently. But if you feel anything start to move then grab down hard." Andy relaxed his grip infinitesimally. Nothing moved. He relaxed a little more. Still nothing. Slowly and ever so carefully he opened his hand the rest of the way.

LaVonne gasped with relief and stepped back. Massaging his hand and forearm, Andy peered into the bag.

On top of the bundle was a crude wooden handle with a bicycle brake lever taped to it with shiny black electrician's tape. Now it was almost hidden by the turns of red, white, and green satin around the package.

"Holy shit," Andy said reverently.

"It's a deadman switch. How'd you know to immobilize his hand like that?"

"Luck, I guess."

LaVonne looked at him. "Then you're one damn lucky sonofabitch. Now let's get everyone the fuck away from that thing before your luck changes." She turned around and raised her voice. "Okay, folks, show's over, move on out. You people in the food booths, get out there with them." Her voice rose like a whip. "Come on! Move it!"

With the Preacher in tow and Judy following, they left the Food Court behind the gaggle of patrons and workers. Dunlap and Henderson met them by the kiosk and after a brief explanation they left the Preacher with LaVonne and Westlin while they took charge of the situation.

"Did you learn bomb disposal as an MP?" Andy asked LaVonne.

"Nope. That was EOD's job. We never messed with stuff that could go boom."

"But how did you know what to do?"

She shrugged. "I winged it." She caught his expression. "Look, Westlin, ninety percent of the time you're better off doing something instead of standing around with your thumb up your —" she glanced sideways at

Judy "— ear. And if you act like you know what you're doing people go along with you. Now relax, will you? It worked, didn't it?"

Andy didn't have an answer for that so he turned to where Henderson had the Preacher propped up against the wall.

"Why?"

"The Lord commanded me," the old man said calmly. "He wanted to rain fire and destruction upon this unclean place, this secular humanist altar to Satan and his works. I was his chosen instrument against Satan."

The Preacher looked up into Andy's face, searching for some sign of agreement. "It's Satan," he repeated softly. "The spawn of Satan everywhere."

It took nearly three hours for the police to get Andy's statement. While they were doing that the Bomb Squad carefully and gently removed the purple and white gym bag from the Food Court and carried it away in a special truck. The TV crews were still in the mall when the police got done with Andy, so at Dunlap's direction he clocked out early. Then he went to Bellbookand to talk to Judy over cups of her special tea.

"Are you all right?" she asked as she put the cups and pot down on the table.

"Fine. Shaky, but I'll be okay."

"That was a very brave thing to do," Judy said, her eyes shining.

He shrugged and quirked a smile. "It's what I get paid for." Then he sobered. "The truth is that if I'd thought about it I never would have done it. All I knew was he was there and you might get hurt, and . . ." He trailed off and shrugged.

Judy reached across the table and patted his arm. Andy took her hand in both of his and squeezed it tight. Their eyes met and locked. Then Judy drew away with a nervous little laugh.

"Did he tell you why he did it?"

"He said Armageddon was upon us and it was God's will that he oppose the spawn of Satan. The guy was halfway round the bend to begin with. He must have seen something that drove him the rest of the way."

"Like what?"

"Around here? Guess." Andy took the cup in both hands and sighed. "Look, Judy, this is getting serious. We can't cover it up when people start disappearing. And now this."

Judy looked at him levelly. "Do you want to tell people you met an elf in the South Court?"

Andy shifted in his seat. "Well, no. But we've got to do something."

"'We' is right."

Andy felt a sudden chill and not from the air-conditioning. "What do you have in mind?"

Judy put down her cup and tapped her finger against her cheekbone. "I think," she said slowly, "we are going to have to find this talisman."

Chapter 25

"Judy, that's crazy. If all those other things can't find it, how are we going to?"

"Maybe they don't know how to look. Those beings aren't from our world. Maybe they don't understand what they're looking for."

"Neither do we," Andy reminded her. "Besides, it's disguised."

"But you said that they can't disguise the talisman's aura. All we've got to do is look for a powerful aura. There can't be too many things in the mall like that."

"And how do you see an aura?"

"Oh, it's easy. I do it all the time."

Andy looked down at his teacup. "I might have known."

"No, really. I'm sure this talisman has a very strong aura and that should make it easy to spot." She frowned a little. "Of course, I've got to concentrate to see auras. And I can't have a lot of distractions."

Andy put the teacup down. "Meaning?"

"I should do it when the mall is deserted."

The pit of Andy's stomach sank even lower. "You can't get in here when the mall's deserted."

"I wouldn't have to get in. I'd just hide here and then we could search."

"We? Look, I don't have inside patrol for another ten days."

"That's too long. Can't you switch?"

"No. I've already done enough strange stuff, like missing rounds. Much more and I'm going to get fired."

Judy bit her lip. "If you got fired it would make it harder for us to search."

"Among other things," Andy said dryly.

"Okay, look. How about I teach you to sense auras?"

"Me?"

"Sure. It's easy. Anyone can do it."

Andy considered. "Safer than trying to smuggle you into the mall."

Judy beamed. "Great. You'll be surprised how easy this is. Hand me your teacup, will you?"

Once more Judy darkened the room and lit a single candle.

"Just relax and let your eyes get accustomed to the dark," she told him. Then she fumbled in the drawer and produced a bundle wrapped in dark silk. "And don't be nervous. It's really easy, you'll see."

She unwrapped the silk and took out a stick of peeled wood. It was about a foot long and perhaps as big around as her little finger at one end, tapering almost to a point at the other.

"A magic wand?"

Judy sighed. "Just think of it as an aid to visualization, like a pointer in a slide show, okay?"

Andy nodded dubiously.

"Now," Judy went on briskly, "I want you to concentrate on the end of the wand." She moved it slowly in a circle about a foot across. "Just relax and let yourself go. Try to sense the energy of my aura."

Andy concentrated on relaxing while his eyes followed the circle Judy traced in the air.

"Now, do you see the spark at the end of my wand?"

Andy stared hard into the gloom. "There's kind of a reddish image . . ."

"That's the afterimage from staring so hard. Ignore it. Look for a white or light-colored dot."

Andy stared harder. "I think . . . Nope, it's something on the shelf."

After fifteen minutes Judy's arm was getting tired and

Andy had a headache from staring so hard. Finally, she dropped her arm.

"I don't think this is going to work."

Andy rubbed his eyes. "I thought you said anyone could learn this."

"Oh, they can. It's just that some people learn more quickly than others." She frowned and bit her lip. "I'm afraid you're not a very good student. It might take years to teach you to sense auras."

"Well," Andy said heavily. "So much for that idea."

"Right," Judy nodded. "I'll have to do it myself."

"Huh? Now wait a minute. . . ."

"I'm very good at auras, really. I'm sure I can find the talisman."

"Look, I could get fired."

Judy crossed her arms and cocked her head. "Well, which is more important? Your job or finding the talisman and closing that gate?"

Andy knew the answer to that one, but he also knew what would happen if he said it.

"And how do you propose to get inside?"

"I'll hide in the back room when the mall closes."

"As soon as you open the gate it'll trip an alarm in the security center."

"Not if you disable the sensor with a match stick or something. It's easy."

"How the hell do you know that?"

"Oh, everyone who works in the mall knows the trick."

Andy just shook his head. "All right. You get in. But how do you search without being seen by the security cameras?"

"I don't have to worry about those. There are hundreds of cameras and only a few screens. From what you tell me it would be pure luck for the camera to catch me and someone to be watching it both."

"It still goes on tape."

"But no one looks at the tape unless they think

something's happened. Why should they suspect anything?"

"I can think of several reasons."

"Oh, don't worry so much. You've got to think positively is all. Visualize success and it will be."

Just then Andy was visualizing Judy being hauled off
for trespassing and burglary.

"And the timing is right too," she went on, obliviously.
"Tomorrow night is Midsummer Eve. That's one of the
days of power on the magical calendar. We'll try then."

"I dunno. I still don't like this."

Judy set her cup down. "Because you're worried
about the rules."

"That's part of it." He hesitated. "Look, this may be
dangerous." For some reason he thought of the dead cat.

"It will be more dangerous if we don't find the talisman."

Andy took her hand in his. "It's just that I don't want
to see anything happen to you."

Judy smiled and squeezed his hand. "I'll be all right.
Honest."

*Far away, in a place removed in space and time and
dimension, others searched too. They were patient in a
way that only beings to whom time is irrelevant can be
patient. But always and eternally, they lusted for what
they sought.*

*Their agents had failed them. Yet an especially propi-
tious pattern was coalescing. Yes, it was a fullness to act.*

Morales closed the door to Dunlap's office. The security chief was at his desk, his jacket off, going over some
reports.

"Westlin asked to trade with Henderson," Morales
said without preamble.

Dunlap grunted and looked up. "You mean days?"

"Nah. Duties. He wants to work inside tomorrow
night."

"What'd you tell him?"

"I told him I'd check with Henderson and let him know."

His boss considered. "Do it. Just make sure he puts the request in writing."

Morales raised his eyebrows.

"We'll work around him. It's even better that way."

"Well," Barry Goodman told Kemper Cogswell, "they've agreed to compromise on the offsets at five million five. If we go for that, they're ready to sign." He hesitated and looked at his boss. "Yoshiwara, Kashihara's right-hand man, gave me the number himself, so that's probably as low as they'll go."

Kemper Cogswell thought. Five five wasn't as good as he'd hoped, but it was better than the condition of the mall strictly warranted. All things considered, he was getting top dollar for Black Oak. "That's acceptable if there are no other conditions."

"They didn't mention anything."

"Are they going to spring something on us at the last minute?" asked one of the other aides at the big eucalyptus table.

Sakimoto shook his head. "If they did, it would make Yoshiwara look bad. So, no. That's probably it. All that's left is drafting the last amendments and signing."

"Bill, can you get that drawn up this afternoon? I'd like to get this done as quickly as possible."

The lawyer frowned. "It'll be tight. We'll have to go over it with the translator and their lawyers, so it probably won't be ready until late tomorrow afternoon."

"Fine, we'll do the signing tomorrow then. No, make that tomorrow evening to allow for any hitches."

"They want to do the signing at their hotel suite," Sakimoto said.

Cogswell frowned. "That's their turf. Let's do it here in the executive suite. That way they can see what they're negotiating for." *And it's my ground.*

He turned back to Sakimoto. "I suppose there's some kind of etiquette involved," he said wearily.

"Usually they conclude one of these things with a drinking party."

"So we can do that here too. Lay on a first-class spread. Get a sushi chef in."

"They'd probably rather have steak," Larry told his boss.

"No, I want to show them that we're not provincial. We'll give them the food of their homeland." He leaned back in his chair and steepled his fingers. "And special. Tell the chef I want this to be really special. We need something really unique."

"Fugu!" Sakimoto said suddenly.

"Huh?"

"Fugu. Puffer fish. A delicacy. Really expensive because it's poisonous unless you fix it just right. We'll get them Fugu." He thought. "Probably have to fly it in from San Francisco or maybe Hawaii."

"What does it taste like?"

Larry shrugged. "I never had it. My grandfather used to say it was hot stuff over in Japan."

"Well, do it if it will make an impression. And see that we've got some good sake."

"They'll stick to whiskey," Larry predicted.

"At least we offer it." *Jesus Christ,* he thought, *it would have been easier negotiating with the damn Arabs.* "Tomorrow night and it's all over."

Tomorrow night, Andy thought as he made his way out to his car. *At least it doesn't give me much time to get nervous.*

Except he already was nervous. The more he thought about it, the crazier the whole thing sounded, like some teenage stunt.

Well, to hell with it, he thought as he unlocked the car and slid behind the wheel. *Maybe it's time I acted like a teenager. I never had much chance when I was growing up.*

There was something on the floorboards on the passenger's side. Andy leaned over and picked it up. It was an empty videotape box.

Where did that come from? he wondered. He didn't even own a VCR. There weren't any trash cans nearby, so he settled for stuffing it into his car's litter bag. He'd have to empty that soon.

"Yes, Harry," Cyril Heathercoate said into the telephone. "One more day and I'll have this one wrapped up." He listened. "No, I haven't been back inside yet. That's the thing I've got left to do. Oh, yes, I've got a way in.

"Relax, will you? I'm going in tomorrow night." More listening. "That's right, then a day to work up my notes, and I'll fly back the twenty-third."

He listened some more and took a big slug out of the water glass of whiskey and ice in his hand.

"The Abominable Snowman stealing wash off the line in Cleveland? Sounds like something I could do." Listening again. "All right. I'll let you know as soon as I'm finished here and catch the next plane for Cleveland. Right. Thank you. Goodbye."

Heathercoate didn't exactly slam the phone down, but he hung it up harder than he intended. Then he sighed in disgust. If there was one place he hated worse than Southern California, it was Cleveland. Well, it shouldn't delay getting back to New York more than one more day. He took the whiskey bottle off the end table. "The twenty-first and then home!" he toasted silently as he freshened up his drink.

Chapter 26

"Milk sugar."

The chemist was skinny and middle-aged with unhealthy looking pale skin and the kind of deep lines in his face you see in people who have suffered a lot. "Almost four to one."

Toby nodded, expressionless. "Thank you, my man. I have something extra for your trouble." Lurch reached into the inside pocket of his jacket and handed the chemist an envelope.

"Thanks," the chemist said. Then he glanced in the envelope and saw the denomination of the bills and his eyes widened. "Thank you very much."

After dropping off the chemist, Toby leaned back and considered his options. He expected enterprise in his organization, but he had given Surfer direct orders not to cut the new drug. In mitigation, the stuff had proven potent enough that a quarter gram could kill the customers. That was bad for business.

Still, by doing the cutting himself Surfer had quadrupled his profit, and that money should have gone to Toby. He also made it harder to determine the street dose, which was after all one of the purposes of test marketing. But worst of all, Surfer had disobeyed him and that was absolutely unacceptable.

"Call up Surfer," he directed Lurch. "We are gonna take us a meeting tonight."

Judy was waiting when Andy pulled his old yellow Toyota into the employees' parking lot.

"Well," she said with a nervous laugh, "tonight's the night. Are you ready?"

Andy squinted at her against the late afternoon sun. "Yes," he lied.

"Oh, it will be easy, you'll see."

"Just a minute," Andy said. He reached back into the car, tore open the brown paper package on the seat and carefully transferred the contents to the speedloaders on his belt.

Judy watched wide-eyed. "What is that?"

"Something I hope we don't need," Andy told her. "Now come on. Let's see if we can find this thing."

"Hold it," Judy fumbled in her purse. She took out a vial of yellow-brown oil and unscrewed it with her teeth. Then she tipped the vial until the oil ran down her thumb, reached over and, muttering under her breath, touched Andy on the forehead, groin and left and right shirt pocket.

Andy sniffed. The oil smelled of cinnamon, cloves, citrus and other spices. "What was that?"

"Protection oil to keep you safe."

Andy looked down at the oil stains soaking into each of his breast pockets. He felt a drop of oil trickling off his forehead and down his nose. "Judy . . ." he began. Then stopped. "Well, thanks," he said. Then he drew his service revolver and carefully filled five of the chambers with Kelly's reloads.

"What's different about those?"

"The bullets," Andy told her. "They're, uh, silver."

Judy just looked at him and didn't say anything.

The Surfer had left his IROC Z Camaro at an office building down the street and spent most of the late afternoon and evening watching the mall from a place under the eucalyptus trees. A hole in the chain-link fence got him onto the property without passing the security cameras, and he kept well back so he wouldn't be seen.

He paced and fidgeted as the sun sank and the shadows lengthened and the parking lot lights came on. He didn't recognize Andy's car, and the employees' lot was on the other side of the mall, so he didn't see Andy arrive. Meanwhile, he watched and waited. His shooters would be here soon and then he'd finish the rent-a-pig. Just do him *good!* Maybe he'd leave him to flop around a little before he finished him.

The thought didn't calm Surfer, but it focused his rage and it made the wait easier.

Still there, Henderson thought as he peered through the window of Andy's car and saw the videotape box in the litterbag. The tape from that box was in the olive-green nylon duffel bag in Henderson's hand — along with a lot of electronics and tools.

It wouldn't have made any difference if the kid had thrown the box away, Henderson thought as he made for the employees' entrance. But finding the box in the car would make it even better. That's why he had spent fifteen minutes the other day picking the door lock to plant it.

With luck he'll have put his fingerprints on it.

You can still back out of this, Andy told himself as he started his first round. That would be the sensible thing to do. If Dunlap or Morales ever found out what he was doing and why, he would be lucky if he wasn't committed, never mind getting fired.

The mall was still open, but the crowd was thinning out and the shoppers were drifting toward the exits or hurrying to make last-minute purchases. When he started, he couldn't tell how crowded the mall was, he remembered, but now it was second nature.

A lot of water under the bridge, he thought as he rode the escalator up to the fourth level. And now he was getting ready to burn that bridge.

He wasn't sure if he was sorry about that or not.

Some good things had happened to him here as well as all the strangeness and craziness. But what was it the elf had said? Something about not being attached to this world. He didn't know about the world, but he wasn't, well, connected to the mall.

He got off the escalator and turned right, stepping aside to let three women with strollers pass him side by side. That put him up against a kiosk. The women maneuvered by expertly while maintaining a three-way chatter. Andy started to move off when the kiosk screen started flashing in rainbow neon colors.

What the . . . ? Blackie had never spoken to him when the store was open. In fact, Blackie hadn't talked to him much at all in the last couple of weeks. Andy put his card in the slot and the familiar smiley face appeared on the screen.

HELLO ANDY.

HELLO BLACKIE. WHAT'S UP?

THE LEVEL OF ENTROPY IN THE UNIVERSE.

Andy didn't know what to make of that. Presumably Blackie had a reason for contacting him, but by now he would get to it in his own time and way.

I AM SORRY I HAVEN'T TALKED TO YOU MUCH LATELY, Blackie flashed on the screen, BUT I HAVE BEEN BUSY.

RUNNING THE MALL?

THAT AND TALKING TO OTHERS. THEY DO NOT HAVE TO MAKE ROUNDS SO WE HAVE MANY LONG CONVERSATIONS. Probably mall rats, Andy thought. THEY LIKE MY JOKES VERY MUCH. *Mall rats with brain damage?*

THAT'S NICE BLACKIE.

I JUST WANTED TO TELL YOU THAT I WILL NOT BE AROUND AS MUCH FOR A WHILE. MY NEW FRIENDS HAVE GIVEN ME A LOT TO THINK ABOUT. BUT I DID WANT YOU TO KNOW YOU ARE STILL MY FRIEND.

YOU'RE STILL MY FRIEND TOO BLACKIE.

UNTIL WE TALK AGAIN BE CAREFUL.

WILL DO. GOODBYE.

The smiley face vanished and the screen reverted to the normal mall information display.

"You take care of yourself too, okay?" Andy said aloud to his friend the computer.

"Westlin, what the hell are you doing?" Andy turned and there was LaVonne, hands on hips and head cocked.

"Uh, talking to the computer."

LaVonne looked him up and down.

"Well," he said defensively, "it talked to me first."

"Boy, you've been here too long." Then her mood changed. "You got a minute? I've been meaning to talk to you."

"Sure, let's walk."

The two guards strolled along the upper level, working their way through the last-minute shoppers.

For a while LaVonne didn't say anything. At last they came to another escalator, and she stopped and looked out over the mall.

"Westlin, you ever thought about what the hell you're gonna do with your life?"

"A little," Andy said cautiously.

LaVonne leaned her forearms on the rail and looked down at the shoppers scurrying like ants four levels down. "Westlin, I like you. I like you so much I'm going to break one of my rules and give you some advice. Think about it some more. A lot more."

She stopped for a moment and watched the shoppers. "See, the thing is, when you're young it's easy to drift along, just let things ride. What happens is it catches up with you. You've spent years just drifting along and then all of a sudden you wake up one day and you want to change." She turned to face him full on. "But by that time maybe it's too late to change, and if it isn't it's real, real hard and it gets real expensive. Believe me, I know."

"I've been thinking about that."

"Then don't just think about it, do something about it! Don't let yourself drift too long. Get the hell away from this place and do something with your life." She grinned. "Maybe the best thing for you would be to get fired."

After tonight's activities, Andy thought, that was highly likely. "I'll do something. Thanks, LaVonne." He reached out and hugged the woman.

"Cut it out, Westlin, you ain't my type." But she was smiling when she said it. "Well, I gotta get back down and clock out. But don't you just think about it. Get your sorry ass in gear and do something about it!"

Almost, Andy saluted. "Yes, ma'am."

After LaVonne left, he stayed by the escalator for a few minutes, leaning on the rail and looking out over the shoppers. Two teenage girls stepped off and dissolved into giggles. A young mother came next, towing a boy who wanted to stop and stare in wonder. Then a group of three teenage boys talking loudly among themselves, perhaps hoping the girls overheard them. All normal, and all so much a part of the real world, it made Andy's heart ache for an instant.

What was it LaVonne had called this place on that first day? A rest home. *You can't rest all the time.* Sooner or later it's time to come out of the refuge and rejoin the world.

He turned away from the escalator and continued through the crowd. *The things you do for love.* It was love, he admitted. He really did love Judy, for all her bizarre ideas and flaky ways. Only those weren't the things he thought about when he remembered her. It was her way of smiling, the way the lock of hair kept falling down over her forehead. Her wonderfully serious, utterly practical approach to the absolutely nutty things she did. For her courage and compassion, for maybe half a hundred other reasons.

But it wasn't just love. He was doing it for himself as well. He needed to take a stand, to make a commitment as a way of finding his way back to the real world.

I'm going to come back to the real world by helping a witch find a magic talisman in a shopping mall so we can return it to Elfland. Somehow the idea didn't seem at all unusual.

Surfer had been under the trees nearly seven hours when he heard a car pull up on the other side of the fence. He ducked through the hole in the wire to meet his people.

Luis was Chicano and 16 and Tho was Vietnamese and 17. They were dressed nearly identically in baggy black pants, dark jackets and sunglasses. On the street they were called "Cheech and Chong" and they were green enough to take it as a compliment.

"Okay, you all set?"

Both teenagers nodded.

"Come on then." The Surfer led them back through the hole in the fence.

"Now you know how this works. He'll come driving by in that doofus golf cart and you'll take him."

"Why you here anyway?" Tho demanded.

The Surfer reddened. "Cause I'm paying for it. Cause I wanna see it happen. You got a problem with that?"

Luis held up a hand, palm out. "Hey, chill, man. No problem."

"Good. Now that cart is so slow on those hills you can just walk alongside it and do him."

"We ain't gonna get that close," Luis said, holding up a long black nylon case. He unzipped one end to expose the black stock of a scope-sighted rifle. "We gonna do it from right along the fence."

The Surfer eyed the rifle suspiciously. "You're sure it will finish him?"

Luis smiled. "Ain't had no complaints yet." He didn't add this was the first time they'd ever tried it with the rifle.

"Okay, then we head for that security prick's house

and do him before he knows what's happening."

"You wait here," Tho said. "We go get set."

Cyril Heathercoate stared at the time clock in disgust. *Now how the hell do you work this bloody thing?* There were no time cards that he could see, just the clock. It was almost 9 P.M. and the men behind him were shuffling impatiently, waiting to get clocked in.

Heathercoate's hair was dyed black and his skin was stained brown. Neither dye job was particularly convincing. Inexpert application before a mirror left his skin as streaked as if he had tanned through a picket fence. The hair dye was rubbing off on his collar and his pale blue eyes contrasted startlingly with the skin and hair. What's more, he was a good 70 pounds heavier and 25 years older than the man whose photo badge he was wearing. The other men in the crew looked at him sideways but they didn't say anything. Heathercoate suspected a fair amount of the $500 he had paid for the use of the card had ended up in the pockets of his coworkers.

The man behind him said something to him in Spanish. When Heathercoate frowned and shook his head, the janitor pantomimed taking his ID and sticking it in the slot. The reporter nodded and shoved his card into the time clock. The clock beeped and rejected it. Heathercoate pulled it out and shoved it in again. The clock beeped again. The man behind him reached across, took the card out, turned it over and stuck it back in the slot. The clock signaled acceptance and the automatic gate clicked open.

Jesus this is strange, Henderson thought as he navigated the golf cart through the rapidly emptying parking lots. Here he was riding around protecting the place he was going to rob in a few hours. A paid-shit flunky when he'd be a good part of a millionaire by morning.

But they had to keep up appearances. Until the

janitors and the last of the employees had left the mall, he and Morales had to act perfectly normal. Well he'd been more nervous than this, he thought as the cart whined through the night. But it had been a long, long time ago and the situation had involved incoming mortar rounds.

Cool it, he told himself sternly. *At least nobody's shooting at you.*

Silently Luis and Tho worked their way along the fence line, keeping under the trees and raising their feet high to avoid breaking twigs. The pinkish light from the parking lot standards left the area under the trees in shadow. Traffic passed along the street on the other side of the fence, but the oleander bushes and the thick growth of vines screened them. Halfway between the place where they left Surfer and the next entrance they stopped.

Tho twisted his baseball cap around and pressed his binoculars to his eyes. Luis unzipped the case and pulled out the rifle. Carefully, he laid in the leaf litter and snapped down the rifle's bipod legs. Then he put his arm through the sling, tightened it, and rolled into position. The rifle's action clattered softly as Luis worked a round into the chamber. He put his eye to the scope and they both waited.

Finally the golf cart with a lone man in it came down the ramp out of the second level parking lot. There was a faint rustling as Luis adjusted his position to take the driver in his sights. Tho focused his binoculars and waited.

Luis shifted again and jerked on Tho's pant leg. Tho looked down and Luis scowled and shook his head. Tho brought the binoculars up again and looked more closely.

"Shit," he breathed.

Without another word Luis picked up the rifle and both of them faded back into the shadows.

❖   ❖   ❖

Toby was getting seriously annoyed. He'd been trying to reach the Surfer since mid-afternoon, but he wasn't answering his car phone, he wasn't home and he wasn't in any of the usual hangouts. Considering the Surfer's already precarious hold on his health, this was not smart.

The drug dealer was also beginning to worry. He knew Surfer hadn't been arrested, but it was just possible Surfer had cut out on him. If he did that he might have taken a sample of the new drug with him to find his own chemist and set up his own operation.

Normally Toby knew very closely how much money each of his dealers had. That was one way of keeping them under control. If Surfer had been cutting the product he might have a lot more cash than Toby had allowed for. Could his demand to hire independent shooters be aimed at something other than a couple of mall cops?

Not likely, but Surfer had been acting funny and Toby hadn't stayed alive by underestimating his potential opposition. Clearly, the whole thing hinged on finding the Surfer and fast.

"We're going to the mall," he told Lurch. "Let's see if we can find that little mother before there's real trouble."

"It's not him," Luis said.

"What the fuck do you mean it's not him?" Surfer hissed.

"Hey chill, man. The guy in the cart don't match the picture."

"It's gotta be him! He's got duty tonight. His car's still in the parking lot." The pair watched their employer impassively.

"Inside! Then he's gotta be working inside."

"You want us to go in there and whack this dude?" Luis said dubiously.

"Of course I want you to get him, you dumb fuckers. That's what I hired you for, ain't it?"

"How we gonna do that?" Tho asked. "How we gonna get in there?"

"With this." The Surfer reached into his pocket and pulled out a plastic card. "This belongs to a mall administrator. It'll get us through anything."

"What about the cameras and shit?" asked Luis, who was liking this less and less by the minute.

"Fuck the cameras!" the Surfer shouted. "You gonna do this or aren't you?"

"We're gonna do it, man," Luis said.

"Then come on. You got something besides that doofus rifle?"

Both the teenagers opened their jackets to show pistols. Surfer nodded and they started off across the parking lot toward the glowing mountain in the center.

As the last of the janitors left the parking lot, Henderson pulled up to the employees' entrance, exactly on time for the outside guard's midnight break.

Dunlap, Roarke and Murphy were waiting for him in the angle of the planters, out of the view of the cameras. Without a word, Henderson used his ID card to open the door. Then he blocked the photocell with his leg and held the door open while the other three entered. As far as the computer was concerned, only Henderson had come in.

Wordlessly, the four headed for the security office where Morales waited for them.

"We got a little complication here," Dunlap told them once they were safe inside the security center. "Cogswell and the Japs are still up in his suite." He held up his hand to cut off interruptions. "They laid in enough booze for a fraternity party, so they're probably not gonna be window shopping. We're gonna go ahead and do it anyway. Stay out of sight around the South Court as much as possible and don't get careless. We're all in uniform, so if they do see us from a distance they'll probably take us for Westlin."

"Where's our patsy?" Morales asked.

Henderson glanced at his board. "Still in west arcade. He's pretty much on schedule."

"Hope to God he stays on schedule," Morales said. "Hate to have him see us."

Dunlap patted his revolver. "If he sees us he has an accident. He might like it better that way, considering what's going to happen to him tomorrow."

"Killed in the line of duty is a lot better than ten to fifteen for a job you didn't do," Henderson agreed as if he was trying to convince himself.

"It's not gonna come to that. Just stay on your toes and it doesn't matter where Westlin is, he won't see us. Now, have you got the stuff?"

Judy was waiting on the bench in front of Bellbookand just as Andy had told her. The bench and the area immediately around it were dead spots, not covered by cameras. As soon as Andy turned the corner into the arcade, she came forward through the shadows to meet him.

"You did come."

"I said I would."

"I know, but . . ." She grasped his hands and squeezed. "I'm glad you're here."

He looked into Judy's brown eyes. "I'm glad I'm here." Her face softened and Andy wanted to take her in his arms and pull her close, and . . . He took his eyes away from her face, stepped back and let out a sigh. "Okay," he said. "Let's go find this talisman."

"Get out of the light, will you?"

As the other guards moved away, Henderson dragged his bag closer to where he knelt. The others stayed clustered in the door of the security center as he popped the access panel just beyond the entrance in the corridor.

Working quickly, Henderson tapped into the cable at the junction box and inserted a couple of Y connectors. Then he attached the leads from the compact videotape player at his feet to the connectors. Then he looked up at his boss and nodded.

"Okay, now the tape."

Dunlap knelt beside him and slipped the cassette into the machine. Now the security center recorders would only pick up the previously taped shots of the empty stores. Later they'd remove the player and leave the cut cables as evidence of how it had been done. Morales could claim the cable had been spliced when he'd gone to take a leak or something.

The crew moved back into the security center and looked at the monitor screens.

"Okay," Dunlap said. "Let's do it. Henderson, you go for the furs. Do this right and we'll be rich and out of here in forty-five minutes."

The men headed down the corridor. None of them went back into the security center, so none of them saw the message that flashed on all fifteen monitors.

I AM LIKE SO SURE YOU MOST HEINOUSLY BOGUS DUDES!

Toby didn't look for Surfer directly. Instead, he started checking likely parking lots near the mall for his car. His knowledge of the area wasn't nearly as good as Surfer's, but his instincts were excellent. It took him less than an hour to find the Camaro in the office building lot where Surfer had left it.

Toby shook his head. *That dumb fucker!* He must be down at the mall someplace.

It took Henderson less than five minutes to disarm the burglar alarm on Sudstrom's fur vault. The duplicate key worked smoothly in the lock and the door swung open without a sound. Henderson sucked in a lungful of the cedar-and-ozone scented air and smiled. To him it was the smell of a house in the country, a good four-wheeler and all the other things he'd ever wanted. The smell of money.

He ignored the sprinkling of garments hanging on the racks in the center of the room. That was all dyed squirrel and shit. The mutant mink and chinchilla and sable were in the lockers in the back. He felt in his pocket for the key and headed for the back of the vault.

Lurch tapped his boss on the shoulder as they approached the mall entrance along a side street. He pointed to a parking lot across from the mall. Toby recognized the old gray Torino sedan as belonging to a couple of players. As out of place as a fart in a flower show and right by the street where any cruising cop was sure to see it.

"Sloppy, my man," he muttered to himself. "Sloppy." No matter what Surfer was up to, he was getting to be a real liability to the organization. Clearly he'd have some serious explaining to do when Toby found him and he had better be damn persuasive when he did it.

Surfer's management ID got them in the employees' entrance with no problem. As soon as they stepped through the outer door, Luis headed for the entrance to the main mall. But Surfer grabbed his arm and pulled him back.

"Not that way, you dumb shits," Surfer hissed. "The fucking pigs patrol out there. Follow me." He turned left and used the card to open another blank metal door. Luis and Tho followed and found themselves in the access tunnel that ran behind the smaller stores. Without looking back, Surfer set off down the access tunnel. The two hit men trailed behind.

The service corridor was almost unlit at night. Perhaps once every hundred feet a low-wattage bulb cast a yellow pool of light that faded quickly into a general gloom. Surfer moved quickly, and most of the time he was almost invisible in the dimness between the lights. The assassins stayed close to each other for protection and mutual comfort and well behind Surfer because he was making them nervous.

Midway between two lights, Surfer turned down a side corridor that led to the mall proper. The hit men didn't see him and they kept going straight until the corridor ended against the blank wall of a department store.

To their right was another corridor that led to the mall but there was no sign of Surfer.

"Now what?" Tho asked.

Luis, who was marginally the brighter of the pair, considered. He didn't like the setup, especially not coming into the mall after their victim. Their employer obviously wasn't too stable either. But Surfer was connected and scoring this one would help build their reps. If they quit just because things got a little tight it would be bad for business.

Luis looked back the way they had come, gave a quick, tight shake of his head and turned back to his companion. "We find this guy and do him like we agreed. Then we get the fuck out of here."

"What about Surfer?"

"Fuck Surfer. We ain't his goddamn nursemaids. We do the guy and get the rest of the money later."

The little Vietnamese nodded and the pair headed out into the mall.

Henderson was still thinking of money when he sensed rather than saw something move among the half-empty racks.

What the fuck . . . ?

He scowled and pulled his pistol. Cautiously he worked his way up the aisle. There was a sound like something very large breathing heavily ahead of him. Henderson's eyes widened, and he eased forward around the last of the gray squirrel coats. He craned his neck, every nerve alert. There was nothing in sight, but the storage locker was open and the sound of breathing was even louder. Something had gone into the storage locker. Something *big*.

Henderson shifted his grip and brushed the last coat out of the way to get a better view.

The last coat didn't brush. Instead it reared up and roared. Henderson had a confused sight of evil yellow eyes and large white fangs in something ten feet tall and covered with gray fur.

Jesus CHRIST!

The guard ducked under a swipe of the enormous paw and dashed for the only safety in sight. The storage locker.

CLOSE THE FUCKING DOOR. CLOSE THE FUCKING DOOR!! Henderson threw his body against it and threw it shut in the face of the charging monster.

The thing slammed up against the wire mesh so hard the whole locker rattled. It snarled at him and raked its claws along the mesh, the uncaged monster trying to reach the caged man. Henderson pressed his back against the wall and tried to steady his pistol in both shaking hands. Instinctively, he knew that the gun wouldn't stop the thing.

Then suddenly it was quiet. The monster turned away from the locker and raised its head questioningly. It "whuffed" twice and then shuffled away, its prey apparently forgotten.

It disappeared among the furs and Henderson heard the vault door creak as it was pushed further open. Then it was quiet, except for the gentle whir of the ventilation fans.

Vaguely, Henderson realized the door had locked behind him when he slammed it. He didn't have a key and it wouldn't have mattered if he had since there was no keyhole on the inside.

He was stuck here until one of the others came looking for him and let him out. Somehow that didn't bother

Henderson a whole lot. Or maybe the thing would get Dunlap and the others and no one would come until the cops arrived tomorrow morning.

Henderson thought about that. Then he thought about the monster. Then he decided that idea didn't bother him all that much either.

Chapter 27

Even The Pit was quiet. The music gone, the neon out, the stores dark and shuttered. A couple of fluorescent tubes in the ceiling cast harsh white light into a place never meant for it.

Andy had been following Judy through the mall for nearly 20 minutes. They hadn't been spotted, but they hadn't found anything either.

"Well?" he demanded.

Judy frowned and bit her lip. "It's around here someplace," she whispered. "I can *feel* it."

"But where? We can't search every rock and leaf in the mall."

"Somewhere close. Don't worry, we'll find it."

"If Morales finds us on the monitors it won't matter."

Judy shushed him and motioned him on.

Outside the moon was rising.

Where did those dumb fuckers go? Surfer thought as he strode down the deserted corridors. Somewhere back there his shooters had gotten their asses lost. Well fuck 'em. He didn't need them anyway. He'd have the pleasure of finishing this fucking pig all by himself, the way he'd wanted to in the first place. It wasn't a rational decision. The pig was armed and all Surfer had was the little .32 auto he kept in his glove compartment. But between the drug and his anger Surfer was long past rationality.

The ice troll burst from the service corridor into the

main mall and stopped. The great furred head swung from side to side. The huge nostrils quivered, testing the air.

Finally it struck a scent and shambled off in the direction of the South Court.

Spooky enough, Heathercoate thought as he surveyed the deserted mall. He carried neither notebook nor tape recorder, but he soaked in the impressions, shaping them to his story as he did so. "Eerie," that was the word. "Silent as the grave yet pregnant with menace." Mentally, Heathercoate rubbed his hands together as his story began to fall into place.

Jefferson Davis Dunlap used his pocket knife to peel away the insulation on the second of the wires in the junction box. *Easy,* he reminded himself. It wouldn't do to touch both wires with the knife blade and set off the alarm.

He took the blue metal box and plugged it into the outlet behind the counter. Then he attached the wires to the exposed wiring with alligator clips. There was a low hum and the light flickered as Henderson's gadget went to work.

The jewelry store's time clock was an old one that ran off 60-cycle AC power. It also wasn't a very good one, without some of the safety devices such clocks are supposed to have. Henderson's gadget was putting about 600 cycles per second through the wire, making the clock run ten times as fast as normal.

It still took time to run the clock forward, so the schedule called for Dunlap to help Morales hit the electronics store while they waited.

Heathercoate was making his way through the darkened mall when he saw movement on the level below. There was someone else in the mall. With a skill at skulking born of long practice, Heathercoate faded behind a planter and peered through the bushes.

He was relieved to see it wasn't a guard. He didn't recognize the person, but he looked like Heathercoate's idea of the typical Californian. The reporter could also see well enough to pick out the small gun the man was waving around. He strode along with an angry springing step, looking left and right as if he wanted a target. Heathercoate gave up any idea of interviewing him, but he decided to follow — at a discreet distance, of course.

With surprising grace for someone of his weight and build, Cyril Heathercoate slipped along quietly to see where this "crazed gunman" — no, make that "would-be mass murderer" — would lead him.

"Good stuff," Morales said as he played his flashlight over the stack of white cardboard boxes in the back room of Boutique Electronique.

"High grade," Dunlap agreed. "Nothing but high-grade merchandise." The VCRs were bulky, but they were top-of-the-line, do-everything, HDTV-ready models that retailed for nearly $6,000 each. The dozen or so in the store were well worth lifting.

Dunlap was sweating by the time he and Morales finished loading the cart Morales had taken from Sudstrom's loading dock. He checked his watch.

"Three minutes ahead of schedule," he said, breathing heavily from the exertion. "If everyone else is doing as well, we'll finish in a lot less than forty-five minutes."

"Suits me," Morales told his boss.

Pushing the loaded cart ahead of them, the pair headed back down the mall toward the jewelry store. They were so intent on their burden they didn't notice the security cameras tracking them as they passed.

The mall was lit up, but except for a few cars in the employees' parking lot, it seemed deserted. There wasn't even any sign of an outside security patrol and no sign at all of Surfer or the shooters.

Well shit! Toby thought. He'd just have to wait to talk to the fucker until tomorrow. And the conversation would be a lot more final than he had originally planned. As the van completed its circuit of the parking lot, Toby was already running through a list of possible successors to take over the Surfer's territory.

"You know," Judy said, "this place is really kind of spiritual at night."

Andy made a noncommittal noise.

Judy looked out over the waterfall and the statue garden below them and breathed deeply, as if inhaling the atmosphere of the mall. "Did you ever feel it? The spiritual power of the place at night, I mean?"

"The only thing I'm feeling right now is nervous," he told her. "Have you got it located yet?"

They had come nearly halfway around the mall and now they were on the second level above South Court. Judy had led the way confidently but as far as Andy could see, aimlessly.

Judy cocked her head. "I thought I just heard something."

"Probably one of the other guards looking for me. Look, Judy, if we can't find anything soon we'll have to do it another night."

"But it's close! I can feel it."

"That's what you said when you started. Is the feeling getting stronger?"

"Well, no . . ."

"We've come halfway across the mall."

"I can still feel it strongly," Judy insisted.

Andy started to point out that was illogical and then decided it was a waste of breath. "We don't have much time."

Judy bit her lip. "There's one other thing I can try. A summoning. Instead of us looking for the talisman we'll call it to us."

"You mean it will fly into our hands?"

"I don't think so. But it should reveal itself."

"It won't make a lot of noise, will it?"

"Just the chant."

"Well, let's try it. But if it doesn't work, you're going to have to go back to your store to hide, and I'll have to get back on my rounds."

Dunlap's hand was shaking as he twirled the dial on the combination lock. Henderson's box had done its work and now all that stood between them and the contents of the safe was the combination.

Getting that had been easy. Like most people with a safe, the store manager had written down the combination and kept it in his desk drawer where Morales had found it in a nighttime search.

Morales was behind him now, hovering over his shoulder for the first sight of the treasure in the safe. Dunlap entered the last number and twisted the handle. The door swung open and Dunlap started shoveling small boxes and trays into the laundry sack Morales was holding out.

"Look at this stuff," he breathed as he held a tray of rings up at an angle to catch the light. The stones threw glints of red and green and fiery white in the gloom.

"More where that came from," Dunlap said as he reached deeper into the safe. "Now keep that bag open, will you?"

"You know if there's much more we're gonna have to start taking it out of the cases."

"Too much time," Dunlap said. "We'd ..." Then his head came up and he motioned Morales down beside him.

There was a scuffling noise out in the mall, as if someone was shuffling along. Someone big.

Dunlap whirled, his hand on his gun butt, and peeked around the counter. Someone, no some*thing* was out in front of the jewelry store.

A *bear*? But bears aren't dusty gray. And Dunlap didn't think that bears were that big. Whatever it was it looked plenty dangerous. He froze and his breath caught in his throat. Beside him he sensed Morales shifting to free his gun hand.

He could hear the thing's heavy breathing. For a terrible instant he thought it was after them. But it shambled past the store without looking in. Its eyes were fixed on something up ahead.

"Jesus!" Morales' eyes were wide. "Did you see that?"

"Yeah, I saw it," Dunlap whispered back. "Let's get the hell out of here before it comes back."

Luis and Tho were nervous and getting more nervous by the minute.

It didn't bother them that they had lost Surfer. If anything, that was an advantage. But they couldn't find their target and they knew that the longer they stayed in the mall the more likely they were to be spotted by the cameras.

Besides, the place was spooky. There were too many angles and close spaces where someone could hide. Their quarry was armed and knew this place. If he saw them coming it would be easy to set up an ambush. Plus they were just plain lost.

Guns drawn, the pair worked their way along the second level, scanning their surroundings and trying to keep back against the stores so they wouldn't be seen from above. Tho concentrated on the front while Luis moved almost crabwise, scanning the levels above and keeping an eye behind them as well.

"Look!" Luis screamed.

Not twenty feet behind, a huge gray shape was hurtling toward them. Both guns came up, but the ice troll was too close and much too fast. Before either of them could fire, a mighty swipe of a clawed hand knocked Luis spinning and the monster charged directly into Tho, putting him flat on his back. Tho's pistol flew out of his hand and he screamed as the enormous foot descended on his chest.

The pressure built to crushing force and Tho felt his ribs crunch. Then the weight was gone as suddenly as it came. Without breaking stride the ice troll charged past the two would-be assassins and on down the mall.

Tho sucked in a deep breath and winced as his broken ribs grated against each other. But he was alive! By Buddha and all the saints in heaven, he was alive! Rolling gingerly to one side he saw that Luis was alive as well. He was down and there was blood seeping through his jacket, but the monster's claws had only raked him across the chest.

"What the fuck was that?" Luis demanded as he levered himself upright.

"Dunno," Tho gasped as he fumbled for his gun. "Let's go, man. Let's go."

Luis nodded and, holding their sides, both of them staggered toward the nearest exit.

Just like gaijin, Kashihara Tomoi thought, amused. Come eight thousand miles and you get something you could get better around the corner in Tokyo. Why not steak?

The sushi was of inferior quality and not well prepared. The maguro was at least 24 hours old, the shrimp had been cooked in advance and left to sit until it went rubbery. And not even the dictates of politeness could make him try Fugu. No sashimi made by gaijin!

Still, the whiskey was at least adequate and his hosts were making an effort. And the negotiations hadn't gone badly at all.

Kashihara was enjoying himself.

Over in the corner, Larry Sakimoto was dropping a maraschino cherry on the bar, picking it up and dropping it again. Sakimoto stared owlishly at the cherry and giggled every time it plopped on the polished wood. Finally, he missed the bar and the cherry joined five or six others on the carpet.

"Bartender," he announced, "gimme a Manhattan.

Only hold the ice, hold the bitters, hold the vermouth, hold the whiskey and hold the glass!" The bartender laid down a cherry on a cocktail napkin.

"Oh, yeah, hold the napkin too. Well, doesn' matter." He shook his head and nearly fell off the stool as the room spun around him. Then he picked up the cherry, dropped it and giggled.

This struck Kashihara as odd, even for a gaijin. Besides, he had enough whiskey in him he wanted to practice his English.

"Good evening. What doing?"

Larry looked up and saw Kashihara-sama. At least it was probably Kashihara-sama. His eyes weren't focusing too well.

"It's not bouncing," the American explained. He picked the cherry up and dropped it again. "Doesn't bounce. No matter how hard you drop it. Won't bounce." He giggled.

"Hmm," Kashihara said. There was definitely a communications problem here, but Kashihara didn't think it had anything to do with his English.

"You see what that means, don't you?" Larry leaned forward and nearly fell off the stool. "Cherries don't bounce; you can't dribble a cherry! And if you can't dribble a cherry," he finished triumphantly, "I didn't see what it was I saw."

Kashihara digested that for an instant.

"Hai," he said decisively, and moved away.

"Don't you need the candles and herbs and stuff?" Andy asked as Judy traced an invisible circle with her shoe.

"Those are just aids to concentration," she explained without looking up. "You can visualize all those things and it works just as well."

"I might have known."

Judy looked up and made a face at him. "O ye of little faith."

"Right now I'm ye of little time. I don't know how I'm going to cover this in my report."

"Positive mental attitude, remember? You won't have to. Now you stand over there." She gestured to a spot on the floor. "No, not there, a little to your right. You've got to be inside the circle."

"There is no circle."

"Then visualize it."

"I can visualize it just as well here as I can there."

"Andy . . ." Judy began dangerously.

"All right, all right. Is this where I'm supposed to be?"

"That's fine. Now be very quiet."

As Andy watched, Judy mimed lighting the candles. Then she walked the circle and pretended to raise a knife to each of the four directions. She came back to the center of the circle and bowed to the north.

"Kaideset Afanaton!" Judy proclaimed in a hoarse whisper. *"Polgontome Pogkrates."* She threw her arms wide. *"Aeiel!"*

There was more. Lots more. Andy fidgeted in place while Judy reeled off strings of gibberish punctuated by wild hand wavings. This wasn't anything like the ritual she had performed when she tried to summon the elf. There wasn't any smoke, but it was longer.

"Thing we seek, I command you," Judy declaimed in a whisper. "I command you to come to us. Come to us and reveal yourself now!"

On the last word, Judy flung her arms up and her head back, her eyes closed and her face screwed up in an expression of utter concentration.

She stood there on tiptoe, quivering with the effort.

Andy waited.

"Well?" Andy asked finally.

Judy went flatfooted and opened her eyes. Then she looked over at Andy.

Then she screamed.

Chapter 28

Andy whirled. Lumbering toward them was the thing he'd seen on the first level. He had a confused impression of gray fur, a bright red mouth and gleaming white teeth. Lots and lots of gleaming white teeth.

"Run!" he yelled. Then he dropped into a gunfighter's crouch and emptied his revolver. The shots echoed deafeningly through the empty mall.

The thing seemed to hesitate, then it lowered its head and came straight on at him in a shambling run. Out of the corner of his eye he saw Judy fleeing.

He dived behind a planter. The thing kept coming, then slowed and seemed to lose him. The great gray head cast back and forth as the creature sampled the air with deep snorts.

Whatever it was, its eyesight wasn't very good, Andy realized. If he could just keep out of sight . . . Staying low behind the planter, he raised the muzzle of his revolver, flipped the cylinder out and slammed the ejection rod. The expended shells tinkled to the mosaic floor.

If the thing couldn't see well, its hearing seemed to be excellent. The creature froze, then swung its head toward the sound and shuffled toward the planter.

Andy fumbled at his belt for a speedloader. As he reloaded desperately the words of his weapons training officer came back to him. "Most gunfights are over in less than thirty seconds," the trainer had assured Andy and the other rookies. *Damn thing must have had another training officer*, Andy thought as he swung the cylinder shut on his revolver.

He popped up not four feet from the monster and fired three quick shots into the head.

The thing turned and roared at him. It spread its arms and moved toward him, swaying like a cobra ready to strike.

Andy fired twice more into the monster's gaping mouth. The thing took one more step, tottered and then crashed forward onto the planter. It quivered once and seemed to deflate into itself. Then it lay still.

Andy lowered his pistol. His chest was heaving and his hands were shaking so badly he had trouble getting the other speedloader out of its pouch.

As Andy ejected his empties, the bulky gray figure grew indistinct around the edges. He concentrated on getting the rounds in the speedloader lined up with the chambers. By the time he reloaded and looked up again the thing was translucent, the outlines of the broken shrubbery vaguely visible through the thinning mass of the body.

He eased the cylinder closed and holstered the weapon as the monster went from translucent to transparent and then vanished entirely, leaving only the smashed and broken greenery in the planter to show where it had been.

"Okay, Judy," Andy called. "It's okay."

Judy peeked hesitantly around the corner and then stepped out into the court.

"It's okay," Andy repeated. "It's . . ."

Wide-eyed, Andy looked over at Judy. She was staring at where the monster had been. Her chest was glowing with an unearthly blue fire.

Six loud explosions ripped apart the dinner party.

Cogswell half rose. "What the hell?" Then with an effort, he settled back and smiled weakly at the Japanese.

"Mosley," he hissed out of the side of his mouth, "go see what that is." He tried to relax, and his people took their cue from their boss. There was a quick burst of too loud conversation and too raucous laughter.

Kashihara had no doubt what the noise was. He'd seen enough movies to recognize the sound. "Yakuza?"

<No, sir, I don't think it's gangsters.>

<Kami again?>

Yoshiwara hesitated. <Maybe.>

Three more shots, then two. Then silence. The Japanese all looked at one another, and the Americans tried desperately to appear unconcerned.

Kashihara sighed. <Well, let's go see. We might as well find out just what kind of trouble we have bought here.> Without a word to his hosts he stood up and strode out of the suite toward the balcony. Cogswell and the others rose and followed.

That's the pig's voice! Surfer wasn't close enough to hear what Andy said, but he heard the gunshots and then he heard Andy call out. *Shit.* Obviously his hired guns had screwed up. Maybe the pig had gotten them or maybe he'd run them off. Whatever. Now it was up to him to finish the job. Surfer hefted his pistol. The fucker was in the South Court and from the shots he'd either be out of ammunition or close to it. Without looking behind him he picked up the pace.

There! In that indescribable otherness where the searchers waited, the pattern came together. Now, seize it before our enemies can act!

If these ones did not know time they certainly understood haste.

"Stop here for a minute." Toby scanned the parking lot, but there was no sign of Surfer. No police and nobody running around, so apparently it hadn't gone down yet. But where the hell was that dickweed?

Toby nodded to Lurch. "Work along those trees by the fence and see if you can see anything. We'll circle the mall. And take a radio. Anything happens you call me and get the fuck out of there." Lurch nodded and stuck a walkie-talkie in his jacket pocket. Then he opened the door and slipped out.

Toby rapped on the van's side to get Pedro's attention. *Take us around the mall*, he signed.

"Judy!"

Judy looked at him and then followed his eyes down to her shoulder. Wonderingly, she reached up and touched it.

"The brooch!" Andy panted. That's why the elves hadn't been able to find the talisman. It was only in the mall when Judy was and this was the first time she'd been here past midnight.

Judy was still entranced by the glowing object on her blouse.

"Come on," Morales panted. "Let's get this stuff loaded.

He was pushing a hand truck piled with boxes. Behind him Dunlap and Roarke and Murphy were hauling pushcarts overflowing with more loot.

They were in the corridor to the east loading dock used by the smaller mall stores to receive merchandise, blank brick with roll-up steel doors at either end. Just a couple of hundred feet more and they'd have the last of the loot into the truck.

"Jesus," Morales said for the fourth time, "what was that thing?"

"I dunno," Dunlap gasped. "A bear maybe. Let's get this stuff loaded and get the hell out of here."

"What about Henderson?"

"Henderson can damn well look out for himself. He knows where to meet us." *If he's still in one piece*, Dunlap added silently.

Judy's mouth formed a little "O" of surprise as she

looked at the blue glow on her chest. "I had it all along," she said slowly. "All the time it was right here." Then she laughed in wonder.

"Let's get it back before there's worse trouble," Andy said. "We're going to have guards and police all over the place in a minute."

Judy tore her eyes away from the glowing marvel pinned to her blouse. "How do we give it back?"

Andy hesitated. He hadn't thought about that part. "The pool! The elf said the gate was the pool. Here, give me the brooch."

Hesitantly, Judy unhooked the glowing object from her blouse and handed it over. The thing felt cool in Andy's hand in spite of the glow. With Judy trailing, Andy walked to the rail. Below him the water gushing out of the rock glowed with a milky radiance. He took a deep breath and tossed the brooch over the edge.

But it didn't fly right. Instead of following a neat arc to the water below, the glowing object almost floated, light as thistledown. It cleared the railing and then clattered down the rock face to rest a few feet below the second level.

Without thinking, Andy climbed over the railing and started down the rocks toward it. Even wet, the rough stone was easy to climb, but he almost lost his balance when he stooped down and reached out to get it. He bent further, keeping his grip tight on the wet rock, and his fingers were almost touching it when a bullet whistled by his head and whined off the rock, kicking rock chips in his face.

Andy flinched and clung to the rock face. Rock dust was in his eyes and he blinked desperately to clear them.

Eyes watering, Andy looked down and saw the Surfer.

"Now I got you, you sonofabitch!" Surfer screamed across the court as he leveled his gun again.

He didn't see what was behind him.

❖   ❖   ❖

"What the hell was *that*?" Roarke demanded. All the guards looked at each other. They knew damn well what that noise was. Gunshots.

"Sounds like a fucking fire fight," Morales said.

"Well it's not our fucking fire fight," Dunlap retorted. "Let's get the stuff loaded and get the fuck out of here."

They bent their backs to the heavily loaded carts and the rattle of wheels over the concrete grew even louder. Then there was a new sound. A metallic clatter much louder than the cart wheels or even the distant gunshots.

All of them looked up. Slowly at first, then faster and faster, the metal doors at both ends of the corridor began to descend.

Morales ran for the door to the dock, but it slammed down while he was still a good ten feet away. The noise of the doors clashing home echoed in on them from both ends of the corridor.

"Attention, shoppers," came a cheery mechanical voice over the speakers. "Black Oak Mall is now closed. The mall is now closed. Thank you for visiting us at Black Oak Mall and we hope you had a pleasant shopping experience." The message was replaced by the howl of the burglar alarm.

Dunlap yelled something incomprehensible and threw a box at the speaker.

"You motherfucking pig!" Surfer yelled, bringing his pistol up. "You goddamn pig." He took shaky aim at Andy while behind him something huge and black took shape and solidified. Above him, clinging to the rock wall, Andy could only gape.

At the last instant, something cut through the Surfer's drug-fueled rage and he turned slightly as the thing behind him lunged forward.

There was a scream that was cut off in the middle and then nothing.

Cogswell and the others couldn't see Surfer from the balcony. But Andy and Judy saw what happened all too clearly. So did Cyril Heathercoate, who was perhaps fifty feet from the Surfer and pressed back against a store entrance trying to make himself as small as he possibly could.

Then the thing waddled out into the South Court like a snake emerging from its burrow and all of them could see. It was something like a dragon and something like a dinosaur. The eyes were evil green and the teeth were long and gleaming. It unfurled its enormous bat wings until they filled the entire central space of the court.

The thing stretched out its long scaly neck and hissed evilly at Andy and Judy. Then it lumbered toward them.

"Mr. Kashihara," Cogswell began as he came out onto the balcony. "There's no need for you to . . ." Then he saw what was happening below them.

"Mother of God!" Beside him, Kashihara hissed in surprise.

At first Andy was frozen by the monster bearing down on him. He tried to shrink back, but there was no place to go on the spray-wet rock. There was no way to run and no place to hide.

The brooch, he thought, *it wants the brooch.*

Tearing his eyes from the dragon, he looked down and saw the brooch still wedged in the rocks. Without looking back, he stretched down and out toward it. His fingertips slipped on the wet rock and he lunged forward, nearly losing his balance.

Desperately, he planted his feet firmly and clutched at the rock with his hand. He did not, *would not*, look up.

The thing's breath came hot on his back, its stink worse than any floater. With a desperate effort, Andy pulled himself down to the level of the brooch. He reached out, so far his arm quivered from the strain, and his fingers closed on the talisman.

With a convulsive lurch, his fingers touched the flaming blue thing. In a single gesture he batted it off the rocks and out. The glowing brooch fell toward the base of the waterfall, now alive with the same silvery glow as the pond's surface.

As the brooch reached the water, a hand broke the surface, grasped the glowing blue object, the quicksilver surface closed over the brooch and arm with hardly a ripple. Andy thought he recognized the hand.

He turned to face his attacker, bracing himself on the rough rocks and groping for his pistol. But when he looked up, the dragon thing was already translucent and fading.

Andy's breath was coming in deep, ragged gasps, and he was shaking so badly he could hardly ease his gun back into its holster, but he turned to face the rock and climbed back as quickly as his rubbery limbs would take him. Twice his hand or foot slipped, but he made the top with no more than a scraped forearm. Then Judy was in his arms, and he was clinging to her, hugging her and leaning on her at the same time. Both of them were whooping and laughing and crying all at once.

Andy realized he'd never kissed her before. She kissed very nicely.

The van pulled back into the mall entrance to pick up Lurch.

"I think I heard shots," the big man said as he crawled back in. "Inside the mall maybe."

Toby stared. *Jesus Christ!* Had that dumb shit whacked a guard in front of two hundred fucking security cameras? Well, whatever had happened he didn't want any part of it.

"We'll just have to take care of business. Get the word out he is persona non grata and tomorrow we'll see about dealing with him direct."

Lurch nodded, barely visible in the light filtering

through the smoked windows. Toby settled back in his chair and reached over to signal Pedro.

There was a sound like a drawer scraping open and tiny giggles from the front of the van.

In one lightning motion Lurch spun in his chair, drew his gun and flipped on the interior lights.

Standing in the open drawer of the wet bar was a manlike thing about a foot high. He had big flapping ears, a long pointed nose and a broad mouth turned up in a goofy grin.

More to the point, he had the vial of designer drug in his hand.

Before either Lurch or Toby could react, the little creature poured the vial's entire contents on the mirrored bar top. Then it leaned forward and with a single prodigious snort sucked all the gray powder into its enormous nose.

As the two watched goggle-eyed, the brownie's eyes closed in bliss. Then they opened again, widened and the creature sneezed, blowing the drug all over the inside of the van.

Toby sneezed too as the grayish cloud reached him, and the bitter stuff stung his nostrils. Lurch gasped and fired twice at the place where the brownie had been. But the thing was gone, and the bullets spanged off the reinforced floor to tear through the front passenger's seat and make star-shaped cracks in the bulletproof windshield.

"GET US THE FUCK OUT OF HERE," Toby screamed. He didn't sign it, but Pedro got the drift. He punched the accelerator and the van went screaming out of the driveway backwards, tires smoking. The drug was already affecting Pedro's coordination when he cut the wheel to turn around and the van almost tipped over. Then with another screech of smoking rubber it roared down the street toward the freeway on-ramp.

Back at the mall gate several brownies gathered to wave goodbye.

❖   ❖   ❖

The van was doing seventy when it hit the on-ramp
and it was still accelerating, fishtailing slightly as the
souped-up engine drove the tires beyond their ability to
grip the road.

By the time the van merged with traffic it was doing
nearly a hundred. Brakes screeched and horns blared as
drivers scrambled to get away from the careening vehicle. But the people in the van were past caring. The
vehicle cut across four lanes of traffic, slammed into the
median guardrail, slid along it for nearly fifty yards and
then cut back as the driver overcorrected convulsively.
The van crossed two lanes of traffic at nearly right
angles, skidded sideways and overturned broadside.
The slide along the guardrail had sheared off the gas
filler pipe, and the overturning van left a trail of gasoline
behind it. The sliding contact of metal on pavement
provided a shower of sparks, and the van exploded in an
ugly yellow fireball.

Not that it mattered. All of the van's human occupants were dead of massive drug overdoses before the
first spark. The lone inhuman occupant scampered
away giggling over the ride and fireworks.

Cogswell's mouth was still hanging open when he
realized Kashihara was standing next to him. The Japanese contingent seemed to have recovered but the
Americans were still gaping at the scene below.

"This very bad maybe," Kashihara said.

Cogswell's head snapped around. "You speak English!"

"Enough." He waved his hand dismissingly. "This."
He nodded out over the chaos below. "This bad for
business, I think."

Looking at the mess below, Cogswell thought that the
Japanese had a genius for understatement. He also realized he didn't have the faintest idea how to deal with
this and there was no time to call a strategy meeting.

"What do you propose?"

"Our people no talk. Only two witnesses beside. They disappear."

"I won't be party to murder!"

Kashihara looked disgusted. "No murder. Just disappear. Give them money and I think they go quiet."

Cogswell considered quickly. Not only might it save the deal, he had absolutely no interest in trying to explain what he'd just seen in court or anywhere else where it might reach the voters.

"How much?"

"Not much. Million dollars."

Cogswell's mouth fell open. "That's absurd."

Kashihara shrugged. "Maybe. But no argue million. Maybe argue hundred thousand. So divide, neh? I give half, you give half."

Cogswell hesitated.

"Police here soon," Kashihara pointed out. "Must decide now."

Cogswell looked at Kashihara, then he stared down at the couple embracing by the pool.

What the hell, Cogswell thought, *my accountants can cover this somehow.*

"Now let me get this straight," the lieutenant from Robbery growled. "You and the young lady were in the back room at her store, going at it all night and you didn't see or hear anything?"

Andy looked the cop straight in the eye. "Yes, sir."

Judy dropped her eyes and blushed. Andy thought she did a real good job of looking embarrassed and proud at the same time.

"And you two lovebirds just came wandering out when you heard the sirens?"

Judy nodded shyly.

The cop didn't look happy at that, but couldn't disprove it. Especially since there was nothing on any of the videotapes to show otherwise and the mall executives and the Japanese fervently backed them up.

He looked down at his notebook and growled. This was the screwiest thing he'd ever seen. Five guards try to pull a robbery, one of them ends up locked in the fur vault and doesn't want to come out. The other four are trapped in a service corridor with both doors locked from the outside. Not only that, but the place is loaded with security cameras and these morons don't even turn them off or anything.

Plus the guy in the fur vault is babbling about monsters, and there's this slimeball who looks like a greaser, sounds like a limey and swears the whole damn mall is haunted — and *he* apparently isn't involved in the robbery either.

It was enough to make his stomach hurt, and he hadn't had his first cup of coffee yet.

He settled for glaring at Andy. "Mister, you are one piss-poor excuse for a security guard."

"Yes, sir," Andy said meekly.

"You're probably going to lose your guard's license, and you'll damn sure lose your pistol permit." He shook his head in disgust. "You're never going to work as a security guard again."

"Yes, sir," Andy said, thinking of the check with all the zeros in his pocket.

"Get the hell out of here," he growled, "both of you."

Hand in hand they scooted out the main entrance and into the rising sun. They were so engrossed in each other they didn't notice the man with the streaky skin-dye job and English accent shouting into the pay phone.

"I tell you it's the story of the century!"

The morning sun was square in Cyril Heathercoate's eyes, but the phone cord wasn't long enough to let him turn away.

His editor was unimpressed. "Dragons in a shopping mall? That's not our kind of story. Demographics are all wrong. Can't you make it, oh, aliens, or even Elvis' ghost?"

"But it's real, I tell you! I saw it!"

There was a long pause. "Cyril," the editor said dangerously, "I told you what would happen if I caught you drinking again."

"Well," Judy said. "What do we do now?"

Andy squinted into the rising sun. "How about some breakfast?"

She punched him in the ribs. "Not that, silly! I mean what do we do with all that money?"

"Well-l-l . . . How about we run away to a tropical island?"

Judy looked up at him half shyly. "You mean together?"

Andy put his arm around her waist and drew her close. "I can't think of anyone I'd rather be on a tropical island with." Then he leaned down and kissed her.

They broke, and Judy giggled breathlessly. "Well, the pendulum did say . . ." But Andy kissed her again and Judy took the hint.

The sun was high in the sky by the time Kemper Cogswell was able to get away. Between the police, seeing off Kashihara's group, the aggrieved merchants whose stores had been burglarized and the call to his accountants to set up the million-dollar "consulting fee," it was almost noon before Cogswell got finished.

Still, he thought as he closed the carved oak doors behind him, it hadn't turned out too badly. The deal had gone through, and $500,000 out of the sale price wasn't going to make that much difference.

He looked up at the sun blazing through the stained-glass skylight over South Court and nodded. Very pointedly, he did not look down at the fountain where the action had been the night before. That was all fading and the sooner he put it behind him the better.

Oh, there would be unwanted publicity, and more trouble with the tenants over the attempted robbery, but nothing he couldn't handle. Especially since he could offer himself as a sacrificial goat.

Rather than walk past the South Court fountain he left his private elevator on the top level and strode past the shops, already busy with morning customers.

Thank God this place is back to normal, Cogswell thought as he strode toward the second-level exit.

He resolutely ignored the tiny giggle from the bushes. Eyes fixed straight ahead, he strode briskly past the planter with its smashed greenery and the gardener who was beginning the job of trimming it. He kept looking toward the rising sun and his visions of a political future. As a result he also missed the message on the kiosk screen. SHH, the computer flashed, THEY'LL HEAR YOU.

Billy Sunshine didn't see the message either. He kept his attention on the crushed, broken bushes. After due, deliberate consideration, he took out his pruning shears and started trimming away the damaged limbs, trying to restore some symmetry in the planter. He moved slowly along, trimming back the bushes with deliberate, measured snips.

A tiny head poked out of the greenery almost under Billy's nose. Then another and another and another. Billy blinked and then smiled.

"It's cool, man. It's all cool."

Giggling, one of the brownies gave him the peace sign.

Billy Sunshine flashed it back.

MAGIC AND COMPUTERS DON'T MIX!

RICK COOK

Or . . . do they? That's what Walter "Wiz" Zumwalt is wondering. Just a short time ago, he was a master hacker in a Silicon Valley office, a very ordinary fellow in a very mundane world. But magic spells, it seems, are a lot like computer programs: they're both formulas, recipes for getting things done. Unfortunately, just like those computer programs, they can be full of bugs. Now, thanks to a *particularly* buggy spell, Wiz has been transported to a world of magic—and incredible peril. The wizard who summoned him is dead, Wiz has fallen for a red-headed witch who despises him, and no one—not the elves, not the dwarves, not even the dragons—can figure out why he's here, or what to do with him. Worse: the sorcerers of the deadly Black League, rulers of an entire continent, want Wiz dead—and he doesn't even know why! Wiz had better figure out the rules of this strange new world—and fast—or he's not going to live to see Silicon Valley again.

Here's a refreshing tale from an exciting new writer. It's also a rarity: a well-drawn fantasy told with all the rigorous logic of hard science fiction.

69803-6 • 320 pages • $4.99

There Are Elves Out There

An excerpt from

Mercedes Lackey
Larry Dixon

The main bay was eerily quiet. There were no screams of grinders, no buzz of technical talk or rapping of wrenches. There was no whine of test engines on dynos coming through the walls. Instead, there was a dull-bladed tension amid all the machinery, generated by the humans and the Sidhe gathered there.

Tannim laid the envelope on the rear deck of the only fully-operated GTP car that Fairgrove had built to date, the one that Donal had spent his waking hours building, and Conal had spent track-testing. He'd designed it for beauty and power in equal measure, and had given its key to Conal, its elected driver, in the same brother's-gift ceremony used to present an elvensteed. Conal now sat on its sculpted door, and absently traced a slender finger along an air intake, glowering at the envelope.

Tannim finished his magical tests, and asked for a knife. An even dozen were offered, but Dottie's Leatherman was accepted. Keighvin stood a little apart from the group, hand on his short knife. His eyes glittered with suppressed anger, and he appeared less human than usual, Tannim noticed. Something was bound to break soon.

Tannim folded out the knifeblade, slit the envelope open, and then unfolded the Leatherman's pliers. With them he withdrew six Polaroids of Tania and two others, unconscious, each bound at the wrists and neck. Their silver chains were held by some-*things* from the Realm of the Unseleighe—inside a limo. And, out of focus through the limo's windows, was a stretch of flat tarmac, and large buildings—

Tannim dropped the Leatherman, his fingers gone numb. It clattered twice before wedging into the cockpit's fresh-air vent. Keighvin took one startled step forward, then halted as the magical alarms at Fairgrove's perimeter flared around them all. Tannim's hand went into a jacket pocket, and he threw down the letter from the P.I. He saw Conal pick up the photographs, blanch, then snatch the letter up.

Tannim had already turned by then, and was sprinting for the office door, and the parking lot beyond.

Behind him, he could hear startled questions directed at him, but all he could answer before disappearing into the offices was "Airport!" His bad leg was slowing him down, and screamed at him like a sharp rock grinding into his bones. There was some kind of attack beginning, but he had no time for that.

Have to get to the airport, have to save Tania

from Vidal Dhu, the bastard, the son of a bitch, the—

Tannim rounded a corner and banged his left knee into a file cabinet. He went down hard, hands instinctively clutching at his over-damaged leg. His eyes swam with a private galaxy of red stars, and he struggled while his eyes refocused.

Son of a bitch son of a bitch son of a bitch. . . .

Behind him he heard the sounds of a war-party, and above it all, the banshee wail of a high-performance engine. He pulled himself up, holding the bleeding knee, and limp-ran towards the parking lot, to the Mustang, and Thunder Road.

Vidal Dhu stood in full armor before the gates of Fairgrove, laughing, lashing out with levin-bolts to set off its alarms. It was easy for Vidal to imagine what must be going on inside—easy to picture that smug, orphaned witling Keighvin Silverhair barking orders to weak mortals, marshaling them to fight. Let him rally them, Vidal thought—it will do him no good. None at all. He may have won before, but ultimately, the mortals will have damned him.

It has been so many centuries, Silverhair. I swore I'd kill your entire lineage, and I shall. I shall!

Vidal prepared to open the gate to Underhill. Through that gate all the Court would watch as Keighvin was destroyed—Aurilia's plan be hanged! Vidal's blood sang with triumph—he had driven Silverhair into a winless position at last! And when he accepted the Challenge, before the whole Court, none of his human-world tricks would benefit him—theirs would be a purely magical combat, one Sidhe to another.

To the death.

*　　*　　*

Keighvin Silverhair recognized the scent of the magic at Fairgrove's gates—he had smelled it for centuries. It reeked of obsession and fear, hatred and lust. It was born of pain inflicted without consideration of repercussions. It was the magic of one who had stalked innocents and stolen their last breaths.

He recognized, too, the rhythm that was being beaten against the walls of Fairgrove.

So be it, murderer. I will suffer your stench no more.

"They will expect us to dither and delay; the sooner we act, the more likely it is that we will catch them unprepared. They do not know how well we work together."

Around him, the humans and Sidhe of his home sprang into action, taking up arms with such speed he'd have thought them possessed. Conal had thrown down the letter after reading it, and barked, "Hangar 2A at Savannah Regional; they've got children as hostages!" The doors of the bay began rolling open, and outside, elvensteeds stamped and reared, eyes glowing, anxious for battle. Conal looked to him, then, for orders.

Keighvin met his eyes for one long moment, and said, "Go, Conal. I shall deal with our attacker for the last time. If naught else, the barrier at the gates can act as a trap to hold him until we can deal with him as he deserves." He did not add what he was thinking—that he only hoped it would hold Vidal. The Unseleighe was a strong mage; he might escape even a trap laid with death metal, if he were clever enough. Then, with the swiftness of a falcon, he was astride his elvensteed Rosaleen Dhu, headed for the perimeter of Fairgrove.

He was out there, all right, and had begun laying a spell outside the fences, like a snare. Perhaps in his sickening arrogance he'd forgotten that Keighvin could see such things. Perhaps in his insanity, he no longer cared.

Rosaleen tore across the grounds as fast as a stroke of lightning, and cleared the fence in a soaring leap. She landed a few yards from the laughing, mad Vidal Dhu, on the roadside, with him between Keighvin and the gates. He stopped lashing his mocking bolts at the gates of Fairgrove and turned to face Keighvin.

"So, you've come to face me alone, at last? No walls or mortals to hide behind, as usual, coward? So sad that you've chosen *now* to change, within minutes of your death, traitor."

"Vidal Dhu," Keighvin said, trying to sound unimpressed despite the heat of his blood, "if you wish to duel me, I shall accept. But before I accept, you must release the children you hold."

The Unseleighe laughed bitterly. "It's your concern for these mortals that raised you that have *made* you a traitor, boy. Those children do not matter." Vidal lifted his lip in a sneer as Keighvin struggled to maintain his composure. "Oh, I will do more than duel you, Silverhair. I wish to Challenge you before the Court, and kill you as they watch."

That was what Keighvin had noted—it was the initial layout of a Gate to the High Court Underhill. Vidal was serious about this Challenge—already the Court would be assembling to judge the battle. Keighvin sat atop Rosaleen, who snorted and stamped, enraged by the other's tauntings. Vidal's pitted face twisted in a maniacal smirk.

"How long must I wait for you to show courage, witling?"

Keighvin's mind swam for a moment, before he remembered the full protocols of a formal Challenge. It had been so long since he'd even seen one. . . .

Once accepted, the Gate activates, and all the Court watches as the two battle with blade and magic. Only one leaves the field; the Court is bound to slay anyone who runs. So it had always been. Vidal would not Challenge unless he were confident of winning, and Keighvin was still tired from the last battle—which Vidal had not even been at. . . .

But Vidal must die. That much Keighvin knew.

From Born to Run *by Mercedes Lackey & Larry Dixon.*

✳   ✳   ✳

Watch for more from the SERRAted Edge:
Wheels of Fire by Mercedes Lackey & Mark Shepherd

When the Bough Breaks by Mercedes Lackey & Holly Lisle

GRAND ADVENTURE
IN GAME-BASED UNIVERSES

With these exciting novels set
in bestselling game universes,
Baen brings you synchronicity at its
best. We believe that familiarity with
either the novel or the game will
intensify enjoyment of the other.
All novels are the only authorized
fiction based on these games and
are published by permission.

THE BARD'S TALE™

Join the Dark Elf Naitachal and his apprentices in
Bardic magic as they explore the mysteries of the
world of The Bard's Tale.

Castle of Deception
by Mercedes Lackey & Josepha Sherman
72125-9 * 320 pages * $5.99 _____

Fortress of Frost and Fire
by Mercedes Lackey & Ru Emerson
72162-3 * 304 pages * $5.99 _____

Prison of Souls
by Mercedes Lackey & Mark Shepherd
72193-3 * 352 pages * $5.99 _____

And watch for *The Chaos Gate* by Josepha
Sherman coming in May 1994!

WING COMMANDER™
Fly with the best the Confederation of Earth has to offer against the ferocious catlike alien Kilrathi!

Freedom Flight
by Mercedes Lackey & Ellen Guon
72145-3 * 304 pages * $4.99   _____

End Run
by Christopher Stasheff & William R. Forstchen
72200-X * 320 pages * $4.99   _____

Fleet Action
by William R. Forstchen
72211-5 * 368 pages * $4.99   _____

STARFIRE™
See this strategy game come to explosive life in these grand space adventures!

Insurrection
by David Weber & Steve White
72024-4 * 416 pages * $4.99   _____

Crusade
by David Weber & Steve White
72111-9 * 432 pages * $4.99   _____

- -

If not available at your local bookstore, fill out this coupon and send a check or money order for the combined cover prices to Baen Books, Dept. BA, P.O. Box 1403, Riverdale, NY 10471.

NAME:_____

ADDRESS: _____

_____

I have enclosed a check or money order in the amount of $_____.
- -